Praise for Anna Pitoniak's

NECESSARY PEOPLE

A BOOK OF THE MONTH SELECTION
A *CRIMEREADS* BEST CRIME NOVEL OF THE YEAR

"That book-blurb saying 'I couldn't put it down' is usually bullshit, right? For me it was true of Anna Pitoniak's *Necessary People*. I literally couldn't stop reading. Murder, ambition, toxic friendship. What's not to like?"
—Stephen King

"Stella and Violet are college besties from opposite backgrounds… When the two take jobs at the same cable-news station, their feisty friendship morphs into a powder keg of jealousy—catastrophically so. Pitoniak delivers a pitch-perfect exploration of class, family, and female friendship, along with a gripping peek inside the inner workings of the TV-news business." —*People,* Book of the Week

"Two women meet in college, become best friends, and follow each other to New York City—where one of them starts single-white-female-ing the other. An inevitable crime takes place, a cover-up and investigation ensue, and then things get…dark. By which I mean completely effed up. In other words, welcome to *Necessary People,* a juicy thriller that will make you side-eye your friends and wonder if they're capable of doing crimes."
—*Cosmopolitan,* Best Book of the Month

"A delicious story about the ambitions that can lift us up or tear us apart." —Mehera Bonner, *Woman's Day*

"Smart and stylish...Pitoniak creates a compelling world of haves and have-nots that plays out in the cutthroat world of cable news. What begins as a sharp story about best friends... develops into a darker tale of rivalry, hubris, and deadly desire." —*Town & Country*, Best Book of the Month

"A story that transported us away from ourselves...Something you can escape into...Let's just say not everyone plays nice— and it's thrilling." —*Goop*

"Take the simmering jealousy found in many female friendships, ratchet it up, and mix in some seriously Ripley-esque longings for upper-crust lifestyles, and you'll land at Anna Pitoniak's utterly enthralling novel." —Elena Nicolaou, *Refinery29*, Best Book of the Month

"Competition on...Stella and Violet are polar opposites. And also best friends. Things take a turn when they get jobs at the same company and the roles they've always held in each other's lives begin to flip. They get competitive and will do whatever it takes to succeed—even if means throwing each other under the bus along the way. Think: *Bride Wars* meets *The Devil Wears Prada*." —*The Skimm*

"Another novel for anyone who misses the Ferrante novels for their portrayal of an intense, rivalry-prone female friendship...A psychological thriller in which two college friends graduate to a TV newsroom where (it appears) only one can thrive." —Emily Temple, *LitHub*

"Sheer pleasure...Pitoniak is an astute social observer, and the novel...is a twisting delight with a haunting punch. Deceptively nuanced and impossible to put down, this is escapism with substance."   —*Kirkus Reviews* (starred review)

"Pitoniak's riveting and gripping novel nails the big personalities, intense competition, and high drama of TV newsrooms. I was sucked in by the dark friendship of these two ambitious women and did not see the final twist coming!"
—Alisyn Camerota, anchor of CNN's *New Day* and author of *Amanda Wakes Up*

"Fantastic...This stirring character study and treatise on the dark sides of ambition, friendship, family, and privilege will hook readers from the get-go."
—*Publishers Weekly* (starred review)

"The writing and ride made this a page-turner. If you like writers like Megan Abbott...this should be right in your wheelhouse."
—*BookRiot*

"A complex, sharply written novel...Everything I want from a novel and more. Rife with plot twists and rich with insights, this is a book that will leave you desperate for whatever Anna Pitoniak writes next."   —Julie Buntin, author of *Marlena*

"A juicy, all-too-familiar tale."   —*Good Housekeeping*

"If your book club enjoys reading about and discussing frenemies, look no further than *Necessary People*."
—Kelly Gallucci and Elizabeth Rowe, *Bookish*

NECESSARY PEOPLE

a novel

ANNA PITONIAK

BACK BAY BOOKS
Little, Brown and Company
New York Boston London

ALSO BY ANNA PITONIAK

The Futures

For Ed, Kate, and Nellie

Copyright © 2019 by Lost Lake Productions LLC

Back Bay Books / Little, Brown and Company
Hachette Book Group
1290 Avenue of the Americas, New York, NY 10104
littlebrown.com

Originally published in hardcover by Little, Brown and Company, May 2019
First Back Bay trade paperback edition, May 2020

Back Bay Books is an imprint of Little, Brown and Company, a division of Hachette Book Group, Inc. The Back Bay Books name and logo are trademarks of Hachette Book Group, Inc.

The Hachette Speakers Bureau provides a wide range of authors for speaking events. To find out more, go to hachettespeakersbureau.com or call (866) 376-6591.

ISBN 978-0-316-45170-3 (hc) / 978-0-316-45172-7 (pb)
LCCN 2018952530

10 9 8 7 6 5 4 3 2 1

LSC-C

Printed in the United States of America

PART ONE

CHAPTER ONE

I WAS NINETEEN years old the first time I saved Stella Bradley's life.

One of the older boys who lived in a shabby off-campus house had managed to capture Stella's attention. When Stella needed rescuing from these situations, from these men who couldn't resist monopolizing her, she would signal to me. Tuck her hair behind her ear, tap a finger against her chin. But for the better part of an hour, she'd ignored me entirely.

Ascending the stairs, she caught my eye. *He's cute, right?* her shrugging look said. *This one is worth it.* Earlier that year, Stella had declared that she was finished with men. Immaturity and frattish antics aside, the men at our college were simply *boring*, and Stella couldn't stand that. "You know what I mean, don't you?" she had said. "It's just not worth it."

"Totally," I had replied. Which was a lie, and wasn't. Stella's intelligence often surprised me. Her categorical statements seemed silly but were in fact insightful. Are the men you meet when you're eighteen really worth the effort? Well, I had no experience with boys, so what did I know? But I could also see the truth she was getting at.

See, this was why I loved Stella Bradley. There's a lot of bullshit in life, and not many people who can cut through it.

"You're sure you want to drive?" I had asked, on our way to the party.

"It's freezing," she had said, backing out of the lot near our dorm. "And anyway, I'm too hungover to drink tonight." It was a cold night, a Saturday in the slump of February. She parked her SUV in the driveway outside the house.

Later that night, with Stella occupied, I went home alone. The snow made for a long and slippery walk, but I was warm in a plush down jacket with a fur-trimmed hood—a jacket Stella had lent to me a few months earlier and insisted I keep. I stamped the slush from my feet on the sodden entrance mat to our dorm and fitted the key into our door. Midnight was an oddly quiet hour. The partygoers were still absent, the conscientious students already asleep.

Over the years, I would grow used to this feeling. Empty bed, ticking clock: the chilly vacuum created by her absence. I was who I was because of her. I wanted the sight of her smile, the sound of her laughter, the warmth of her hand on my arm, the sense of her within easy reach. On quiet nights when I was alone and Stella was elsewhere, I wondered how pathetic this was. I mean, really: was it normal to think about another person so much?

But this night, this particularly cold and snowy February night, was only five months into our friendship. As the months turned into years, questions like that would lose their sharpness, and the answers would become irrelevant. What we had—eventually, I would see this—was nothing like a normal friendship.

Around 3 a.m., unable to sleep, I began to worry. Stella had been tired that day. She'd been planning to sleep in her own bed. She said that she had sex like men did, leaving afterward, refusing to spend the night. She had been sober when I left, and would have driven herself home. The boy, behind her, had bounded up the stairs two at a time. He had looked so pleased with himself. Too pleased.

"It's me," I said into the phone. "Again. Call me, okay? I'm worried."

But my texts and calls went unanswered. Another hour passed before I started to panic.

Something was wrong.

———

It had been the last stop on my trip. A small New England college, second tier and expensively manicured, what I imagined a country club looked like. On that trip to tour colleges, certain differences stood out. At some schools, I could imagine seamlessly fitting in. The bigger schools, those with vast student bodies and ample scholarships for people like me, room for a democracy's worth of differences.

This school wasn't like that. The smaller the club, the harder it is to blend in—I'd learn this repeatedly in the years to come. I lingered at the back of the group. Then someone approached, a shadow blocking the April sunlight in my peripheral vision.

"Nice shoes." She nudged her foot against mine. We were both wearing black Converses.

I turned and took her in. She was tall and blond and beautiful in a way that suggested glamour and globe-trotting, and radiated the possibilities of serious money. She pulled down her sunglasses, revealing cool blue eyes, and leaned closer. "I'm so bored I want to kill myself," she said.

"Don't do that," I said. "You'll never get the blood out of that white shirt."

Her laugh was harsh but amused. "What's your name? I'm Stella."

"I'm Violet," I said.

"Well, Violet, I'm afraid I have no choice." With a sigh, she hung her sunglasses from her shirt. A white Oxford, top three buttons undone. The weight of the sunglasses tugged the fabric down, revealing an arc of lacy bra. "This is the only place I got in."

"It's a good school," I said.

"It's a good school for people like me," she said.

"Which means?"

The tour group was moving on. We followed, slowly.

"Rich," she said. Then shrugged. "And lazy."

It was my turn to laugh. She smiled.

"Live your truth," she said. "Isn't that what the gurus say?"

"A quarter million bucks in tuition is a lot to pay for your truth."

Stella laid a hand on my arm. "See that woman?" she said, indicating an older but similarly attractive woman at the front of the group. "That's my mother. You know what *she* always says? You can't put a price on respectability."

"Honestly, I don't know what that means," I said.

Stella laughed again. "Me, neither. But she says it with conviction."

The group was rapt as the tour guide described a stone gargoyle. But Stella was looking at me, squinting. The quality of her attention was at once sincere and ironic, unlike anything I'd experienced before. *Keep talking*, it said. *We're just getting started.*

"So what's your deal, Violet?" she said. "Are you going here, too?"

———

I could hear the thumping music from a hundred yards away. The windows were bright against the darkness. I told myself I was being paranoid. Stella was probably fine. But then the driveway came into view, and sure enough, her car wasn't there.

The boy from earlier was in the living room, his shirt rumpled and eyes rimmed with red. The die-hard handful of remaining partyers didn't notice me, or the blast of cold air from the open front door. The room was humid with whiskey and sweat.

"Hey," I said, grabbing the boy's arm. "Where did Stella go?"

He swayed as he turned toward me. "Who are you?"

"Her roommate. She never came home."

"Dunno. She left a while ago."

"How long? Like, minutes? Hours?"

"I told her to stay. But she was all, *Ew, no. Your house is disgusting.*" He laughed at his own impression. Another boy was passed out on the lumpy couch, and someone was drawing in Sharpie on his forehead. The boy started to turn away, but I grabbed his arm again.

"Hey," I said. "Her car isn't in the driveway."

"She said she was fine to drive," he said. "I guess she can really hold her liquor."

"She wasn't drinking tonight."

"Oh yeah? Señor José Cuervo would say otherwise. Yo," he shouted as I hurried toward the door. "Tell that chick to call me."

At the end of the driveway, I whipped from left to right, my heart hammering. There hadn't been a single car on the road from our dorm. Stella must have gotten confused, driven in the wrong direction. I started walking that way, deeper into the woods, carefully but quickly. The road was icy and tunnel-like between the tall snowbanks, curving as it hugged the edge of the river. The moon was bright and full, and the stars were thick as spilled sugar.

"Stella?" I called into the empty woods. The sound of my voice, almost erased by the wind rustling the evergreens, was small and useless. She could be anywhere. How the hell would I find her? "Stella?" I shouted, louder this time.

The road dead-ended. I retraced my steps, and turned down another road. It was nearly 5 a.m. Calm down, I told myself. Maybe Stella was safe and sober. Maybe she'd taken another way home and was already asleep in bed.

After another dead end, then another, my fingers and toes had gone numb. That's when I saw a glimmer down the road. A shine of metal and glass, easy to miss in the snow.

New York plate, Mercedes medallion, MTK and ACK bumper stickers. The car had veered off the road, coming to a stop against a tree. "Stella!" I shouted, running to the front door. She was slumped over the steering wheel. A trickle of blood descended from her hairline.

"Wake up," I said, shaking her. She was breathing, but her skin was cold. The blood on her forehead had started to dry. "Wake up!" I shouted again, pushing her into an upright position, shaking her even harder.

She blinked several times. Then she shook her head, her eyes sliding back into focus. "What?" she said. "What happened?"

"Are you okay?" I said. "Is it just your forehead?"

"I'm so tired," she said.

"Jesus," I said. "Slide over. I'm going to drive."

"Last night was crazy," Stella said the next day, over a late brunch in the dining hall. She didn't remember how she'd gotten that drunk. When I asked if something had gotten into her drink—"you know what I mean," I said darkly—she rolled her eyes and said I watched too much TV. She took dainty bites of her toast, stirred a packet of sugar into her coffee. She kept recognizing people across the dining hall, smiling and waving at them.

"Stella," I said. "This is serious. You could have *died*."

"You're so dramatic," she said. "You shouldn't worry so much."

"But what if I hadn't found you?"

She laughed. "That's my point. You did find me. So who cares?"

———

"You're sure about this?" Diane Molina said, when I told her about my decision.

This was the week after I'd returned from seeing colleges. Mrs. Molina, my history teacher, had encouraged me to apply to the best schools, to every possible scholarship. The fact that I was throwing away a full ride at Duke surprised her as much as it did me.

"I already sent in the paperwork," I said.

"What do your parents think?" she said, cutting a square of lasagna from the pan, the melted cheese stretching into strings. I had dinner with the Molinas at least twice a week.

"They won't even care," I said.

"Of course they will." Diane frowned. She insisted I call her Diane at the dinner table. "Sometimes you're too hard on them, Violet."

"Well, they're hard on me." Like a reflex, my finger touched the scar above my eyebrow. My mother liked to throw things— bottles, plates—to make her point. Years ago, when my father took me to the clinic to get the gash on my forehead stitched up, he smiled and told the nurse how clumsy I was, falling on the playground.

"I think you have to be the bigger person here, sweetheart," Diane said.

Diane was the closest thing I had to a friend in my hometown in Florida, but sometimes she was too nice. Too forgiving. Her kindness didn't prevent my mother from resenting her. "Teacher's pet," she spat, every time I went over to the Molinas'. "You act so high and mighty, Violet. But they're trash, you know. Those people are trash."

No matter that the Molinas had college educations and a tidy split-level ranch, and we lived in a mildewed apartment with roaches. Despite how poor we were, my mother was a snob of the worst kind. Teachers weren't better than her. She paid taxes, which meant teachers *worked* for her.

"Not possible," I said to Diane.

"People can change," she said. "You'd be surprised."

Diane knew what it meant to be stuck in the wrong place. She had followed her husband to Florida for his job, and she was determined to make the best of it. Corey Molina was a reporter for WCTV, the CBS affiliate in Tallahassee. Before school, during the segments at 7:25 or 7:55, I'd watch him reporting on local robberies or fires or car crashes. He always arrived late to the dinner table, sighing with exhaustion. My fascination with Corey's work was the real reason I liked spending time with the Molinas.

That night, I was grilling Corey for more detail about his latest story when he laughed and shook his head. "You ask a lot of questions," he said, serving himself more lasagna.

"Sorry," I said.

"Just an observation, not an accusation," he said. To Diane, he cocked an eyebrow. "She'd be a good reporter, wouldn't she?"

She smiled. "She's going to be too busy with her Rhodes Scholarship for that."

"That is ridiculous," I said, though I was flushing with happiness. Those spring days on the eve of my departure felt heady with liberation. I was leaving behind a miserable town and miserable family forever. The freedom was intoxicating. I had just picked a school, and a future, based on a five-minute conversation with a stranger. But when you've grown up without money, and therefore without options, it's liberating to finally make this kind of reckless choice.

"Plus," Diane said, "she's got too much moral integrity to be in your business."

Corey looked at me, ignoring his wife's teasing. "I mean it," he said.

———

As luck would have it, Stella and I were in the same dorm. Within a week, Stella decided that she disliked her assigned roommate. Within a week and a half, the school happily accommodating, given her parents' donations, I'd switched places with this girl, taking her bed while she took mine. Stella told people that her old roommate had sleep apnea and the machine kept her up at night. The truth, which she told me alone, was that she found this girl pious and mousy.

Got it, I remember thinking. *Avoid those things.* When I passed this mousy girl in the dining hall or library, I gave her a sympathetic smile. I felt sorry for this girl, but I wouldn't have changed a thing. My position came with advantages.

"You're Stella's roommate?" people always said. "She's so cool."

A lush bouquet of adjectives described Stella: cool, funny, clever, outspoken, beautiful. Life was a party when she was around. But her personality had byways and channels that were invisible from most angles. Picture a river from above, and the canals and locks that only open when the conditions are right. I saw the parts of her that most people never did.

"Fair warning," Stella said, as we drove to her house for Thanksgiving that first year. "My parents aren't really huggers."

"Mine weren't, either," I said.

She laughed. "You talk about them like they're dead."

I shrugged. Instead of saying what I was about to say—*they might as well be*—I turned up the radio. Stella liked my cynicism, but only to a point.

"Violet," Anne Bradley said, shaking my hand as we stood in the foyer of their house in Rye, New York. "It is so wonderful to finally meet you."

During the pleasantries, I tried not to gawk. To describe the Bradley home required a vocabulary that would take me months and years to accumulate: a majestic white Colonial overlooking Long Island Sound, with a circular driveway and a carriage house. A sprawling green lawn with an orchard of Bosc pear trees, a swimming pool edged in travertine, a dock jutting into the water.

Through that week, I gave them reasons to like me. Stella's mother found me cleaning up the kitchen after breakfast. Stella's father saw me reading *The Portrait of a Lady* and complimented my taste; Thomas Bradley had always regarded Henry James as one of our greatest novelists. Anne and Thomas watched me, their polite-but-cool judgment evolving into warmth. They had oysters as an appetizer one night. When Anne demonstrated how to slip them loose from the shell, her guidance was free of condescension, like I was an exchange student from a foreign country.

In good palate-cleansing Protestant manner, the Bradley family always capped Thanksgiving dinner with a brisk walk through the neighborhood. It was freakishly cold that year. Stella looked at my thin jean jacket and said, "That won't work. Take this," handing me a parka from the hall closet. It was tomato red, heavy with down filling, the lining slippery smooth. Expensive clothes were like camouflage, or alchemy. During the walk, the Bradleys waving at the occasional neighbor, I liked the idea that—from afar, at least—I blended right in.

"Keep it," Stella said, later. "You're going to need a real jacket. I've got others."

Stella had treated it as a fait accompli that I'd come home with her for Thanksgiving. I hadn't even considered going back to

Florida, and Stella didn't question that, which was another reason to love her. "Thank God we saved you from those people," she sometimes said, which was the closest we ever got to talking about my family. My home seemed to exist in her mind as a dense jungle, a tangle of sinister mysteries.

"And my parents love you, by the way," she said, after Thanksgiving. "I can tell."

"Oh!" I said. "Good. Well, I love them, too."

Stella snorted. "You don't have to say that."

"But it's true."

"Really?" She arched an eyebrow. "Then you're a better person than me."

It was, in fact, only half true. I loved the calm and comfort of the Bradley family. But what I couldn't admit to Stella, what I could barely admit to myself, was the underlying calculation. It whirred constantly in the back of my mind. To wind up at a private college like this was luck enough, but to wind up best friends with the most dazzling girl on campus? It wasn't that my personality changed when I met Stella. It was that it *became*, it flourished, because I could say things to Stella that I wouldn't have said to anyone back home—knowing they would only respond with bafflement, or laughter—and she always volleyed right back, sharpening me like a whetstone to a knife. I didn't just want the friendship of this dazzling girl. I wanted the world that had made her so dazzling in the first place. This was a golden opportunity not to be taken for granted. So I paid attention. I studied everything. I learned the vocabulary and the syntax. It was hard work to win over people like Anne and Thomas Bradley. But in the service of a larger ambition, hard work is nothing.

Besides, genetics dictated that I had inherited the streak of darkness in my parents. Overcoming that would take deliberate effort. I'd rip the weeds out by the root, leave the soil rich and bare. I was certain that if I played the game correctly, I could become someone better. The past could be overcome. Outcomes could be changed.

And through the years, new things grew. My role became firmly established. "Violet's the responsible one," Stella told people, slinging her arm around my shoulder, spilling her drink in the process. "And I'm a mess."

Everyone came to agree on this. Stella Bradley didn't care about anything. That's what made her so *fun*. Stella's credit card paid for spontaneous road trips, lavish meals, and hotel rooms. She made cutting remarks about her family's net worth as she handed over the platinum AmEx. She liked being rich, but she knew that it wasn't really *her* money, so she expurgated her guilt with fits of generosity. The fun we had was genuine and real, but Stella was also strategic when she declared me to be the responsible one. My responsibility had a particular utility. Stella had a unique tendency to get herself into binds; I got her out of them. I retrieved her when she was stranded, brought her money when she'd forgotten her wallet, held her hair back when she vomited from drinking too much. I saved her, over and over. *See?* she'd say, when I rescued her from yet another scrape. *See how right I am?*

———

There was an assumption, shared by nearly every student at our expensive college, that anything was possible. No careers, no avenues were off-limits. Your ambition didn't have to be circumscribed or compromised. Stella had taught me how to live in this world of long horizons. I imagined the years ahead, the two of us gradually becoming equals. Look at how well the system had taken care of the Bradleys. If I worked hard, wouldn't it take care of me?

But that, I eventually realized, was naive.

Stella opened doors for me. She showed me how confident and outspoken a person could be. Even a young woman, whom the world is not inclined to take seriously. I learned by watching her, witnessing the power of her charm and confidence. I loved Stella, and beyond that, I needed her. This life wouldn't have been possible without her.

But the things you need when you're nineteen years old aren't the things you need later. People change. Relationships change.

There would be a test in the years to come. Could I do it without her?

Or, more accurately, could I do it in spite of her?

CHAPTER TWO

BACK WHEN I was in high school, Corey Molina described what it felt like to walk into the CBS offices for the first time. The walls were lined with portraits of legends—Edwards, Cronkite, Rather, Stahl—and it was thick with the aura of seriousness and *60 Minutes*. He had gotten his first job by showing up and not leaving until someone gave him something to do. "You need two things to succeed in this business," Corey had said. "A news instinct, and a little bit of masochism."

I had moved to New York the summer after graduating from college. I struck out at the page program at CBS. Ditto for NBC, and ABC, and CNN and Fox and MSNBC. My résumé lacked the right internships and connections, but it didn't faze me. My mother was always falling for those law-of-attraction scams: think like a millionaire and you'll become a millionaire! She assumed it was as easy as ordering a pizza. But I believed in my own version of the law. You can become a millionaire if you really want it. You just have to bust your ass to get there.

There was a relatively new channel called King Cable News. It had no ideological bent, nothing that made it stand out, except for a wealthy owner—Mr. King, of King Media—who was happy to run the company in the red for as long as he had to. For the decade of KCN's existence, Mr. King had been poaching stars from other networks, wooing them with massive paychecks, complete editorial independence, and equity in his privately held media conglomerate. When King Media eventually went public, the star anchors wouldn't be wealthy in the usual multimillion-dollar-contract way. They'd be wealthy like tech titans, or hedge funders. KCN had won several Peabodys and Emmys in the past few years and had started gaining respect in the industry. Their audience was growing, too; they were often in third place, sometimes in second. More to the point, they were the place that offered me a job.

Rebecca Carter had been a network star, a White House correspondent and then a morning show anchor, and one of Mr. King's original hires. Her innate seriousness, which she'd had to shelve for morning television, was on full display at *Frontline with Rebecca Carter*, the flagship program in the 8 p.m. hour. And it worked: she was on a hot streak lately, moderating a primary debate in the last presidential election, scoring big sit-downs.

After arriving at KCN's headquarters in Midtown on my first day in August, I took the elevator up to the floor that housed *Frontline*. There had been no instructions about an orientation or who to ask for. Within seconds, a woman spotted me—and the bright lanyard that held my new ID badge—and shouted, "Intern!"

"Me?" I said.

"Who else? I need you to photocopy this."

She was waving a sheaf of paper like an urgent white flag. I took it from her, but before I could ask where the copier was, she had disappeared.

"Over there." At the desk next to me, a guy with his phone pinned between ear and shoulder gestured across the room. "The copier's around that corner."

"Ah—thank you," I said, and ran toward the copy room. As I was squinting at the machine's instructions, my forehead pricking with sweat, panicking at the options to collate and staple and double-side, the woman reappeared. "Actually, I need ten copies of that," she said. She snapped her fingers. "*Now*, not yesterday."

After leaving the copies with her, I wasn't sure what to do next. Across the bullpen, the nice guy who'd given me directions was now off the phone. I walked back over.

"Success?" he said, eyes glued to his computer screen, typing with disarming speed.

"Thanks again," I said. "It's my first day. I'm an intern."

"I'm Jamie," he said. He had a Southern accent, and it came out like *ahm Jay-mee*.

"Violet," I said. "I'm not sure who I'm supposed to report to."

"It doesn't really work like that," he said. "People will figure out who you are and they'll just tell you what to do. Although you're lucky. You're starting at a quiet time."

"Really?" I said, looking around the newsroom—the ringing phones, the people running back and forth. There was a guy on crutches, following a group into the conference room. Even he was hobbling as fast as he could.

"Relatively quiet," Jamie said. "Rebecca's on vacation until Labor Day. It'll get a lot busier when she's back."

"But that's three weeks from now," I said.

"Correct."

"Well, I thought anchors hated being off the air for that long."

Jamie stopped typing. He looked at me for the first time. "Violet what?"

"Violet Trapp."

"You did your homework, Violet Trapp. *Most* anchors hate being off the air. But Rebecca would rather be on vacation. Normal people don't care. That's what she says. The only people who care about anchors taking long vacations are those rabid media-watcher types. And they're all out in the Hamptons right now, too."

"Oh," I said. "Smart lady."

"The smartest." His phone started ringing. "All right, next thing. Could you run down to the cafeteria and get four coffees? Two black, two with milk and sugar. Keep the receipt."

———

The days went fast. There was no time to train the interns, so we were assigned to the simplest tasks: fetching coffee, answering the phone, running scripts to the control room. Or seemingly simple, because the tasks had to be done perfectly and they had to be done *now*. On Friday, one of the production assistants approached our cluster of interns and said, "Which one of you made it through the week without fucking up?"

The other five interns had each been reamed out by somebody and laughed nervously at the question. Except for me. I stepped forward. "What do you need?" I said.

The assistant was maybe a year older than me, but hierarchy was hierarchy. "Bring the guest from the green room to the set before the D block," he said. "You can handle that?"

"I'm on it," I said, ignoring his snotty tone.

The guest was a consumer safety expert, there to talk about the latest changes in airbag technology. The executive producer wanted the anchor to stretch the interview to fill the block. It was amazing how much could be learned just by eavesdropping.

"Here you are," I said, pushing open the swinging door that led to Studio B. Terrance, the substitute anchor while Rebecca was on vacation, was shuffling papers on the desk and humming to himself. He looked up at the guest and nodded, then went back to his notes. Terrance wouldn't bother engaging until the cameras were on. It was a waste of energy.

"Hey, lady," the floor director said. "Are you staying or leaving?"

"Am I allowed to stay?" I said.

"As long as you stand in the back and don't get in anyone's way," he said. "But if you're staying, close the damn door."

It was dark around the edges of the studio, and freezing cold. The cameraman to my left was wearing a fleece sweatshirt and a hat, and the one to my right was drinking hot tea. The consumer safety expert squinted into the bright stage lights. "Can I get a glass of water?" he said.

"Two minutes back," the floor director yelled. "Water's under the desk."

The door swung open. "Home stretch, Hank," Jamie said, cuffing the floor director on the shoulder. "Almost the weekend."

"Airbags," Hank said. "Christ. They didn't have airbags when I was a kid. You just had to hold on."

"Did they even have cars when you were a kid, Hank?" Jamie grinned. Then he spotted me, standing at the back. "You're staying to watch?" he said.

"Is this your segment?"

"Yup," Jamie said. "How's the first week been?"

"Good. Great, actually. It's been fun."

"Thirty back!" Hank the floor director yelled.

Jamie stepped forward. "Hey, Terrance. You're giving us a quick intro, throwing to package, then four minutes for the interview. Got it?"

Terrance narrowed his eyes. "I've done this before, James."

"Better safe than sorry," Jamie said.

"Hey!" the airbag expert said. "That's exactly my motto."

"And we're on in five," Hank shouted. He finished the countdown with his hand. The red light on the camera went on. Terrance sat up straight, relaxed his face into a confident expression, looked into Camera One, and began talking. After he introduced the previously recorded package and the camera cut away, he sighed and went right back to shuffling his papers.

"Long week, I guess. So, do you like the other interns?" Jamie said.

"Sure," I said. "I guess."

Jamie smiled. "You sound enthusiastic."

"We don't have a lot in common," I said. "Everyone seems... connected."

"How so?"

"This one girl—her father used to be a producer. Tim Russert's producer."

"Ah," Jamie said. "Yeah, I'd say that's a useful connection."

"She kept calling him 'my late uncle Tim.' Oh, you know, the time my late uncle Tim was talking to Yasser Arafat. Finally someone said, Tim who? She had been *dying* for one of us to ask."

Jamie laughed, and I blushed. "Never mind," I said. "I shouldn't be talking trash."

"Don't worry about it. Those connections only matter at the beginning. Most of those people will wash out," he said. "I didn't know a single person when I started in news. Eliza completely took a chance on hiring me six years ago."

Hank waved at us to shut up. The prerecorded package was over, and now Terrance was introducing the guest. During the interview, Terrance nodded and made eye contact and thoughtful "hmm" noises. It was a skillful performance, although when Hank started making "wrap it up" hand gestures, Terrance's genuinely delighted smile undercut his previous posture of interest. *This* was what he was actually interested in—going home. "Well!" he exclaimed. "I'm afraid that's all the time we have tonight."

"And we're clear," Hank yelled when the red light switched off.

The studio was one floor below the newsroom. As Jamie and

I climbed the stairs, he said, "They're not stuck up like that. Rebecca and Eliza, I mean. They could be, with the success they've had, but they aren't."

I was intensely curious about Eliza. She was the executive producer of *Frontline*, her office adjacent to Rebecca's corner suite, her shelves lined with a collection of news & doc Emmys. I'd googled her, of course, but this was the difference between talent and producers: Rebecca's every movement was plastered across the internet, while Eliza remained almost anonymous. Mostly I knew that Eliza Davis was an exception in a business still dominated by white men: a powerful black female EP.

"I'd think that helps," I said. "Not being snobby. Right? It keeps you outside the bubble."

Jamie looked over at me. "Where do you come from, anyway?"

When I started telling him where I'd gone to school, he shook his head. "No, I mean, where are you actually *from*. Your hometown."

"Oh." I responded as I always did: "You've never heard of it."

Back in the newsroom, Jamie said, "A bunch of us are going for drinks across the street. A Friday tradition. Want to join?"

I hadn't gotten a paycheck yet, and my bank account was nearly bare. But I could afford one beer. I'd eat rice and beans for the rest of the weekend. "Sure," I said.

"Good," Jamie said, smiling. "More time to figure out what your deal is."

"Honestly, it's a nowhere town." Didn't moving to New York mean I'd never have to talk about my past? Then again, Jamie's job was to ask questions. "On the Florida Panhandle. Barely even a real place."

"Everywhere is a real place."

"I haven't lived there in a long time." There was a tightness in my chest, and I was feeling uncomfortably defensive. "It's not home anymore."

"Okay, okay. You're pleading the Fifth, then?"

I laughed. "Yeah."

"We can talk about it some other time," Jamie said. "But you know, I'm from nowheresville just like you. Small town in South Carolina, in my case. My momma would murder me if she thought I was disrespecting it. Here, look." Jamie pulled out his phone, flicked through a stream of photos. "From the Fourth of July parade. See that lady dressed up like Martha Washington?"

"*That's* your mom?" I said. This woman was wearing a powdered wig and a hoop skirt.

"You don't get to choose them," he said, but his bashful smile showed real pride.

———

The week before I started at KCN, Stella's mother asked me to meet her at the apartment to discuss the—as she put it— "arrangement."

It was a gorgeous two-bedroom on a leafy block in the West Village. A chef's kitchen, a wood-burning fireplace, a terrace, a doorman. Anne and Thomas Bradley had their waterfront mansion in Rye, but they were looking ahead to retirement, to eventually wanting a pied-à-terre in the city. At least, this was their excuse for buying Stella the apartment. Even the wealthy feel pressure to justify these kinds of decisions.

"Violet," Anne said, kissing my cheek. The kitchen was empty except for her Birkin bag, resting on the white marble counter. "So nice to see you."

Living with Stella was the only way I could afford to be in New York. After graduation, Stella planned to travel with friends for an indefinite stretch. She was in Cannes, then Lake Como, then wherever the wind took her. "But so what?" Stella had said. "Obviously you should move in right away. That's what the apartment's there for, isn't it?"

Anne Bradley seemed to see things differently. From her bag she pulled a folder, and from the folder a stapled document. "We took the liberty of drawing up an agreement," Anne said. "Just to formalize things."

"Okay," I said. There were several pages filled with dense clauses and subclauses. As I attempted to decipher the first paragraph, Anne slid a pen across the counter.

"Could I read the whole thing through?" I said. "Just to be sure."

"Oh," Anne said. Then she smiled. "Take all the time you need."

From what I could tell, it looked like a standard tenant agreement. But on the last page, a number jumped out: fifteen hundred dollars per month in rent, to be paid no later than the first of the month, by check or wire transfer to Mr. and Mrs. Thomas Bradley.

I swallowed. When her parents first came up with this idea and I'd asked Stella how much my rent would be, she'd shrugged and said, "I don't know. Nothing, probably." I should have known, by now, that Stella's assurances were worthless. Her parents controlled the money, not her. Or maybe, to her, fifteen hundred *was* nothing. But still, the price came as a shock.

"Everything okay?" Anne said. The pen was in my hand but hadn't yet touched paper.

I took a deep breath. "Mrs. Bradley, I'll be honest. I can't afford this. After taxes, I'm only bringing home about fourteen hundred a month with this internship."

"Oh!" she said. "Oh, Violet, I didn't realize. We'll change it, of course."

"Thank you," I said. "I really appreciate your understanding."

"What would work for you? Let's see. What if we halved it to seven hundred fifty?"

I ran through the mental calculation. Seven hundred fifty on rent, plus two hundred on student loans. That left four hundred and fifty to live on. Fifteen dollars a day. I'd walk to work; I'd eat cheap. Tight, but I could manage.

"That would be great," I said.

"Oh, good," Anne said. "Phew."

"Should I just cross this out?" I said, pointing at the number. "And write in seven fifty?"

"Well." Her smile slackened. "Actually, why don't you give me that. I'll have our lawyer type up a new version. It's more official that way."

But the process dragged out. Anne e-mailed me with updates. Just waiting for our lawyer to revise the agreement, she wrote. Then, I have the agreement! Thomas wants to look it over one more time. And then, I'm sorry for the bother, Violet, but could you please send us your employment letter from KCN?

Can you talk for a sec? I texted Stella. By this point I was staying at the apartment, in a sleeping bag on the floor, but Anne and Thomas probably only agreed to this because I had nowhere else to go. An employment letter? Did they think I was scamming them? I felt mildly panicked. If the Bradleys decided to pull the plug, I had no other plan.

Stella would reassure me. She would laugh and say that her parents were crazy, we just had to humor them. *You know how rich people are,* she'd say. *Obsessed with every dollar.* If she ever texted me back, that is—which she didn't. She often forgot to check her phone, and while she was frolicking in Europe, who could blame her? But her silence stung a little.

In the end, it was fine. I signed the revised agreement and handed it to Anne. She nodded, her lips set in a tight line. "Thanks for your patience, Violet," she said, tucking the papers into her bag. "You see, Thomas pointed out that it's a... somewhat *unusual* arrangement."

I wrinkled my brow, offered a vague smile of puzzlement.

"Stella isn't living here, after all," Anne said. "It's a bit odd, don't you see?"

"But she'll be back soon," I said.

"You're practically like a second daughter, of course. But still. It's a big expenditure. The maintenance alone! Well, you know what it's like in New York."

It's official, I texted Stella that night. I am a tenant of Anne and Thomas Bradley.

Lol, she texted back. Now you know how I feel.

Where are you, anyway? I wrote, hoping to catch her while her phone was still in her hand. But there was no response. Not that day, or the next day, or the day after.

In September, one of *Frontline*'s senior producers quit. The gossip was that he had waited until Rebecca returned to give notice, in the hopes that she would make some grand gesture to counter his offer from another network. Instead she told him goodbye and good luck. Rebecca valued loyalty.

This created a ripple effect. Jamie was promoted to senior producer. Someone was promoted to fill his old job. It resulted in an opening for an assistant, a job with a real salary and benefits and security. To say that each of us interns wanted that job was like saying that America wanted to beat the USSR during the Cold War. It was a question of existential purpose.

"Are you busy right now?" I said, stopping by Jamie's desk one afternoon. There were several rungs between us, but I still went to him with my constant questions. Plus, we were becoming something like friends.

"Always," he said, typing on his phone. "What's up?"

"I need some career advice." I lowered my voice and glanced around. The newsroom was competitive but not cutthroat, so you couldn't be too blatant. "I want that assistant job."

He laughed. "Oh? I never would have guessed."

"What can I do to make sure I get it?"

He put his phone down. "Memorize the difference between a cappuccino and a cortado. The other interns just don't seem to get it."

"Very funny."

"Partly it's luck. But you should try to make yourself indispensable. It needs to be *you* that producers think of when they need something done, not someone else."

The vacant desk sat there like a shiny prize. There was no urgency in making a decision. At this point, several of us interns were capable of carrying out the work of an assistant. There was script-running and lunch-fetching, but there were also the complex systems that we had finally mastered: searching the archive, pulling stock images, monitoring alerts in iNews. Every minute of programming required a staggering amount of technical work. It wasn't hard, but it was finicky, and a lot of it trickled down to us.

The lack of timeline drove some of the interns crazy. A few of them quit. That just showed they weren't cut out for the work. If you wanted predictability, this was the wrong business.

"Is it a test?" I asked Jamie, at one point. "Like, *Survivor: Newsroom Edition*?"

He laughed. "Really? There's a hurricane in the gulf and two wars in the Middle East and wildfires in California. You think the bosses have time to think about the *interns*?"

"Fair enough," I said.

One day I walked past the empty desk and noticed that the phone was ringing. No one else made a move to answer it, so I sat down and picked up. "KCN, this is Violet speaking."

"*Who?*" the voice shouted. "Never mind. We've got a big problem. I've got the camera crew here and I've got this lady mic'd and lit but she's getting cold feet." His voice was familiar: one of the field producers. "Major problem. We're going to have to scrap this from the rundown."

"Don't hang up," I said. "I'm going to put you on hold, okay?"

I sprinted to find the senior producer for the segment. Her eyebrows shot up when I relayed the message. "What else did he say?" she said. "What were the exact words?"

"I've got him on line three," I said, pointing at her blinking phone.

"Oh!" she said. "Nice. Thank you."

I wound up as the go-between all day, bringing scribbled messages to the senior producer when she was in meetings, relaying precise instructions back to the field producer. It was such a scramble that when the editor was cutting the tape, the producer asked me to record the scratch track, the narration that the reporter—who was en route back from the field—would later replace with his own voice. In the end, the interview was salvaged. Hours of frenzy were distilled into a neat three-minute package in the C block. After the broadcast, the senior producer thanked me and said, "It's Violet, right? Good work today."

The next week, the job was mine.

———

What's our address? Stella texted me one morning that fall.

It was a busy day at work, and by evening I had forgotten about the text, or what her reason for it might be. When I got home, the lights were on. A pair of ballet flats and a quilted jacket were discarded near the front door. "Stella?" I called out.

A girl emerged from the kitchen. A brunette, who I didn't recognize. "Are you the roommate?" she said. "Stella mentioned you might be here."

"I'm sorry," I said. "But who are you?"

"A friend of hers," she said. She was wearing an oversize button-down and, apparently, no pants. There was a cigarette between her fingers, with a delicate column of ash. "She said I could crash for the night."

"You can't smoke in here," I said automatically, thinking of paragraph 5, subparagraph B, in my agreement with the Bradleys.

She took another drag. "Seriously?" she said, stretching out the word. Bad vocal fry.

"It's their apartment, not mine," I said.

"I can see that." She stared at me appraisingly, like she was sizing up an untagged item at the flea market. I followed her into the kitchen, where she flicked her cigarette into the sink and opened the refrigerator. "Don't you have anything to drink?" she said, scanning the shelves. "Don't you *live* here?"

"How do you even know Stella?" I said.

"Isn't Stella the best?" she said. Her purse had spilled its contents across the kitchen counter. Lipstick, eyeliner, crumpled bills, matchbooks. She lit another cigarette. There were always girls like this, blasé and affectedly cool, who buzzed around Stella like flies around rotting fruit. They made me feel prickly, territorial. Stella was *mine,* not theirs.

The girl said she was only spending one night. But that turned into two nights, and three. I couldn't help texting Stella to vent. Not that I had any grounds to complain; she'd invited this girl, after all. And this was her apartment. But that night my phone rang.

"Is she still there?" Stella said, the connection clear despite the ocean between us.

"Yup," I said. From down the hall came the smell of cigarette smoke and the tinny sound of a TV show playing on her computer.

"What the fuck?" Stella said. "Go get her. Put me on speaker."

"Oh," the girl said, startling when I opened the door.

"Hey," Stella said. "I said you could stay one night. *One.* Why are you still here?"

The girl glanced back and forth between me and the phone in my outstretched hand. Her eyes went wide. Her mouth opened and closed, swallowing her panic.

"Hel-*lo?*" Stella said. "Can anyone hear me?"

"We're here," I said. "But it seems our friend is at a loss for words."

"You told on me?" the girl hissed.

"Violet happens to be honest," Stella said. "She happens to be a *good* person. The kind of friend who warns you about shady shit like this."

"You should really pack your things," I said, almost laughing at the look on this girl's face. "I'll ask the doorman to get you a cab."

"See how nice she is?" Stella said. "I would've just thrown your crap out the window."

Stella insisted on staying on the phone until the girl had gone. "Chop-chop," she kept saying, her voice beaming through the black screen. When the front door finally closed behind the girl, both of us burst out laughing.

"God," I said. "Thank you."

"Are you kidding?" Stella said. "That was fun."

"She was the worst."

"The *worst.* I mean, I barely know her. She was in Cap d'Antibes a month ago, same time as me. I owed her one."

"Owed her for what?"

"We were on this guy's yacht. He was a creep. He wouldn't leave me alone. She made an excuse so that we could leave."

"Ah," I said. "That trick. Instant case of food poisoning?"

Stella laughed. "It's just not the same without you, Violet."

We talked for a long time that night. Stella was a natural storyteller, and traveling had given her plenty of material. The jealousy that had accrued over the past few days, listening to this girl talk about Stella (they were so much alike, they were always on the same *wavelength*, you know?), washed away. This was just the long-distance phase of our relationship—that's what Stella said. We knew couples from college who had moved to different cities on opposite coasts, determined that nothing would change. "They can do it, why can't we?" she said. "It's only temporary." I didn't want to point out how much work it took. How rare it was that both people put equal energy into maintaining the relationship.

"Wait, so where are you? In France?" I asked.

"Paris," she said. "Currently lingering on the balcony, avoiding the world's dullest dinner party. Guess what I'm looking at right now."

"The Eiffel Tower?"

She laughed. "How did you know? What about you, what are you doing?"

I looked down at my pajamas, at the sponge in my hand, which I was using to wipe down the kitchen counters. It was immensely satisfying to have the apartment to myself again, to restore order to it. "Cleaning the kitchen," I said.

"That's my girl," she said.

It could have been a split screen in a movie, two women in opposite settings. Both of us had been itching to graduate, bored with school for different reasons. But even as Stella told me more about Paris, the shopping and the beautiful people and the dinner parties that began at midnight, it struck me that I didn't want to be there. I missed her, but I was happy with this life in New York, this sense of succeeding on my own terms.

She wasn't sure when she was coming home. She wasn't sure *if* she was coming home. The European lifestyle suited her. This she said jokingly, but also not. Climbing into bed that night, I thought of Anne Bradley handing me the paperwork. *An unusual arrangement.* Luck can vanish as suddenly as it appears. If Stella never came back, would they keep subsidizing this apartment just for me?

"She wants a hard copy of the script in front of her," one of the producers said. "Run it down to the studio, will you?"

"Rebecca does?" I said.

"Who else!" the producer barked. "Pronto."

In the weeks since her return, I'd only seen Rebecca from afar, through the glass walls of the conference room, or coming and going from her corner office. When I pushed open the swinging door to Studio B, where she was sitting at the anchor desk, she looked up from her phone right away. "Who is that? Is that my script?"

It was hot under the bright stage lights. "Here you are, Ms. Carter."

She had intense green eyes, the color of spring. "It's Rebecca. Never Ms. Carter, got that? Ms. Carter makes me sound like a middle school principal."

"Sorry. Rebecca."

"You're new, aren't you? What's your name?"

"Violet Trapp."

"Violet, could you be a hero and get me a tea? The throat-coat kind they have in the green room. I keep telling them to tone it down with the air-conditioning, but they won't listen to me. Even though my name is on the damn set—isn't that right, Hank?"

"That's right." Hank, the floor director, nodded. "Buncha assholes."

When I returned a few minutes later, Rebecca was marking up the script. Her eye flicked to the tea I slid in front of her, but she didn't look up. She was in the zone. "Thank you," she murmured.

"Thirty seconds!" Hank shouted. He turned to me. "It's you again, huh?"

"Is it okay if I stay and watch?"

He shrugged. "You know the drill."

Rebecca straightened her papers, nodded at whatever Eliza was saying in her earpiece, tucked her phone and her tea beneath the desk. After the cold open ("Tonight, on *Frontline*," Rebecca's previously recorded voice narrated) and the slick theme music, Rebecca followed Hank's gesture to Camera One. "Good evening," she said. "We begin tonight in the Caribbean, where Tropical Storm Lyle has officially become Hurricane Lyle. The storm is predicted to hit the Carolinas next week, and millions of Americans could be affected. For the latest we turn to our meteorologist—"

Rebecca had many things in common with Terrance, the sub-stitute anchor: a warm facial expression that merged curiosity and concern, a beautiful low voice, an easy chemistry with the reporters in the field. But I couldn't take my eyes off Rebecca. That hadn't been remotely true when Terrance was anchoring.

"I can't figure it out," I said to Jamie, later that same night.

"Ah," Jamie said. "Everyone remembers their first time."

"But I watched Terrance that night. Remember, you were there."

"Terrance is Terrance. Rebecca is a star. And the first time you're up close and personal with someone like that—that's special."

"You make it sound like I just lost my virginity."

"It's an appropriate metaphor."

I squeezed the wedged lime into the narrow neck of my Corona. "Well, it was *much* more exciting than losing my actual virginity, let me tell you."

Jamie laughed, and I felt a ripple of uncertainty. Why did I say that? It sounded flirty, and I hadn't intended flirty. We were at the bar with our colleagues, the Friday night ritual to ease the transition from week to weekend. For the workaholics who thrived at KCN, the cadences of normal life could be difficult. Some dealt with it by working all weekend. Others dealt with it by drinking and going out too much. And then there was Jamie, the rare producer who maintained a semi-normal life, and his psychological health, in addition to his career.

It was like Jamie's wick burned slower than everyone else's. He accepted the imperfection of the work we did, which didn't make him love it any less. I had read once that the South was the only part of America that understood tragedy, because it was the only part of the country to experience defeat in war. This was grandiose, I knew, to leap from a calm voice in a Midtown bar to the sweep of history. But after a beer or two, my thoughts tended toward the grandiose. So did Jamie's. That was part of the reason I liked him so much.

"What about you?" I said. "The first time you met Rebecca. What was it like?"

He held up a finger. "Let me ask you a question. Tonight, when you were watching. Who did you want to be? Rebecca, behind the anchor desk? Or Eliza, in the control room?"

"That's easy," I said. "Eliza."

"Why?"

"I don't know. A gut feeling. Eliza's job seems more interesting. And harder, in a way."

"But you were saying that you couldn't take your eyes off Rebecca. That she had something that made her different from Terrance. Better than him."

"That's true," I said. "But whatever that thing is, I know I don't have it."

Jamie snapped his fingers. "Exactly."

"Hey," I said. "You could at least *pretend* to disagree."

"You know what a producer can do? She can take mediocre talent and make it good. She can take good talent and make it very good. But she can't take good talent and make it great."

"You mean stars are born, not made?"

"Sort of," he said. "Mostly my point is that a producer has to know his or her limits. Self-awareness. That's what separates us from the talent. That ineffable thing you were talking about— you know what I think it is? Delusion."

I laughed. "This is Rebecca you're talking about."

"I mean it in the kindest possible way," Jamie said. "If you *think* you're special and chosen, if you deliver the news believing that you possess some unique authority, guess what? It looks great on camera. People buy it." Jamie shrugged. "But you and I, we know what we don't have. We're too honest with ourselves to feel like we deserve the spotlight."

"Because no one deserves the spotlight?"

"Precisely." Jamie lifted his beer in salute.

"This Socratic method of yours," I said. "Is this how you haze all the new assistants?"

Jamie looked around the bar, at the tables covered in beer and nachos, at our colleagues gossiping energetically despite the dark circles beneath their eyes. "You see these people? Two or three years from now, most of them won't be here," Jamie said. "But I have a feeling you're in this for the long haul."

CHAPTER THREE

ON A SATURDAY morning in November, sitting in the kitchen with coffee and the news, I heard the front door open.

"Hello?" a voice called from the other room. "Anyone home?"

"Mrs. Bradley?" I called back. In the foyer stood Anne, and a second woman. Anne was wearing leather driving shoes, a field jacket, and a silk scarf. The other woman was wearing a wrap dress, a trench coat, and kitten heels. Both of them had perfect blond bobs. I was in yoga pants and a threadbare T-shirt, my unwashed hair in a ponytail.

"I see what you mean," the second woman said to Anne, with a frown.

For a moment, I thought she was talking about me. Then she started walking the perimeter of the living room, craning her neck to look at the ceiling, running a hand along the mantel-piece. "Great bones," she said. "Southern exposure."

"It just seems a shame to have this place sitting so empty," Anne said. "Oh, Violet, let me introduce you to our decorator."

The decorator had a practiced smile and a firm handshake. She also had a chipless peach manicure and expertly applied makeup. Her whole look was impeccable, in the way of someone whose livelihood depends on aesthetics.

"So what are you thinking?" Anne said, trailing the decorator from the living room to the kitchen. The decorator nodded as she took in the marble countertops, the white cabinets, the six-burner range. "Kitchen's in great shape," she said. "This place must have been renovated a few years ago. New lighting, some open shelving and glass doors, and it'll look fabulous."

She sniffed, then peered into the sink, where a cast-iron skillet was soaking. "Do you cook?" she said to me.

"A little," I said. I'd bought pots and pans from the thrift store, and had been teaching myself with cookbooks borrowed from the library. It was the cheapest way to eat, and I liked the transformation of it, how the lowliest ingredients could become luxurious with time and effort.

"How lucky for you," she said. "A professional-grade kitchen like this."

"I thought Stella should come back to something more homey," Anne said, as we followed the decorator down the hall toward the master bedroom. "Who can blame her for staying away? This is daunting!"

There was a keenness behind Anne's laughter. For a woman like Anne, having a daughter like Stella was the ultimate achievement, a testament to good genes and good parenting. Her love was possessive, as attuned to Stella's absence as I myself was. She wouldn't admit it, but I could tell the months of Stella's sporadically answered calls and texts had hurt Anne.

After surveying the master bedroom, the decorator turned to the next door in the hall. "Oh no," Anne said, putting her hand on the woman's elbow. "That's Violet's room. We don't have to worry about that."

"I see," the decorator said. "My mistake."

"You've probably put your own stamp on it by now. Haven't you, Violet? You've had the run of the place."

"Yes," I said. "I'm very grateful."

"Well," Anne said. "I'm sure it won't be much longer until Stella is home for good."

After the decorator finished jotting down measurements and notes, she said to Anne, "I have a team of painters who can get the place done in a few days. Then we'll get everything delivered and installed. Less than a week and this place will be transformed."

"Wonderful," Anne said. "Violet, when do you leave for Thanksgiving?"

"Thanksgiving?" I said.

"It's only a few weeks away," Anne said. "You must have booked your flights by now. You know they get very expensive if you wait too long."

"Oh," I said. "Right."

"You *are* going home, I assume?" She arched an eyebrow. "Given that your parents didn't even come for graduation? They must miss you terribly. Violet is from Florida," she said to the decorator. "That's why I thought Thanksgiving would be the best time to get this done."

The decorator nodded. "It's much easier when the home is unoccupied."

"So when do you leave, Violet?" Anne said. "Monday? Tuesday?"

"Uh," I said. "Tuesday. Tuesday night."

"So we can get the painters in here by Tuesday morning," the decorator said. "If you don't mind taking your things with you, so you don't have to come back here after work."

"Perfect," Anne said, clapping her hands. "It's about time we make this place livable."

———

Over the past four years, I'd gone home with Stella for almost every holiday. I perfected the role of polite, self-sufficient houseguest. I did the dishes and ran errands, and expressed frequent gratitude for their hospitality. Even with Stella gone, I suppose I'd been unconsciously counting on an invitation from the Bradleys for Thanksgiving. My other friends from college knew that I always spent holidays with them. It was too embarrassing to disprove that. And it seemed better to go along with the lie I'd told to Anne.

I texted Stella: Classic Anne Bradley encounter today.

It took her twenty-four hours to respond: What happened?

I wrote back immediately: She's decorating the apt. Every decision is life-or-death important. It's like HGTV except they kill you if you pick the wrong shade of eggshell.

For days after that, I opened the messages on my phone to check whether her response had somehow failed to pop up on the screen. One sleepless night I scrolled through our text message history. For so long our words went back and forth with a steady *thwock,* like a tennis ball in a rally. When Stella left about six months ago, our exchanges became sporadic. When she was awake, I was asleep. When I was lonely, she was too busy having fun.

But I wasn't lonely, for the most part. Childhood had accustomed me to my own company. If I had one person who really understood me, that was enough. I didn't need a big group of friends, didn't need anyone beyond Stella—and I still had her, even if we didn't see each other every day. I trusted that.

It was only when Stella's absence was invoked by other people that I felt self-conscious, stripped of my passport to this world. News of her travels filtered through the social grapevine, and I was at the outer reaches. "I heard she's having a crazy time in Mykonos," a girl from college said, with an arched eyebrow. She was like the girl who had stayed in our apartment; she mistook gossip for intimacy, but she did so with such conviction that I felt compelled to nod along, pretending to know exactly what she meant.

Earlier that fall, during one of our Friday nights at the bar, Jamie was quiet for a while, and then he said, "Fair warning. At some point, I'm probably going to have to yell at you."

"Where did that come from?" I said. "Because I took the last mozzarella stick?"

"When it happens, I don't want you to think it's personal," he said. "This is the weird part about becoming friends with your coworkers. The screwups."

"Me, screw up?" I made a mock-offended face, but at the same time I felt a flush of gladness at that simple declaration, *friends*. "Maybe I'll just be perfect."

But then in mid-November, for a story about an American track runner who was charged with taking steroids, I had to find a photo of the coach who ran the doping program. A quick search produced the perfect image: the athlete and the coach, embracing after the last Olympics, gold medal around the athlete's neck. The story ran at the bottom of the hour, in the D block. The picture—it really was perfect; the pride, the hubris!—sat above Rebecca's shoulder for the better part of the two-minute story. I was pleased with my work.

Right after the broadcast, at 9:07 p.m., Jamie's phone rang. As he listened, his face turned redder and redder. When he hung up, he took a deep breath, and turned to me. The transformation was rapid, almost Hulk-like. I'd never seen Jamie like this.

"What is it?" I said, alarmed.

"How did you not double-check it, Violet?" His anger was tightly coiled, barely contained by his words. "Are you kidding me? How did you let that happen?"

"Let what happen?" My stomach flip-flopped.

"The goddamn *photo!*" he said. "That was the wrong person!

That wasn't the coach. That was another athlete. A retired athlete who happens to be incredibly famous."

"Oh," I whispered. "Oh my God."

"*And*," Jamie said. "*And*. In addition to being incredibly famous, this other athlete has staked his entire reputation on never doping. *Ever*. He's unimpeachable. He's like Mother Teresa. How could you not check that?"

"I'm sorry," I said. "Jamie. I'm so sorry. I'm—"

"Don't apologize to me," he snapped. "Apologize to him. We just smeared his reputation in front of a million people."

"What do I do?" I said, panicked.

"Start working on a correction," he said. "Rebecca will have to read it tomorrow."

It was the worst day I'd ever had at KCN. Eliza, rolling her eyes as Jamie explained the situation. Rebecca's visible exasperation as she read the correction during the next night's broadcast. It had been my mistake, but Rebecca had to own it. The lawyers had to sign off on a precisely worded letter of apology to the retired athlete, which performed the delicate dance of expressing genuine remorse but also avoiding a lawsuit. After the horrible twenty-four hours were over, Jamie collapsed into his chair with a sigh. "So, are you okay?" he said, with a look of genuine concern.

I nodded. I would have burst into tears if I hadn't cried so much already.

"I'm sorry I lost my temper," he said. "But we have to get these things right. It's a really, really big deal when we make a mistake like that."

"I know," I said quietly. "It won't happen again, I promise."

"We've all been there. Everyone has at least one colossal fuckup in their first year."

"It's an awful feeling." After a moment, I added, "Thank you for warning me, though."

"About the yelling? It happens, but I don't like it. Makes you feel like an asshole." He shook his head wearily. "Sometimes this job can drive you crazy."

———

I worked late on the Tuesday night before Thanksgiving. Around 11 p.m., Eliza passed my desk on her way to the elevator.

"Burning the midnight oil?" she said.

It was the first time Eliza had spoken to me. There were too many layers of hierarchy between us. But from afar, I had developed something of a crush on her. Where Rebecca was chatty and friendly, Eliza was intimidating and cool. My spine instinctively straightened as she stopped at my desk. She was a woman who forced you to be on your A game. No tolerance for meekness.

"Catching up on some things," I said.

"Remind me of your name?"

"I don't think I ever officially introduced myself." I stood up. She seemed slightly amused as she shook my hand. "Violet Trapp."

"How long have you been here, Violet?" Eliza said.

"I started as an intern in July, and became an assistant in September."

"And you're practically the last person in the office."

"So are you."

She smiled. "True, but we don't pay you enough to justify you working this hard."

"Maybe that's a chicken-and-egg question," I said. "Which comes first?"

"The hard work, or the payoff?" she said. "Good point."

She had a camel hair coat draped over one arm. As she pulled the coat on, flipping her dark hair free from the collar, she said, "Have a good holiday, Violet. See you Monday."

Jamie thought he was doing me a favor by arranging the schedule so that I had Thanksgiving and Friday off. "You work too hard," he said. "Use your vacation days. Take a break." I would have preferred to work all week, but to keep up appearances, I'd come up with a plan. I slept beneath my desk on Tuesday night, which was surprisingly cozy, duffel bag as pillow and coat as blanket. On Wednesday night, I caught the train to Long Island. Deep into the off-season in the Hamptons, hotel rooms were cut-rate. I'd been careful about budgeting, packing lunch and eating plenty of pasta, and I had a few hundred dollars saved up for emergencies. This counted, I suppose: maintaining my fiction for Anne Bradley. The area was familiar from tagging along with Stella in previous summers. If I was going to be alone, at least I could be somewhere scenic.

It was midnight by the time the train arrived in East Hampton. The taxi dropped me off at a motel on Montauk Highway. I didn't realize how tired I was until the next morning, Thanksgiving morning, when I woke up and saw that I'd slept for eleven hours.

In town I found a coffee shop that had stayed open. I caught my reflection in the window. The red parka that Stella had given me years ago was still in good shape, buttons replaced and stains carefully scrubbed away. At the beach, it was a beautiful fall day, cold but made warmer by the sunshine, the ocean glittering and rippling in the wind. There were a handful of people running and walking their dogs. A middle-aged woman, with the radiant health and silver hair of a vitamin spokesperson, emerged from the water in a wetsuit. Far offshore, boats puttered in the waves.

My mind wandered back to Christmas, my freshman year of college. That first time I went home, the house was shabbier than usual. Dishes piled in the sink, rancid black mold in the shower, an intense air of neglect. My mother was wary and skeptical, like

I was a body double sent to fool her. Only when she got sufficiently drunk did she let down her guard.

"Where'd you get that shirt, hmm?" she said, pinching the fabric between her fingers. It was a gray henley, a soft cashmere blend. "How'd you afford this nice little thing?"

"A friend lent it to me," I said, which was true.

The next day, my mother was wearing the shirt. She'd taken it from my room while I was sleeping. "Your *friend* won't mind, right?" she said, a cloying twist in her voice. She was thoroughly enjoying herself, stretching out the sleeves, using the hem to wipe spills, leaning close to the frying pan while she cooked, the grease speckling the fabric. "*Mom,*" I finally snapped, when she purposely sloshed red wine down her front.

A vicious grin spread across her face. "Just...be careful," I said, trying to suppress my frustration. But it was too late; I'd taken her bait.

"Oh, so now I'm not careful?" she said. "There's always something you want to criticize, Violet. We're *never* good enough for you. What's next?"

Teeth clenched, I stayed quiet.

"Hmm?" she said. "You think you can come back here and act like you're better than us?"

I changed my flight and returned to school early, on Christmas Day. It wasn't until then that I could pinpoint what had changed. My parents, my mother especially, were obsessed with status in the way the downtrodden always are. They clung to anything that could assure them of some minor superiority. And once upon a time, I'd been that thing for them. The smart daughter, the good daughter. The only teenager in town who wouldn't end up a deadbeat. They took pride in that. But when I came home, my mother felt the disgust radiating from my skin. She had lost the one thing that had made her special.

I hadn't done what I was supposed to do. I hadn't returned with compassion and love, an ambassador from another socioeconomic land. But this was another thing I admired about Stella: her indifference to what was expected of her. Why did I have to pretend to like my family? Or the holidays, for that matter? What was so great about them? The pageantry demanded was so one-note and unoriginal. If you weren't lucky enough to have a loving family, a long dining table, a bountiful spread—and maybe a crackling fire and attractive dog, to top it off—then you weren't doing it right. You were made to feel deficient.

Wherever Stella was in the world right now, she had probably forgotten that it was the fourth Thursday in November. Drinking champagne in Geneva or shopping in the souks of Marrakech, doing exactly what she pleased. Glamorous, but then again, why should that picture be any more glamorous than this one? I was a young woman alone on the beach, surf lapping at her ankles beneath her cuffed jeans, a weekend of freedom stretching ahead. One picture wasn't better than the other. Stella wasn't happier than me. Mostly she just *acted* that way.

"I won't give them a reason to pity me," my mother used to snarl. This was a bitter catechism she'd recite every few months, when money was tight. Food stamps were normal in our town. So were visits to the church basement, where canned and dried goods were free for the taking. I knew better than to suggest we make use of these resources, so that we could spend our money to repair the car or buy new shoes or pay off the credit card. My mother made it clear how she felt about that. Over time, I understood the point she was making. Pride could be a sin, but it could also keep you afloat. Pity was something you invited by acting pitiable.

On Friday, the day after Thanksgiving, I traced the same route from the motel to the town to the beach. The shops were livelier, windows advertising steep Black Friday discounts. When I stopped into the coffee shop, a barista was standing on a ladder, pinning up pine garlands while Christmas carols played in the background, the month-long milking of the holiday already in full swing.

Most of the restaurants in East Hampton were way beyond my price range. But that night I found a bar at the edge of town, with a Mets pennant and a neon Bud Light sign in the window, which looked more my speed.

"What can I get you?" the bartender asked when I pulled up a seat at the end of the bar.

"A glass of the house red," I said. "And a grilled cheese sandwich."

"That," he said, setting a wineglass on the wooden bar, "is an interesting combination."

"My version of a wine-and-cheese pairing," I said.

"Ah." He had a nice smile. "You're a classy woman."

The bar was about half full, pleasantly buzzing but not too loud. After he had circled around to pour refills, the bartender stopped in front of me, drying his hands on a towel. "How is it?" he said, nodding at my half-drunk glass of wine.

"Entirely serviceable," I said.

He laughed, and extended his hand. "I'm Kyle."

His handshake was warm and firm, ridged with light calluses. I said, "I'm Stella."

"Stella," he said. "I love that name. What brings you to town?"

I cocked my head. "You don't think I live around here?"

"No way you're a local. I've got a radar for these things."

"I needed a break," I said. "From my family. You know how the holidays are."

"Where are your folks?"

"Westchester," I said. "But I live in the city now."

It was an old shtick when Stella and I were at parties: if a guy hit on us, we'd give the other person's name and phone number. Nine times out of ten, this meant my phone would buzz with the persistent advances of a man hoping to get in touch with that gorgeous blonde named Violet. Every once in a while, someone—the less attractive sidekick—would hit on me, and I'd have occasion to call myself Stella Bradley.

But we only did this to keep them away. Tonight, even while shaking his hand, I thought, *I want to sleep with him.* Using Stella's name was part of the seduction. In college, I'd hooked up with guys every few months, enough to make me feel normal. It was easy enough, because Stella created a halo effect. If this ordinary-looking girl was always with the most beautiful girl on campus, then there had to be *something* special about her, right? They were consistently forgettable encounters, but already this felt different. A kind of desire that was almost like a test. Could I do this? Could I convince him that I was someone funnier, cooler, sexier than I actually was?

"So what do you do, Stella?" Kyle splashed more wine into my glass without asking.

"Nothing," I said. The word was pleasant to say; a smooth, easy release.

"Nothing?" he said. "Doesn't that get boring?"

"I've been traveling," I said. "Taking time to figure out what I really want to do."

And why shouldn't I? I thought. *Go ahead, let this guy say something snarky, I don't care. Why shouldn't I do what I feel like doing?* Stella had physical gestures—tilting her head and swinging her long hair over one shoulder, leaning her body across the table—that I found myself now imitating. She had taught me how to flirt, how to carefully mete out your personality, because the person across the bar isn't yet ready to know the real you. Borrowing Stella's name gave me a boost of confidence. I imagined a live wire stretching between me and her, wherever she was.

"An international woman of mystery," he said. "I like it."

"What about you?" I said. "Are you from around here?"

He stuck his thumb over his shoulder. "Grew up about ten miles down the road. I've been working for the owners since I was eighteen. They have another bar over in Sag Harbor. I switch between the two. Keeps things interesting."

"So you're a bona fide local."

He smiled. "You could say that."

"Well," I said, cocking my head. "Maybe you can show me around sometime."

In that moment, Kyle's expression changed. I'd seen this before. That sudden snapping of attention when a girl signals her interest, or there's a fourth down during a tight game.

At the end of the night, when his shift was over, Kyle said, "Can I walk you out?"

He'd been drinking water, and I'd switched to club soda. So many college hookups had been drunk and fumbling. Not this. There was an intensity from our being sober, from the hours of anticipation. In the parking lot, standing next to his car, the night clear and full of stars above us, neither of us had our jacket on. It had been hot in the bar, and the cool air felt good. Kyle was wearing a plaid shirt with the sleeves rolled up. One of the tattoos on his forearm was a silhouette of Long Island. He reminded me, in ways, of the boys from back home. Anchored forever in familiar soil.

Kyle kissed me. His hand slipped under my shirt, and I felt the ridges of his calluses against my rib cage. After a while, he said quietly, "Is your hotel nearby?"

I shook my head. "Let's do it here," I said.

"In my car?" he said. He turned, surveying the parking lot, which at 3 a.m. in November was empty except for us. When he turned back to me—my body against the side of his car, the prospect of gratification right there—he pushed into me and kissed me harder, his erection even more pronounced. It felt good. I thought, *I made this happen.*

After, as the car windows fogged from our breath and we twisted our limbs to pull our clothing back on, he said, "I'm so glad I met you, Stella."

"Me, too." I smiled at him, but a sadness seeped into the edges. The carriage was turning back into a pumpkin.

Kyle wanted to drive me home, but I couldn't let him see my dingy, run-down motel. There was a fancy hotel in town, where I told Kyle to drop me off. He waited in his car, headlights piercing the darkness. I stood at the entrance to the hotel, waving at him, but he didn't move. Only when I opened the door and went inside did I hear Kyle's car pulling away.

The man behind the front desk seemed surprised to see me.

"Hello," I said. "Uh, I'm staying at another hotel down the road, but it's just not up to snuff. I may want to switch. Do you have any availability tomorrow night?"

The man believed me, or he pretended to. "Yes," he said. "We do, in fact. Our deluxe junior suite is available tomorrow night. The rate is nine hundred."

"Great," I said. "Perfect."

"Do you need a taxi?" the man said, as I headed for the door.

"There's a car waiting for me outside," I said. "Good night."

———

Pete, one of the doormen in our building, nodded at me when I returned to the apartment.

"Did you have a good time in Florida, Miss Trapp?" he said.

I must have looked confused, because he added, "Mrs. Bradley mentioned it to me."

"Oh," I said. "Right. It was fine."

"No sunburn." He winked.

"Nope," I said. "The sun is terrible for your skin."

In the elevator, I felt a vague annoyance with Anne Bradley. She had a tendency to do this, to treat the most mundane details like breaking news. Why on earth would Pete the doorman care where I spent Thanksgiving? But people like Pete tended to indulge Anne, to feign interest. Doormen, hairdressers, manicurists, personal shoppers, housekeepers: Anne was a wealthy woman, and earning her tips or year-end bonuses required making her feel that her minor concerns were in fact major. In the past, when Stella chafed at her mother's nosiness, I thought she was overreacting. *Give her a break,* I had said more than once. *At least she cares.*

Now I sympathized with Stella. To financially depend on someone—as I did, with the Bradleys—and to sense them tracking your movements, that was unpleasant. Money bought allegiance, and allegiance bought control. Money also insulated its possessors from what people really thought. Poor Anne. People like Pete the doorman never told her that she was boring them to death. They warned you about these things in leadership books, the danger of yes men. But so far, no one had written a leadership book for wealthy women who exercised compulsively and lived in waterfront mansions in Rye.

I shook my head as I turned on the lights in the apartment. That was a nasty, ungrateful thought. The Bradleys were generous. Take this apartment redecoration—so much effort, and I was the only one who'd get to enjoy it.

It was beautiful. The walls were painted ecru and cream, the floors overlaid with oriental rugs in pale shades. The couches and chairs in the living room were covered in subtly patterned fabric and accented with bright pillows. A glass coffee table held oversize art books. A chandelier hung above the long dining table. In the kitchen, the cabinets were filled with flatware and mixing bowls and wineglasses. On the marble countertop were white ceramic canisters, lids lifted to reveal flour and sugar and rice and pasta. The furniture and artwork I understood, but the thoroughness in the kitchen baffled me. Was this meant for Stella? For me? It was like I'd wandered onto the set of a movie in which I wasn't starring.

I dipped a finger into the sugar. It was real. I'd wondered, for a moment.

The master bedroom was transformed, too. There was a king-size bed with a massive headboard, a vanity table in one corner, an armchair in the other. Lilacs in a glass vase on the nightstand perfumed the air. The flowers wouldn't last longer than a few days. I felt uneasy. None of this was meant for me. It was meant for a girl who wasn't here, and who had no plans to return anytime soon.

The door to the walk-in closet was slightly ajar. I opened it and turned on the light inside. It was filled with Stella's clothing. High heels and ballet flats lined up on shoe racks, sweaters folded and organized by color, dresses on silk hangers. I was light-headed and dizzy. It was too perfect. It was like a diamond necklace in a glass display. It said, *you want this, don't you?* It tempted you into smashing the glass and running off with the goods, even while the bloody shards in your knuckles reminded you that it didn't really belong to you.

I turned off the light and slammed the door closed. My heartbeat was running wild when I sat down on the mattress in my room. The lumpy mattress without a bed frame, the thrift-store lamp and the particle-board bookshelves: they were hideous, but they were mine. If I stuck to this room, I was safe. No one could accuse me of theft. Of leaving fingerprints on another person's possessions.

But over the following days, I kept thinking of those final moments in the car with Kyle.

Can I have your number? That was the last thing he'd said to me, looking eager. I had to remind myself that dismissal came naturally to Stella. In this movie, I was a rich girl visiting from the city, and he was a townie bartender. Rebuffing him gave me a satisfying rush of power. The feeling was so good that I knew it had to come with a price.

With Facebook or Google, it was easy to find out the truth. I waited for the lie to catch up with me, for Kyle to track me down. But days passed, and nothing happened. Maybe it wasn't such a big deal, after all. I was merely channeling what I'd learned from Stella. Her confidence, her verve. Didn't they say imitation was the sincerest form of flattery?

The week after Thanksgiving, I stood in front of Stella's closet. I don't know why this had spooked me so badly last time. They were just clothes. Stella was thinner than me, but some of her dresses had forgiving cuts and loose tailoring. Several of them fit me well. What harm was there in trying them on, enjoying the sight of myself in the floor-length mirror? What harm was there if, sometimes, I felt like sleeping in her king-sized bed instead of my own? Or if I took the occasional bath in her deep claw-foot tub?

It's just stuff. That's what Stella liked to say, when one of her uptight friends got a stain or spill on a piece of expensive clothing. *Who cares about stuff?*

And besides—she'd never know.

CHAPTER FOUR

REBECCA CARTER HAD two reputations: that within the industry, and that within our newsroom. Within the industry she was blazingly competitive, never hesitating to flatten anyone who got in the way of an exclusive sit-down or a big get. She was a shark, our competition at CNN and Fox said with suppressed admiration. As ambitious as they come. If securing an interview meant that Rebecca herself had to camp out in the front yard of a subject's home, groveling and showing obeisance, she wouldn't hesitate for a second. How else were you going to get the ratings?

But within our newsroom, she was like a mother hen. The lack of resentment she engendered was remarkable, because resentment seemed inevitable. She was a celebrity and a multimillionaire who attended state dinners and had appeared in *Vogue*. The rest of us were overworked and exhausted, pickling ourselves in sodium-rich takeout. But Rebecca knew how to prevent jealousy from taking root. When a senior producer was sleepless because of her colicky newborn, Rebecca hired her a night nurse. When someone's parent or child or spouse was ill, Rebecca paid for the best medical care. When someone was burning out, Rebecca sent them on vacation to a lavish Caribbean resort and banned them from e-mail.

But this warm and fuzzy reputation wasn't, in fact, a contradiction of the harder reputation. They went hand in hand. Rebecca's generosity didn't stem from some nurturing impulse. It was politics, plain and simple. She knew that, in order to win, she had to keep the proletariat on her side.

The best example of this came at Christmas, when Rebecca hosted a party for *Frontline* employees at her Park Avenue penthouse. Jamie told me that she gave each employee a personalized gift, hand-selected with their interests in mind. Rebecca's assistant actually did the research and the shopping, but the fact that Rebecca beamingly played Santa Claus was what counted.

"This is what you learn when you work in TV long enough," Jamie said, on yet another Friday night. Halfway through his second beer and he was getting philosophical. "It's all manufactured. Even the serious stuff. You think *60 Minutes* doesn't use clever editing and camera angles to get their point across?"

"Oh no," I said. "Jamie. Are you actually a conspiracy theorist? Are you about to tell me the moon landing was faked?"

"Well, why *haven't* we gone back?" he said. Then he laughed. "No. Here's what I mean. Even if the story is manufactured, even if it's contrived a certain way, the reaction isn't fake. If a viewer starts to cry, or laugh, or get angry—that emotion is real."

"So we're manipulating them? We're tricking them into feeling something?"

"You have to *make* them feel something. Your goal can't be pure verisimilitude. If you just served up the news with no editing or storytelling or tension, the viewer wouldn't feel a thing. And that's bad for them. That's bad for the world."

"Treat the news as advocacy. Is that what you're saying?"

"Treat it as a story. Use the tools at your disposal. Viewers need us to make them care."

I waved to the waitress, signaled for the check. "You ever

think about writing this stuff down? Turn this into Journalism 101. Professor James Richter."

"I'm selective about my students," Jamie said. "Gotta make sure it's worth it."

———

On the night of Rebecca's holiday party, a Saturday in December, Jamie texted to see if I wanted to head uptown together.

Sorry, no can do, I wrote back. Having a wardrobe emergency. Original, right?

Sounds dire. Want company and/or help? he wrote.

Sure, I wrote, then gave him the address and told the doorman to let him up.

My wardrobe could stretch through a workweek. Cotton dresses that didn't require dry cleaning, layered with cardigans and tights in cold weather, scarves and accessories from thrift stores. But the invitation to the party had said "Dress Code: Festive" and there was nothing in my closet that came close to festive. I could show up in one of my Monday-to-Friday dresses, put on some red lipstick and dangly earrings, and that would be fine. But was it a crime that I wanted to feel pretty? This was another TV trick. You dress for the role. The outfit is part of the story. When Rebecca was interviewing strongman dictators, she wore tailored black suits. After a natural disaster, she was in khakis and field vests. With a teary-eyed widow, she wore pastels in soft textures. Tonight, I didn't want to look like my regular self. I wanted to look like the person I was becoming.

In college, Stella let me borrow clothes, but only on her terms—these were *her* things, and she hated it when I didn't ask in advance. There was no time for that now. If I texted her, how likely was she to respond? So I selected several options from her closet and laid them on the bed. Rich silks and velvets in jewel

tones and elegant blacks, infinitely more beautiful than anything
I owned. There was a plum-colored wrap dress with a subtle
gold pattern that fit me well. In Stella's en suite bathroom, I
cranked up the shower and hung the dress from the rod to steam
loose the wrinkles. I was considering her array of shoes and jewelry, humming to myself, when I felt a hand on my shoulder.

"Fuck!" I said, jumping several inches.

Jamie raised his hands in apology. The shower had covered
his footsteps. "Just your friendly neighborhood wardrobe con-
sultant," he said. "This is what you're going with?"

I glanced down at my leggings and T-shirt. "Yes, Einstein," I
said.

"Is this your room?"

"My roommate. I'm raiding her closet."

"That's nice of her." Jamie stuck his head in the closet. "Is she
rich?"

I laughed. "Excuse me?"

"I've been in enough dressing rooms to know how much those
cost." He pointed at a pair of high heels with signature red soles.
"More than any normal person can afford."

"She is rich," I said. "But I'm guessing the apartment tipped
you off already."

He smiled. "I like to give the benefit of the doubt."

"I need another ten minutes," I said. "There's wine in the
kitchen, if you want."

The bathroom was steamy from the shower. I rubbed clear
a circle in the fogged mirror and examined my reflection. The
dress looked good on me. The wrap accentuated my waist,
and the neckline plunged to just the right point, highlighted
by the delicate gold necklace I'd found in Stella's closet. I
slipped into a pair of her nude pumps, and spritzed on her
perfume for good measure. I felt like an entirely different person. I felt confident and attractive—and, at the same time,

ashamed of my own vanity. Wasn't it worrying, how much I'd grown to like these trappings? The clothing, the jewelry, the fancy parties?

Jamie was in the kitchen, leaning against the counter, a glass of wine in one hand and his phone in the other. Until this moment Jamie had only existed in the office, or extensions of the office. It was jarring—strangely and suddenly intimate, like his life had superimposed itself over mine. Jamie was, I realized, the only person I'd ever brought into the apartment.

He glanced up from his phone. "Looks good," he said, giving me a thumbs-up, with no special affection. I felt a private relief: he'd come over as my friend, nothing more.

The elevator opened into the foyer of Rebecca's apartment. It was a small room with colorful wallpaper, a gilt-edged mirror, an umbrella stand, a table holding a miniature Christmas tree. Through the front door I saw a much larger Christmas tree in the living room. It had to be at least ten feet fall.

The party was in full swing. There was a jazz trio, waiters with hors d'oeuvres on silver trays, a crowd at the bar. The living room was a long rectangle, with windows facing south toward the Midtown skyline. The décor was tasteful, the art expensive-looking. Everyone was dressed up and sipping carefully, mindful of the carpets and furniture, not yet buzzed enough to forget that this was the boss's apartment.

The party had self-segregated by occupation. The camera guys and editors were over by the couches; the ladies from hair and makeup were laughing by the bar; the writers were huddled in a serious-looking conversation. Even the producers broke down into distinct groupings: the live producers, who tended to be extroverted and chatty; the field producers, who were adrenaline junkies with intricate war stories; and the tape producers, who had a hard streak of independence. The assistants were scattered throughout the party, identifiable by their timidity. By rights I should have been with them, but instead I stuck with Jamie.

Beneath the ornamented tree was a pile of wrapped boxes and gift bags. "Remind me what she got you last year?" I said.

"A first edition of *The Sound and the Fury*."

I rolled my eyes. "Is that really your favorite book?"

"No," he said, grinning. "But *Light in August* is."

"Are you trying to impress me? Because it's not working."

"Liking Faulkner is a requirement if you're from the South."

"Don't remind me."

"Ironic, huh?" Jamie tilted his head. "Violet Trapp, always rejecting her roots. But isn't Faulkner the one who said that the past isn't dead, it isn't even—"

"Hey, look at that!" I said, as a waiter walked by with a tray of pigs in a blanket. "Excuse me, sir? Could we please try those?"

"Nice save," Jamie said.

"Can't talk," I mumbled through the crumbs. "Mouth full."

A while later, I was ordering a drink at the bar when Rebecca appeared next to me. She was dressed like an off-duty Jackie Kennedy or Audrey Hepburn, barefoot in slim black pants and an oversized white sweater, hair pulled back in a bun. It was a power move. In a room of people wearing their best dresses and high heels, suits and ties, Rebecca's unadorned beauty stood out.

"Your first holiday party," she said, squeezing my arm. "Are you having a good time?"

"Yes! Thank you. Your apartment is beautiful."

"I can't bring myself to care about interior decorating. Eric did most of it. Where is he?" Rebecca started scanning the room, but then she stopped and frowned. "I hate the jazz trio. I truly hate them. We've hired them five years in a row, mostly out of pity. I think they're getting worse. Do you like jazz?"

"I...I don't really know."

"Eric is always dragging me to these awful places in the West

Village. He loves it and I have no idea why. Where *is* he?" She stood on her tiptoes, which wasn't much help for a petite woman in a room full of high heels. "Eric! Come here."

The man who appeared from the crowd was tall and lanky, with thick dark hair and matching eyebrows. Eric was a novelist, a literary man-about-town, often appearing on panels and giving talks at the 92nd Street Y. He and Rebecca had met as undergrads at Harvard and had been together ever since.

"This is Violet," Rebecca said. "She's new. She's a star."

I felt a flush of pride, an electric sense of self-possession. Although, just as quickly, it faded: Rebecca probably said this to everyone. Compliments were cheap. Why not toss a few bread crumbs from your balcony? Rebecca liked the reciprocal adoration that came with making other people feel good.

"Lovely to meet you, Violet," Eric said, shaking my hand.

Rebecca touched my arm. "Excuse me. See that guy? He's in charge of our budget for next year and he needs a little sweet-talking."

Across the apartment, one of the KCN executives was about to leave when Rebecca blocked him from the door, prying his coat away and handing him a freshly procured drink. He obeyed, looking nervous, as she pushed him into a quiet corner of the dining room.

"The poor man," Eric said. "He doesn't stand a chance."

I nodded, confused, and made some general noise of agreement.

"Apparently your corporate overlords want to keep a tighter leash on travel expenses," Eric said. "But it's hard to say no to Rebecca Carter. You must know that by now."

"She's very talented," I said. "Well, obviously, yes, I don't need to be telling you that. I meant—"

"They really ought to give them training," Eric continued, ignoring me. "The way the CIA trains their officers to resist interrogation. Those poor men need some mental toughness.

Otherwise it's not a fair fight. She'll get her way, and he'll run tuck-tail back to the fortieth floor. Then they'll have to fire him, and hire someone new. On and on the orchestra plays."

"Um," I said. "Yeah."

We struggled through small talk for several minutes. I kept thinking Eric would find an excuse to end this painful conversation—didn't he have other people he wanted to talk to? Finally, as a last resort, I said, "I read your piece in the *Times* last week. It was great. I thought it was such a brave stand to take."

He smiled. No, he *beamed*. The op-ed had been completely forgettable. An argument for preserving the freedom of the novelist, as if there was some campaign being waged against it. But it worked. Eric lit up as he told me about the high-minded reason he had written it. Then, with growing animation, he started on the rumors and gossip of the literary world. By the time I finished my drink, Eric was laughing so hard he was wiping tears from his eyes. Rebecca returned, raising an eyebrow. "Are we having fun?" she said.

"Oh, Becky, this one's a keeper," Eric said, as if I was the source of his uproarious laughter for the last twenty minutes.

"Right," she said. "I'm just going to borrow her for a minute, okay?"

Rebecca steered me toward the bar. "You're a trouper," she said. "Thanks for babysitting him. Pretty dress, by the way."

"It wasn't—he was so nice, it just—"

"Of course. He's wonderful. I do love that man. But Jesus, can he talk. Have you read any of his books?"

"Well...no." My cheeks reddened.

"Most people your age haven't. He's a little, let's say, vintage. Had his only big hit over fifteen years ago. But his is the kind of business where you can dine out on one hit for a long time." She laughed. "If only we had it so easy, right? We have to reinvent the wheel every single goddamn night." Rebecca clinked her glass against mine. "Enjoy the rest of the party, Violet."

Jamie and Eliza were across the room, near the windows. "I see you met Eric," Eliza said. Her eyes twinkled with amusement. "And you're still standing?"

"Remember last year?" Jamie said. "When he buttonholed that assistant?"

"His mistake," Eliza said. "That kid should have known better."

"What happened?" I said.

"He told Eric that realism in the novel was dead," Jamie said. "Whatever that means."

"And Eric spent the rest of the party jabbing his finger into this kid's chest, telling him that unless you've actually done it yourself, you don't get to comment upon the form." Eliza smirked. "That's what he said, right? Comment upon the form."

Jamie rolled his eyes. "Which is rich, because you know who considers himself the *real* executive producer of Rebecca's show?"

"It's like clockwork," Eliza said. "We do a segment on the latest celebrity divorce and within thirty seconds, he's e-mailed Rebecca and copied me. Eric likes to remind his wife that this tawdry stuff is beneath her dignity. That she should overrule her producers. Because *Rebecca* is in charge of her own show, not me."

"Wow," I said.

Eliza laughed. "Have you seen this apartment? That Brioni suit he was wearing? Like he doesn't love the life that Rebecca's ratings pay for."

It was 1 a.m. by the time the party died down. When a subway finally arrived at the Lexington Avenue station, it was nearly deserted. Jamie, who was splitting a cab back to Park Slope with a colleague, was worried about me getting home by myself.

"I'm a big girl," I said. "I'll be fine."

"But you're still new around here," he said. "Text me when you get home."

On rare days when it was relatively quiet at work, Jamie and I would take our lunch break together. Him with a plastic container of salad, me with my packed Tupperware, sitting outside if the weather was good. Jamie took to removing his watch and laying it between us. Otherwise, talking and talking, it was easy to lose track of time. We'd come back inside, eyes readjusting after the noontime glare, and I'd feel refreshed and happy. But then Jamie would run into Eliza, or Rebecca. My happiness looked like a cheap imitation compared to what Jamie had with them. A different depth. A sense of trust.

Jamie had stopped asking me directly about my childhood. He saw that it made me uneasy. Instead, during one of our lunches that fall, he described the family vacations they'd taken to Florida. It was a clever technique, a way of drawing me out.

"My brother was fifteen and I was thirteen," he said, shaking his container to disperse the salad dressing. "My parents let us wander Ocean Drive by ourselves. My brother convinced some older girls to buy beer for us. You know what they got us? A six-pack of O'Doul's." He laughed. "We didn't know any better. And the weird thing is, I actually felt drunk. We lay on the beach and talked for hours. It was so much fun."

He had a dreamy look in his eyes. The place he remembered was the Florida of ultramarine Miami skies, candy-colored midcentury architecture, forests of sleek glass condos. Palm trees and fast speedboats and mouth-puckering ceviche. As Jamie kept talking, I had a dizzying, vertiginous realization: he thought that this was common ground. He thought we had the same picture in our minds.

But I had only seen pictures of places like Miami. I grew up in a shitty town that could have been Anywhere, America. The beach wasn't a factor. The beach was for rich people, or nice families who took vacations. And the one time we attempted a family vacation, I could tell there was something weird about this beach. On the Gulf side, there were no crashing waves or cool breezes. Just a flat blank canvas of gray-greenish water, stretching into the void. Water that had gone limp and surrendered to the heat, overtaken by the creeping, ticking life of the state. Mosquitoes thickened the air. Stingrays clustered in the shallows. The day was a bug-bitten, sunburned disaster. "I was trying to do something *nice*," my mother snapped, slamming the trunk after we packed the car up. My father laughed. He was good at drinking just enough to ignore her moods, but not so much that he couldn't drive home. "Nice costs money," he said. As he turned the key in the ignition, he caught my eye in the mirror. "How 'bout you, girlie? You got any money?" My mother snorted. Laughing at me always made her feel better.

I couldn't blame Jamie for not understanding. I hadn't told him anything about it. Most of the time, it didn't matter. We were in New York, we worked in television news, and life was crazy enough that we had plenty to talk about. It was comforting to think how childhood shrank in the rearview mirror of time. That proportion of my life, that giant black hole, would only get smaller and smaller.

As Rebecca's party had worn on, it had segregated itself in a different way: not just by occupation, but by tenure. The old hands, like Jamie and Eliza, kept to themselves. They had different things to talk about. They had seen it all before. I found them so much more interesting than the interns and assistants. When Eliza and Jamie told war stories, their laughter was sanguine. Problems diminished in the long view. Experience could be a breakwater against seasonal storms.

I wanted that. I wanted nostalgic stories in common with Jamie and Eliza, a shared history. Recently Jamie had taught me the phrase "salad days." At first, stupidly, I thought it was a reference to what he ate for lunch. Then he clarified: it meant his earliest years of naive inexperience. "But you seemed to skip those," he said, one day. "How'd you get to be such an old soul?"

Practice, I thought. Years spent with the Bradley family, observing their refined art of omission. In good Wasp fashion, they never dwelled on the bad parts. It worked for them, and I figured it could work for me. But that answer was too depressing, so instead I shrugged and said, "No TV or internet in our house. Only the radio. I grew up like it was the 1940s."

Jamie laughed. Clever enough, and it threw him off the scent. See, I could be like other people. I could toss out occasional filigreed details from the past. And this detail happened to be true. I didn't have to explain that my mother shoved our TV to the floor during an argument with my father and it never got replaced. That our internet was cut off after the bills went unpaid.

———

"Violet," a voice said. And then louder, "Violet." I thought I had dreamed it, but when I opened my eyes, the voice was in the room. A hand on my shoulder. A draft of air from the open bedroom door.

"Jamie?" I said. Because I realized, half awake, that I'd forgotten to text him the night before. Illogically, I thought maybe he'd gotten worried and came to check on me.

"Who the fuck is Jamie?"

I rolled over. She was standing in the doorway, backlit by a brilliant ray of sunshine from the living room. Heeled leather boots, skinny black jeans, oversize cashmere hoodie, and blond hair piled into a messy bun. "Oh," I said. "Stella!"

"Surprise," she said, flatly. She was oddly stiff when I stood up and hugged her.

"When did you get in?" I said. "Just now?"

"A little while ago."

"What is it?" I said. "Is everything okay?"

"You didn't even bother to ask," she said, turning abruptly.

"Ask what?" I said, following her across the hall and into her room.

"This!" she said, flinging her arms wide. "All my shit!"

There were skirts and dresses scattered across the bed from last night, shoes arrayed on the floor. My stomach twisted into a knot. Pure sloppiness on my part.

"Shit," I said. "I'm so sorry, Stell. I should have asked. But there was this work party last night, and it was an emergency, I had nothing to wear, and—"

"You're making it worse," she snapped. She started shoving everything back into the closet. "Are you trying to make me feel stingy? Well, I'm sorry, but this creeps me out. Like, I have no idea what you've been doing this whole time. Do you do this every day? Do you dress up like me?"

"Stella," I said. When she didn't turn around, too intent on jamming her high heels back into the shoe rack, I said louder, "Stella Evelyn Bradley."

It was an old joke, our way of puncturing a petty argument. *You triple-named me,* we'd say, laughing. *No fair.* For some reason, the mock sternness always worked.

She whipped around. There was a twitch in her upper lip. "Really?" she said. "We've only been together five minutes and you have to pull that out?"

"Give it up," I said. "You're not actually mad. You're just hungry, right?"

Her veneer of annoyance receded, and then dropped completely. She laughed and said, "God, Violet. You know what I like about you? None of those bitches I've been hanging out with ever have enough to eat. We go to dinner and we split, like, two salads."

I laughed, too, although there was a subtle sting in that comment.

Stella flopped down on the bed and began rummaging through her purse. Her moods had a liquid quality. She was now fixated on something else, muttering to herself. "I'm out," she said. "Where's my phone?"

When she found it, she pressed it to her ear as she walked into the bathroom. "Hiii," she said sweetly. "It's Stella Bradley. Remember me?"

The conversation was short and cryptic. After, she tossed the phone onto the bed. "That's what I like about New York," she said. "People never leave."

"Who was that?"

"This guy," she said. "Don't worry. He just helps me get Adderall."

I furrowed my brow. "I thought you had a prescription."

"Well, *yeah*, but they're so stingy with it. You know, you should really get a prescription. It's amazing. And if you don't like it you can give it to me." She was now on her knees, emptying her suitcase, piling clothes on the floor. "I really need to do laundry. Do you send it out somewhere?"

"So what's the story?" I said. "Are you back for good?"

"I don't know," she said, sitting back on her heels. "But it's Christmas next week. I can't ditch my family at Christmas. Do you think they're pissed I've been gone so long?"

"Let's do this over breakfast," I said. "Come on. I'll cook."

———

She had no plan beyond the present moment. Maybe she was back for good. Maybe she'd leave again after the holidays. The only thing she knew was that she needed some rest. A break from the cycle of travel and party-hopping, and the relentless performance of fun. A few weeks of peace and quiet—was that too much to ask?

"But that won't satisfy Anne," I said. "She'll want specifics."

"Anne is a pain in my ass," Stella said. "This is good. What is this?"

"Parmesan and thyme." Simple omelets were a staple. On a budget, eggs were a miracle. "See, I could tell that was just the low blood sugar talking."

She laughed. "I missed you."

"So stay," I said, with a surge of hope. "Remember the plan? The two of us, together in the big city?"

She wrinkled her nose, folded her napkin into a careful rectangle, stood up and started rinsing our plates. Neat behavior was her method of avoidance. Stella once scrubbed our entire dorm bathroom to postpone breaking up with a clingy boyfriend.

"Or not," I said. "That's cool, too."

"I just don't know what I want," she said. She stood at the dishwasher, plates in hand. Instead of slotting them at the edge, she put them in the middle of the empty bottom rack. This was the behavior of a sociopath, or someone who grew up with housekeeping staff. "You're lucky," she added. "You always knew."

"Lucky?" I said. "I'm barely making minimum wage."

"But you love it. I can tell."

"How?"

"Come here," she said, and dragged me into the living room, where a mirror hung above the mantelpiece. We stood in front of it, side by side. "Look. Your skin is clear. You lost weight. You're not biting your nails. You look tired and you need some concealer for those under-eye circles, but that's easy to fix."

In the mirror, I saw that she was right. I hadn't noticed it myself. Stella and I had always existed at distant ends of the continuum. Roughly the same height and the same coloring, but she was a hundred times more beautiful. Exquisite features and perfect blond hair, compared to my plainness and dirty-blond hues. A vast gulf remained, but the past five months had brought us slightly closer together.

"Well?" she said. "You must be happy there, right?"

"I guess so."

"See?" She cocked an eyebrow. "And therefore I have to hate you."

In the afternoon, a guy showed up at our door: the person Stella had called that morning. He was tall and preppy, a cable-knit sweater beneath his faded Barbour jacket. Stella explained that they'd gone to Rye Country Day together, and now he worked in finance. "This is Violet," she said to him. "Don't worry. She's cool."

Stella dipped a key into the bag of white powder, sampling the wares. She sniffed a bump of cocaine, smiled, and widened her eyes. The preppy guy lined up several small plastic bags on the coffee table, along with half a dozen orange pill containers. After counting Stella's money, he looked satisfied and impressed with his own efficiency.

"Men have it so easy," Stella said, after he left. "Did you see him? Everyone trusts a guy who looks like that. That's why it's so easy for him to get refills."

"Really," I said, watching as she cut a line of cocaine. "Is that the story."

"Plus both of his parents are doctors. I would *kill* for that. Easy access."

I laughed. "Your father literally runs a pharmaceutical company, Stell."

It wasn't that I was innocent to her habits. She'd done plenty of this in college—at parties, to sober up, to help her endure all-nighters. But it wasn't even 3 p.m., the living room bright with sunlight. Whatever her reasons, it didn't seem like she was doing this for fun.

"Stop it," she said, wiping her nose as she sat up.

"Stop what?"

"Stop giving me that look. You're so *judgmental,* Violet. Has anyone ever told you that?"

"You have, plenty of times."

"Do you know what our problem is?" She went into the kitchen, filled a glass with water and ice, and took a long drink. "Violet, do you know what it is? I just realized it. Take a guess."

"I have no idea."

She pointed a long index finger. "You've got the dirt on me, but I don't have any on you."

"Oh, come on."

"I'm serious," she said, her color rising. "You see me doing bad things, but what about you? You're so *perfect.* You never do anything bad. You could blackmail me if you wanted. But I could never do that to you. This is fucked up, Violet. The power dynamic is all fucked up."

This was Stella on the upswing of a buzz. She drew connections between disparate dots and then got excited by her own intelligence. It was like a game to her. My job wasn't to be offended. My job was to play along. I kept a straight face, because if I smiled she would think I was mocking her. But I was happy. This dynamic felt strangely like home.

"Explain it to me," I said. "Between the two of us, you're the one without any power?"

"Yes," she said. "Yes, yes, that's exactly right."

"Even though your family is worth, like, a billion dollars?"

"That's not the point." She tipped the last of the water into her mouth, crunching on an ice cube. Her phone vibrated. She scanned the screen, then glanced out the window. "Actually, this is perfect," she said. "The weather is perfect, and we have time to walk."

"To where?"

"Dinner," she said. "My friend who lives in Brooklyn Heights. He's having a dinner party and we're going. We can walk across the bridge. Just in time for sunset."

"I'm not sure," I said. "It's a school night."

"What?" Stella squinted, like I was speaking another language.

"Work tomorrow. I have stuff to catch up on tonight."

"You said they barely pay you minimum wage. You can't be that important."

I laughed. "Harsh."

"Come on," she said, tugging my arm. "I'll let you borrow something to wear."

———

Stella's friend lived in a brownstone that backed up onto the Brooklyn Heights promenade. The older woman who owned the building liked that this young man was an artist, that he reminded her of her bohemian days. He rented the top floor, with its gabled windows and creaky floors and spectacular views of Manhattan, for a pittance.

While Stella made the rounds, kissing the cheeks of friends-of-friends, I wandered into the kitchen to get glasses of wine. The counter looked like an old master still life: verdant vegetables, a pile of lemons, bundles of rosemary, a chicken on the cutting board. The host was in the other room, talking about his new work. Dinner was still hours away.

These friends knew me, dimly, as the girl who lived with Stella. They were polite enough, but I always found the conversation slippery and difficult. The usual questions—where you live, what you do—went nowhere. You couldn't effort your way into their world. But even though Stella had been away for months, her reabsorption into the group was instant. No one at the party bothered her with the tedious details: *What's the plan? Are you back for good? What are you going to do?* To them, it didn't matter. Their intimacy was elastic. Stella was Stella, no matter where she was in the world.

"You stayed at Le Sirenuse when you were in Positano?" one girl asked.

"Of course she did," another girl responded. "I told her she had to."

"Loved it," Stella said.

"What about Morocco? Did you make it to Marrakech?"

Stella nodded as she refilled her wineglass, and mine. She was wearing a loose silk tunic with a vibrant tropical pattern that should have been all wrong for December but was somehow perfect. As the dinner party coursed around her, Stella brimmed with a serene worldliness, like an advertisement for the restorative power of globe-trotting.

"La Mamounia or the Royal Mansour?" the host asked.

"Both," she said. "Three nights at each."

He clinked his glass against hers. "That's my girl."

As the conversation moved on to other geographies, I said quietly to Stella, "I thought he was a struggling artist."

"He is," she said. "And apparently a struggling cook. Where's dinner? I'm starving."

"Then how can he afford to travel like that?"

She laughed. "You heard his last name. Take one guess."

"Oh," I said. "*Oh.*"

The shabby apartment, the rickety table and chairs, his boasts of cheap rent, his paint-stained T-shirt and frayed jeans: they had fooled me. When Stella reminded me who he was—more to the point, who his parents were—suddenly it made sense.

"Isn't it depressing?" Stella said. "Fast-forward ten years and all these people will be having the exact same conversation. Nothing will change."

"I thought you liked them," I said.

"I do like them. The trick is you can't think about it too much."

I'd missed her more than I realized. Stella was so good at these parties. I let her fill my wineglass, again and again. She'd touch my arm, she'd catch my eye, she'd laugh at anything. She was at ease in this world, but she hadn't made the mistake of so many: she hadn't forgotten that this world was finite. That other people lived across the border. She could lean her head close to mine, with a perfect sotto voce observation, and suddenly she was back in my world.

We didn't eat until 10 p.m. The meal was long and leisurely, and there were no movements toward the door. A countdown ran in the back of my mind: in ten hours, I'll be at the office. In nine hours. In eight. There was dessert, more wine, cigarettes by the gabled windows, cold air from the December night. The festive feeling of a weekend, even though it was Sunday. Around 1 a.m.—*seven hours,* creeping panic—I said to Stella, "I really have to go."

"Aren't you having fun?" she said.

"I have to get some sleep," I said. "You can stay."

"No, it's fine." She sighed. "I'll come with you."

When I woke up the next morning, my alarm blaring at 7 a.m., I had a pressing headache. My mouth was foul and cottony from the wine, my eyes gritty from exhaustion. While I was waiting for the shower to warm up, there was a knock on the door.

"Gatorade," Stella said, handing me a bottle. "And Advil."

"Why are you awake?" I said, twisting off the lid. Lemon-lime flavor—my favorite.

"Jet lag," she said. "I've been up for an hour."

After I'd showered and dressed, I found Stella in the kitchen.

She spread her arms and said, "I made breakfast! Well, I bought it. Same thing." There was coffee, and a bagel wrapped in wax paper. "Milk, no sugar. Everything, toasted, with cream cheese. Did I get that right?"

"You're my hero," I said. "Seriously. Thank you."

While I unwrapped the bagel, still warm and fragrant from the toaster, Stella removed a stray hair from the sleeve of my sweater, straightened my necklace so the clasp was at the back. These tiny, attentive gestures meant she was about to ask for something. "Do you really have to go to work?" she said.

"That's pretty much the deal."

She pouted. "But I'm gonna be so bored."

By the time I got to the office, the headache had loosened its grip only slightly. There was also the nausea, and the general malaise. Enduring the next twelve hours with this hangover seemed impossible. Jamie saw me and said, "Late night?"

"Is it that obvious?" I said.

I was off my game. It took forever to complete a routine fact-check. I brought the wrong script to Rebecca and had to sprint upstairs to get the right one. I hated doing shoddy work, I resented the fact that I wasn't myself. At the end of the day, I'd missed several calls and a dozen texts from Stella. She wanted to make plans for that night—a late dinner, drinks? No, I texted back. I'm dead from last night. Going straight to bed.

She wrote back right away. PLEASE?

Some of us have to work in the morning, I wrote.

It was an unnecessarily mean thing to say, an eruption of irritation after a long and shitty day. But it was true, and it worked. She didn't bother me again.

CHAPTER FIVE

THE PLAN WAS for Stella, who had been home in Rye a few days already, to pick me up from the station on Christmas Eve. When the train left Harlem, the buildings along the track blurring as we accelerated, I texted Stella to remind her. She didn't respond, but I wasn't worried. We'd talked just that morning.

"Hurry up and get here," she'd said. "They're driving me insane."

"They're your parents," I'd said, my work phone pinned between ear and shoulder. Using the landline at my desk made it look like I was busy with actual work, even when I was just talking to Stella. "That's what they're supposed to do. Anyways, cheer up. It's Christmas."

"Christmas is a fucking sham."

Stella's mood had worsened since she returned to New York. She kept pestering me to go out with her, to stop being so lame, and I kept saying no. Lesson learned from that hungover Monday: Stella and I couldn't revert to old ways if I actually wanted to succeed in my job. "Yeah, yeah, I get it," she interrupted, when I tried to explain. She didn't care. She only saw it as an obstacle.

"It *is* a sham," I said. "But it's our job to play along with it."

"I hate it when you get like this," she'd said.

"Rational, you mean?"

"It's the worst. Okay, whatever, see you at six thirty."

But it was 6:30, and soon the crowds and cars at the Rye train station dissipated, with no sign of Stella. I could imagine the possibilities—Stella waylaid because she'd picked a fight with Anne, criticizing the dinner menu, refusing to change into nice clothing for the guests. In the previous week, when Stella made it clear that she preferred to spend her time in the city rather than the suburbs with her parents, Anne came to her. But their day of lunching and shopping devolved, like always, into argument. What did Stella and Anne have to fight about? They had everything they could possibly want. Their misery was of their own invention.

By 7 p.m., with the night getting colder and Stella failing to answer my calls or texts, I decided to take a cab to the Bradleys'. There were twinkling lights in the shrubbery along the driveway, and bright red poinsettias framing the front door. It was perfect, which is what I'd come to expect from Anne Bradley.

But when she opened the front door, her face fell. "It's only you?" Anne said.

"I'm afraid so," I said.

She stepped outside and peered down the driveway. "I mean, Stella isn't with you?"

"I took a cab from the station," I said. "I couldn't get hold of her."

"It's been hours," Anne said. Her voice was hoarse, on the verge of breaking. "I have no idea where she is. Are you sure you don't know?"

"What do you mean?"

"Who is that?" Thomas Bradley appeared in the doorway. "Oh," he said. His disappointment matched Anne's. "Let's go inside, everyone. No need to put on a show for the neighbors."

The kitchen was aromatic, saucepans on the stove and casserole dishes in the oven, Christmas music playing softly in the background. At the counter, Stella's older brother, Oliver, was flipping through the *Wall Street Journal* and drinking a glass of milk. Milk! Somewhere inside my brain, I could hear Stella snorting with laughter.

Oliver smiled, smarmily. "I'm sorry your delightful friend isn't here to greet you."

"Oliver, please," Thomas said.

"What? It's true. Someone needs to apologize for her awful manners."

"I'm still not sure what's going on," I said.

"They got in a fight," Oliver said. "And then she ran away."

Anne sighed. "She was very upset. She needed some space."

"That was around lunchtime," Thomas said. "Violet, we were hoping you might have heard from her. She's not at the apartment, either. The doorman promised to call if she shows up."

"I talked to her this morning," I said. "Around ten, I guess? But not since then."

"No texts? Nothing?" Anne said.

I shook my head.

The timer on the stove beeped. Anne hurried over, releasing the smell of rosemary and caramelized vegetables from the oven, and Thomas looked at his watch. "Almost seven thirty," he said. "Our guests will be here any minute."

"Violet, honey, you'll want to freshen up?" Anne said, over her shoulder.

"I'm a little surprised your parents are going through with dinner," I said to Oliver as we walked upstairs. I thought my outfit looked okay—work clothes, black pants and a cardigan—but to Anne, "freshen up" meant "put in more of an effort."

Oliver laughed. "I thought you were more insightful than that, Violet."

"So what exactly happened?" I said, stopping outside the guest bedroom.

"She's a brat. What else?"

"Let's stick to the facts," I said. "No editorializing."

"Well, the fact is that my parents are tired of her traveling the world and spending their money. Do you know what her credit card bill was in October? Twenty thousand dollars."

"In *one month?*"

"So they finally decided, enough. Time for Stella to settle down and get a job. The plan was for the four of us to have a civilized conversation about it over lunch. Stella saw it from a mile away. She freaked out. She said she wasn't going to be *bullied* by us. And then she left."

"Just like that?" I said. But it made sense. She hated being backed into a corner, hated being told what to do.

"My father set up an alert in case she uses her credit card. My mother is finding out whether the cell phone carrier can track her location."

"And if that fails, they'll get the CIA to track her down," I said.

Oliver chuckled. "I wouldn't put anything past my parents."

———

Despite all of this, dinner was remarkably smooth. To their guests, Anne and Thomas didn't betray that anything was wrong. "Stella decided to spend Christmas in Paris with her friends," Anne said, as she poured the wine. "We miss her, of course, but I can't blame her. Paris is so romantic at this time of year."

I'd learned this during my time with the Bradley family: cognitive dissonance came easy to the wealthy. Thomas Bradley was the CEO of Bradley Pharmaceuticals, a massively profitable company founded by his grandfather, and the Bradleys had more money than they could spend in a lifetime. And yet they

complained about the tax rate and the price of gasoline. They
donated to Democratic candidates, but they left stingy tips for
bad service when the waitress was making five bucks an hour.
Wealth was not something to be spent. It was to be protected
by trusts and lawyers and tax havens so that it could endure for
generations to come. Part of me admired Stella's ballsiness, in
going against this. She took the money at face value: a liquid
asset, meaningless in itself, that ought to be used to pursue pleasure in this lifetime.

But the truth about Stella—her hot temper and impulsive
spirit—that was too coarse for dinner. The lie was better suited
to the festive spirit of Christmas Eve. Anne directed the conversation like a maestro. At one point she asked me to tell the guests
about my *fascinating* job. They leaned forward as I shared a few
juicy but anonymized tidbits from KCN. The guests around the
dinner table were rich and successful, but our TV stars were in a
different realm: they were famous. When they died, their names
would outlast them. The value I brought, as a guest, was an abil-
ity to induce a delicious feeling of schadenfreude in the Bradleys
and their ilk. They loved hearing about these more famous people losing their tempers, or screwing up an interview, or slipping
in the ratings.

Over time, I realized that the Bradleys may have liked me
as an individual, but they loved me for what I represented.
People who came from nothing, who busted their asses to get
college scholarships, who hustled into a winning career. Look
at me, climbing the ladder at KCN: I was a perfect example
of that bootstrappy, self-reliant, equal-opportunity American
spirit. (Never mind the various advantages I'd had: my skin
color, my good health, my friendship with an heiress.) It allowed the Bradleys to sleep easy at night. To believe that the
meritocracy functioned as it was supposed to. Their generosity
was real, but Anne and Thomas took a calculated kind of pride

in me, like I was proof of a successful charitable experiment, excellent ROI on the money they'd spent.

The next morning, Anne decided that enough was enough. She was calling the police.

A few hours later, the doorbell rang. There was a tall man in a dark overcoat, his face weary and rumpled as if he'd just awoken from a nap. "Detective Fazio," he said, shaking hands with Anne and Thomas. The police had been reluctant to come, but the Bradleys loomed large in town, with their sizable annual donations to the police memorial fund.

The five of us sat in the living room. In the distance, through the wide windows, the skyline of the city rose from the gray waters of Long Island Sound. The presents beneath the twinkling tree were untouched. It felt nothing like Christmas morning.

"Mrs. Bradley, one more time, walk me through what happened yesterday," Detective Fazio said. From the breast pocket of his coat, he took a pen and notebook.

Anne, visibly pleased by this attentiveness, repeated the story: the conversation with Stella, how she'd gotten annoyed and then angry, how she'd grabbed the car keys and bolted. Fazio nodded along. "So what should we do?" Anne said, after she'd finished.

"Just a few more questions," Fazio said. "Has this kind of thing happened before?"

"What do you mean?" Anne said.

"Has she ever run off without telling you where she's going?"

Thomas cleared his throat. "Yes," he said. "A few times."

Anne glared at her husband, but he continued. "Two or three times she ran off in high school," Thomas said. "Always after an argument. She'd spend the night with a friend and turn up the next day. That may be what's happening here."

Anne shook her head. "This was different."

"You said your name was Violet Trapp?" Fazio said to me. "One 'p' or two?"

"Two."

"And you were her roommate in college?"

"That's right."

"And in college, did she ever run off without telling you where she went?"

"Well, there were a few times." Fazio gestured for me to continue. "She'd disappear for the weekend with a guy she was dating. Or she'd go into the city. Usually I'd find out after the fact, when she'd call me to come get her." The room was intensely quiet, and I was aware of how suggestible the direction of the conversation was. "But I think she just forgets," I added. "To tell people her plans, I mean. She gets caught up in the moment."

Thomas nodded, but Anne leaned forward insistently. "She was angry, Detective. Irrationally angry. I have no clue why. I'm worried she'll do something reckless."

"I spoke to her yesterday morning," I said. "She *was* in a bad mood."

"Why?" Fazio said.

"I got the sense she had been arguing with Mr. and Mrs. Bradley."

"Is that true?" Fazio said.

"Yes," Oliver said. "She was acting like a spoiled baby all week."

"So?" Anne said. "What do we do?"

Fazio closed his notebook. "Mrs. Bradley," he said, "we have to account for the circumstances. Your daughter isn't a minor. She has the right to leave. You said she took her phone, her wallet, her coat. She was acting in a sound mind, blowing off steam after your argument. We can't consider her a missing person if she left of her own volition.

"That said"—he produced a business card from his pocket— "I'll leave my number with you. Call me if anything changes. In the meantime, I'd keep an eye on your credit card activity. And get in touch with her other friends. Ask if they've seen her."

"Leaving so soon?" Oliver said that afternoon. He leaned against the doorjamb of the guest room while I zipped my duffel bag closed.

"There's a lot going on," I said. "I don't want to impose."

The truth was, I wasn't sure how the Bradley family felt about me when Stella wasn't there. I could clear the table and wash the dishes, but that wasn't enough to make me a part of their family. There were moments of vague puzzlement when they looked at me, like, *Why are you here, again?*

"You're never an imposition," Oliver said. "But I can't blame you for leaving."

"I don't mean any offense, just—"

Oliver waved a hand. "None taken. There's a weird vibe around here right now."

I attempted to smile. "Maybe that's why Stella left."

"I think she had other reasons. Let me get that." Oliver picked up my duffel bag and ushered me toward the stairs. "You wouldn't guess it," he said, "but Stella can be prone to jealousy."

"Well, sure. Everyone is."

"Of you, I mean. Stella is jealous of you."

My cheeks reddened. "I doubt that," I said.

"Think about it," Oliver said. "Stella comes back to New York and finds you succeeding. Thriving, even. And she's utterly at loose ends. How do you think that makes her feel?"

We were downstairs, in the foyer of the house. Through the window, I could see my cab idling in the driveway, clouds of exhaust drifting through the winter darkness, the driver's face lit by the glow of a phone.

"She feels competitive with you, Violet," Oliver said. "You must know that."

"I don't think that's true," I said. My heart was beating faster. "Anyway, that's my cab. Thank you for carrying my bag, but I should really get—"

"It *is* true," Oliver said, keeping his grip firm on my duffel bag. "And anything can set her off. Like when she found out that you were borrowing her clothes."

My palms broke into sweat. An image of Stella, her features twisted with anger. I had apologized, and Stella had forgiven me. Conflicts like this had always slid easily into the past. But she kept alluding to it, several days later. *Cute dress. Is that yours or mine?* she'd said, snarkily. *You need to borrow anything today, sweetie?*

But why this, out of everything that had passed between us? She and Oliver barely spoke, and yet she'd told him? *Anything can set her off.* His words suggested culpability. But that was ridiculous. Wasn't it?

"That's Stella." Oliver handed me my bag. "No one overreacts like she does."

———

Back at KCN, there was a dead zone between Christmas and New Year's, no news breaking or big stories to report, the content vacuum filled by best-of-the-year recaps. Rebecca was skiing with her family, and Eliza was in an undisclosed tropical location. The newsroom was quiet. But the producers decided this was the perfect time to catch up on the stories we'd missed.

"Evergreen stories," one of the producers said, slapping a stack of paper on the conference room table. Jamie was his boss, but Jamie was on vacation, too, so this producer reveled in lording his temporary power over the assistants. "Divide these up and chase them down. I want at least one good story in the bank by the end of this week. You'll thank me the next time we need to plug a hole in the rundown."

This was our utility as assistants: our time was worth less than that of the producers, so we could afford to squander several hours on a wild-goose chase. These stories had been ignored for a reason. Mostly, they were less important than whatever news was breaking on a given day. Or their importance hadn't yet been revealed, because that required extensive and low-yield digging. Like excavating a fossil with a toothbrush, where we usually preferred jackhammers.

I took my assignments back to my desk. Most were obvious and immediate dead ends. But there was one that looked interesting.

In New Jersey, a company called Danner Pharmaceuticals had filed suit against several former employees for violating nondisclosure agreements. So far, the story had only been covered in a regional Jersey newspaper. But it was strange: the employees being sued weren't high-level scientists or researchers, who might possess proprietary information. Instead they were janitors, and security guards, and cafeteria workers. Why would Danner have these employees signing NDAs at all?

An afternoon spent on research didn't clarify anything. Maybe it hadn't been covered because it wasn't that unusual. Maybe companies like Danner sued gossipy janitors all the time. I drummed my fingers on my desk. Jamie talked about how important hunches were. "If your gut is telling you that there's a story, you should listen to it," he said once. "It means there's more to find out."

I couldn't tell what to think. Then I had an idea.

"Oliver Bradley," he said, after his secretary put the call through.

"Oliver, hi! It's Violet."

"Violet?" His tone went from brisk to puzzled. "What's going on? Is it Stella?"

"Oh—no." Consumed by the routine of work, I'd almost

forgotten about Stella's absence. "I've, uh, been calling and calling. Haven't had any luck. Have you heard anything?"

He sighed. "Nothing."

"She'll be fine," I said. "She always is."

After a pause, he said, "So is that why you called?"

"Actually, no. I have a work question."

Oliver was a lawyer, but he'd spent summers interning for his father, and he knew the pharmaceutical industry well. He'd heard of Danner, but not the story from the regional paper. "Basically," I said, "I need to know if there's a real story there. If this kind of thing is standard practice, or if this is unusual."

"Hmm," he said. "You know, our firm doesn't really like us talking to the press."

"This is just background. I'm only curious about how the industry works. You're irrelevant to the story. No offense."

"None taken." Oliver laughed. Over the years, I'd absorbed Stella's negative view of her brother. But it was much easier talking to him on the phone. He was almost normal.

He explained that while NDAs were common in the industry, it *was* unusual for janitors and security guards. "You have to ask yourself what they're privy to, and why Danner would be so determined to keep it a secret. And the fact that they actually went through with suing these employees is noteworthy. Litigation is expensive. That's a lot of billable hours." He paused. "So what did they say? Who were they talking to?"

"You want to know what the real story is?"

"Well, duh."

That tone—for a moment, he reminded me of Stella.

"Good." I smiled. "This means I might be able to get my producer interested in it, too."

He laughed again. "So you're not going to tell me?"

"I don't have any answers yet. But I'll try."

"Your job sounds fun," he said.

"It is. Mostly," I said. "Some days more than others."

"Do you want to switch? Write this brief for me and I'll take a turn as Murphy Brown?"

"The first and only time in my life I'll be compared to Candice Bergen."

"Well, you're just as pretty as her."

Both of us were quiet for a moment. I was relieved Oliver couldn't see me blushing—but then again, if we'd been face-to-face, there was no way he would have said that. The phone, the office, the topic of conversation, it had neutralized the terrain. He wasn't Stella's big brother. I wasn't her best friend. We were just two people, talking.

From his end of the phone, there was the distant whoop of an ambulance from outside his office. In a minute or two, that ambulance would probably pass the KCN building. In those days between Christmas and New Year's, the city was quiet. Sirens echoed louder through the streets. Some people chose to take vacation, or to be with their families. Other people chose work. Oliver, I decided as I hung up the phone, really wasn't so bad.

A friend from college threw a party on New Year's Eve. Her parents were in Sun Valley, and she was alone in their Central Park West penthouse.

The hostess's smile deflated when she saw me arrive alone. "Where's your other half?" she said, air-kissing my cheek.

"Stella?" I said.

"She still traveling the world? Lucky bitch. My parents won't give me a dime."

She put her hands on her hips and laughed harshly. We were in the marble-floored foyer of the apartment. The ceilings were double height and chandeliered, and there was a round table that held several dramatic orchids and what looked like a small Degas. This girl was skinny like Stella, but I could read the starvation on her body. The bony chest, the bobble-head effect. She had always sucked up to Stella in college. Stella, with her effortless beauty and natural measurements, made look easy what the hostess killed herself to achieve.

I'd arrived too early. There were a few docile boyfriends at the perimeter, but most of the group was girls. The party was still more of a pregame, clustered around the island in the kitchen, which was sticky with spilled tequila and lime husks. It was the moment in the night when the hostess was entirely pleased with herself, with the assembled group of women who reflected back her aesthetic ideals. The best pictures of the night would be taken now, when the apartment was still empty, the fridge brimming with liquor.

The girls kept asking me where Stella was. We'd been invited as a package deal, but they really wanted her. I was a little too plain, too serious, too sober. Everyone liked to say that after high school, popularity contests ended. That was true in most cases. But, like high school, the world of Manhattan trust-fund babies was an artificial construct. Nothing really mattered; everything was signaling; it was as insular and petty as a high school cafeteria. These girls were hungry and anxious, but they had perfect blowouts and designer clothing, and they took comfort in telling one another how hot they looked. Which was true—they *did* look hot. It was possible to envy them, and hate oneself for envying them, all at once.

Around 11 p.m., as the party started to fill up, I slipped out unnoticed. The subway was nearly empty. Most people would stay put, wherever they were, as the clock approached midnight. But being underground at midnight didn't seem like the worst possibility. I'd never liked New Year's Eve. So one year was ending and another beginning—did no one notice that life itself proceeded without interruption, indifferent to your resolutions and reflections?

If Stella were there, I would have leaned over and said this to her. She would have laughed and called me a cynical bitch, but she also would have agreed. Our friendship was built on those moments, when our perspectives overlapped like binoculars twisting into focus. We said to each other what we wouldn't say to other people.

But for Stella, observation wasn't the same as belief. She spent her opinions like she spent her family's money: easily, constantly, but never as an investment in something permanent. She'd say something provocative, and often true, but then she'd abandon it. When pushed on a comment she'd made, she'd shrug and say that she wasn't really serious; she didn't really care. For a long time, Stella's indifference had impressed me. Other people would feel bad about running away from home on Christmas Eve. Stella? She was probably drinking a mai tai on a beach somewhere.

And that was fine. Having Stella back in New York had been exciting, but it was also exhausting. At some point in the last several months, our lives had diverged. She wanted spontaneity and freedom. I wanted routine and discipline. I wanted to care about my work. If this was the new pattern, Stella coming and going as she pleased—maybe that was okay. Maybe we needed some breathing room. To occupy our own separate lives.

Pete, the doorman, was on duty that night. "Just a few minutes to midnight," he said. "Did you race home to catch it?"

"Nah," I said. "It'll be a quiet night for me."

"That's good," he said. "That reminds me, actually. Miss Stella asked me to tell you that she was very tired, and she was going to sleep. She was driving for hours."

"Stella?" I said. "She's back?"

Pete nodded, smiling brightly. "Happy New Year!" he said, as the elevator door closed.

CHAPTER SIX
Nine months later

I'D REACHED THE one-year mark at KCN in August. A year was a solid, respectable thing. Now when I heard the new assistants and interns bragging about the number of months they had under their belts, I thought, *months!* Who were they kidding? Of the six other interns who had started with me, five had already washed out. The last remaining girl was always crying when the senior producers yelled at her. I gave her until October, tops.

At this point, I'd learned the ropes, and figured out how to navigate the personalities within the newsroom. I knew how Rebecca liked her coffee (extra hot, skim milk), and I knew what to talk about with a nervous guest in the green room (pets, children). But when I was at my desk, hours sucked into technical scut work, I enviously watched Jamie coming and going from meetings with senior staff. That world was so much bigger than mine: sources and scoops, competitive bookings and big gets. I didn't want to be an assistant anymore. I wanted to be a producer, helping to make the news.

"Let me give you some advice," Jamie said, one afternoon in September. He'd emerged from yet another meeting, looking dismayed. "You know how you should pick a lane and stick to it?"

"You've said that a hundred times," I said. Jamie was always harping on developing a beat, finding an angle that others weren't covering. "I'm trying, okay? I really am."

He plopped down in his chair and shook his head. "No. What I was going to say is, when you pick a lane, make sure you don't pick a lane that's about to be blocked off for the foreseeable future. Because then you don't have a lane. You're just stuck in traffic, like a chump. And then—I don't know. I give up on this metaphor."

"What's wrong?"

"I've spent five years covering the DoD, and now this administration is going to choke the life out of it. Did you see the latest budget cuts?"

"Yeah, but we're spending that money on other things. Education. Social Security. The NIH. Isn't it kind of a good thing?"

Jamie sighed. His father had been a naval officer, and his older brother worked for the Air Force JAG. Several of his hometown friends had joined up after high school. Jamie had naturally gravitated toward covering the Department of Defense, and in a newsroom where few of the producers had connections to the military, he didn't have any competition. "It's more complicated than that," he said. "But long story short, there's not gonna be a whole lot of news coming out of the Pentagon in the next few years."

He stared idly into the distance, swiveling his desk chair back and forth. "My mom was always saying I should go to medical school," he said. "I could have been a doctor by now. I'd make a good doctor, right?"

"You talk too much," I said. "You'd annoy the patients."

He laughed and pushed his foot against my chair. I'd had chances to move to better desks, those closer to the water fountain or with more sunlight, but I liked sitting next to Jamie. He was so calm. His self-possession, I suspected, came from the fact that he loved this job. All of it, from breaking a big story to writing the perfect chyron. This was his place in the world.

"Jamie!" Eliza called, as she walked over. "Just heard. We got the interview with the football player. His people confirmed for Thursday morning."

"Whoa," he said, sitting up straight. "What did the trick?"

"Rebecca worked her usual persuasive charm."

"And Mr. King's not going to mind? Given that he's friends with the commissioner?"

Eliza half smiled, half smirked. "Fuck 'em. Ginny'll take the heat if need be."

"That's huge. God, what a relief."

"I know. I *really* wasn't looking forward to another Community Cares segment." She rolled her eyes, then she noticed me. "You didn't hear that, Violet."

I cocked my head. "Didn't hear what?"

"Good girl."

Increasingly, I had the sense that she liked me, but Eliza remained an enigma. She was the type of person who, while sharing an elevator, was perfectly comfortable staying silent. Whereas Rebecca would fill that time with a torrent of conversation, bathing you with her relentless attention.

But this didn't mean Rebecca was always warm and fuzzy. More than once she'd snapped at a producer, loud enough for the whole newsroom to hear: "Would you *get* to the *point!*" Or the night when the teleprompter was malfunctioning, and the rundown had changed at the last minute, and with sixty seconds to air Rebecca still didn't know what the lead story in the A block was. When we went to the first commercial break, her face changed from professional warmth to pure rage. "This is my ass on the line, people," she said. "Do you understand that? When we fuck up, I'm the one whose face gets plastered all over the internet. I get blamed. I look like a goddamn idiot because *you* don't have your shit together."

Eliza calmed her down that night, as she always did. It was obvious from the beginning that Eliza was an excellent journalist, but what took longer to reveal itself was her diplomacy. It didn't matter how nasty a situation got. She was smooth and reassuring in the face of disaster. But Eliza's diplomacy, like Rebecca's famous generosity, was not an end in itself. At the root of every behavior, you could find a seed of self-interest.

"She and Rebecca are a package deal," Jamie explained once. "They bring out the best in each other. You put Rebecca with a different producer, or Eliza with a different anchor, and you just don't have the same magic."

"Yeah," I said. "Which is good, right? That makes them untouchable."

"As long as you keep the peace," Jamie said. "Rebecca's temper is the X factor. A newsroom stays loyal to an anchor until it doesn't. The people who light you, who mic you, who do your hair and makeup, who prep the guests—if you really piss them off, sabotage is easy."

"So Eliza needs to make sure Rebecca doesn't alienate everyone?"

"Because if they bring Rebecca down, Eliza goes with her. See?"

I nodded. "Makes sense to me."

Jamie furrowed his brow. "You don't seem bothered by how Machiavellian it is."

"It's not Machiavellian," I said. "It's just survival."

We were running wall-to-wall promos for the interview. He was a retired football player who planned to speak out on the NFL's long-term cover-up of brain damage. In addition to being a Hall of Famer, he was the stoic and silent type. When he spoke, people listened.

Rebecca and Eliza returned to the newsroom around lunchtime on Thursday, after taping the interview. They stood outside Rebecca's office, conferring. The interview must have gone well. If Rebecca was listening this carefully, it meant she was in a good mood.

Rebecca and Eliza spent most of the day in the edit room. After a few hours, Eliza opened the door and stuck her head out. "Jamie!" she yelled. "Come eyeball this for me."

Half an hour later, Jamie returned, looked subdued.

"Uh-oh," I said. "I guess I don't need to ask."

He sighed. "It's not the worst thing I've ever seen. We've got him saying some incendiary stuff. He has proof that officials ignored the data. But it just feels...flat. Lifeless."

"It probably doesn't help that he's so serious."

Jamie shook his head. "No, it's not that. He's good on camera. He's got gravitas. But after the segment's over, you're kind of left thinking—so what?"

"Yikes."

"I know. It needs something."

I drummed my fingers. "It's hideous, when you think about it."

"I agree," Jamie said.

"I mean, children are at risk. Children with young, developing brains. How many teenagers play football in this country? Doesn't Rebecca's son play?"

Jamie had been spinning back and forth in his chair, which he always did while mulling, but he stopped. "Yes. Exactly," he said. He jumped to his feet. "Come with me."

Rebecca and Eliza were in the edit room, standing behind a hassled-looking woman. Eliza was probably itching to grab the controls, but union rules meant that only an editor could do this work. The editors tended to be older and grumpier, and they didn't always appreciate fresh-faced producers coming into the room with a segment to crash. I was scared of this particular woman: she was a chain-smoker from Staten Island who sometimes reminded me of my mother. She did the work well, but with a maximum of grumbling. But with Rebecca and Eliza in the room, she was silent and deferential.

"Yes?" Eliza said, with a look of *this had better be important*. Jamie pushed me forward. "Tell them what you just told me."

"About how many teenagers play football?" I said, and Jamie nodded. I took a deep breath. "I was just saying how outrageous it is. That there are children at risk, whose brains are still developing. If they'd known this sooner, parents might have thought twice about letting their kids play football. Even your son, Rebecca. Doesn't he play football?"

Jamie snapped his fingers. "That's the lead-in. Right there. That's the frame for this whole story."

"It's a public health risk." Rebecca nodded slowly. "It's about our children. Shit. Why didn't I think of that?"

"It's a question every mother has to ask herself," Eliza said. "Knowing what I know, am I willing to let my child do this? Jamie, this is really good."

"It was all Violet."

"*Violet*," Eliza said, grabbing my forearm. "Nice work. Can you chase down the up-to-date stats on how many kids play? Anything you can find on concussions, too."

At 8 o'clock, the newsroom was quiet as the *Frontline* theme played. When Rebecca appeared on-screen, she looked different. Her hair was in soft waves instead of her usual sleek blowout, and her dress was a pastel floral instead of her favored bright solids. This was the Rebecca Carter who remembered her years in family-centric morning television.

"Good evening," she began. "At *Frontline,* we have one

mission. Keeping you, our audience, as fairly and accurately informed as possible. You've probably noticed that I don't often speak about myself. That's because this hour isn't about me—it's about you. But tonight, we're featuring a story that hits close to home. So I want to speak to you personally. I want to speak to you as a mother."

Fifteen minutes later, when the story ended and we went to commercial, the newsroom exploded in applause. Jamie broke into a grin, and slung his arm around me. "You're good at this," he said. "You know? You've got it, Trapp."

In the past year, evidence of my contributions had appeared on-screen in small ways. A statistic that I'd dug up, or a change made after my fact-check. But this was different; this was bigger. A contribution big enough that it might actually compel a viewer to keep watching. It might stick with them. It might change their mind.

After the broadcast, everyone gathered in the newsroom. Rebecca and Eliza believed in traditions, and one of them was marking a big story with good champagne. A few minutes later, Eliza came over with two plastic flutes. She handed one to me, then tapped hers against mine.

"We'll have to wait for the overnights," she said. "But I have a good feeling."

"Rebecca was great," I said.

"Remind me how long you've been here?" Eliza squinted at me.

"A little over a year."

"You're a quick study."

I glanced over at Jamie, across the room. "I've had a good mentor."

"So you're modest, too." Eliza smiled. "Follow me. I want you to meet someone."

Rebecca was in the corner with a handful of executives, some of whom I recognized from her holiday party. There was an older woman, deep in conversation with Rebecca. She looked like the kind of woman who would be friends with the Bradleys: ash-blond hair, a tweed suit that suggested Chanel. Eliza tapped her on the shoulder.

"Ginny," Eliza said. "This is Violet Trapp, the young woman I was telling you about. She's our newest associate producer. Violet, this is Ginny Grass, president of KCN."

"I'm—what?" I said.

"She just got promoted," Eliza added. "Approximately five minutes ago."

"Congratulations," Ginny said, shaking my hand. Her voice had a crisp delivery that reminded me of old black-and-white movies. "Lovely to meet you."

"Thank you," I said. Then to Eliza and Rebecca, I said. "Wait, really?"

"So what do you think, Gin?" Rebecca said. "Think we beat MSNBC?"

"Let me worry about that," Ginny said. "Just enjoy yourselves tonight."

"Oh please." Rebecca rolled her eyes. "Give me the numbers as soon as you have them."

"You'd think a Peabody and six Emmys would help with her obsession, but you'd be wrong," Eliza murmured to me.

"Don't let her fool you," Rebecca said, hitting Eliza on the shoulder. "She's a whore for the ratings just like the rest of us."

Ginny wore a strained smile. I got the sense she disliked my witnessing this level of candor—and insecurity—among my superiors. "It's an achievement no matter what," she said. "We should all feel proud of this story."

"I can feel proud and still envy Fox's audience, can't I?" Rebecca said.

Eliza nudged me. "Go on, go celebrate. You don't have to hang with the old folks."

Jamie was by the kitchenette, which had been turned into a makeshift bar. He refilled my plastic flute. "You look like you have some good news to share," he said.

I paused. "Did you know?"

"Just a few minutes before they told you." He grinned, then leaned forward and kissed my cheek. "Congratulations."

I touched my cheek in surprise. I blushed, and so did Jamie. The moment stretched on for several long beats, until Jamie glanced away. "Your phone," he said.

"Huh?"

"Your phone." He pointed at my hand. I'd gotten into the habit of bringing my phone everywhere, even the bathroom. "Someone's calling you."

"Oh," I said. "Just a second."

I stepped away, stuck my finger in the other ear. "Hey," I answered. "I can't really talk."

"Violet!" Stella had to shout over the music in the background. "You need to get down here, stat. This party is crazy."

"I'm still at work."

"It's nine thirty. The show's over, isn't it? You can bring that guy, you know, whatshisname. Frank. Isn't his name Frank?"

"His name is Jamie."

"Okay, sure. I'm putting your names on the guest list."

"Stella, I can't—"

"Nope," she said. "Just one night. I'm forcing you not to be lame for just one night. Don't be such a baby, Violet. Get your ass in a cab."

"You talking about me?" Jamie said, after I hung up.

"Will you come to this party with me?" I said, before I could think better of it.

The party was at the Boom Boom Room, at the top of the Standard Hotel.

"The *what?*" Jamie said, as we rode the E train downtown, swaying back and forth from the rhythm of the tracks. "That's really what it's called?"

Stella may not have known the difference between Sunni and Shia, or Myanmar and Mozambique, but she did possess a specific and potent kind of vocabulary: the name of every chic restaurant and club and boutique and designer on the island of Manhattan. She always assumed I knew what she was talking about, because it was unthinkable not to know these things. What is New York if not the places where the wealthy and beautiful go to exercise their wealth and beauty? Her mental map of the city must have been a funny thing. Clusters of bright pinpoints in SoHo and the West Village and Chelsea, a few along Madison Avenue on the Upper East Side. The rest of the island just darkness. Although we had been sleeping under the same roof since January, Stella and I lived in virtually different cities.

"I've never been," I said. "But she's there all the time."

"It's kind of a ridiculous name," Jamie said.

"Well, she's kind of a ridiculous person."

"She works in fashion?"

"Part time, a few days a week. She's what you might call a lady of leisure."

We walked west down Thirteenth Street toward the Standard. It was a Thursday night, which meant the neighborhood was thrumming. The lobby was packed with people waiting for the elevator to the rooftop club. "Wow," Jamie said. "Doesn't anyone have work tomorrow?"

"We do. And we're here. We're guests of Stella Bradley," I said to the woman with the clipboard, who crossed off our names and gestured us into the elevator.

At the top of the elevator, a mirrored and carpeted hallway led to the club. I stood on my toes, trying to catch a glimpse of Stella. A gorgeous redhead in a tight white dress appeared next to Jamie and me, holding a silver tray with glass flutes. "Champagne?" she said, towering in her stilettos. She smiled and laid a manicured hand on Jamie's arm.

I shook my head. Who knew what a drink at this place cost? Payday was eight days away, and I had to make the seventy dollars in my bank account last until then.

"Okay," Jamie said, watching the woman walk away. "I get it."

"You know, they're paying her a lot of money to flirt with you. It's her job."

Jamie looked around, taking in the dramatic golden-lit pillar behind the bar, the shimmering ceiling, the view of the skyline. "Should we try and find your roommate?" he said.

Pushing through the crowds, I savored the sound of that phrase. My roommate. I was always the nameless friend, never the other way around. Jamie knew very little about Stella. I rarely talked about her. This suddenly struck me as a terrible idea. Why on earth had I invited Jamie? So that he could see us side by side, and realize how superior Stella was?

"I always thought that was a cliché," Jamie said.

"What?"

He pointed at two girls dancing on the bar. "I thought that only happened in the movies," he said, a look of innocent awe on his face. In this particular slice of the world, he was Dante and I was his Virgil. The two girls on the bar were teetering in their high heels, grinding to some smash hit from the past decade. One was a brunette, the other a blonde. I squinted and said, "Shit. That's Stella."

"*That's* your roommate?" Jamie yelped.

"Please try to contain yourself. Stella!" I called, waving at her.

"Violet!" she shouted. She hopped down from the bar and squeezed through the crowd. Her hug smelled like cigarettes and perfume and mint. "And you're Jamie," she said, grabbing his hands and kissing him on both cheeks. I relaxed, a little. Of course they would get along. Stella could charm anyone when she felt like it. "I've heard a *lot* about you."

"Really?" he said.

"You both need drinks. Excuse me?" Stella said, waving down another white-dressed waitress. She plucked two glasses from the tray and passed them to us.

"We don't have to pay for these?" I said, holding the drink hesitantly by the stem.

She laughed. "Of course not."

Stella tossed her hair over her shoulders. Her dress was stiff and boxy and asymmetrical, interesting rather than beautiful. That was what her boss, a young fashion designer, was known for. His work was experimental and not remotely flattering, and therefore it was only feasible to wear his clothing if you were already thin and gorgeous.

"What's this party for?" Jamie asked.

"An after-party," Stella said. "We had our show tonight."

"Show?" he said.

"It's Fashion Week." She arched an eyebrow. "You didn't know that? I am *so* ready for this week to be over. It's been endless."

"It seems like really hard work," Jamie said, smiling.

"It is!" Stella said, sailing past the sarcasm. "You try pulling off a runway show when half the designs aren't even finished by the night before. And looking good on no sleep." She drained her glass, handed it to another passing waitress. "Anyways. We might as well have some fun." She draped her arm around my shoulders, considerably taller than me in her high heels. "Violet was so much fun in college," she said to Jamie. "You should have seen her freshman year. She was *wild*."

"Let's talk about something else," I said.

"I know how it looks now. She probably seems so professional. So put together. But back in the day, oh my God." Stella laughed. "Straight out of the Everglades. Barely civilized."

"Stell, come on," I said.

"Is she like this with you, too, Jamie?" She tilted her head, faux innocent. "She'd never tell me anything about home. She never wants to talk about it. So mysterious, right?"

My mind flashed through a carousel of images, any one of which Stella might choose to conjure. The obvious candidates were the embarrassing moments, drinking too much, fumbling encounters with boys. But I hadn't accounted for the times, again and again, when I dodged her questions about home. I thought my evasions were clever. I thought, on some level, that Stella wasn't really listening.

But she was always listening, even when it didn't appear that way. Tucking away that knowledge for future use. There was a greedy, excited sparkle in her eye.

"I don't blame her," Jamie said. "You get old enough and you start to realize that no one really cares where you're from."

Stella looked annoyed. "That is not remotely true," she said. Then she smiled, reassuming her power. "So this one time, freshman year, we went to this party and—"

"Jesus, is this a roast?" I snapped. "Did I miss the memo?"

Stella laughed and kissed me on the cheek, leaving a sticky press of lipstick. "So *sensitive*. You've gotten so boring, Violet. Is she like this at work, too?"

"Actually," Jamie said, "Violet's kind of a big deal these days."

Stella laughed. "Oh, really? Pray tell."

But Jamie ignored her tone. "You're looking at *Frontline*'s newest associate producer," he said. He was smiling at me, pleased and proud.

My stomach churned. *Stop*, I thought, *please stop*. Didn't Jamie see the look on Stella's face? This wasn't my role in our relationship. She could only stand the spotlight being on someone else if that spotlight was unflattering.

"She was just promoted tonight," Jamie continued. "Youngest AP in KCN history."

"Huh," Stella said, turning to me and arching an eyebrow. "So this means, what? No more getting people coffee? Because that's basically what your job has been, right?"

Sometimes it frightened me, how perceptive she was. She knew precisely where a person's vulnerabilities lay hidden. She knew exactly where to angle her knife, for maximum pain. Maybe I loved Stella because she was the opposite of everything I'd grown up with. Or maybe I loved her because she was, at some level, just like my parents. More likely to mock me than believe in me. Moments like this, I thought, *Either she's an asshole or she's right, and the world sure doesn't treat Stella Bradley like she's an asshole.*

"I'm going to the bathroom," I said.

"You're single, right?" Stella said to Jamie, looping her arm through his. "Come on. There are some models you should meet."

Half an hour later, my dignity somewhat restored by hiding in the bathroom and responding to e-mails on my phone, I pushed back through the crowd in search of Jamie. But Stella appeared at my side and grabbed my arm.

"*There* you are," she said. "Where have you been?"

"I've been here this whole time," I said. "You just haven't noticed."

She put her hands on her hips. "It's because of what I said about the coffee, isn't it? But that's what you always say, Violet! You've complained about the coffee, like, a hundred times." Stella laughed. "You're always saying how, what do you call it, *underutilized* you are."

"I know," I said, although the sting was still there. "It's fine."

"Violet!" She squeezed my hand. "I was just kidding. Of course I'm happy for you! *Duh.* What kind of friend would I be if I weren't?" She took the glass from my hand and sipped. Then she made a face. "Is this club soda? Are you sober right now?"

"More or less," I said.

"But we need to celebrate. And these places suck unless you're drunk!" She dragged us to the bar and ordered a pair of tequila shots. "Cheers," she said, clinking her glass against mine.

As Stella was about to order a second round, a colleague asked her to say hello to some VIP from *Vogue*. "I'll find you later!" she shouted. I finally spotted Jamie in the corner, chatting with an older woman. She had cropped gray hair and purple-framed glasses and a black kimono. When I waved at him, he smiled. Jamie and the woman shook hands, and Jamie gave a slight bow as he stepped away.

"Did you just *bow* to her?" I said, after he came over.

"I don't know," he said. "These parties are confusing, okay?"

"Who is she?"

"Kind of famous, I think. I didn't catch her name. But she's a designer. She was friends with Andy Warhol, once upon a time."

I laughed.

"What?" Jamie said.

"Nothing," I said. "I just love that at this party, with a room full of models, you wind up talking to the only octogenarian."

He smiled. "She's the most interesting person here. Present company excluded."

Outside the hotel, we were greeted by a cool September night. Even though it was past 2 a.m., I felt awake and alert, and strangely relieved. My two worlds had collided, and it wasn't that bad. I took a deep, satisfied breath.

"Walk with me for a little while?" I said. "It's such a nice night."

As we made our way east, after a long silence, Jamie said, "So that was Stella."

"That was Stella."

"She's something, isn't she?"

"That depends on what the meaning of something is."

"Ha ha, Bill Clinton." He elbowed me. "Is she always like that? She's so *on*."

"She loves an audience," I said. "Especially a brand-new audience. You don't know her tricks. And you're not her friend yet. So she'll try harder to impress you."

"But why does she care what I think?"

"Okay, it's like this. One time in college she was worrying about her new haircut. I told her it looked great, which it did, by the way. But she didn't care. She said, 'Your opinion doesn't mean anything to me, Violet. Of course you think it looks good. You love me.'"

"Ah," Jamie said.

"But the upside," I said, "is that, when you get to know her, she stops trying to impress you. Because what's the point? And then she's a lot more fun to be around."

After another stretch of silence, Jamie said, "Know who she reminds me of? Rebecca."

"Rebecca *Carter?*"

"It's that energy. Rebecca's more polished now, but she wasn't always like that."

"Are we talking about the same Rebecca Carter? The one who once dodged bullets in Sierra Leone?"

"You'd be surprised. You drop Stella Bradley into a war zone, I bet she does pretty well."

It seemed like an absurd thought, on its face. Stella, a journalist?

"Her ego is already big enough. Don't ever tell her that." I was laughing like it was a joke. But then why did I feel a distinct ping of panic, somewhere deep in my brain?

I promised Jamie a nightcap in exchange for walking me home. Upstairs, I studied the contents of our liquor cabinet and called into the other room, "Any preferences?"

"I'll have whatever you're having," he said.

When I carried two glasses of wine into the living room, Jamie was studying the photographs on the mantelpiece. Like the rest of the décor, these were selected by Anne. She'd included a few photos of me and Stella from college, but mostly the images were of the Bradley family. Jamie squinted at a towheaded Stella, aged three or four, her arms wrapped around the family's old golden retriever. "Cute kid," he said.

"Do you want to sit?" I said, nodding at the couch.

After we sat down, Jamie lifted his wineglass, the red liquid remaining level as his glass tilted toward mine. "To your promotion," he said.

"God," I said. "I'd almost forgotten."

"It's been a long night."

I set my glass on the coffee table. "Thank you for coming with me," I said. "You didn't have to do that."

"Are you kidding? And miss a chance to see the famous Boom Boom Room?"

Jamie set his wineglass down, too. He shifted, angling his body toward me. His knee brushed against mine. "Although it is kind of nice," he said. "Just the two of us."

"Oh," I said. Suddenly seeing what was happening.

Jamie leaned in, his face growing more detailed. His freckles, his unkempt eyebrows. As he kissed me, his hand cupped the back of my head. It was gentle but deliberate, as if to show he'd been thinking about this for a long time.

It's not that the kiss wasn't nice. It's not that I hadn't occasionally considered it, given how close we'd become. But in that brief moment, his hair smelling like the cold outdoors, his lips tasting faintly of red wine, the kiss was just a kiss. Nothing more. No spark of chemistry, no jolt of excitement. An ending, rather than a beginning.

After a second, Jamie sat back. "Too fast?" he said.

I shook my head, stared at my lap. Looking him in the eye felt cruel.

"Oh," he said. "Oh, God, Violet, I'm so sorry. Did I totally misread the situation?"

"I'm not good at this stuff," I said.

Jamie took his hand off my knee. I wanted to be honest, but how? Because the real truth blaring through my mind, the real calculation underneath, was *your career is more important than this.* At best, being with Jamie would be a distraction. At worst, it would fuck everything up.

"I mean," I continued, staring at my hands, as if the answer lay there. "We work together. And you're one of my best friends. I'd have no clue how to navigate that."

When I finally looked up, Jamie was shaking his head and smiling. "You're right," he said, a note of palpable relief in his voice. "You're completely right. This is ironic. I always suspected you were too smart for me, and this proves it."

"So we're okay, then?"

"Of course," he said.

I didn't really have to ask. Jamie was an awful liar, and if he had been upset or embarrassed, it would have been obvious.

"Good," I said. "Because I mean it. About being one of my best friends."

After we said good night—Jamie texted me a simple "thank-you" from his cab—I felt a stinging flash of loss. The knowledge of what I'd just given up, of the door I had just closed. There would have been simple ways to navigate the conflict. We could tell HR. One of us could transfer to another show.

But that would mean putting my ambition second. I wanted to succeed, to prove that I could do this. I wanted that more badly than I'd ever wanted anything. The world is shaped by powerful forces—politics, finance, media—from which most people live distantly, feeling the ripple effects but never understanding the origin. In the past year, I had finally crossed a crucial threshold. I was standing on the side of actor, not acted-upon. I sensed myself getting stronger, sharper, better. But I also sensed how desire fed on itself. It ballooned inside of me, until it squeezed out room for anything else. Sometimes I wondered whether it was deforming me.

But maybe that was backwards. Maybe you had to be deformed in the first place to be capable of such blistering want. Things weren't getting pushed out. It was that there'd never been anything else in there. Just a void, waiting to be filled.

CHAPTER SEVEN

ON A SATURDAY night in late October, Anne and Thomas had a party to celebrate their thirtieth wedding anniversary. Anne didn't like birthdays—"They make me feel so *old,*" she said, wrinkling her nose—but she did like throwing big parties. For this one, they spared no expense: they rented out the Rainbow Room, hired a twenty-piece band, and invited a hundred friends.

Stella and I were in a cab crawling north along Sixth Avenue. It would have been faster to take the subway, but after ten months of living in New York, Stella no longer believed in taking the subway. It wasn't for her, she said, with the same dismissive conviction that her mother took toward birthdays.

"I can't believe *this* is my Saturday night," Stella said. She kept rolling the window up and down, over and over. It was raining, and I could see the cab driver flinching every time she did it.

"Stop," I said, putting my hand over Stella's. "The window. Everything's getting wet."

She raised an eyebrow. "What's it to you?" Then she opened it again.

I met the driver's gaze in the mirror. *Sorry,* I mouthed. He frowned.

"Why couldn't they have the party on—I don't know—a

Tuesday? Don't old people love throwing parties during the week? And I can't believe you agreed to come to this." Stella glared at me. She was in a bad mood, bored in this moment and bored in general. "I mean, they're my parents. I have to be there. But if Anne hadn't literally given birth to me? Forget it."

The cab dropped us off at Rockefeller Center. Stella paid, but she left a stingy tip. I wanted to slip the driver something, but I only had a twenty-dollar bill in my wallet, which I couldn't afford to part with. The windows on the ground floor of 30 Rock were lined with posters of NBC's biggest stars: the anchors, the morning-show hosts, the late-night comedians, looming beneficently over the sidewalks. We were inside the atrium, shaking the rain from our umbrellas, when Stella said abruptly, "She's not *that* pretty."

"Who?" I said.

"That woman, what's her name." She gestured vaguely. "The lady on the news. I mean, she's okay. But she's very plain-looking."

"Believe it or not," I said, as we stepped into the elevator that would whisk us up to the Rainbow Room. "It's not entirely about looks."

Stella snorted. "Oh, please. Then why don't you see any ugly women on TV? I read somewhere that, like, half of all the women on TV started off as beauty pageant winners."

"Well, the other half went to law school." I frowned. "And where did you read that?"

"Who cares?" Stella said. "You're just annoyed because I know something about the TV business that you don't know."

When we arrived, Anne was frustrated. "This is awful!" she said, pointing at the rain-streaked windows and thick gray clouds. "Of course the one day it rains this month is during our party. I timed this whole thing around sunset. But it seems like the *weather* had other plans." She spat out the word like the weather was an uncooperative vendor who was violating their contract.

"It still looks beautiful," I said. The room sparkled, like a jewel nestled in the gray cottony clouds. "And so do you, Mrs. Bradley," I added.

"Well, thanks, Violet. You're sweet. Do you mind terribly getting me a martini? The waiters seem to be neglecting this corner of the room."

"Oh, sure. Of course."

"Stella, sweetie, do you want Violet to get you anything from the bar?"

Stella looked up from her phone. Anne often dispatched me for her little tasks, treating me like a hybrid of family friend and hired help. But if this was what it took to keep my rent at $750 a month, so be it. "Vodka soda," Stella said, then went back to texting.

By the bar, I found Oliver with a whiskey in one hand and his phone in the other. "You and your sister are exactly alike," I said, bumping my shoulder against him.

"Violet!" He kissed me on the cheek. "So nice to see you."

"Although I'm guessing you're attending to more serious matters." I nodded at his phone. "Not texting your dealer, like Stella."

Oliver looked horrified.

"I'm just joking!" I said. "Completely joking." I wasn't, though. It continued to surprise me, how little Stella's family knew about her life.

"Oh. Well." He smiled tightly.

I ordered three drinks from the bartender, and said, "Don't worry, they're not all for me."

"Honestly, I wouldn't blame you," Oliver said.

"You know, you and Stella might think these parties are boring, but I'm pretty impressed."

He smiled, this time more genuine. "I've been meaning to ask you," he said. "Remember that thing you called me about? It

was a long time ago. You had some question about NDAs at—
Danner Pharmaceuticals, right?"

"Yeah. I'm surprised you remembered," I said.

"So what happened with that?"

"I got in touch with some of the people they sued, a few janitors and security guards, but they didn't want to talk. I mean,
they couldn't. That's why they'd been sued in the first place."

"Aren't you curious, though?"

"Of course. But you can't overthink it. You'll start convincing
yourself there's a story when there isn't." I shrugged. "In Danner's case, an overly litigious company that takes itself too seriously? Annoying, maybe, but not a capital crime."

Oliver lifted his glass toward me. "I heard about your promotion, by the way."

"Stella told you?"

"She told my mom, and my mom told me. Congratulations."

"Oh—well, thank you."

"We're proud of you, Violet," Oliver said. "You're a credit to
the Bradley name."

It was delicate work, maneuvering through the crowd with
three drinks in hand. I supposed it was nice to hear that from
Oliver. The Bradleys' affection was contingent and changeable,
and I liked knowing where I stood with them. The music, the
laughter, the tuxedos and gowns and glittering lights: this world
was hard to earn, easy to fall in love with. But sometimes I
wanted to run in the opposite direction. What if I didn't want to
be a credit to the Bradley name? What if I wanted to be a credit
to my own name?

"*There* you are," Anne said. "Thank you, Violet. I'm parched."

Anne was holding court with a group of women who looked
just like her: moisturized, fastidiously slender, impeccably pre-
served from the disappointments of middle age. In a low voice,
Stella said to me, "I'm dying, Violet. Literally dying."

I laughed. "Should I call 9-1-1?"

"Honestly, I'd rather ride around New York in an ambulance than stay here all night. At least that's *exciting*. Do you realize we're the youngest people in this room by twenty years?"

"Except for Oliver," I said.

Stella snorted. "Oliver's the oldest person here. Look. He's turning into our father."

Oliver and Thomas Bradley were standing together at the bar, surveying the room. And it was true: they had the same serious mien, the same aristocratic height, like an English peer and the son who would someday inherit his title. Although if you looked at Stella and Anne side by side, you might say the same thing. Stella maintained that she was the black sheep, but with each passing year she grew into the family resemblance, like a tree bending to the sun.

"How long do you think we have to stay?" Stella said.

"No idea. Your family, not mine."

"Can you pretend to be sick? Say you have to go to the hospital and I'll come—"

"Wait a second, is that Ginny Grass?" I said, spotting a familiar face across the room.

Stella swatted me on the arm. "*Rude.* Don't interrupt."

"See that woman in the blue dress? Is she friends with your parents?"

Stella squinted. "Oh yeah," she said. "Ginny. She's an old family friend. She has a place down the road from my grandparents, in Maine. How do you know her?"

"She's the president of KCN. My boss's boss's boss."

"Huh." Stella tilted her head. Gears seemed to be turning. "You wanna go say hi?"

"Oh God, no. I have no idea what I'd say."

But Stella had already started pulling me across the room. "What are you so scared of? She's just a normal person."

"To you, maybe."

"Ginny!" Stella said loudly, from a dozen feet away.

Ginny turned, and exclaimed, "Stella!" She kissed her on the cheek. "You look beautiful, my dear. You never change."

"Neither do you," Stella said. "You have to tell me your secret. And, oh my goodness, I *love* your earrings. Where are they from?"

Ginny touched the diamonds dangling from her earlobes. The most remarkable thing about Stella's charm wasn't just the force of it; it was the way she turned it on from zero to sixty in a second flat. No one could have guessed her bad mood of moments ago.

After a while, Ginny noticed that I was hovering awkwardly. With a practiced smile, she turned to me. "Hello," she said, extending her hand. "Are you a friend of Stella's?"

A small part of my chest collapsed. A pinprick, air hissing out. Stella looked too amused to offer clarification. "Violet Trapp," I said, keeping my head high and voice steady. "Actually, we've met before. I'm an associate producer at *Frontline*."

"Oh!" Ginny said. "Of course. Of course, you look very familiar. But you two are friends?" She touched Stella on the forearm. "What a small world."

"Violet always makes her work at KCN sound so interesting," Stella said. "Much more interesting than my job."

"It's a calling, really," Ginny said, nodding.

"You know, I've been thinking," Stella said. "Fashion has been fun, but it's not really for me. I've been considering a career change. Maybe getting into news."

"You *have?*" I said, my hand jerking, nearly spilling my glass of wine.

"What a splendid idea!" Ginny clapped her hands. "Oh, you'd be perfect for it."

Stella looked like a cat that ate not just one canary, but an

entire cage of them. "Do you really think so?" she said in a sac-
charine voice, her eyes fixed on Ginny.

They spent most of the night sequestered in the corner, their
heads tilted together. When the party ended, Stella slipped her
arm through mine. As we rode the elevator down and hailed a
cab on Fifth Avenue, she said, "Don't be mad at me."

"Why would I be mad at you?" I said, but I closed the car
door harder than I needed to.

"Don't be like that. You should be flattered. You heard what I
said."

"Why haven't you mentioned this before?"

She shrugged, muting the TV in the back of the cab. "It never
came up."

"That's awfully convenient."

"And," she said. "You don't exactly have the power to hire me."

"*What?*"

"Ginny set it up. I have an interview on Monday. What should
I wear?" She got a faraway look in her eye. "I should go shopping tomorrow."

"Stella, this is crazy. Have you even *thought* about this?"

"Why can't you be happy for me? This is fun. We're going to
work together!"

What I wanted to say was *you don't have the job yet.* But that
wasn't really true. With Ginny as her backer, Stella's hiring was
basically guaranteed. The interview, the résumé, the references,
it was just a paper trail. Plausible deniability against charges of
nepotism.

"Aren't you coming?" I said to Stella, when the cab stopped at
our apartment.

"We'll be making a second stop," she said to the driver. "I'm
meeting some friends downtown. Let's have brunch or something tomorrow, though?"

"I'm busy," I said, and this time I slammed the door before she could respond.

The alarm clock glowed red in the darkness. The raindrops struck the air conditioner in my window with a pinging pebble-like noise. I was too hot with the duvet, too cold without it. I couldn't sleep. Eventually, around three thirty, I got up.

The apartment was dark, Stella's bedroom empty. She often spent the night elsewhere, in the bachelor pads of the men she slept with, or with friends whose parents had housekeepers to cook them breakfast. I thought this was abnormal, but sometimes I wondered if I had it backwards. We lived in an elegant prewar building on one of the few quiet blocks between Union Square and Washington Square. It was some of the most expensive real estate in the world—and yet I rarely saw the other residents of our building. Passing through the lobby, it was often just me and the doorman. I'd never seen another person taking out the trash, carrying groceries, fumbling with keys. When I walked down our block at night, most of the windows were dark. The richest parts of Manhattan were emptier than they appeared.

In my childhood home, I'd hated the thin walls, the sound of my father snoring at night. My mother's bleached hair collecting on the floor and clogging the shower drain. I'd hated how the kitchen was constantly infested with carpenter ants, and the bathroom was always damp, and cars backfired on the street outside. But too much quiet could be just as exhausting as too little.

When I was restless with insomnia, I liked to bake. Bread, cakes, cookies, anything. In those 3 a.m. and 4 a.m. hours, I could look at the clock on the oven and imagine that I was doing this for a reason. Rising early with the invisible fellowship of other bakers, so that the world could have their muffins and scones ready in time for breakfast.

That night, I made soda bread. I measured and mixed the ingredients, kneaded the stretchy dough, brushed the rounded loaf with milk. The waiting, the actual baking, was my favorite part. Here was the only thing I had to worry about: sitting on a stool in front of the warm oven, the timer ticking, watching to be sure the bread didn't burn. Music playing in the background (Billie Holiday, that night), the dishwasher swishing quietly. Cooking was improvisational, but baking was precise and predictable. The sweet, life-giving scent of bread was a product of my own two hands. It was rare to feel this way—to stand still and enjoy it, for a minute.

Especially in New York, especially in this business, getting ahead was the cost of entry. Working was a way of being. Time not spent in pursuit of a larger ambition was time wasted. When asked whether I liked my job at KCN, I always said yes, but I thought, Why are you asking that question? Why is *liking* the metric? The job was both more than that and less than that. It wasn't a source of peace and contentment, that was for sure. But it was my means of survival. It paid for rent and food and clothing. It propelled me further and further from the life I'd known before.

The timer went off, and I slid the loaf onto a rack to cool. There was the misery of having too little, but there was also the misery of living among those who believed there was no such thing as too much. Surely there was an in-between. If I were a different kind of person, maybe this could have been my life. Live in a village in the French countryside, apprentice with a local baker, eventually open my own B&B, where I'd bake bread to serve with soft cheese and wine, and keep bundles of lavender in every room. I'd learn to be content with the simple pleasures of life itself, not tortured by the notion that I wasn't keeping up. This, by the way, is the fantasy of every person who has spent too many late nights at the office under buzzing fluorescent lights.

Perhaps Stella suffered from the inverse fantasy. She had spent the past year living the dreamy life of a glossy magazine. She stayed out late, she slept in, she met friends for languorous meals. She spent money like it was water, her bank account one small tributary that flowed into the coursing river of Manhattan commerce. Taxis, bottles of wine, bouquets of flowers, new dresses, new shoes, massages, facials, haircuts, highlights, spin classes. And those were just the basics. Her days were a chick-lit fantasy come alive.

A lot of my mental space was taken up by the slicing and dicing of my paycheck into rent and loan payments, groceries, occasional savings. But look how frictionless it was for Stella. Look at how much spare time she had to think. To let her mind wander. To plan her next move.

Of you, Oliver had said, last Christmas. *Stella is jealous of you.*

You couldn't beat Stella Bradley at her own game. So I had found a separate game, one where we wouldn't compete with each other.

It hadn't occurred to me that Stella could look at my life— the long hours, the grunt work—and actually feel something like envy. But that was my own stupidity. Everyone wants what they don't have. Everyone wants more.

PART TWO

CHAPTER EIGHT

STELLA STARTED AS an intern at KCN in the new year. When she got her first paycheck in January, she came over to my desk and said, "Am I supposed to do something with this?"

"You're supposed to deposit it," I said.

She furrowed her forehead. "But what are all these things? Social Security? Does this look normal to you?" She thrust the check toward me. When I registered the dollar amount, there was the momentary satisfaction of seeing how much bigger my salary was than hers. I had to take my victories where I could get them.

"Perfectly normal," I said. My phone started ringing, but as I moved to answer it, Stella said, "Can I ask you something else?"

"I have to take this call."

"Please, Violet? I need your help."

"Fine." I watched the call go to voice mail, imagined my source annoyed at having to leave a message, the apologizing I'd have to do when I called back. "What is it?"

She led me to the copy room, where a red light was flashing on the copy machine. There was a crumpled, ink-stained piece of paper jammed into the feeder. With wide eyes, Stella said, "I think I broke it."

"*This* is what you need help with? Why didn't you ask another intern?"

She frowned. "Because you're my friend."

"I'm also a producer, and in case you can't tell, I'm a little busy. Ask one of the interns or assistants." Walking away, I added, "I haven't even used that machine in months."

"You look pissed," Jamie said, when I returned. "What is it this time?"

I sighed and dropped into my chair. "The copy machine is jammed."

"Have a little sympathy for her. She's still new."

"You want to take a turn helping her? Be my guest."

Jamie had been witness to my bad mood all month. I could sense him hesitating, holding back advice that, honestly, I could have used: *get over yourself,* or *you're wasting energy on being mad.* But Jamie was practiced in the art of self-preservation, and knew better than to get between us.

When Stella applied to KCN, there were two internship openings: one on the morning show, and one on *Frontline.* "Well, obviously I'm choosing *Frontline,*" she'd said. "Waking up at 3 a.m.? No thank you." At first, I'd held out hope that Stella might lose interest. This was grinding, grueling work. How long could she possibly last?

It had taken me months to feel secure in the newsroom, to stop automatically reminding people of my name, to stop apologizing reflexively when they didn't remember it—like it was my fault. Being a young intern or assistant, it was safer to assume that people saw you as an interchangeable part in the machine. Because, in fact, that's what you were. But from day one, Stella assumed that people knew her name.

And the thing is, they did. Her haplessness only enhanced her charm, especially among men. Right away, she was the most popular intern in the newsroom.

On Sunday morning of that week, Stella called me.

"Can you come uptown?" she said. "I don't have my wallet."

"Isn't your lover picking up the bill?" I said. Stella called him that as a joke, but it stuck. Her lover, the older man, married but getting a divorce. "Can't you just borrow money from him?"

"He had to go to the emergency room. His kid broke his arm."

I sighed, turning off the kettle that I'd just started for tea. "I'll get on the subway now."

Stella was waiting in the hotel lobby when I arrived thirty minutes later. "Thank God," she said, springing to her feet. "The concierge has been giving me the weirdest looks."

She turned around and smiled at the serious man behind the ornate wooden desk. She waved her monogrammed wallet and said loudly, "See? Nothing to worry about. I told you I wasn't going to run out on the bill."

"Unlike lover man," I said. "I'm surprised he stuck you with this."

"He's weirdly cheap," she said, as she slid her credit card across the desk. "He always talks about how hard he works for his money. Whereas I'm just a spoiled princess. Born with a silver spoon in my mouth."

"He says that?"

She laughed. "He doesn't have to."

The hotel where they met on weekends was on Madison Avenue in the seventies, chosen for luxury and relative distance from the man's family, who lived downtown. He was a hedge fund type, a loft in Tribeca and a house in East Hampton, three kids in rapid succession, crazy rich but still covetous: next he wanted a ski house, a Gulfstream. He'd do anything to close the deal—flowers, jewelry, whatever it took—but he grew neglectful once the ink dried. Recently, his wife had looked at her prenup and decided the payout was better than a life of obedience to this man. But she was still his wife, and the mother of his children, and when one of his children broke a bone on the playground, it was his paternal duty to rush downtown and, in a harried-rich-man way, question the competence of the doctors.

Stella had met him the year before, when she was working in fashion. They saw each other a few times a week. When I asked her why she liked him, she shrugged and said, "I don't know. Something about him, it's a turn-on. The sex is great." He was worldly and successful, and handsome. He often promised to make her wife number two, not that Stella would ever agree to it. But the relationship was mutually exciting. She got to act like a sexy spy, sneaking in and out of luxury hotels. He got to fantasize about a hot new wife.

"I'm hungry," Stella said, after she signed the bill. "Let's get food. I'll treat."

Across Madison Avenue from the hotel was an Italian restaurant, the type of place where young women like Stella flocked. Wide windows, flattering golden light, dramatic floral arrangements, an overpriced menu. After Stella ordered the omelet and I ordered the spaghetti carbonara, I shook my head and said, "How many times have we done this?"

"Done what?" she said.

"The morning after," I said. "Your wild night on the town, and my quiet night at home, and then I come get you when something goes wrong."

She smiled. "You know how much I love you, right?"

"Sure."

"I *need* you," she said. "You know that."

Even after years of friendship, even after the countless times Stella had purchased my patience and forgiveness with those words, and cheapened them in the process, they still meant something to me. I was loved, I was needed. Isn't that all anyone wants?

"Okay," I said. "I have to ask the inevitable. When are you going to end it with this guy?"

She sipped her cappuccino. "If I wanted to, I could marry him and retire tomorrow."

I laughed. "One whole month of work. You must be exhausted."

"I know," she said. "But still. Sometimes I think about it."

"You'd lose your mind," I said. "You'd be so bored."

Her smile turned into a frown as she stared at the milky foam of her cappuccino gradually dissolving into the tan liquid. "I'm not sure people at KCN like me," she said.

"That's not true," I said, startled. Glimpsing the softer side of Stella was rare enough that, sometimes, I forgot that part existed. "Of course people like you."

"No," she said, shaking her head. "Like, in that meeting the other day. The way people were looking at you, Violet. The way they were *listening* to you. I don't have that."

I smiled, gently. "That's not because they like me. That's because they respect me."

"Well, fine," she said. Irritation crept into her voice. "Whatever."

The waiter placed our food before us. Stella cut into her omelet, and I twirled the pasta around my fork. The smoky pancetta, the rich coating of egg. It was overpriced and unoriginal, but it tasted good. It tasted great, in fact. I took a deep breath. Even with Stella at KCN, maybe everything would be okay.

"It took me a long time to get there," I said. "And, you know, it's still not exactly easy. I'm still not sure if I'm actually any good at this."

"What do you mean?" Stella said.

"I keep striking out," I said. "They haven't liked any of my pitches. Not a single one. I don't know if I'll ever manage to get an idea through."

"Well, that's the dumbest thing I've ever heard."

I laughed, confused. "What?"

"It's obvious they think you're smart," Stella said, pointing at me with her fork. "So what if they haven't liked your ideas? They'll like the next one. Or the one after that."

"You don't know that."

"But that's the way the system works, isn't it? Or, what, do you think every producer above you has some magical special talent that you don't have?" Stella reached her fork across the table and twisted pasta around it. "I'm planning to eat at least half of this," she said. "Carbs don't count when they're on some-one else's plate, right?"

Partway through the meal, Stella spotted a friend. They air-kissed and traded pleasantries, and the whole time, Stella looked radiantly beautiful. Her hair in the perfect messy bun, her smile relaxed and confident. The thorny romance, the insecurities we'd just been talking about: none of that was visible. For Stella, a restaurant like this was a clubhouse. It was a place to be among her own kind, but that also meant she couldn't show a single crack. These people would notice.

It was places like this, this stretch of Madison Avenue on the Upper East Side, that made me keenly aware of how different our lives were. Restaurants served food that was too expensive for anyone but the one percent. Stores sold goods that theo-retically served a practical purpose—baby clothes, candles, bed linens—but wealthy shoppers insensitive to price had caused these objects to attenuate into pure signals of luxury. Walking to the restaurant, we had passed stores selling leather jackets for toddlers, sheets too delicate to sleep on. There was one time my mother came home with a new handbag, and when my father found out what it cost, he went ballistic. "You spent fifty dollars on a *bag*? A goddamn *bag*?" he sputtered, right before she slammed the bedroom door in his face. At the boutique across the street, handbags started at seven thousand dollars.

So how was it possible, the two of us coming from such different worlds, that Stella often had exactly the right answers to my questions? *That's the way the system works.* It was a key slipped right into a lock. This was her strange intelligence. Stella tended to be terrible with the details. But, maybe as a result, she saw other things. She saw the connections that the rest of us missed.

———

The next week, Stella came by my desk with a paper in hand, looking worried. I was on a phone call, taking hasty notes. After several seconds of my ignoring her, she waved the paper at me. "Hello? Violet?"

Jamie sprang to his feet. I half listened as he said, "She's busy. What's up?"

"Oh," Stella said. "The archive. Do you know how to use it?"

"I think I can remember," Jamie said. "Show me what you need."

Last week, when I'd snapped—*you want to take a turn helping her? Be my guest*—I hadn't meant for Jamie to take the suggestion literally. After hanging up, I watched the two of them across the newsroom: Stella at her computer, Jamie standing behind her, pointing over her shoulder. Jamie was a senior producer, and therefore way too valuable to spend time teaching an intern the ropes. But he was also a nice guy, and he genuinely liked helping people.

"Jamie," I said, walking over to Stella's desk. The two of them looked at me in unison. "I can help her with this. You don't have to."

"I got this," he said. "I needed a break, anyways."

"And you're a good teacher," Stella said, twisting in her seat to look up at him.

"Um, okay," I said. They looked so cozy, Stella pleased to have his attention. "Don't forget we have that meeting in ten minutes. Eliza wants new pitches from everyone."

"I'm finally getting somewhere on that Medal of Honor story," Jamie said.

"The guy whose brother defected to Russia?"

"Two brothers, working for two enemies. Can't you see the movie already?"

"This sounds interesting," Stella said. "Can I come?"

"Sorry," I said. "It's for producers only."

Her eyebrows arched. The hardness in my voice caught both of us by surprise.

"You can come," Jamie said, and then he looked at me. "What? She can come. I need help on this story, anyway. It's going to take a lot of legwork. You're okay with that?"

"Of course!" Stella said.

"Well, good. Then you should be in the room when I tell Eliza about it."

Later, after the meeting ended and Jamie and I returned to our desks, Jamie said, "It's nothing I didn't do for you, too, you know. I brought you along to those high-level meetings, back when you were an intern. Don't you remember?"

"That was different."

"Why?"

"Because I take this job seriously."

"And she doesn't?"

I thought about Stella sipping her cappuccino, kidding-but-not-kidding about her early retirement. "How about this? Ten bucks says she's not working here at this time next year."

Jamie shook my hand. "You're on."

"You seem awfully confident," I said.

"I'm imagining how I'm going to spend that money."

Stella was now across the room, talking to a male assistant who, like most of the guys at *Frontline,* had an obvious crush on her. She leaned back against his desk, her long legs emphasized by her heeled boots and short dress. He propped his feet on his desk. The two of them were laughing, indifferent to the mounting chaos that occurred every afternoon as we approached airtime. Our show was a well-oiled machine, and it was impossible that this machine wouldn't chew her up and spit her out. "What are you seeing that I'm not?" I said.

Jamie glanced up from his computer and followed my gaze. "I'm seeing the exact same thing as you," he said. "I'm just more realistic about it."

CHAPTER NINE

SO MUCH OF the first two years of climbing the ladder in cable news was simply about surviving. The elimination burned slowly but consistently. I was the only person who remained from my class of interns. Most of the old assistants were gone, too. The ranks thinned as one moved up. There were fewer producers than assistants, and fewer senior producers than producers, and at the very top there were just two people: Rebecca, the star, and Eliza, the executive producer.

Climbing that ladder, I began to have a sense of my strengths and weaknesses. What I was good at: I was detail-oriented, thorough, consistent, reliable. My assignments got more interesting because I was trusted to carry them out. What I was okay at: I was still shy about networking and developing sources. It took a delicate touch, and more than anything, it took time. Jamie always reminded me of this. Trust was our currency with sources, and to gain that trust, you needed to put in the time. Weeks and months, not minutes and hours.

"It can't feel transactional," Jamie said once. "A source won't just hand you a story. You can't just call them when you need something. Like your Danner story"—Jamie was my sounding board on this, as on all things—"they're nervous. They're not ready to talk. But if you keep in touch, maybe someday they'll get there."

Trust was a thing we talked about a lot. It was a buzzword, part of the KCN brand, crucial to our relationship with our audience. At our biannual corporate town halls, the bosses talked about the importance of our mission. We were journalists. We had a role to play. In order to have a healthy democracy, one that shared objective truths, people like us were essential.

And this was what I feared I'd always be bad at: believing in that mission. It's not that others were Pollyannas and I was a cynic. They were all cynics, but only to a point. Sure, the world could be an unjust and cruel place, but if you told the story, if you presented the facts, if you delivered the truth—that would help correct the balance. A fair outcome wasn't guaranteed, but it was possible. There was still a fundamental optimism at work.

And how could I not agree with that? I was the case in point: a girl from a poor family, the first to go to college, now living in New York City and working as an associate producer at KCN, steadily climbing the ladder. No wonder the Bradleys loved me.

There were times I'd come close to believing it. If I played by the rules, if I did the right thing, if I put my trust in the mechanism of meritocracy and if I worked hard enough, I could do anything. This was America, after all.

But any trajectory can be interrupted. And my problem was Stella.

———

In June of that year, after dozens of shoddy pitches that gradually got stronger, my first story aired. The business beat had become my domain at *Frontline,* because it played to my strengths: I could spend hours combing through documents and financial statements, invigorated rather than bored by the dry facts at hand. When the story aired, I felt relieved: I could really do this, after all.

The next morning, Stella was in the kitchen, already showered and dressed and drinking a mug of coffee. The night before, when our group went to the bar and toasted me—Rebecca had also given me a special shout-out, after the broadcast—I'd been giddy with success, and Stella had been in a bad mood, sulking over her vodka soda. Now she held a yellow highlighter, which she ran over an article in the *Wall Street Journal*. Scattered across the counter were copies of the *New York Times,* the *New York Post,* and the *FT.*

"You're up early," I said. Pouring myself coffee, I thought, *Stella knows how to use the coffee machine?* "What are you doing? Is this for work?"

Stella nodded, staring at the paper. It seemed like an affect picked up from an old movie, this ink-and-paper highlighting in an age when everyone read the news online.

"I don't get it," I said. "Is this an assignment?"

She looked up, annoyed. "Do you not think I'm capable of taking initiative?"

I held up my hands. "Sorry. I was just curious."

"I'm trying to get better at this." She sighed, capping the high-lighter. "It's like," she said, "everyone just *knows* everything. In a meeting the other day, someone said—what was it—a tax holiday. And everyone in the room was like, 'oh yes, of course, a tax holiday.' What the fuck does that mean? Where do you even learn this stuff?"

She seemed genuinely irritated, which irritated me in turn. What I wanted to say was *you learn this stuff by paying attention, Stella.* You pay attention because you have to pay attention. The world isn't going to unfurl itself for you. You have to pry it open. I wanted to say *a tax holiday is a simple concept.* The meaning is encoded in the phrase itself, and your ignorance is your own fault.

Instead, I smiled and said, "Don't worry. You'll pick it up over time."

Stella's initiative wouldn't last. I was certain of that. It was a reaction to that brief moment when everyone was looking at me, not her. Her earnest newspaper-reading, the newly alert way she answered the phone, the speediness with which she ran scripts to the control room: it was a performance for my benefit, wasn't it? Sometimes our relationship felt like one long game in which we were constantly keeping score. This was just another way for Stella to rack up a few points. She could be the eager-to-please intern that I had once been, too.

But I was wrong. Stella was putting on a performance, but it wasn't for me.

The story of our friendship was always the story of opposites. Yin and yang in every regard. The pretty one and the plain one; the rich girl and the poor girl; the social butterfly and the book-ish nerd. For every possible measurement, we stood at far ends of the spectrum. And there was one particular metric that clocked a vast gulf between us, that, for years, had allowed us to exist in harmony.

Ambition.

Every decision I made was designed to distance me from my origins. Stella, on the other hand, always knew that she belonged. When you already have everything you could ever want, what good is ambition? Stella never had to think about how to dress, what to say, where to put her hands, whether to laugh or smile, whether to act smart or play dumb. It came naturally, like breathing. It was like that famous line. A fish, asked how the water is, responds, "This is water?" That was life, to Stella. A medium one could move through without even considering what the medium was, or how that medium might feel to other people.

Until, that is, she got to KCN.

This is life? I could see the dismay on Stella's face, during her early months of work. *This* is life? This uncontainable and roiling thing, chock-full of complicated ideas and obscure terms? Conflict, avarice, war, incompetence: when you paid enough attention, life had a way of showing its ugly chaos. For the first time, Stella didn't understand what she was supposed to do.

And now what did Stella want? She wanted the thing she had once possessed, which had been wrenched away from her. That sweet, velvety sense of belonging.

The rich girl and the poor girl, the pretty girl and the plain girl. If we were characters in a story, Stella was the one you always wanted to be. The girl who is quick to laugh, good at making friends, charming to strangers, comfortable in her own skin; the girl whose beauty is equated with virtue. Her heart open and capacious, not curdled by desperate ambition.

Real trust, Jamie said, can't be transactional. And what is ambition if not a constant transaction? Hard work—days, weeks, months—in exchange for more money, more power, more influence. I wanted to succeed, and that was my problem: people could see that desire. They could smell it. How can you trust someone who reeks of ambition?

Stella's newly polished performance at KCN worked. The bosses noticed. It all happened within the span of a few weeks. She was promoted to assistant. She was invited to more meetings. People trusted her. Why? They knew she was rich, that she didn't *need* this job. So she was doing it out of pure love for the work. Wasn't that admirable?

I'd had more than a year's head start on Stella. But by that summer, she was closing the gap between us, and her shadow was looming over me again.

Stella was a distractible driver, checking her phone and texting as we lurched through Friday afternoon traffic on I-95. It was a long drive to the house in Maine, where we were spending the week with her family. When we arrived after midnight, the house was mostly dark, but the porch light was on. The front door opened and a woman stepped out.

"Nana?" Stella squinted. "Oh, Nana, you didn't have to stay up for us."

"Don't be silly, my dear," her grandmother said. She was a petite woman, dressed in slacks and a cardigan and a string of pearls, her silver hair neatly bobbed. I shivered, still in the cotton dress I'd worn to work that day. It was August, but it felt more like fall.

"Nice to see you again, Violet." Mrs. Bradley smelled like lily of the valley as she brushed a dry cheek against mine. "You haven't changed a bit."

"Oh," I said. "Thank you."

Inside, the house was as I remembered it: grand but relaxed, with dark wood floors and white walls. There were family photos everywhere, Oliver and Stella in Kodachrome, ancestors in faded sepia. The property was set far down the driveway, at the tip of a peninsula, surrounded by water on three sides, the neighbors invisible. The house sat atop a prow of land, the lawn sloping down toward the rocky beach. As we passed through the wide living room into the kitchen, the windows were open to the night air and the roar of the ocean.

It was inherently elegant in a way that made Anne and Thomas's home in Rye look overdone. Anne, I had gathered, didn't particularly enjoy spending time with her mother-in-law. Stella's parents had their own beach house in Watch Hill, but the Bradley grandparents insisted that each branch of the family spend at least a week at the Maine compound, adhering to strict rituals of tennis matches and cocktail hours and dinner parties.

The elder Mrs. Bradley was a far better Wasp than Anne would ever be, and this made Anne insecure.

"Did my parents already go to bed?" Stella asked.

"They were tired," Mrs. Bradley said, placing a loaf of bread on the kitchen counter. "Did you eat? You look thin, Stella. Your mother doesn't feed you enough."

"My mother doesn't feed me at all." Stella laughed. "That's Violet's job now."

"Oh?" Mrs. Bradley said, pulling a serrated bread knife from the knife block.

"Violet's a great cook," Stella said. "Among her many talents."

"She is?" Mrs. Bradley said, with a faint smile that suggested *of course she is, just look at her.* "Well, Violet. You must cook for us sometime."

After Mrs. Bradley had fixed us chicken salad sandwiches (awfully dry, without mayonnaise or mustard) and said good night, Stella opened the refrigerator. "Aha," she said, holding up two bottles of beer. "Let's go eat outside."

As we left behind the radius of light that spilled from the living room windows onto the lawn, the night was dark and clear. The grass, when we sat down on it, was parched and spiky. Mrs. Bradley had said it was one of the driest summers on record.

"God," Stella said, leaning back on her elbows and kicking off her sandals. "Aren't you so fucking happy to be away from that office?"

"I suppose," I said.

Stella laughed. "*I suppose,*" she said, in a singsongy voice.

"What?"

"You're so serious. Loosen up, Vi, we're on vacation."

Stella pulled a joint from her pocket. As she sparked the lighter and raised a questioning eyebrow at me, I shook my head.

"I'm okay," I said.

"Miss Goody Two-Shoes," she said. "Here, take it."

"No, really." I pushed her hand away. "It'll just put me to sleep."

She shrugged and took a long inhale. "Your loss, loser."

My phone buzzed against my leg: an e-mail from a senior producer, about a segment I'd been working on. I was typing a response when Stella reached over and grabbed the phone, tossing it on the grass between us.

"Hey!" I said. "That was work."

"No phones at meals. Nana's house, Nana's rules."

"Does your dad know about this rule? I bet you ten dollars we come down for breakfast tomorrow and he's already glued to it."

"Rude, Violet."

"I bet you a hundred dollars."

"Look," she said, pulling out her own phone and dropping it next to mine. "Even though you're being *very* snarky—here. A show of good faith."

"Fine," I said.

"Fine," she said. After a second, she started giggling.

"How high *are* you?" I said.

"I got it from some skeeze at the gas station," Stella said. "It's probably laced."

We lay on our backs for what felt like a long time. In Maine there was no light pollution, and the sky was bright with stars, so regular and dense that it looked like a dark colander studded with thousands of holes. There was silence, except for the roar of the ocean and the occasional rasp of Stella's lighter.

My phone vibrated again. I couldn't resist, and sat up to see what it was. The screen was alight with a text message from Jamie. I was reaching for it when Stella grabbed it first. That's when I realized it wasn't my phone—it was hers.

She curled over the phone, her body angled away from me.

"Jamie's texting you?" I said.

"He's funny," she said. The light from the screen illuminated her smile.

"What is it?"

But she was standing up, sliding her feet back into her sandals. She bit her lip, then pushed a button and held the phone up to her ear. "I'll see you in the morning," she called back over her shoulder. "Take the guest room at the end of the hall."

"What about you?" I said.

She was already halfway back to the house. "Hey!" she said, her voice clear and sweet. Then she was laughing. "Yeah, I know. I know."

Her voice faded into the distance. A knot formed in my stomach. Jamie and Stella were texting each other? They were calling each other? After midnight on a Friday? I had always assumed that Jamie disliked Stella, that their friendship only existed because they had me in common. But lately I'd been working harder than ever, determined to stay at least a step ahead of Stella in the KCN hierarchy. I'd been spending less time with both of them.

I started to gather the dishes. Stella had left behind her beer bottle, her plate with her half-eaten sandwich. Her joint, too. It was smoldering where she'd dropped it, the grass around it starting to smoke. The orange glow of the ember was like a firefly trapped in the darkness, a dangerous remnant of Stella's routine carelessness.

For a second, I thought about leaving it there. Maybe the flame would catch, ripping across the bone-dry lawn toward the Bradley compound. A horrible, magnificent inferno. A lesson to her. If I kept cleaning up her mistakes, Stella would never learn.

The days in Maine felt expansive. I'd wake without an alarm, the guest bedroom flooded with sunlight. Stella aside, the Bradley clan were chipper morning people, eating breakfast on the porch and chatting while they read the *Wall Street Journal*. Breakfast, like every meal, was a civilized affair. A glass bowl of fruit salad, a silver pot of coffee, scones and muffins baked that morning by Louisa, their efficient housekeeper.

Stella would wander downstairs in late morning. We'd go for a swim off the end of the dock, or we'd play tennis on the Bradley's court, or we'd take the boat to the next town over. Occasionally we ran into someone Stella knew, locals Stella had befriended in previous summers. "Tenth grade," she said, waving as she reversed the engine and we pulled away from the gas station dock. The manager of the marina waved back, beaming at her. "I blew him in the back of his car."

"Really?" I said. He was scruffy and potbellied, and definitively not her type.

She put on her sunglasses. "He sold me coke. It was a fun summer."

In the afternoons, we'd return to the house for a late lunch and then fall asleep reading on the shady porch, the thrillers and spy novels that lined the Bradleys' bookshelves. As the day faded, we'd go for another swim. Mrs. Bradley had us gather for cocktails at 6:30 p.m. precisely. We had to be showered and dressed. The housekeeper would have dinner waiting for us afterward.

The first time Stella had invited me to her house, Thanksgiving of freshman year, I was convinced I'd never fit in. Pop culture had taught me how easily the poor girl embarrasses herself in the company of the wealthy. But this, it turned out, was a myth propagated by the wealthy themselves. Rich people love their shibboleths. They love to act like their language is impossible to learn. The truth was that anyone with halfway decent powers of observation could pick it up in five minutes.

This was how I purchased my way into Stella's family: with good manners. To keep a toehold in this world required careful behavior. The worst thing I could do was to flout the rules. Old money hates, *hates* the nouveau riche because the nouveau riche haven't bothered learning the rules. They're having too much fun getting drunk and riding Jet Skis. They've got their money, which is more important than social acceptance. Anyway, if you give it a few generations, their money will look like anyone else's.

It wasn't so bad, really. The Bradleys were boring and uptight, attached to ritual and manner, but at least they were predictable. Not like my own parents, with their constant eruptions of anger. Here, as long as you followed the rules, you were okay. As long as the conversation was polite, it didn't matter what was being said. Of course, this led to a lot of boring conversation, a lot of dull iterations of the name game. You know how old houses always look good? Whether mansion or tenement or saltbox, if it was built more than a century ago, it has a certain air of elegance. But when you think about the small rooms, the out-dated layouts, the bad electrical wiring, you realize you'd never actually want to live there.

That was like the world of the rich. From far away, it looks enchanting. Up close, you realize the elegance is just a prod-uct of stasis. It's easy to be tricked into thinking something is beautiful.

Toward the end of that week, Stella and Oliver and I took the boat out after lunch. It was a perfect day: the sky bright blue, the air hot, the sea glassy and calm. Hundreds of yards offshore, Stella cut the engine. We bobbed in silence for a while. I closed my eyes. This sense of peace, this calm solitude amid pristine wilderness—I'd admit, the wealthy did this well.

I heard Stella laugh. "What?" I said, opening my eyes.

"This freak," she said, pointing at Oliver, who had just taken off his T-shirt. "Jesus, Oliver, do you *ever* go outside?"

"You are pretty pale," I said. His bright white skin made him look like some nineteenth-century German aristocrat down from his schloss. Possibly tubercular, probably just delicate.

"You're supposed to be the nice one, Violet," Oliver said. He placed his sunglasses atop his carefully folded T-shirt. "Anyone else coming in?"

"I just ate," Stella said. She lay on the bow of the boat in her bikini, her stomach taut and hip bones protruding, her slender legs crossed like drinking straws.

Oliver climbed onto the edge of the boat. "Violet?"

"Sure," I said. When I jumped in, the water was so cold that it made my breath catch.

Oliver lay on his back, moving his hands just enough to stay afloat. "My grandmother taught me to swim. In the summers, when I was little," he said.

"Don't bore our guest," Stella called from the boat.

"Don't eavesdrop," Oliver called back. He flipped over and faced me. We were both treading water, eggbeater-style. "She taught me and Stella. She drilled us when we got older. She'd ride next to us in the boat and time us on a stopwatch."

"I can picture it," I said.

"Nana doesn't fuck around." Oliver smiled. He took a precise satisfaction in swearing. Then his smile disappeared. "Actually, it's a sad story."

"What happened?"

"When she was a little girl, her older brother drowned. He took the boat out, the weather turned, and he capsized. He wasn't very far offshore when it happened. If he'd been a stronger swimmer, he might have made it back. His body washed up the next day. She was five years old, I think. It's one of her first memories."

"That's awful."

"Sad, isn't it? That's been her obsession ever since."

Oliver flipped onto his back. I joined him, spreading my limbs like a starfish. With my ears filled with water and my eyes look-ing only at the sky, I felt hyperaware of how far out we were, how deep the water was beneath me. Hundreds of cubic meters of water separated me from the ocean floor, but if I went mo-tionless, the water meant nothing. Dead weight, sinking right to the bottom.

When we climbed back aboard, Stella was lying on her stom-ach, paging through a gossip magazine. "Why are you reading that trash?" Oliver asked as he toweled off.

"I don't know if you've heard, Oliver, but I'm a journalist. I need to keep up."

He rolled his eyes. "Violet, I thought you'd be a better influ-ence on her."

"Get fucked, Ollie," Stella said lightly, using the nickname he hated.

"Don't worry," Oliver said to me. "This is just her thing. Whenever she fought with our mother, she'd go out in this boat and sulk for hours. Bobbing around and stewing."

"I can *hear* you," Stella said.

"It's Pavlovian. This boat brings out the bratty teenager."

"Or maybe it's because you won't stop giving her a hard time," I said.

Oliver looked surprised. I shrugged. "It's vacation. You're being kind of harsh."

Stella clambered over the windshield onto the deck of the boat. She smacked her brother on the arm. "*Yeah,*" she said. "That's for being a paternalistic asshole."

"Ow," Oliver said whiningly.

"You should listen to Violet," Stella said. "She's smart. If she says there's something wrong with you, there's something wrong with you."

"There's nothing wrong with me," Oliver muttered, pulling his T-shirt back on.

Later, as the sun was sinking and the air was growing cooler, Stella drove us back in. She'd had her boating license since she was little, and she handled the boat deftly, much better than she did the car. She steered with one hand, her blond hair streaming in the wind. Oliver and I were sitting on the bench seat in the back.

"I'm sorry about earlier," he said. "I didn't mean to start a fight."

"It's okay," I said.

"No, it was rude. You shouldn't have to sit through our bickering. But I guess we both revert to childhood when we're together. I guess it's inevitable."

"I'm an only child." I shrugged. "What do I know?"

"I worry that you have this distorted view of me. Stella probably says otherwise, but I'm actually a nice guy."

Oliver looked genuinely distressed, and I felt bad. He was oddly old-fashioned, but he also had an endearing sincerity—the opposite of Stella's cool sophistication.

"I know that!" I said, touching his hand. "Of course I know that."

The waves had picked up, and occasionally Stella hit them at the wrong angle, bouncing the boat violently. She whooped with delight.

"Slow down!" Oliver shouted at her. "This is way too fast."

"Can't hear you!" Stella shouted back.

Oliver edged forward to where Stella held the wheel. He said something inaudible, and she rolled her eyes, but the boat slowed down slightly. As Oliver made his way back to the bench seat, Stella shouted, "Sorry my brother's such a pussy, Violet."

"She's insane," he said. "I have to remind her that not all of us have a death wish."

"She's too confident for her own good." I thought of the

smoldering joint the other night. "Maybe you should let it happen. One bad accident and she'll be scared straight."

"And get another lecture from Anne and Thomas about how I failed to take care of my little sister?" He laughed bitterly. "No, thank you. They still think it's my fault that she disappeared at Christmas two years ago."

"How was that your fault?" I said, surprised Oliver was bringing this up. Like anything unpleasant, that episode had become taboo in the Bradley family. Maybe it was the setting. When she ran away that Christmas, Stella had come here, to the house in Maine. She was right under her family's nose the entire time. It was too easy to fool them. Later she told me that she returned to the city mostly because she'd gotten so bored.

Oliver frowned. "Who knows? Stella can do no wrong." His tone was acidic, and his stare contained real contempt. "That's the way it's always been."

Anne was waiting as we pulled up to the dock. She wore a bright Lilly Pulitzer sheath and held her hand over her eyes, shading them from the sun. "You'll never guess who I ran into," she said, as Stella knotted the rope around the cleat. Stella was surprisingly dexterous with the anchors and ropes and engine. In another life she could have been a mechanical engineer. Or maybe this was just how you turned out when you grew up around fancy boats.

"Who?" Oliver said.

"Ginny. Ginny Grass! I bumped into her at the market. Isn't that a funny coincidence?"

"Not really," Stella said. "She lives down the road."

"Well, she's coming for dinner tomorrow night. Won't that be nice?" Anne said. "Violet. You must know Ginny, too, of course?"

"Of course," I said. When Ginny passed through the newsroom, the most she'd give me was a bland smile. I was too many rungs down the totem pole to matter.

"I'm starving," Stella said.

"Cocktails in fifteen minutes," Anne said, starting back up the lawn to the house. "Hurry, please. Your grandmother doesn't like wet bathing suits."

There was a corner of the porch that Grandmother Bradley liked in the evening: on the western side of the house, looking over the inlet that separated the peninsula from Maine proper, the sky and the water flamed with a blood orange sunset. There were Adirondack chairs, a wooden table with fixings for cocktails, and a silver bowl filled with nuts. The bowl, Mrs. Bradley had explained, was a family heirloom. It dated back to the nineteenth century. When Mrs. Bradley refilled the bowl, she did so with a Costco-sized, generic-branded plastic container of mixed nuts. I'm not sure whether anyone else found this as funny as I did.

That night, Mr. Bradley was mixing a pitcher of martinis, and Mrs. Bradley was supervising. She took a sip. "Too much vermouth," she said, wrinkling her nose.

"*There* you are," Mrs. Bradley said sharply to Anne, when she breezed in. "Anne, I wish you had consulted me before inviting Ginny Grass to dinner."

"What do you mean?" Anne's smile faded. "I thought you loved Ginny."

"Tomorrow is Louisa's night off. We won't have any help."

"Oh." Anne went pale. This was serious. "Oh, I'm so sorry. I can take care of it. I'll pick something up from the market. Pasta salad and corn on the cob. Ginny won't mind."

Mrs. Bradley emitted a mirthless laugh. "It's a good thing Ginny's mother is no longer with us," she said. "She's probably spinning in her grave. The Bradley family serving her daughter corn on the cob. My goodness."

Anne looked miffed. "Well, times *have* changed."

"Hmmph," Mrs. Bradley said. Then she looked at me, and her expression changed. "Actually, I have a better idea."

So this was how I spent my last day of vacation: cooking dinner for eight people. I went to the market that morning, Anne's credit card in my pocket. "Spare no expense," Anne had said, winking like she'd just given me a wonderful gift. She loved Mrs. Bradley's idea. It was the perfect chance to show me off. Planning menus, cooking gourmet meals—look at how far Violet Trapp had come! I was tempted to throw the game. To remind them that they couldn't count on me to be their performing monkey.

But I hadn't gotten this far in life by being a spiteful jerk, so I settled on an heirloom tomato tart for an appetizer, followed by sirloin steak, zucchini gratin, roasted potatoes, and blueberry pie for dessert. At the wine store in town, I asked the clerk to recommend a pairing. When he asked about a price point, I repeated, "Spare no expense." He steered me toward a thirty-five-dollar bottle of sauvignon blanc. I bought a case of it, threw in a few bottles of Bollinger champagne, and took pleasure in handing him Anne's platinum credit card.

When I returned from town, Stella and Oliver were playing on the tennis court, which was right near the driveway. I hefted a paper bag into my arms from the trunk and squinted into the bright sunlight. "A little help?" I called.

"It's match point," Stella called back. "I'm about to finish him off."

"Please? The ice cream is melting."

She ignored me, bouncing the tennis ball with one hand, touching it to the racket and rocking back on her heels. She raised the racket above her head, and smashed it down in a powerful stroke. It was a perfect serve, the ball landing just shy of the service line, but Oliver returned it with a drop shot. Stella sprinted toward the net, but she was too late.

"Ha!" Oliver said. "Deuce."

"God*damn* it," Stella said.

"You're both useless," I shouted.

The steady thwack of their game continued as I carried groceries into the house. The Bradley family avoided the kitchen all day. By the time everything was done—the tomato tart and blueberry pie baked and cooling, the steak ready for the grill, the gratin and potatoes ready for the oven—it was nearly 6 p.m. Promptly at 6:30, I heard the crunch of tires over gravel. I was wearing my best dress, had put on makeup and jewelry. Tonight could be an opportunity to impress Ginny. To be charming and interesting, to lodge myself in her awareness as more than just another employee.

"How do I look?" I said to Oliver, who was mixing a drink on the porch.

He smiled. "Lovely."

As I was about to say hello to Ginny, Stella swept onto the porch and cut me off, wearing the same ratty sundress she'd worn all day, her unwashed hair in a bun. This is the harshest advantage of the truly beautiful: the less effort they put in, the more they distance themselves from the rest of us. Stella managed to monopolize Ginny for the entire cocktail hour. The Stella charm offensive was at work.

Later, Anne clapped her hands. "What do you say, Violet? Are we ready for dinner?"

Everyone turned to look at me, including Ginny. She nodded, gave me her bland *it's-you-again* smile. Grandmother Bradley took my elbow and tugged me away from the group. "We ought to serve the food in the kitchen," she said. "I can't stand buffet-style. Too messy. Then I suppose I'll help you carry the plates out." She said this last as if it was an enormous favor, not a basic courtesy.

But when his grandmother approached the table with two

plates of tomato tart in hand, Oliver sprang to his feet. "Oh, Nana, you shouldn't be doing all that," he said.

"Violet can handle it, can't she?" Stella said. "Here, Nana, sit next to me."

I carried the rest of the plates out by myself, and twenty minutes later I cleared them, and then brought out dinner by myself, too. The group was too absorbed in conversation to notice my to-and-fro. As I returned to the table, I saw Stella turn to Ginny, who was seated next to her. She touched a finger to Ginny's wrist. "What's this bracelet?" Stella said.

"Oh," Ginny said. She fiddled with it. "It's a medical bracelet. I have a heart condition. A form of arrhythmia."

"Is it serious?" Stella said, her eyes wide with fake concern.

"If I keep an eye on my diet, I'm fine," Ginny said. "You're sweet to ask, my dear."

"Violet?" Anne said. "Could you please bring out another bottle of wine?"

It was so easy for them: even though it was Louisa's night off, they didn't need to adjust any of their usual routines. The dinner was perfect—the white linen tablecloth, hurricane lamps flickering in the breeze, dahlias from the garden, the food exactly right—but beneath it persisted a sour taste. This had been a mistake. I should have stood up for myself, should have asked for help. Where was my backbone? I was letting them walk all over me.

"Oh, my favorite," Ginny said, when I brought out the pie. "Is this from the bakery?"

"Violet made it," Anne said.

"You did?" Ginny said, looking at me with new attention. "It's delicious."

"Thank you," I said, refilling my wineglass with a generous pour.

"My sister and I would pick blueberries all through our

summers up here. We'd eat them until we were sick," Ginny said, wistfully. "That feels like a long time ago."

"Remind me, was your sister older or younger?" Stella said.

"Younger, by a few years."

Stella smiled. "I always wanted a sister."

"We were close, growing up, but I suppose we drifted as we got older." Ginny twisted the stem of her wineglass between her thumb and index finger. "We only lived twenty blocks apart in the city, but I rarely saw her."

"You said she used to work as a model?"

"Quite a successful one." Ginny smiled. "She was a muse to a whole contingent of designers. She saw something in their clothes that even the designers hadn't seen."

"Why did she stop?" Stella asked.

"You know, I never had the chance to ask her."

Stella paused, then said quietly, "How did it happen?"

"A few weeks went by," Ginny said. "Two, maybe three. She wouldn't answer her phone. I started to worry. The doorman finally let me in to her apartment. It was very peaceful, in a way. It was winter. She turned the radiators off and opened the windows. The apartment was cold. There was no smell. The pills were on the nightstand. The strangest thing was, she looked so *alive*. So pretty. She looked like she was sleeping."

The candlelight caught in Ginny's brimming eyes. From the distance came the roaring ocean. From closer, the sound of crickets in the garden. When Ginny spoke again, her voice was quiet. "I don't tell many people about my sister." She smoothed the napkin in her lap. "A lot of people don't even know that I had a sister. But it's nice to say these things out loud."

Stella put her hand on Ginny's. "It's clear that she meant a lot to you."

Ginny smiled softly. After several long moments of silence, she sighed and said, "I think you have a knack for this, my dear."

"What do you mean?" Stella said.

"You're very good at getting people to open up to you, aren't you?"

My stomach lurched. Stella shrugged, but there was the slightest curl to her lip. Her supplicant curiosity, her personal questions, it had all been part of her plan. I knew exactly how charming and convincing Stella Bradley could be. And she knew it, too. How could I have been so stupid not to see this coming?

"If you can get me to talk about the dreadful situation with my sister," Ginny said. "Well. I'm not exactly an easy nut to crack. And I think your talents might be going to waste at KCN."

"Oh, but Ginny, I love my job," Stella said, her tone sickeningly sweet.

"You'll love it more when you're in a position that suits your talents. I'll make a few calls next week. I don't see why we should be squandering this"—Ginny gestured at Stella—"when we could have you in front of a camera."

CHAPTER TEN

STELLA BEGAN AS a general assignment reporter for KCN, working the 5 a.m. shift four days a week and a shift on Sundays. It was the gruntiest of grunt work: getting man-on-the-street interviews, banking live feed that would go unused, enduring ridicule every time she flubbed a line or threw it back to the wrong person.

But glamour is relative. Stella was now Talent, capital T. She had an office, a small one, but it had a door and a window. She hired an agent to negotiate her contract. She used the Talent Only entrance at the side of the building. She spent a fortune upgrading her wardrobe, and several hours a day in hair and makeup. She hired a vocal coach; she wore whitening strips on her teeth every night. And none of this was silly or vain, because it was now her job to look good. Because if viewers liked watching her deliver the news, it meant they would keep the channel tuned to KCN, which meant we could charge steeper rates for advertising, which meant the rest of us could receive our salaries and health insurance and afford to buy groceries.

For someone in Stella's position, cable news had a benefit: twenty-four hours of airtime to fill meant plenty of opportunities to get hits. A reporter could rise through the ranks on cable far more quickly than at a network. Stella's big moment came in November, just a few months into her new role. A gas main exploded in Hell's Kitchen and a fire tore through nearby apartment buildings. Stella was the first reporter on the scene. KCN had it up at least five minutes before anyone else. She held her stick mic, looked confidently into the camera, and delivered flawless live shots every thirty minutes for the next twelve hours straight.

"Who is that?" Rebecca said, looking at the wall-mounted screen in the newsroom. Night had fallen, and Stella was delivering yet another live shot in front of the smoldering buildings. The chyron blared BREAKING: TWO DEAD, SIX MISSING. "Is she new?"

"She used to be an assistant here," I said. At least Rebecca didn't remember who Stella was.

"You sure she didn't come straight from the Mattel factory? She looks even younger than you, Violet." Rebecca crossed her arms and watched in silence as Stella read the latest statement from the NYPD. "She's not bad, actually."

"Who is?" Eliza said, as she walked past. Then she followed Rebecca's gaze to the screen. "Oh," she said. "Give credit to Jamie on that one. That's his new girlfriend."

———

They had started dating right around Labor Day, and told me soon after. The careful choreography annoyed me even more than the news itself: their gentle voices, their glances back and forth, loaded with meaning. *Is she okay? You go first—no, you go first. But be careful.* They acted like I was so fragile I might shatter.

"We don't want this to be weird," Stella said, brow knitted in sympathy.

"Why would it be weird?" I shot back.

"It won't affect our friendship," Jamie said. "Or our working together."

Stella took his hand, nodded earnestly. She often absorbed the mannerisms of the men she dated. For the moment, at least, Jamie was turning her into a heart-on-her-sleeve idealist. "You know how important you are to us."

Us. They wrapped that word around themselves like a cozy blanket. Jamie began spending the night at our apartment. Once a week, then twice, then almost every night. One morning I ran into him in the kitchen, where he was clad in boxers and a T-shirt. Instead of sitting with me, he smiled sheepishly and carried two mugs of coffee back to Stella's bedroom.

After he closed the door, I could hear them laughing. It was painful, how vividly I could imagine the rest of it. The mugs of coffee set aside, the minty toothbrushed kiss—Stella standing on her tiptoes to press her lips to his—then the kiss turning into more, the T-shirt and boxers easily shed. Stella had told me several times how good Jamie was in bed. How attentive, how generous, how unlike the men she'd been with before.

That fall turned into a long, dark, trudging winter. January, February, March. I bought earplugs so I could sleep through the night without hearing them. I wondered if it would be better to leave—find a new city, a new industry, or at least a new apartment, where I wasn't constantly in the shadow of Stella Bradley. But at the same time, I was doing well at KCN. I got a raise, and then another. With my cheap rent, I was saving plenty of money. Rebecca and Eliza gave me more responsibility. They liked my pitches. I had that news instinct, they said. I loved the work.

And what was the issue, anyway? Why couldn't we both succeed? I had no desire to be on camera. I had no desire to date Jamie Richter. So what was it to me if Stella succeeded in those arenas? But any attempt to be happy for her was an intellectual exercise. And there was no one to talk to about this, because I had lost my two closest friends to each other.

Rebuffing Jamie had been easy for me, because what he was offering—love, affection—didn't seem necessary. But that's because I already *had* love—I had it from Stella. It was such a given that I didn't even think about it. Not until Stella and Jamie started dating did I realize the comfortable assumption that had formed my bedrock for so long: Stella wasn't the type to settle down with a man, and I was too busy with work to meet anyone. It was perfect. It would be just the two of us; we were all the other person needed.

Now, that assumption was smashed to pieces. The resentment was suffocating. I mean this literally: muscles clenched behind my breastbone, making it difficult to breathe and drink and swallow. And along with this I felt guilty, too. Why couldn't I be a better friend? Wasn't that what friends were supposed to do—support one another, love one another, take pride in one another?

There was this economics class I'd taken in college. One day, we learned about the concept of a zero-sum game. "Of course," the professor said, standing at the front of the room, "not every situation is zero sum. Most situations aren't. The real world is infinitely more complex than this abstraction. And the more complexity there is, the less likely it is that zero sum obtains."

That lecture lodged in my memory: the dusty chalkboard, the professor in her black sweater and gray slacks. She was pretty, young, on the tenure track. A diamond ring glittered on her left hand as she paced back and forth across the front of the room. But what I remember most was walking out of that classroom and thinking: she doesn't get it. Of course the world is zero sum. Every gain demands a loss. The loser may not be aware that she is a loser. But the loss will reveal itself at some point. This pretty young professor was the type of woman to bake cookies for faculty meetings, to write thank-you notes after dinner parties. The type to believe that she didn't have to be like the other guys—selfish, cutthroat—in order to get ahead. That there was such a thing as a win-win, as a rising tide.

I looked her up online after graduating. She had been denied tenure.

———

During the broadcast one night in mid-May of that year, my phone buzzed.

It was over two years ago, during that week between Christmas and New Year's, that I had first read the Danner Pharmaceutical story. None of the employees had been willing to talk at length, but I'd kept in touch with one person: Darla, a former cafeteria worker. She was the kind of sweet older woman who you worried scam artists might rip off. She texted me pictures of her dogs and grandchildren. "It's like buying lottery tickets," Jamie said once. "You cultivate sources. Most of them go nowhere. But hey, sometimes you hit it big."

I read and reread the text from Darla. Then I called her after the broadcast wrapped.

"And he's not worried about getting sued, like you were?" I asked.

"Oh, honey, of course he's worried about that. But he's so young." Darla coughed wheezily. She was prone to seasonal allergies. "He's got a lifetime to pay back legal bills. Not like me. This debt is following me to the grave."

"Don't say that, Darla," I said. "You've got plenty of time left."

"George always stood in my line at the cafeteria, even when the other lines were shorter. He's a good boy, Violet. You'll talk to him, won't you?"

"Of course. If that's what he wants."

"He needs to get it off his chest. That's what he said to me. He said, 'Darla, I need to get this off my chest. I can barely stand it anymore.'"

"And this thing he needs to talk about—this is what got you in trouble, too?"

Darla was silent. I could hear the faint sound of her breathing, in and out.

"Fair enough," I said. "I'll call him right now."

The next night, I met George at a bar several blocks away from the KCN radius. I spotted him at the bar—brown hair and blue tie, as he'd described—and he sprang up when he saw me approaching.

"Thank you for meeting me," George said, pumping my hand eagerly. Darla had said he worked in sales at Danner.

"I'm glad we're getting the chance to talk," I said, taking the stool next to him.

"What are you drinking?" He waved at the bartender. There was a nearly empty wineglass at his elbow. "This chardonnay is good. Are you a chardonnay fan?"

"Just a club soda, actually," I said.

"Oh," George said, his smile deflating slightly. "Sure. That works, too."

George was good at small talk: sports, weather, television, what I was reading. Nearly thirty minutes passed, and he showed no signs of slowing his chatter. He'd probably remain in salesman mode all night if he could.

"George," I said finally, interrupting his spirited analysis of last night's Yankees game. "Darla said you had something you wanted to tell me."

"Isn't Darla the best? I remember this one time—"

"Look," I said. "George. If you're not ready, we can do this another night. I'll just get the check and be on my way. Excuse me?" I started waving for the bartender.

"No—wait." His smile disappeared. "I'm sorry. I'm a little nervous, I guess."

"That's understandable," I said. "But tell you what. We're off the record. I won't even write this down. We're just having a conversation for now, okay?"

He hesitated for a moment. Then he sighed. "I'm going to quit," he said, his voice low and defensive, so different from his good-old-boy twang. "I am. It's just that I have these student loans, and my mom needs the money—my dad's out of the picture—and this job pays really well."

He was quiet for a while. "There's a but, isn't there?" I prompted.

"But I can't do it anymore," he said.

"Can't do what?"

"You know how pharma works," he said. "Our customer isn't really the customer. It's the doctor. That's who we're selling to. We need them to write prescriptions for our drugs. So you've got guys like me, your district sales managers, to wine and dine the doctors. Tell them how great this new drug is, so they can tell their patients the same thing. That's what the system hinges on. But guys like me—well, we weren't getting the results that Danner wanted."

George sat up a little straighter. "I went to Georgetown, you know. I majored in marketing. I'm *good* at my job. Danner used to pride themselves on their sales force. But suddenly the people they're hiring—not so much. They laid off the guys I'd worked with and they replaced them with four very pretty girls. And do you know what else those girls had in common?"

I shook my head.

"My team—me and those four girls—we'd take a group of doctors out to dinner. It's just business, right? Then we'd wind up at the hotel bar, have a few nightcaps. The numbers always worked out. After a while, each of the girls would lead a doctor upstairs. Two by two they left. They were former call girls. High-end. Slick. It felt totally natural. And then I'd wait in the hallway, in case anything happened. Do you know what that makes me, Violet?"

His face crumpled in anguish.

"It makes me a *pimp.*" His voice cracked. "I pimped those girls out. I let these twenty-one-year-old girls go alone into these hotel rooms with these drunk old men just so that we could get an edge on Pfizer and Bayer."

"You were told to do this?" I said. "By your boss?"

"Our district was the guinea pig. Sales were way up. After it started working for us, they rolled it out across the country. Five-star service, that's what my boss called it. White-glove client management."

My heart was thrumming with a sudden, hyperalert instinct. I had to be careful not to betray this, not to spook George. "How long has this been going on?" I said evenly.

George was shredding his cocktail napkin into tiny pieces. "Two years," he said. "But a few months ago, it got really bad. There was a rough night. One of the girls wound up with a black eye and a broken arm."

"Did she report it to the police?"

"And tell them what? Danner would claim she was acting irresponsibly. That she'd picked up the doctor on her own accord. They'd fire her, and for good measure, they'd say that she had lied to the company about her previous—let's call it—work experience."

"This girl, the one who broke her arm, where is she now?"

"She's lying low. She quit, obviously. And it's not like she could do her job anymore, the shape she was in. She wanted to disappear. That's what she said."

"Was this when you decided you needed to tell someone?"

George scrunched his forehead. "I know that makes me an awful person. What the fuck? Someone almost needs to get *killed* before I'm willing to speak up?"

"You signed an NDA, I assume?" I asked gently. "And Danner obviously takes that seriously. Is that—that, uh, white-glove management—why Darla and the others were sued?"

He shook his head. "That's the crazy thing. They didn't even know about this. But Danner is so secretive, they'll sue over anything. For, I don't know, talking about what was on the cafeteria menu that day. I bet that's why they sued Darla. Some unbelievably stupid bullshit."

"So that story that ran in the paper a few years ago—"

"It was nothing. Half the people in central Jersey have been sued by Danner. I'm surprised that you've kept sniffing around for so long." He squinted at me. "How did you know?"

"I don't know," I said.

George took a morose sip of chardonnay. He looked like he was on the verge of tears. "What a clusterfuck," he said.

"George," I said. "You're speaking up now, right? Some people wouldn't say anything. And you want this to stop, don't you?"

"Of course."

"Then I'd like your permission to share this with my bosses at KCN. They'll need to talk to you about this, too. Sooner rather than later."

He nodded. "Okay," he said.

I debriefed Jamie the next morning. His eyebrows climbed higher as the story went on. "And this came from that woman who sends you pictures of her beagles?"

"She's like a second mother to George. They stayed close."

"Jeez, did you hit the jackpot." Jamie shook his head. I felt a twinge of irritation: it was luck, sure, but it was also a persistent two-year-plus pursuit. "It's almost too salacious to believe," he said. "How confident are you? You checked this guy out afterwards?"

"Thoroughly. He's on Danner's website. There was a press release last year that said he won some big award at their annual sales conference."

Jamie grimaced. "I bet he did."

"Are you skeptical? Why would he make this up?"

"Who knows? A ploy for attention. Payback for some slight in the past." Jamie opened his laptop to search for Danner Pharmaceuticals. "Wow. He wasn't kidding about their stock price, though. So when can we talk to him?"

We called George that afternoon. On the phone, he repeated the same story to Jamie. Jamie asked more questions, the wheres and whens and whos, if there was a paper trail to prove that this was a coordinated strategy—a memo, an e-mail, anything. George said that the initial instructions had been given verbally, one-on-one. E-mails and memos were left purposely vague. "Closing the deal" could mean anything. Maybe it meant cigars and brandy after dinner. Maybe it meant an à la carte fuck with a call girl.

"George won't be enough, obviously," Jamie said, after we'd hung up.

"I *know* that," I said.

Jamie raised an eyebrow. "I know you know that. I'm not second-guessing you, Violet."

"Right." I sighed. These days I was more easily annoyed by Jamie. It wasn't fair. He was just doing his job, thinking out loud. "You're right. I'm just—"

"You're excited." Jamie smiled softly. "This is big. It's important."

That night, after the broadcast, Jamie followed Eliza into her office and closed the door. He wanted to get her guidance on what came next. After a few minutes, my phone rang, and Eliza asked me to join them.

"Have a seat," Eliza said, gesturing at one of the chairs across from her. "Jamie says you trust this guy."

"I do," I said.

"To start, see if you can corroborate what he's saying," Eliza said. "Right now it's just one guy, and we have no idea what his agenda might be. If you get someone else on record, we can add more resources. But I only want you two working on this for now."

"Understood," Jamie said.

"What about tracking down the girl who went into hiding?" I said.

"She'll be hard to find. She wouldn't have used her real name," Eliza said. "And, first, I'd like to find out whether this really was a top-down plan. Do you remember Jerome Kerviel?"

"Ah—no?" I said.

"That's because no one does," Eliza said. "He was a French trader, convicted for fraud. But Société Générale painted him as a rogue actor, and the rest of the company was untouched. He goes to jail, the world moves on, and nothing actually changes."

I tried contacting other sales managers at Danner, under the guise of seeking comment for a story about digital innovation in the pharmaceutical industry. But e-mails went unanswered, and phone calls ended in abrupt hang-ups. George was right; Danner had done a thorough job of training its employees to never speak with journalists.

Jamie had slightly better luck. He selected his tools like a surgeon choosing an instrument: flattery, appeals to ego, horse-trading, subtle bullying. He convinced one of the sales managers to meet him for lunch. But Jamie returned a few hours later, looking frustrated. The man had only wanted to talk about his college basketball career, and how KCN really ought to do a documentary about the time Bucknell made it to the Final Four.

By June, several weeks into it, we were without a single lead. The days were too busy with regular work to get anything done, so after the show wrapped at 9 p.m., Jamie and I would put in a few more hours. After another fruitless night, as we were waiting for the elevator, Jamie sighed. "So there are two possibilities. Either Danner is running the most airtight operation I've ever seen, with fewer leaks than Seal Team Six. Or George is just making this up."

We stepped inside the elevator. "Or," I said, "the story is true, and the others are too scared to talk about it."

"And, what, George is sneaking around like Deep Throat? Those things only happen in the movies."

"But George *hasn't* been sneaky. That's why I believe him."

"Okay. Occam's razor. What's the simplest explanation? That there's a massive cover-up happening, which two persistent journalists haven't found a shred of evidence for? Or that one guy is a little bit off his meds? So to speak."

"I don't buy that. You should have seen how upset he was." I paused. "Why don't we meet with him in person? Both of us. Ask him who else we should talk to, beyond the obvious."

The elevator opened. Our footsteps echoed at this midnight hour, the lobby quiet and empty except for a lone security guard behind the front desk. Jamie sighed again. "You know I'd only do this for you, Violet."

The next night, a Friday night, Jamie and Stella had a dinner reservation at an obscenely expensive sushi restaurant in the East Village. On Friday, Stella was out covering a story on Staten Island. Jamie left several messages asking her to call him back. "She's been talking about this place for weeks," he said. "She's not going to be happy."

"We don't have to do it tonight," I said. "We could meet George another time."

"Sooner is better. This has to take priority." Jamie avoided my gaze, scribbling aimlessly on his notepad as he tried Stella yet again. He'd always been a bad liar.

That afternoon, I saw Stella across the newsroom. When she spotted me, she held a finger to her lips. She crept silently behind Jamie's chair and put her hands over his eyes. "Guess who?" she murmured into his ear. Time moved twice as quickly in cable news, and the tranquil honeymoon phase of their relationship had passed. As reality set in, Stella had become both flirtier and more demanding of Jamie.

Jamie jumped. In the moment between Stella's hands dropping from his eyes, and him turning to her, his expression flickered with dread. Then he forced a smile.

"What's up?" she said. "You left, like, a million messages."

"Yeah," Jamie said. "I'm sorry, Stell. I can't make dinner tonight."

Her face darkened, quick as a cloud moving in front of the sun.

"I have to meet a source," Jamie continued. "It's a last-minute thing. I'm so sorry. I know you were excited about this place."

"No way. It was *impossible* to get this reservation. I had to drop Rebecca's name."

"Isn't the name Stella Bradley hot enough for them?" He smiled.

Oh, Jamie, I thought. *You're a dead man walking.*

"Do *not* make a joke about this," Stella said. "You've had this on your calendar for a month. And now what am I supposed to do?"

"I know, it's just—"

"You and your never-ending excuses." Stella whipped around. "What do you say, Violet? You in the mood for sushi? Want to be my date, because my boyfriend bailed on me *again*?"

"She can't," Jamie said.

"She can speak for herself," Stella snapped.

"We have to meet with a source," I said. "Both of us."

It was barely perceptible, but Stella flinched at those words. Genuine injury: *us*. She curled her lip into a defensive sneer. "It's this story, right? This big, important, mysterious story that you refuse to tell me anything about?"

"We can't," I said. "You understand that."

"Understand *this*," she said, flipping me the finger. Several people nearby turned at the sound of her raised voice, watching as she stalked away and nearly collided with a coffee-toting intern, yelling at him to get out of her way. Lately her temper had grown shorter and shorter. She couldn't stand it when something didn't go her way. The more success she had on camera, the greedier she became. The addictive, sugary thrill of attention brought out the worst in her.

"You in trouble, bro?" one of the assistants said to Jamie, once she was out of earshot. Jamie rolled his eyes and said, "You didn't see that. Get back to work, all of you."

That night, we met George at the same bar in Midtown. "How are you?" he asked, shaking our hands with the earnest vigor I remembered.

"Fine," I said. "Listen, George, let's—"

"I really appreciate it," he said. "Both of you working on this with me."

He was back in deranged salesman mode, blathering about the weather, about his plans for the Fourth of July, about the NFL preseason. *Who gets excited about the NFL preseason in June?*, I thought. As Jamie's eyebrows arched, I panicked. Maybe he *was* off his meds. When our drinks arrived, I took my chance to interrupt.

"George," I said. "*George*. Listen to me. We have a meeting back in the office in thirty minutes. So we don't have much time."

"What? You have a meeting at ten o'clock on Friday night?"

"Yes," I said. "Our schedules are crazy."

"Everyone at Danner is stonewalling us," Jamie said. "Our boss is going to pull the plug on this, and soon, if we don't get some corroboration for your story."

"We need you to think," I said. "Who else can back up what you're saying?"

George, now with a concrete task at hand, calmed down. He cocked his head and ran through the list of obvious suspects, all of whom we had already tried. It was when George was musing about whether the hotels had security cameras that Jamie snapped his fingers.

"The footage?" I said. "There's no way they'd turn that over to us."

"Not the footage," Jamie said. "The staff. They might have seen something."

At the hotel in New Jersey the next day, Saturday, we started by ordering lunch in the bar, talking with the bartender—he would have had a front-row seat to the unfolding drama. But it turned out he was new, only a few weeks into the job. We paid the bill quickly and moved on.

Over the next few hours, drifting through the hotel as inconspicuously as we could, we tried talking with the maid, the concierge, the bellboy. Each was polite and helpful, until our questions moved from the general to the particular. Once they sensed an agenda, they backed away and shook their heads. This was turning into another dead end. I looked at my watch. Almost 5 p.m. The traffic back into the city would be bad.

Five p.m. A sign had said that the hotel bar opened at 10 a.m. That meant—

"Jamie," I said. "Let's go back to the bar. I bet the shift is about to turn over."

Sure enough, there was a new person on duty. We took two seats at the bar.

There was something different about this bartender. He looked me straight in the eye when I ordered, but his manner was abrupt. The drinking he oversaw at this blandly corporate hotel was intense and joyless, drinking designed to make you forget that you were exhausted and wearing a rumpled polyblend suit, and that your alarm was going off at 6 a.m. Prostitution was practically legal at a hotel bar like this. Jamie cut straight to the chase and told him why we were there. The bartender nodded, and said, "Yeah, I remember."

I felt a jolt of adrenaline. Our first confirmation that George was telling the truth.

"Can you tell us what you saw?" Jamie said.

He cocked his head like, *do you think I'm an idiot?* Jamie removed a stack of twenty-dollar bills from his wallet, folded them in half, and slid them across the bar.

"Appreciate it," the bartender said, pocketing the bills. "What I saw was eight or nine people come to the bar for a nightcap. There was a younger guy who was buying the drinks. A bunch of young women and a bunch of old guys. They paired off pretty quickly. One of the old guys told me he had dibs on the redhead."

"How long did they stay?" I asked.

"A few hours. The old guys were drunk, and getting grabby. I almost had to kick them out. They were making the other guests uncomfortable. The younger guy stayed to close the tab." After a pause, he added, "You should talk to the night manager who was on duty that night."

"Why?" I said. "Did she see something?"

"Ask her yourself. Her shift starts at ten."

We stood in a far corner of the parking lot, near the dumpsters and the back door to the hotel kitchen, propped open to let in the mild night air. I could hear the clatter of pots and pans, the rat-a-tat of a knife chopping, the tinny radio and shouted Spanish. The night manager crossed her arms, waiting for us to begin.

"You might remember a group of guests who stayed here a while ago," Jamie said. "Five rooms, reserved by Danner Pharmaceuticals. They had dinner in the restaurant."

"We've got 206 beds in this hotel," she said. "Average length of stay is one night. And you're talking about how long ago, so you do the math."

"Maybe it's unlikely," I said, "but if you recall anything—"

She waved a hand. "Relax. I remember. Jesus, how could I forget?"

There had been noise issues, she said. A guest had called the front desk to complain about shouting and raised voices. The first time the night manager knocked on the door, it settled down for a while. Then it started back up, and it was worse. The guest next door said she could hear loud thumps, something shattering. Sobbing and screaming.

The manager went back upstairs, this time with a security guard in tow. She passed a man in the hallway. He was sweaty and out of breath, his shirt unbuttoned and flapping open, but she had no cause to stop him in that moment—he was a guest, after all.

When she reached the room, the girl was alone. She had two black eyes, a broken arm. Bruises around her throat, blood dripping from her nose. The doctor had already gotten a taxi and was long gone. The night manager wanted to call the police, but the girl insisted that George could just drive her to the emergency room. She was okay, she said. She'd drunk too much and tripped over the furniture. She was clumsy like that.

"He tried to pay me off," she said. "That kid, George. His hands were shaking like crazy. Here was five hundred dollars for the cleaning fee, he said. The cleaning fee! Give me a break. I did have to replace the carpeting in that room, by the way. Her blood was everywhere. No way to get the stains out."

"So you didn't take the money," Jamie said.

"Take a bribe from a jackass like that? No way. He let this girl get beat to a pulp and then pretended like all she had was a bump on her forehead. The Danner guys don't stay here anymore." She grimaced. "Too ashamed to show their faces."

CHAPTER ELEVEN

AFTER THE BREAKTHROUGH, Eliza assigned two more producers and a handful of assistants to the story. But even with added resources, so much of our reporting hinged on serendipity. An assistant had a friend at Bayer who had heard about unfair tactics at their rival. Another producer knew a guy who had once dated a girl who worked at Danner, a very pretty girl who carried Gucci handbags and leased a BMW and didn't know a thing about pharmaceuticals.

For my part, I was working on the woman from the hotel. George had finally gotten hold of her new number. She called herself Willow, and now lived in Florida. She was skittish and unpredictable, responding to texts but not phone calls, Facebook messages but not e-mails, vanishing for long stretches of time. Jamie offered to try speaking with her, but I felt protective. If she wanted to live far away, with a new name and a new identity, starting over—who could blame her?

A story like this, Eliza explained, was delicate. It took a long time to convince sources to go on the record. If our competitors heard what KCN was working on, they might try to scoop us. For that reason, Eliza insisted we keep the circle small. "I don't want some intern spilling the beans at happy hour," she said. "Only tell the necessary people."

Stella still didn't know what the story was, but she no longer seemed to care. In August, she anchored the Saturday morning news program while the regular host was on vacation. A year into her work as a reporter, it was becoming obvious that the KCN executives had bigger plans for her. Her assignments got better, and she was no longer on the morning shift. She appeared on shows across the network, often in prime time. Our lobby was lined with larger-than-life posters of Rebecca Carter and her ilk: the chief White House correspondent, the morning show anchors, the Peabody-winning investigative reporter. The bona fide stars of the network. A few weeks after Stella's first turn in the anchor chair, her poster went up in the lobby. Stella, with a royal purple sheath dress and shiny blond hair, arms crossed and gaze serious, with the KCN tagline, *The News You Need.*

In the past, at least Stella had the grace to behave with self-awareness. When she vacationed in Gstaad and St. Barts, she downplayed the glamour. When men competed to buy her drinks, she dismissed them as shallow and dumb. Even just last year, when she and Jamie started dating, she broke the news conscientiously. Stella always made an effort to bridge the socioeconomic and aesthetic gulf that separated us.

And why did she do this? Because she needed me. Because I was loyal. Because I was the only person who gave her the steadfast attention she craved. Because she was most alive when she had an audience, and I made her feel alive. Who else could see past her vanity, her temper tantrums, her mood swings, and give her what she needed in order to feel like herself? She had to make those efforts, because if she were to alienate me completely, who would she have left?

Well, I'll tell you who. The most loyal audience there is: viewers of cable news.

"A toast," Thomas said, lifting his glass. The six of us—the Bradley family plus Jamie and me—were seated around their dining table on a Sunday evening in October. Thomas glowed with the pride of a parent whose once-problematic child has, by succeeding unexpectedly, erased every painful memory of the past. "To our Stella."

"We're so proud of you, sweetheart," Anne said.

Stella smiled. "Don't forget the best part, Daddy. We won the demo last week."

"Like winning a beauty pageant judged by a blind man," Jamie said quietly.

"Oh?" I whispered. "You mean eighteen- to forty-nine-year-olds aren't flocking to cable news in droves at 9 a.m. on Saturdays?"

"What are you two talking about?" Stella said. "You know it's rude to whisper, Violet."

"Nothing." I lifted my glass. "Just toasting to you."

It was chilly for October, and there was a blazing fire in the dining room fireplace. So many meals like this had peppered my years of friendship with Stella: the finely embroidered napkins, the heirloom silver, the distinctive taste of oregano in the roasted Cornish game hen. The world could change, years could pass, but there would always be these constants. Thomas often boasted of how his Bradley ancestors fought in the Revolutionary War. And, really, how different was this life from that of his ancestors? Strip away the changing technologies and fashions, and what remained was the comfort and the power of wealth. And especially the endurance of wealth: the system we lived in produced certain victors, and pointed to those victors as proof of its own efficacy. Just look at Stella.

"You must hear all sorts of buzz about Stella," Anne said,

looking at me as she cut her food into small pieces. "Ginny tells me she's really putting her mark on the place."

"Of course," I said. "Although I've been a bit distracted lately. It's been busy."

"Violet's being modest," Jamie said. "She's working on a big story."

My cheeks grew hot. A year into their relationship and he still hadn't learned how to avoid pissing Stella off. "We'll see if it turns into anything," I said.

"Oh, it will," Jamie said. "It's the kind of story that makes careers."

Stella leaned over. "But you can't say anything about it," she said. "Right?"

"Right," I said.

"So I guess we'll have to wait and see." Stella smirked.

"I think that's work." Jamie pulled his buzzing phone from his pocket and stood from the table. "Would you excuse me for a minute? I should take this."

A few minutes later, I excused myself, too. In the hallway en route to the powder room was Thomas's study. The door was ajar, and Jamie was inside.

I pushed the door open. "What are you doing?" I whispered.

"Come here," Jamie said. "Look at this."

I hesitated. "Thomas wouldn't want us in his study."

"I came inside to take my phone call but then I got distracted. Here, look." He pointed at a framed photograph on the bookshelf. "Do you recognize that man? At the edge of the group. Gray hair, blue tie."

I peered at the picture. "Gray hair, blue tie, that describes every guy in this group."

"This one," Jamie said, pressing his finger against the glass, leaving an oily smudge.

"He looks familiar," I said. "But why?"

"Remember when we were looking up the executive team on Danner's website the other day? That's where you've seen him before. This is the CEO of Danner Pharmaceuticals."

"Whoa." I squinted. "You're right."

"I Googled it. Looks like this was a dinner given by the pharma lobby. There was some industry recognition award, excellence in leadership or whatever." Jamie rolled his eyes. "Both Thomas Bradley and the Danner CEO were among the recipients."

"So they don't necessarily know each other," I said. "Maybe they do, or maybe they just happened to be in this picture together."

Jamie paused, turned to me. "Have you told Stella about the story?"

I laughed. "Do you think I'm an idiot?"

"I'm sorry, Violet, I have to ask."

I put my hands on my hips. "Have *you* told her about it?"

"Oh, give me a break."

"You're the one sleeping with her, *James*. You never slip up during pillow talk?"

Jamie shook his head. "I'm being paranoid, I know. I just—I don't like how murky her loyalties are."

"Well, it's a good thing she's not working on this story."

"Imagine after it breaks. Do you think we're really going to be welcome here, in the Bradley household?"

"You're being dramatic," I said.

"Am I?" Jamie said. "This is big, Violet. You can't predict the ripple effects."

A few weeks later, Willow finally agreed to meet me in person. She wasn't saying yes to an on-camera interview yet, but this was the most important step before that.

Eliza looked pleased when I told her. "Good," she said. "I knew you'd get there eventually. How soon can you meet her?"

"The day after tomorrow, it looks like."

"And you and Jamie will both go? Where does she live?"

"Florida," I said. "The Panhandle."

"So if you can get her on the record, we'll have"—Eliza started counting on her fingers—"George, Willow, the hotel employees, the voice mail from George's boss, the guy from Bayer. What am I forgetting?"

"We're working on the other girl, the BMW girl. And one of George's old friends from Danner. He's on the verge of quitting. I'm telling him that he should get out ahead of this."

"The right side of history. No one can resist that line."

"So what do you think?" I said. "Do you think we have it?"

"Just about," she said. "Get Willow to commit to an interview, and we'll start putting the package together when you're back."

Jamie and I were on a flight to Panama City the next afternoon, the sky already darkening as the plane took off from JFK. As I watched the fading ribbon of sunlight across the western horizon, I was aware of a vague panic gathering underneath my rib cage, my pulse and breath quickening. The airplane was climbing a steep trajectory into the sky. The engine revved and slowed, the cabin rattled in the thinning atmosphere. I closed my eyes and tried to breathe through my nose. A moment later, I felt Jamie's hand squeezing mine.

"You okay?" he said.

"I don't like flying."

"Is that really what's going on?"

I opened my eyes just long enough to see Jamie's look of concern. Then the plane gave another violent rattle and I shut them again.

"When was the last time you went home?" he continued.

We can talk about it some other time, Jamie had said, years ago. That meant now, apparently. "It's been a while," I said.

"But you must think about it," he said. "Isn't this right around where you grew up?"

The plane was bouncing like a kite in the wind, my hands gripping the armrest. "You really know how to pick your moments," I said.

"Maybe if we have some time tomorrow, we can take a drive and—"

"*Jamie,*" I said. "Jesus. Just leave it alone, okay?"

It had been cold in New York, sterile and chilly on the plane, so when we stepped outside in Panama City, the warm humidity came as a relief. It washed over me like a familiar greeting: the pudding-like night air, the glow of sodium lamps in dark parking lots, the constant buzz of mosquitoes. Jamie heard my sigh and turned to me.

"You okay?" he said.

"Yeah," I said. "Sorry I snapped at you."

He spread his arms wide. "Who can stay mad when you're in the South? I love this place. I'm sick of winter and it hasn't even started."

"Does Florida count as the South?" I said, dropping my bag in the trunk of the rental car.

"The Panhandle does," he said.

When we checked into the Marriott, Jamie asked the woman at the front desk where we should eat. "Well," she said, hesitating. She knew we were from New York; I was wearing black and had just asked if the hotel had a gym. "The only thing nearby is an Applebee's."

Jamie slapped his palm against the counter. "Applebee's it is!"

"Really?" I said, after we turned from the desk.

"Oh, come on," Jamie said. "Let's live a little."

It was across the highway from the hotel, glowing like a beacon, in a strip mall that included a Piggly Wiggly, a Hobby Lobby, a bank with a drive-through ATM, and several vacant storefronts.

"Is it bad that I'm perversely excited for this?" Jamie said, as we walked across the mostly empty parking lot. "I haven't had a blooming onion in years."

"That's Outback Steakhouse," I said. Why did I know these things?

"Good God," he said, grabbing my arm in mock horror. "You're right."

"You're becoming one of those obnoxious New Yorkers we hate so much."

He grinned. "I suppose it takes one to know one."

Jamie goaded me into ordering half the menu with him: fried things, cheesy things, several sugary cocktails with names like Bahama Mama. After two hours, we were drunk and happy. Our waitress was an older woman with bleached hair who kept giving us freebies. "I like you kids," she said, with a smile that lit up her whole face. Jamie called her "ma'am" and exclaimed "God almighty" whenever she delivered a new dish.

"Your accent has suddenly gotten a lot stronger," I said. "Is it the booze or the zip code?"

"Both," he said. "This feels like home."

"Coronaries and alcoholism," I said, picking up a French fry. "I'd say so."

He grinned. "You're having fun. I can tell."

Of course I was. This feeling of nowhere else to be, so might as well have another drink—it was more fun than I'd had in months. But that was only the first layer. A deeper part of me was watchful and wary, unsettled by how close we were to my hometown. What if I ran into a high school classmate? It wasn't inconceivable. What would I do? What the hell would I say?

We never talked about it, but I knew that Stella and Jamie assumed that what I did was easy. Making a clean break with your past was dramatic, but it simplified things. Just think of the complications I'd avoided: holiday visits home, weekly phone calls, the fraught negotiations of a child growing older. But they didn't know how the past, even after such merciless severing, could follow you like a phantom limb.

Diane Molina, my high school history teacher, had sent me long and earnest e-mails during college, filled with questions. How was I? How was school? What was I reading? At first, I liked getting those e-mails because they made me feel less alone. Then I liked getting them because they made me feel smart, telling Diane about books and ideas that she'd never heard of. Eventually, though, I came to dread those e-mails. Even the sight of Diane's name in my in-box gave me claustrophobia. When I graduated, my college e-mail expired. The bounceback did the work for me. I didn't tell her where I was going next.

That's why Jamie's questions on the plane had bothered me. I wasn't one of those corn-fed country girls who pined for home; didn't he know that by now? But maybe he didn't, because his experience was so different. Jamie was lucky. In New York, his smooth manners and mellow accent were charming. It set him apart from the cold Yankee workaholics, even as he kept pace with them. It didn't work that way for women. Keep your Southern accent and sweet tea smile, and you are placed in a very specific category.

And so our business was filled with people like me, accentless and delocalized. Most reporters rose through the ranks with itinerant gigs at Middle America affiliates. Climbing the ladder gradually allows your oxygen levels to acclimate, Fargo to Denver, Denver to Chicago, and finally to the big leagues. It's also a useful way to exfoliate the past. By the moment of arrival in New York or Los Angeles or D.C., the accent is gone. All that remains is a hard and untraceable delivery.

When they appear on-screen, reporters and anchors remind those back home of just how far they've come. For some people, that's a motivation. For me, it was terrifying. I didn't want my parents to see my success, or understand what it meant. I had an irrational fear of them tracking me down, coming to New York to demand money or attention. The best disguise was staying behind the scenes. If my name and reputation was only known within the industry, all the better. It was a language that wasn't even open to them.

Jamie's phone was ringing. He put down his drink mid-sip and started patting himself. When he finally located his phone, he frowned at the screen and silenced the call. The phone rang again, and this time he switched the ringer off.

"Who was it?" I said.

"Excuse me, ma'am?" He waved to our waitress. "Could I trouble you for another strawberry margarita?"

"Of course," she said. "Another for you, sweetheart?"

"Ah," I hesitated, because the hangover was already looming.

"She'll take it!" Jamie said.

Then I heard my phone ring. I reached for it and answered it automatically. Jamie's eyes went wide. Too late, I realized what was happening.

"Hey, Stell," I said. "What's up?"

"Why isn't Jamie answering his phone?" she said. "He's there, isn't he?"

"Um, I don't—"

"What the *fuck*," she said, "is wrong with him? Is he bleeding? Has he been hit over the head? Because that's the only reason he should be ignoring my calls."

"He's in the bathroom right now," I said. "He's, uh, been in there for a while. I think he ate some bad food on the plane." I grimaced, and Jamie mouthed a thank-you.

"So what? He brings his phone into the bathroom with him. He's attached to that thing like it's an umbilical cord."

"I don't know, Stella. Honestly."

"Well, *whatever*. I had a shitty day at work, thanks for asking. I had—"

Lately, her tirades had gotten worse: slights minor or imaginary, which she perceived as mortal wounds. This time, she had gone to New Jersey to record a stand-up, but her segment had gotten cut at the last minute. This happened all the time to young reporters at KCN, but Stella didn't measure herself against them. She measured herself against stars like Rebecca Carter, who never had to put up with this shit. "I'm too good for this place," she'd said, more than once. "I go down the street to another network and they'll triple my salary." Her confidence was so brazen that I'd started to wonder if she had some secret leverage over the executives. After a while, I said, "Oh, look, Jamie's back."

"God, finally. Put him on, will you?"

Jamie kept the phone a few inches from his ear. Even over the music in the restaurant, I could hear Stella's loud haranguing. He unenthusiastically said, "Uh huh" and "Yeah, totally" and "Okay, yeah, love you" and finally hung up with a sigh.

After a long pause, he said, "I don't get it."

I kept quiet. My policy was to remain neutral during their fights.

"It's like she's a different person," Jamie continued. "I mean, you must see it, too. Right? You see how ridiculous she's being? I'm not allowed to miss a single phone call from her, even when I'm on assignment?"

"She wants what she wants," I said. "And she's used to getting it."

"Well, when is someone going to finally say no?"

I looked at him, pointedly.

"Good Lord." He sat back and gripped the edge of the table, as if bracing himself for the sudden plunge of a roller coaster. "I thought that dating Stella Bradley would be fun. I didn't sign up for—I don't know—personality rehab."

"I hear you," I said. "But I've never found the solution."

Jamie leaned forward and sucked at the last inch of his drink, the straw making a harsh guttering sound. A grown man inhaling a pink margarita like his life depended on it was an objectively funny sight, but this wasn't an appropriate time to laugh.

"She's going to drive me insane, Violet," he said. "She makes me so angry. Sometimes I feel like I'm about to lose my mind. Like I'm going to snap."

"Jamie," I said. "If it's really that bad, why don't you just end it?"

Silence. From the way Jamie looked at me, I could tell he was thinking the same thing. Why didn't he end it? Well, why didn't *I* end it? Being Stella Bradley's best friend had always rested on a delicate formula. There were the bad parts, and there were the good parts. Lately the balance had shifted. The good was almost gone, and it was almost enough to break me.

But there were things it was safe to talk about when you were several drinks deep at an Applebee's in Panama City, and this wasn't one of them. Jamie knew that, and I knew that, and despite the Bahama Mamas and strawberry margaritas, we were still smart enough to turn back from the edge of this cliff.

We picked at the remnants of dessert, then went home. We said good night in the hallway of the Marriott—my room on the left, Jamie's on the right—and as I lay in bed, hearing the distant mechanical churn of the ice-making machine, all I could think was *if Stella finds out that I planted this idea in his head, she is going to kill me.*

About twenty minutes outside of Panama City, the highway led to a paved road, which led to a dirt road, which snaked through the forest. At the yellow mailbox we'd been told to look for, I turned down the driveway. It was rutted with potholes, and pebbles and rocks pinged against the undercarriage of the car. The light was filtered and dappled by the cypress trees. At the end of the driveway was a small bungalow, the clearing illuminated by a shaft of sunlight.

It was a few minutes before noon. Ours was the only car in the driveway. "I'm going to look around," I said to Jamie, who stayed in the car and nodded behind his sunglasses.

Willow lived inside the confines of a water management area. The trees were tall and vibrant green, and the lakes and creeks we'd passed were filled with crystal-clear water. Signs along the road pointed to hiking trails and canoe launches. This had always confused me about Florida: that a place of such overwhelming natural beauty could contain so much man-made ugliness. It felt like a perfect metaphor for something.

The ticking chorus of birds and insects was interrupted by the sound of an approaching car. I rapped on the window and Jamie startled awake. The car, a modest gray compact, came to a stop. Willow stepped out, but she stood behind the open door like it was a shield.

"You're the newspeople?" she said.

I waved. "We talked on the phone. I'm Violet Trapp, and this is Jamie Richter."

She slung a bag over her shoulder. "I'm guessing you want to come inside."

As we followed her through the front door and my eyes adjusted to the indoor dimness, I was struck by how clean and spare her living room was. The walls and floorboards were painted white. There was a brightly colored Mexican rug, three minimalist armchairs, a few pictures tacked above the desk in the corner. I'd been expecting simplicity, but the kind that reflected panicked transit: a suitcase, a mattress on the floor. This was not that. This was a life that had been arrived at carefully, after rigorous purification.

"Thank you for talking with us," Jamie said, as Willow

emerged from the kitchen holding a glass of water. She was beautiful, and her clothing aligned with her simple home décor. Like a Calvin Klein model in the nineties: jeans, a white shirt, sleek dark hair.

"Willow," I said, "at this point, we've turned up a lot of information about—"

She rolled her eyes. "That's not my real name."

"What would you prefer?" Jamie said.

"Nothing. You should just know that I hate the name."

"Okay," I said slowly. "That's fine. What I was saying is, we've got plenty of evidence against Danner. If you choose to go on the record, you won't be taking them on alone. Several other people have spoken out. And you'll have reporters and producers and KCN executives—every resource we have will be behind you."

She stood up and left the room. From the kitchen came the sound of running water. The living room was oppressively hot and still. My forehead was dotted with sweat, I was thirsty and craving air-conditioning, and the heat made me feel slow and exhausted. Willow took her time in the kitchen. Jamie caught my eye and shrugged.

When she returned, she was holding an orange. She stood between the kitchen and the living room, leaning against the doorjamb. The scent of citrus spiked the air as she dug a fingernail into the skin and began slowly peeling it away from the fruit.

"You realize how much I don't want to do this," she said.

"I understand," I said.

She raised an eyebrow, like, *do you?*

"Violet probably explained this," Jamie said, "but there are things we can do. We can keep your face in shadow during the interview. We don't have to use your name, or your location. The world doesn't have to know where you are, *who* you are, today."

Willow peeled the orange in one long spiral. She hefted the

naked fruit in the palm of her hand, like she was testing its weight. She broke the orb into two symmetrical halves, then handed one to Jamie and one to me.

"Oh," I said. "Thank you."

Jamie looked at her quizzically. "Do you have any questions for us?"

"I sleep with a gun in my nightstand," she said to me. "Did George tell you that?"

"He did," I said.

She crossed her arms. "Let me guess. You were thinking you'd come down to Florida and find some ruined woman. Drunk off her ass in a trailer."

"I didn't think anything," I said, although she was exactly right. This picture—white floors, scent of oranges—it was not what I'd imagined.

"I'm in school now. I'm getting my business degree. That's where I was this morning. I happen to be at the top of my class. Did he tell you *that*?"

"George spoke highly of you," I said.

"I bet he did. What a knight in shining armor."

"Willow, we won't force you. You don't have to do this if you don't want to."

She held my gaze. "I don't *want* to do anything. I have to."

After a long pause, Jamie cleared his throat. "We can do the interview tomorrow," he said. "We'll film you here. Violet and I will be with you the whole time."

Jamie drove us back to the hotel, where we would call Eliza and tell her that the interview was set for the next day. But in those final moments of quiet in the car, I felt an anticipatory letdown. Wrung out by the heat, plagued by a thumping headache. Willow, in her little white house. There it was: the answer to the question we'd been chasing for months. It was both sadder and more ordinary than anything I'd been expecting. The world leaves people broken, but they find a way to put themselves back together again.

Jamie interrupted the silence. "That poor woman," he said.

"I was surprised," I said. "Weren't you? Her house. The business degree."

"That's what worries me. The tough guy act. It's not real."

"It seemed real to me."

He shook his head. "It's going to crack at some point. You don't go through what she went through without a reckoning."

"So, what, you think she's doomed? She can never have a normal life?"

"I'm just saying, she needs to take the measure of what happened to her. Didn't that freak you out? She should be angry. She should be *pissed*. But it's like she's been lobotomized."

"Maybe she already dealt with it and now she's fine." For some reason, Jamie's reasoning irritated me. I wanted to believe in Willow's life. I wanted to believe in the possibility of her reinvention. "Maybe she managed to put everything behind her."

"Maybe," Jamie said. "But I doubt it."

CHAPTER TWELVE

BACK IN NEW YORK, we showed the raw interview footage to Eliza and Rebecca. Rebecca grew wide-eyed at Willow's graphic descriptions of the doctor's violence. Eliza wore a grim frown, which deepened as it went on.

"What a fucking bastard," Rebecca said, when it was over.

"It's awful," Eliza said. "It makes you sick."

"I was sure she was going to bail on us," Jamie said. "She almost backed out that morning. Violet calmed her down."

"She wanted to be sure it was worth it," I said. "That her talking would actually help to change something. Not just result in her getting sued."

"Christ Almighty. If a story like this doesn't change something," Rebecca said, "then I don't even know why we're here."

Ginny joined us later that afternoon. In the conference room, Eliza and Rebecca showed her everything we'd assembled: the interviews with Willow, George and the other sources, the scattered bits of evidence that finally added up to something coherent, and damning.

"When are we going to Danner for comment?" Ginny said, clasping her hands atop the table. Her lack of emotion was normal. Rebecca got hot with outrage, Eliza was fiercely competitive, but Ginny was the ballast that kept the whole ship steady.

"Monday," Rebecca said. "We'll give them twenty-four hours."

I spent the weekend working. There were several producers on the story by now, but it didn't stop me from obsessing: double- and triple-checking every fact and quote, asking the beleaguered editor to try dozens of variations. I sat with the writer who was polishing Rebecca's script, even though Rebecca would inevitably rewrite it herself just before airtime. On Sunday evening, Eliza stopped by the office and saw me at my desk.

"You're still here?" she said. "Violet, you have to get some sleep."

"I'm just checking one more thing," I said.

"Direct orders," Eliza said, placing a hand on my shoulder. "We're in good shape. It's diminishing returns at this point."

Darkness came early in November. I wrapped my scarf tight as I walked home, shoved my hands deep in my pockets. It was good to breathe the fresh air, to watch taxis speeding through intersections, to smell the sweet roasted chestnuts, to let normal life serve as distraction from the somersaults in my stomach. The thought of waiting another two days for the story to air was almost unbearable. I was confident that the story was good, that it was important, that it was ready. What I didn't know was how the world would react to it.

When I got home, Stella was in the living room, paging through the Sunday Styles. She pretended to be interested in the articles, but really she was just looking for pictures of herself amid that week's social scene. "*There* you are," she said. She folded the newspaper, a perfect facsimile of a responsible adult. "You've been ignoring my texts all weekend."

"I've been a little busy," I said. How much had changed from years ago, when I was alone in this apartment, eagerly waiting for Stella to text me back.

"Hungry?" she said.

"Yeah," I said. I hadn't eaten since breakfast. "Starving, actually."

"Good," she said. "Let's go out."

On the walk to the restaurant, Stella huddled close, her arm looped through mine. She smelled like the sweet chemical tinge of hairspray from her hit that morning, and the same musky perfume she'd worn for the last seven years. The bistro was on a quiet street near our apartment. It was authentically French, the kind of place that had no menu, just a chalkboard listing the day's items. We ordered a bottle of Burgundy, and when the waiter filled our glasses, Stella lifted hers to touch mine.

"It's been a million years since we did this," she said.

"Well, we've both been busy," I said. "Occupational hazard, I guess."

She tilted her head. "You know, Violet, you seem different."

"What do you mean?" I took a chunk of bread from the basket, spreading it with a thick coat of butter. Stella wouldn't touch it; she was exceptionally weight-conscious these days. She subsisted mostly on wine, lettuce, and green tea.

"I always thought we were the most important thing in each other's life," she said, gesturing across the table. "This. Our friendship."

"Of course this is important."

"But I feel like you don't *love* me anymore." She furrowed her forehead sulkily as she sipped her wine. It was manipulative, but nonetheless it worked.

I sighed. "It's temporary, Stell, I promise. The story airs on Tuesday."

"Why won't you tell me what it is?"

When I hesitated, she rolled her eyes. "Seriously? Half the

newsroom must know by now. I saw you guys meeting with Ginny. So you can tell Ginny, but you can't tell me?"

"Well..." I said. Once upon a time, Stella and I had told each other everything. And she was right: word was getting out, she'd know the story soon enough. "Okay. But promise me, you have to keep this close to the vest."

"Duh," she said. "So what is it?"

She listened attentively as I talked. Her eyes grew wider and wider. She didn't interrupt, which was an accomplishment for her. "Wow," she said, at the end. "Wow. That's *crazy*. Danner—that's, like, a household name."

"Yup. And it's been going on for years. The whole company is rotten." A flash of worry, remembering the picture in Stella's father's study. "But Stella, listen. You really can't tell anyone. Especially not your family."

She arched an eyebrow. "Give me more credit than that."

"I know, it's just that—"

"I'm a little offended by your implication," she said. "But never mind. This is impressive, Vi. You did all of this? You tracked these people down—the girl in Florida, everything?"

"Not alone, of course. Jamie has been a huge help."

"Speaking of Jamie," she said.

My stomach twisted. "Is everything okay?"

She looked puzzled, almost annoyed. "Why would you say that? Everything is great. In fact, what I was going to say is that—"

"Excuse me?" An older woman approached our table, with a big smile and the excited air of someone overstimulated by visiting New York for the first time. "Excuse me, Stella Bradley? I'm a huge fan. I just love you on KCN."

"Oh, wow," Stella said. "I love meeting my fans."

"Could I"—the woman blushed—"could I have a picture with you?"

"Of *course,*" Stella said.

"Do you mind?" the woman said, handing me her phone. "Oh, thank you so much," she said afterward, her adoring gaze fixed on Stella. "I just *love* you, I really do. I had to come over and say hello."

"You're so sweet," Stella said. "Enjoy your dinner. And don't skip dessert! The crème caramel is amazing. It's my favorite."

The woman blushed again. "Oh, but I'm on Weight Watchers. I can't spare the points."

"I won't tell," Stella said, raising an eyebrow. "If *you* won't tell."

The woman laughed. "This is the highlight of my whole trip! Stella Bradley. I can't believe it. You are just so wonderful. God bless you, honey."

"God *bless* me?" Stella said, after the woman walked away. "Blech."

"You're pretty good at faking it," I said.

"So where was I?" Stella poured more wine into our glasses. "Right—Jamie. He told me he wanted to talk."

"Oh." I coughed. A sharp flake of baguette caught in my throat.

"Yeah." Her eyes glimmered. "You don't schedule a talk, not unless it's major. We're having a late dinner on Tuesday. He told me to set aside the night."

I gulped water from my glass, attempting to dislodge the painful lump.

"I have no idea what it is," Stella continued. "No, that's not true. I have a few theories. You want to hear them? I bet he's asking me to move in. Don't you think that's the most likely thing? Although, you know, it did occur to me that he might ask me to marry him. But then I thought, that's crazy. That's way too fast. Right?"

"I don't know, I—"

"Or maybe not. I'm so curious!" Stella's laughter was thin and giddy. She was not good at recognizing her own emotions and was probably mistaking her anxiety for excitement. "He's been acting so nervous lately. I mean, it's been over a year. That's not actually that fast, is it? And wait a second." She narrowed her eyes. "Are you in on this? On whatever he has planned?"

"I promise you, I'm not."

She smiled. "Well, you'd have to say that no matter what, wouldn't you?"

On Monday morning, I made the call to Danner's public relations team, running through the litany of allegations and asking for their comment on each one. If the woman on the other end of the phone was surprised, she didn't betray it. "I'll have someone get back to you," she said crisply. "Could you please spell your name for me?"

"How'd it go?" Jamie said, after I hung up.

"Cool as a cucumber," I said. "I have to say, it was weirdly anticlimactic."

"So they have twenty-four hours to comment, otherwise we're going ahead."

"And what do we do now?" I said.

"We wait," Jamie said.

The day passed with excruciating slowness. I managed to get through all of my work—calls, e-mails, follow-ups, fact-checks—and it was still only noon. I was either insanely productive, or I was losing my mind.

"How do you stand it?" I said to Jamie, who was calmly reading a report about cancer research. He was making notes and highlighting things, engaging his brain in a level of deep thinking that was currently inconceivable to me.

"This is your first real baby." He didn't look up from the document. "The second one's less exciting, I promise."

Throughout the day, I caught glimpses of the KCN feed on

screens in the newsroom. Promos for the story were running during commercial breaks. Rebecca was going to appear on KCN's morning show to tease the story. She was also planning to tip to it at the end of that night's broadcast. Hank, the floor director, let me watch from inside Studio B.

"And be sure to tune in tomorrow night," Rebecca said, as the D block edged toward the close, "when we'll take you inside the explosive story of how far one Fortune 500 company was willing to go to increase their profits. You won't want to miss it. Until then, I'm Rebecca Carter. Thank you for watching, and we'll see you tomorrow. Good night."

"Clear," Hank yelled.

Rebecca's smile vanished. She glared into the camera. "Who the hell booked that idiot? I told you a thousand times I can't stand those people from the Heritage Foundation."

The guest in the last segment had been particularly pompous, extolling the virtues of privatizing Social Security. Rebecca kept her cool during the interview, but if you knew what to look for, her twitching frustration was obvious. She shook her head at whatever Eliza was saying into her ear. "I don't give a shit, Lizey. Never again, got it?"

Rebecca yanked out her earpiece. She spotted me as she made for the studio door. "Was that guy as big a blowhard as I thought he was?"

"Worse, actually," I said. "You should read his latest white paper."

"I've had enough masochism for one day, thank you," she said, as we walked up the stairs from the studio, back to the newsroom.

Eliza was waiting outside Rebecca's office. "You were good tonight," she said. "That color really works on you."

Rebecca glanced down at her hot pink blouse. "I hate this. I look like Barbie."

"Pink tests well," Eliza said. "The viewers think it makes you look sassy."

"Jesus Christ, Eliza, are you *trying* to kill me?"

Eliza smiled. "Maybe just a little."

She followed Rebecca into her office. A moment later, their laughter echoed into the bullpen. With Rebecca and Eliza, there was always a clean separation between their professional rancor and their friendship. They could yell at each other, no-holds-barred, but within a minute or two, it was like nothing had happened. For this dynamic to work, the two of them had to be equally and fully confident in themselves. Both Rebecca and Eliza knew how good they were. And I suspect that each believed—in her heart of hearts—that she was slightly smarter than the other. But only slightly. Close enough that no one else would notice. This led to a certain generosity in their friendship, a constant forgiving of the other person. Jealousy was a non-factor, because why be jealous when you knew that you had it better?

Later that night, as the office was emptying out, my phone rang. It was a blocked number. "*Frontline,*" I said. "This is Violet Trapp."

"They only gave me your number." The woman's tone was icy and impatient. "I need to speak to Eliza Davis."

"Can I ask what this is about?"

"Put me on with Eliza."

"I'll have to check—"

"*Now,* please."

I punched the hold button and stuck my head into Eliza's office. "Call for you on line one," I said.

She glanced at the clocks on her wall—New York, Los Angeles, London, POTUS—and then raised an eyebrow. "Someone from Danner?"

"I think so. I tried to ask, but—"

"It's just an ego thing," Eliza said. "They want to talk to the person in charge. Makes them feel better. Here, sit down."

Eliza pressed the blinking button and put the call on speaker. "This is Eliza," she said.

"Eliza. This is Mary. I'm the head of communications here at Danner."

"What do you have for us, Mary?"

"These are serious allegations you're making. We don't take any of this lightly."

"I should hope not."

"We believe there has been a fundamental misunderstanding. This story doesn't reflect the truth, which is that the culture of Danner is a healthy and supportive one, for all employees. There were a few reckless actors, driven by greed, who did unforgiveable things. We have every intention of dealing with this in a manner that reflects the severity of their actions."

"Is this your statement? Should I be writing this down?"

"I'm doing you one better. Our CEO wants to sit for an interview. He was extremely upset by these allegations, and he feels that he should explain Danner's side of the story."

"Okaaaay," Eliza said. "But this wouldn't be softball."

"Nothing is off limits," Mary said. "We only have one condition. We get to select the interviewer."

"It would be Rebecca, obviously."

"We had a different person in mind."

"You know that Rebecca will give him a fair shake."

"It has to be Stella Bradley," Mary said.

"*What?*" Eliza said.

"Oh my God," I whisper-choke-coughed, but Eliza waved at me to shut up.

"Stella Bradley. He likes her work."

"Stella Bradley is approximately ten years old."

"She's an excellent interviewer, and from what I understand, she's a rising star at KCN. Your bosses probably wouldn't be happy to hear you speaking about her in that way."

"I don't give a shit what they think. Mary, come on."

"I'm serious." There was a long pause. "It's Stella, or no dice."

Eliza pressed her index fingers against her temples. "She may not be available on such short notice. She could be out on assignment."

"I have a feeling she'll make herself available for an opportunity like this."

Eliza stared at her phone, at the digital readout that showed the seconds ticking by. "Okay. I'll talk to my people and call you back."

After the call ended, Eliza was quiet. My heart was pounding.

"Eliza," I said, my voice high and shaky. "This isn't a good idea. We can't do this."

She looked up at me, quizzically. "I thought you two were friends."

"We are," I said. "But this just isn't—"

"It doesn't matter," Eliza said. "We have to take this seriously. Can you find Rebecca and Jamie? And I'll get Ginny on the phone."

"I don't like this, Gin," Rebecca said. We had assembled in her office, and she was seated behind her desk, talking to the speakerphone. "Why does he get to call the shots?"

"We have to let Danner respond to these allegations." Ginny's voice was cool and controlled. "It's their right, and our duty. It would be irresponsible to run the story without it."

While Ginny spoke, Rebecca pressed the mute button. "What the fuck, Lizey? When have you known Ginny to give a plum like this to some JV player?"

"You know how Ginny is," Eliza said. "Stella's one of her favorites."

"This is bullshit," Rebecca muttered. She unmuted the call, and said, "Yeah, okay, I hear what you're saying. If you think this is the right thing to do."

"Thank you, Rebecca," Ginny said. "I knew you'd understand. Eliza, you'll call them back? And someone will get hold of Stella?"

"Violet can wrangle her," Eliza said. "Then let's regroup, okay?"

When I texted Stella, she was just wrapping up a hit in the 9 p.m. hour. Several minutes later, she arrived at the newsroom, looking especially glamorous in her full hair and makeup. Exactly like the person you'd want conducting a high-powered interview with a CEO. "What is it?" she said to me and Jamie. "You didn't say in your text."

"Let's go into Eliza's office," Jamie said. "She'll want to explain it herself."

When I didn't follow them, Stella said, "Aren't you coming?"

"Some stuff I need to catch up on," I said, my jaw clenched tight.

Jamie paused for a moment, looking back at me. He knew exactly how much this was crushing me. He also knew how pointless it was to fight their decision. "I'm sorry," he mouthed, his eyes sympathetic.

When Stella emerged from Eliza's office a few minutes later, she was grinning from ear to ear. "Holy shit," she said. "Violet. *Holy shit.* You heard, right?"

"Can I talk to you?" I took her hand and dragged her toward the kitchenette. This was my last-ditch attempt. If I couldn't stop this from happening, Stella still could. I jabbed at some buttons on the coffee machine, hoping the noise of it would cover our conversation.

"You can't do it," I said. "Please."

"What are you talking about?"

"The interview. Say no. Say you're not comfortable with it."

"Are you insane? This is, like, career-making. This is my big break."

"This is supposed to be *my* big break," I said. "It's my story."

"It's not *your* story. It's KCN's story." Stella put her hands on her hips. "You should know that, Violet. And this is very selfish of you. Why aren't you happy for me?"

"Because you're going to get all of the credit," I said, my voice splintering.

What was I hoping for? If she wasn't going to change her mind, at least I wanted her to admit to the unfairness. She would have done that, in the past. *I know this sucks. I wish it hadn't worked out this way.* The words running through my head were too pathetic to say out loud: *You're my friend, Stella. You're supposed to love me. What happened to us?*

She smirked. "Well, I'm the one who landed us this interview, right?"

The interview was scheduled for 2 p.m. the next day, giving us just enough time to cut the tape and edit the package before broadcast. I knew the story better than anyone, so it was my job to brief Stella ahead of the interview. As the night went on, the newsroom emptied. Eventually it was only the guy at the overnight desk and us in the conference room, papers and coffee cups scattered across the table.

"Say that one more time," Stella said, around 3 a.m.

"Danner's market cap increased to $150 billion last year."

"Wait, slow down. Market cap? What's that?"

I was tempted to slam my forehead against the table. It was like that all night: stop, start, stop. Either Stella was being extra diligent, or she was in way over her head. And which scenario was worse? That she blew the interview and the story along with it—or that she nailed it?

The next morning, Stella had a rack of clothing wheeled into her office. She enlisted Ginny's help in selecting the right outfit: she had to look authoritative and tough, but not too tough, because she also had to be a stand-in for the regular viewer at home. Ginny, president of KCN, undoubtedly had more important things to do than parse wrap dresses and cap sleeves. But she didn't seem to mind. As Stella held up options, pressing them against her torso, Ginny's affectionate gaze was like a scene from a gauzy movie: a mother watching her daughter trying on wedding dresses, the big day on the horizon.

"Let's never forget," Jamie said. "We're the real story, not them."

"Huh?" I'd been staring through the frosted glass walls of Stella's office.

"How is it possible you've never seen *Broadcast News*?"

I shook my head. "Sorry. I'm spacing out."

"You don't want that," Jamie said, nodding in Stella's direction. "It's a shitty bargain. The second you appear on camera, you've got a giant target painted on your back. That's why they're all so insecure, you know. They know people are gunning for them to screw up."

"It's not like I wanted the interview for myself," I said. "I just don't want her to have it."

"You have to let it go," he said. "This is too important for that."

I had heard it said that there were only so many stories in the world. That everything could be distilled to an archetype. The hero embarks on a journey. Boy meets girl. The fatal flaw leads to tragedy. I wondered about the truth of this. Did every story follow these patterns because there were, in the end, only so many paths that human behavior could take? Or was it that the storytellers were responding to the demands of the audience?

See, the demands were obvious to us—we knew exactly what people liked to watch, and what they didn't. The ratings bore that out, every single week. The audience liked clean takeaways. They liked black-and-white, heroes and villains. They liked the truth, but only kind of; they liked the truth packaged in a way to make them feel better about their own lives. Too much murkiness, and they are reminded of their own murk: their own mistakes, their own shortcomings, the times they, too, misbehaved and mistreated others. Those stories didn't rate well. If you wanted people to watch, if you wanted to win the demo and get the blockbuster numbers that your bosses demanded, you needed a story with a good ending.

And Stella had delivered that. Jamie field-produced the interview, and after several hours in the edit room, he emerged looking exhausted but relieved. "It's good," he said. "I was worried we'd have to redo the entire package, but the interview slots in neatly. It works."

"Nice job, guys," Eliza said, as she walked past. "I just watched it. It's almost like that interview was exactly what the story was missing." She tapped her watch. "Ten minutes till show time."

The second half hour of the broadcast was devoted to the Danner story. It was my name and Jamie's name that appeared after "Produced by" in the corner of the screen, and it was Rebecca's voice that narrated over the B-roll. But it was when Stella and the CEO appeared on-screen that the energy changed. Everyone in the newsroom stopped talking and typing. They stared at the TV, rapt with attention.

Whatever that thing is, I had once said to Jamie, *I know I don't have it.*

Stella asked the questions in a stern but fair-minded way, her head tilted at a thoughtful angle. The CEO leaned forward, contrite pain on his face. "Look," he said, "I'm the father of two beautiful teenage girls. They are the strongest, smartest people I know." It was a horribly hackneyed line, but when I glanced around the room, no one else was rolling their eyes. "Violence against women demeans all of our sisters and wives and daughters," he continued. "The thought of it, frankly, makes me sick to my stomach. We will do everything in our power to prevent it from ever happening again. Not just in our industry, but in any industry."

The other parts of the segment—the interviews with George and Willow, footage of the hotel with Rebecca's voice-over describing the assault—had been significantly reduced to make room for Stella's interview. My stomach sank as it went on. The whole tenor of the story changed. Sin, repent, repeat. It was the most basic kind of story, the kind the audience loved most. The interview was what everyone would talk about the next day—not Willow, not the other girls. They wouldn't be remembered for more than a few minutes.

Stella pressed the CEO just enough to deliver some sizzle. "But how could you let this happen?" she said. "You're in charge. Doesn't the buck stop with you?" I blinked, feeling hot tears in my eyes. The meager territory I had claimed as my own, the little patch of land free from Stella Bradley's shadow—it was gone, invaded, colonized. Our friendship only worked when we had our own turf. But now Stella had discovered the thrill of a big story. The appeal of the nice guy at the next desk over. I would never get these things back, not with her around.

After the story ended, over the loud sound of the newsroom applauding, I said to Jamie, "You can't honestly say that was an improvement over what we had before."

He raised an eyebrow. "Of course it was. Do you know what I wanted to know, after we reported the story? So what. So what's going to change? What's Danner going to do about this? And now we've got that answer."

"But it lets them off the hook. It makes them look good."

"How does this make them look good? Everyone just learned that Danner was systematically enticing doctors with prostitutes."

"And we gave them a platform to gloss over all of that."

"It's not our job to have an agenda against them," Jamie said. "Our job is to report on what really happened. That includes covering their response."

After a beat of silence, Jamie said, "Look. I know you're frustrated by the Stella thing. But you still produced a great story. This is still your moment."

It was a nice thing to say, but it wasn't true. The applause wasn't for me, nor was the champagne after the broadcast. Stella swept through the newsroom toward us, receiving a stream of compliments on the way. She threw her arms around Jamie. "My agent already e-mailed. NBC and CNN want a meeting. Can you believe it?" She laughed with delight. "Are we still going to dinner?"

"Oh," Jamie said. He stepped back. "I figured you'd want to stay and celebrate. We can have dinner another night, right?"

Stella looked confused, but at that moment, Ginny Grass came over. "Oh, *Stella*. My God. You were fabulous. We need to talk." Ginny rested a jewel-heavy hand on Stella's forearm. "We're adjusting our lineup, and I have something in mind for you."

Stella smiled. Her contract was set to expire at the end of the year. She held the best cards at the table.

"Let's have lunch this week," Ginny said. "Better to talk somewhere more private."

Ginny kept her hand fixed possessively on Stella, like she was the owner of a Thoroughbred that had just won the Kentucky Derby. Which, I suppose, she was. Rumor had it that the bosses wanted a new host for KCN's morning show. The executives had cycled unsuccessfully through a series of bland anchors.

They needed someone with personality, with star quality, someone relatable to a millennial audience. Stella fit the bill. She
was twenty-six years old. She would be the youngest anchor in
KCN's history.

On Wednesday, I had an appointment to meet with a broker. I
explained my situation: I'd had a roommate for the last three
years, but now I wanted—needed—my own apartment. Where I
wouldn't have to worry about the other person railroading my
career.

The broker's offices were depressing and sweatshop-like, in a
nondescript part of Midtown. Low-walled cubicles that were completely anonymous, nothing except a computer and a business-
card holder. The broker had responded to my e-mail in about
thirty seconds.

"Hmm," she said. "With your budget, you're not going to find
much in Manhattan. Maybe a studio, way uptown."

"Uptown is fine."

"How about this?" she said, turning her screen toward me.
"This is a good example of what you can expect for your price
point. Up near St. Nicholas Park."

I squinted. The pictures were small and fuzzy, like they'd been
taken with a ten-year-old flip phone. The apartment was one
room, a minuscule galley kitchen along one wall, a door that
presumably led to the bathroom. "Oh," I said.

"You're on the sixth floor, so you get good light."

"The sixth floor?"

"Actually—whoopsie," the broker said. "Never mind. Looks
like that one is in contract already. And they got more than the
listing price. Wow. Okay, let's try again."

On the walk back to the office, I wondered if I was being
rash. The places were awful, and multiples more expensive than
my $750 rent. Seven fifty was a lot to me, but pennies to the

Bradleys. I often thought about those checks going into their bank account, barely changing the balance, a few raindrops falling on the Atlantic Ocean. But they always cashed the check promptly, and the one time I was late to send it in, Anne had sent me a precisely worded reminder on the second day of the month. Would the Bradleys be offended when I left, after so many years of treating me like family and subsidizing my rent? Would Stella?

But for the first time, those questions seemed stupid. Naive, misguided. I finally saw how things were. Had Stella let our friendship stand in the way of an opportunity? Of doing what was best for her?

On Thursday night, Stella went out to dinner with Jamie and was planning to stay at his place. I had been sound asleep when, around 4 a.m., there was a crash down the hallway.

I opened my eyes. There was another crash. Thudding footsteps. My heart started pounding. When I stood up from my bed, my legs were shaking. Another *bang*. The footsteps were getting louder. Back in Florida, my father had always kept a gun in the house. I cursed my younger self for ever judging him about this. Right now, all I wanted was a gun.

More crashing, more thumping. How had this person gotten past the doorman? Maybe they wouldn't make it back here. Maybe I'd be okay if I hid in the closet. I had my phone unlocked, about to dial 9-1-1, when I heard the voice.

"Violet!" she shrieked. "VIOLET!"

"What the FUCK!" I flung open the door. "You almost gave me a heart attack!"

Stella stood at the end of the hallway, silhouetted by the light from the living room. "What are you doing?" I said. "Why aren't you at Jamie's?"

Up close, I saw that the living room was a disaster zone. Framed pictures had been smashed. A lamp had been knocked over, its bulb shattered. Stella collapsed on the sofa, breathing hard, her face flushed red. "What happened?" I said.

"He broke up with me," she said. "*He* broke up with *me.*" Then she burst into tears.

I tiptoed through the broken glass—the framed photos of Stella and Jamie that had lined the mantel—and sat down. The bottoms of Stella's bare feet were cut and bloodied from the glass. When I put my hand on her back, her skin was flushed and sweaty through her blouse. After a long time, when her sobs finally slowed down, I said, "Do you want to tell me about it?"

Stella looked up. Her face was swollen and puffy. She rarely cried, and never like this.

She inhaled deeply. "I thought we were celebrating, you know?" she said. "We went to dinner at Daniel. We were talking about how great the ratings were, and I never thought"—her voice broke, a fresh spill of tears—"I never thought, for one second, *that's* where the conversation was going. I mean, what the fuck? Who breaks up with someone over a six-hundred-dollar dinner at Daniel?"

Granted, Daniel had been her idea. She'd snagged a last-minute reservation using Rebecca's name (again). Jamie never would have picked a place like that.

"I was so happy. I was *so* happy. Did you hear the ratings? Almost four million people watched. That's insane. Those aren't cable news numbers. It wasn't until dessert that I remembered Jamie had wanted to talk to me about something.

"So I asked him. Then he said, why don't we wait 'til we get home. I said, are you sure? But he was being all quiet and, like, *sketchy*. He wouldn't look at me."

"So you knew something was wrong," I said.

"I thought he was about to propose! The dinner and everything, acting weird. I thought he had a ring in his pocket. I'm serious. Don't look at me like that."

I rearranged my eyebrows, which had arched on their own accord.

"You probably think I'm so stupid," she snapped. "Well, fuck you, too."

"No! I'm just as surprised as you. That's all."

"*Ugh.*" She flung her arms out and whacked them against the back of the couch. "So, we're leaving the restaurant, and that's when he says it. He just doesn't think it's working. We're both so busy. Neither of us is making the other person a priority. Well, speak for your *fucking* self, Jamie. All I've done is prioritize him. I've bent over backwards to make that asshole happy. And this is how he repays me?"

This, I suppose, was the fundamental problem. Stella's charm, her glow, her energy—it was so powerful that anyone who stood close enough could feel it. People were happy when they were near Stella. She saw that, and she took credit for their happiness. So when the shtick eventually wore off, when a person started to see Stella for who she really was, she couldn't understand what had changed.

But the difference between me and Jamie? Jamie was brave enough to say it to her face. To cut bait, to make a clean break. Me, I didn't have those guts. Stella was the vine wrapped around the limbs of my tree, and even though I had branches that were dead and dangling and should have fallen off long ago, she kept them in place. Jamie was a better friend to me than Stella had ever been. In that moment, I should have defended him.

But no one ever said doing the right thing was easy. Instead, pathetically, I crinkled my forehead and said, "That's horrible, Stell. I'm so sorry."

She stood up and started pacing, ignoring the crunch of broken glass beneath her feet. Little bits of her blood smeared the rug. "What is wrong with him? Does he realize what he just threw away?" She stopped and put her hands on her hips. "Look at me. You're telling me Jamie Richter is going to do better than this?"

Her face changed, and she snapped her fingers. "This is some guy thing, isn't it? They get bored and they want to fuck someone new. He's going to get this out of his system, and then he'll come crawling back, but he can forget it. I'm not taking him back."

Over the years, I'd endured hours of Stella whining and complaining, but this was new. Raw anger. A wounded animal. Stella had a deeply rooted sense of self, a security and desirability that the world constantly confirmed back to her. But where life had failed to make a dent, Jamie had finally succeeded. Something at her very core had been disturbed.

"I have to pack," she said, all of a sudden.

"Why?" I said.

She pulled out her phone, and after a moment, she was barking into it: "This is Stella Bradley, I need my car brought up. A silver Mercedes SUV. License plate—" When the call ended, she threw the phone onto the couch and walked out of the room. "We're getting out of here," she called over her shoulder.

CHAPTER THIRTEEN

HER GRANDPARENTS HAD closed up the house after Columbus Day, but Stella had a key. She didn't tell them we were coming. She waved her hand and said, "I can't get into all of that with them."

I'd only been to Maine in the summers. Their small town looked different at this time of year. Stores that were cheery and bustling during the high season—buckets of cut flowers outside the grocer, cases of rosé stacked in the wineshop window, sweet yeasty scents from the bakery—were now closed and darkened. As we drove past the ice cream parlor, the T-shirt shop, the movie theater with faded posters of summer blockbusters, I wondered where everyone went. Were the baker and grocer and wine merchant still here, tucked away in their homes, living frugally through the off-season? What did they do, during the long winter months? The town was eerily quiet, the only open businesses the 7-Eleven and the motel near the highway. As Stella climbed out of the car to open the gate to her grandparents' compound, it struck me: in this deserted town, who were they trying to keep out?

The driveway was long, and when we reached the house a few minutes later, it, too, looked different. The lawn was patchy, the trees bare, the windows shuttered. The net had been taken down from the tennis court, and the flower beds were covered in burlap sacks. The house looked harsh and isolated without the soft, verdant beauty of summertime.

I shivered while we stood on the doorstep. When Stella finally found the right key and opened the door, an alarm started chirping. "Oh, shit," she said. "Oh, fuck."

"You don't know the code?"

"I used to." She was frozen, staring at the blinking panel on the wall.

"Shouldn't we call someone? Before it triggers—"

The alarm got louder. *Warning,* an automated voice said. *Warning.* Stella was just standing there, biting her lip. I started to say something, but she held up a hand, then leaned forward and punched in a six-digit code. A moment later, the alarm stopped.

"My dad's birthday," she said, exhaling.

Stella moved through the house, turning on the hot water heater, resetting the thermostats. "You remember that Christmas, the first year after college?" she said.

"Which one was that?"

"When my family ganged up on me and I came up here. I couldn't figure out how the heat worked. So I kept a fire going and slept in front of the fireplace. Did I ever tell you that?"

On the long drive from New York, the sun rising over Connecticut, stopping for gas with the morning rush on the Massachusetts Turnpike, Stella had been intensely quiet. She barely spoke a single word. Now her mood was different. Lighter. She seemed pleased to be back in familiar territory. She went from room to room, humming to herself, running a finger through the layers of dust that had accumulated on the tables and shelves.

"Aren't you going to get some sleep?" I said, following her into the kitchen.

"I'm not tired," she said. "Besides, I have to make some calls."

"To who?" I said. Stella had opened the liquor cabinet and was examining the contents. She shut the cabinet, waved a dismissive hand at me, and left the room.

In the guest room, I lay down in the dim afternoon light, the gauzy curtains pulled shut against the sun. My eyes were growing heavy when I heard Stella's footsteps in the hallway outside the door. Pacing back and forth, her voice sharp and irritated.

"I just needed to get away for a while," she said. "Mom. I'm *fine.*"

A pause. "God, no. Don't come here. Why would I want you around? That's the whole reason I left, don't you get it?"

Another pause. "Well, Violet doesn't really count. You know how she is. She always tags along."

After a while, the footsteps faded, the voice disappeared.

When I woke up in the darkness, my phone said it was 5 p.m.

"Stella?" I called, stepping out of the bedroom. The house was silent. The door to the master bedroom stood ajar. With the light spilling in from the hallway, I could make out a sleeping form on the bed. A glint on the nightstand, wine bottle and wineglass. The sound of Stella's steady breathing. I closed the door quietly and went downstairs.

There was a box of pasta and canned tomatoes in the pantry, and I made enough so that Stella could have the leftovers. In the living room, I turned on the TV, but the signal from the cable box was scrambled. The Wi-Fi didn't appear to be working, either, so my laptop was useless. The sole source of entertainment was a wicker basket full of old issues of *The New Yorker*, water-rumpled from last summer.

The evening crept by. After glancing up one too many times and jumping at my reflection in the dark windows, I'd finally drawn the curtains. The quiet house gave me the creeps. It was made worse by the fact that I didn't know why I was here. Like a bad riddle, or a video game: what was the goal, anyway? What was I playing for?

Around midnight, my phone buzzed. From Jamie: Where are you?

I had forgotten to tell him that I wasn't coming into work that day, but he could put two and two together. I explained the impromptu road trip, Stella's need to get away from it all. Back in the city by Sunday, I think, I texted.

There was comfort in knowing that, soon, this weekend would only be a strange memory. Sunday morning, we'd be in the car driving south. Monday morning, we'd be back in the office. It ran through my head as I splashed water on my face, rummaged through the linen closet for a towel, pulled back the covers on the guest bed: I had a life to return to. I would be done with this, soon enough.

My phone wasn't there when I reached for it. Darkness, disorientation, strange sounds from downstairs. I had no idea how long I'd been asleep.

This time, the door to the master bedroom stood wide-open, the lamps inside blazing. "Stella?" I said tentatively, peering in. The bedroom was empty, and a mess. The contents of her bag were splayed across the floor, there was a stain of red wine on the carpet near the bed, and several cigarettes were stubbed out on the windowsill.

The closet door was open, and it caught my eye. Inside the closet was a safe, and the safe was open, too. I took a step closer. The safe looked empty. I was curious what had been inside, although I wasn't about to crouch down and start examining it. What if she came in, and caught me snooping? When Stella was in a mood like this, anything could set her off.

But when I turned around, the answer was on the nightstand. Right next to the wineglass Stella had knocked over. A compact, metallic shape that clarified into a gun.

My heart thudded. Why did she need a *gun?*

Loud music was thumping through the ceiling. Downstairs, it smelled like cigarettes. I found Stella in the kitchen, perched on a stool at the counter. There was a bottle of vodka in front of her, an empty glass ringed with lipstick, a square of rolling paper that she was fashioning into a joint. She was wearing a silk bathrobe—shell pink with a pale lace trim, the knot lazily tied, the curve of her breast visible beneath the loose fabric. Jamie had bought it for her birthday just a few months ago. He'd asked for my help in picking it out.

"There you are," she said, raising her voice over the music. The deep bass caused the ceiling to vibrate. "I was wondering when you'd finally join us."

She stared skeptically at the faded pajama pants and oversize T-shirt I slept in. I crossed my arms over the lumpy, braless softness of my chest. "Us?" I said.

"You're very popular." She gestured with her cigarette to the counter: my phone. I must have left it on the couch. "Jamie hasn't responded to any of *my* texts. But maybe he doesn't need to talk to me. He has you. You can just tell him everything I'm doing."

"He only wanted to know why I wasn't at work."

"Well, why don't you call him?" she said. "Right now. Call him and explain."

"It's the middle of the night."

"I knew you'd say that," she said. "You always have an excuse, don't you?"

When I stepped forward, Stella snatched my phone away. "Not so fast," she said. Then she laughed. "You do realize you're a guest in this house, Violet," she said. "You have to do what I ask. It's only the polite thing."

"Give it back."

"What else is in here, hmmm?" Stella said. "Your texts with Jamie. Your e-mails. Everything you've been saying behind my back."

"You're being paranoid," I said. A picture of Willow flashed through my mind, in her little house outside Panama City. The clean living room, the business classes, the gun she slept with. I felt a smoldering curl of anger. There were people who actually needed protection. People who actually feared for their safety. To Stella, this was all just a game.

"Why are you here?" she said. "Really, Violet, why?"

"Because you asked me to come with you," I said. "Seriously. Give it back."

"Did I?" She tilted her head. "I don't remember asking you to come. But there you were, with your sad little duffel bag. You just can't let it go, can you?"

"I'll leave if you want me to leave."

"Ugh," she said. "See, this is your problem. You're no fun. You give up so quickly."

"Jesus, Stella, what's *fun* about this?"

She looked momentarily confused. She was actually *surprised* that I wasn't going along with her routine, despite how twisted it had become. In the time she took to gather herself, the phone in her hand buzzed. My phone. A smile spread across her face. "Well, well, another text from Jamie. Ahem," she said. Then, in a simpering voice: "Let me know how you're holding up."

"So I guess he's awake," Stella said. "Should I call him, Violet? Should we just—"

I lunged for the phone. I managed to grab Stella's wrist but she twisted it away and sprang up from the stool, which tipped over and hit the tiled floor with a loud smack. She ran through the door and into the cold night air. "What are you doing?" I shouted, but she was already halfway down the sloping lawn.

The frozen grass was cold and rough against my bare feet as I ran after her. At the bottom of the hill, she reared her arm back and threw the phone as far as she could.

The night was dark. Cloud cover, no moonlight. I couldn't see where it had landed.

"You want it so bad?" She spun around. "Go find it."

"You're horrible," I said, as she walked past me, back to the house.

"Fuck you," she shouted over her shoulder. "Do something by yourself, for once."

In the summer, there were buses in town that ran south to Portland and Boston, but service ended after Labor Day. There was a local taxi service, but when I called that Saturday morning, their phone just rang and rang. Without a car, you were virtually trapped.

And the next morning, when I woke up, the driveway was empty. Stella's pattern was to run away after a fight, lick her wounds and disappear for a while. Hours, or days, depending on how much she wanted to punish the person who had mistreated her. She wasn't answering her phone, but she surely wasn't gone for good. Her clothing was scattered across the bed, her shoes across the floor. The nightstand still held her Cartier watch, and the gun.

Over the years we had argued and bickered and squabbled, but never had we spoken so plainly. Never had we been willing to look directly at the problem, and call it what it was. Despite her paranoia, despite being stuck in this house, I felt strangely relieved. The friendship was ending. Even if Stella's star continued rising at KCN, that was fine. I could endure envy. It was the in-between that drove me crazy: pretending to love her, pretending to be happy for her, when the whole thing was a slow torture.

As the shadows grew long and the sun sank toward the

horizon, there was the crunch of tires over gravel and the slam of a car door. When Stella came into the house, she looked strung out. She'd slept even less than me that weekend. In the kitchen, she pulled a bottle of wine from the wine rack, and twisted the corkscrew into the neck. The cork emerged with a soft pop. She took two glasses from the cabinet, and held one toward me.

"Aren't you going to drink with me?" she said.

"I'm not really in the mood."

"Come on." Her tone was one part teasing, two parts pleading. "Be a friend."

A few minutes later, when she had emptied and refilled her glass for the first time, I said, "Do you want to talk about what happened last night?"

"Not really," she said. She pointed at my glass. "You need to catch up."

I took a small sip. The wine was expensive, set aside for a special occasion. But that was Stella's way. It didn't look like alcoholism when you were drinking fine wine instead of rotgut vodka. Money could disguise just about anything.

"Are we leaving tomorrow?" I said.

"I haven't decided yet," Stella said.

"Okay. I can find my own way home."

"I don't think so." Stella laughed harshly. "I think you do what I tell you to do."

She finished the bottle and drummed her fingers against the counter. "I'm bored," she said. She stood up, tucked another bottle of wine under her arm, put the corkscrew in the pocket of her jeans. "Come on."

"Where are you going?" I said.

"Jesus," she said. "When are you going to stop asking so many questions?"

It was dusk by now, the last light fading from the sky. I followed her down the sloping lawn, toward the water. The ocean was a deep, dark shade of blue. The wind had picked up, and there were whitecaps in the distance.

Attached to the dock was a boathouse, where the Bradleys kept their watercraft: kayaks, paddleboards, windsurfers, and the speedboat. Stella hauled the door open with a long, loud creak. Inside, the speedboat was rocking in its berth. Stella undid the ropes that tied it in place. The slosh of the water was louder in here, echoing off the walls. It smelled like cedar and paint and gasoline. Stella pointed at the door at the other end of the berth, which rolled up onto a track, like a garage door. "Get that open, will you?" she said.

"Is this such a good idea?" Nightfall, the wine, the whitecaps.

"Just do it," she said.

Stella climbed into the boat and started the engine. Even half drunk, she deftly maneuvered it out of the berth. I hesitated for a moment. But when you were with Stella, it was easier to go along. To get swept up, and follow the path of least resistance. I knew that better than anyone.

She was glaring at me, waiting. At the last second, I jumped into the boat.

Stella revved the engine. The boat accelerated so suddenly that I was thrown from my feet. She whooped with glee, and behind us the lights from the house shrank to a pinprick. The high whine of the engine was punctuated with the *thunk, thunk, thunk* of the boat slamming against the swelling waves. By now we were far beyond the shelter of the peninsula, in the open ocean. Twilight had given way to nightfall, the first stars glittering overhead. After a long time, Stella finally slowed down and cut the engine.

The silence came as a relief, and then a menace.

The only sound was the water slapping against the boat. Stella let go of the wheel and opened the wine she'd brought along. She drank directly from the bottle and, this time, didn't offer any to me. She stood in a wide-legged stance, her knees bending reflexively when the boat dipped up and down from the waves beneath.

Minutes passed. Finally, she said, "You knew, didn't you?"

"Knew what?"

"That Jamie was going to dump me."

And there it was: this whole weekend had been a game. A chance for Stella to bat me around, like a kitten with a ball of string. Who had held her as she sobbed on the couch? Who had been there for her, no matter what, over the last seven years? But it didn't matter. It was easier for Stella to blame someone else for this anguish. It was easier to ignore her broken heart and focus instead on my betrayal.

I chose my words carefully. "I knew that he wasn't happy."

"And you let me embarrass myself," she said. "You should have told me, Violet."

"It's not my business. I didn't want to interfere."

Stella laughed. "Now you're definitely lying. You interfere all the time."

"What are you talking about?"

"It's creepy. Everyone sees it except for you. You've been following me around for *years*. You think it doesn't freak me out? The way you've attached to my family like a leech? I mean, seriously. With you around, I feel like I need a goddamn *gun* to protect myself."

She took another long pull of wine. "Aren't you going to say anything?" she said. Her voice was thick and slurry. "Aren't you going to defend yourself?"

"You're drunk," I said. "You're being an idiot."

"No. You're jealous. You're jealous of me and Jamie. You wanted him all to yourself. So you ruined it. This is your fault."

"He was my friend first, Stella."

"I knew it!" she shrieked. "I knew it. You've been jealous the whole time. But you realize that *I'm* the one he's been fucking."

"Stop it."

"*I'm* the one who's had his dick in my mouth every night."

"Shut up!" I shouted.

"Oooh, look. I made Violet Trapp mad!" Stella laughed. She took another swig of wine and wiped her hand across her mouth. Her gestures were getting looser, messier. "You think you're so smart. So in control. Don't you?"

"Not all of us can afford to have other people clean up our messes."

"That, see?" She pointed at me. "That's exactly what I'm talking about. You're so *smug*. Everyone's beneath you. No one is as smart as you. Well, then, riddle me this. Why did I get the Danner interview and you didn't?"

"Because you got lucky," I said. "Because pretty blondes rate well."

"Of course you would say that. But I made that happen. *Me*. It was all me."

"No, it wasn't, it was the—"

"Remember when you told me about the story, at the restaurant? And you made me *swear* not to tell anybody?" She smiled. Her teeth glowed white in the darkness. "That was a mistake, Violet. See, my father knows the Danner CEO. So I got in touch with him. I knew he would never agree to an interview unless it was with someone he could trust. And he trusts me. I planted the idea." She laughed. "Not bad, huh?"

The blood was roaring in my ears. My throat was tight, my eyes pricking with tears. The hatred I felt was like an annihilation. I had to get away from her. Not just now. Forever.

"Oh, little baby Violet." Her voice was a sickly sneer. "Am I going to make you cry? Am I being too mean?"

"Take us back," I said.

"Not until I feel like it."

I stood up. "Give me the keys."

She stepped back, pressed herself against the windshield. "Fuck off."

"Give them to me!" I shouted, grabbing for them. She yanked her wrist free from my grasp, then scrambled over the windshield, standing on the bow. Our friendship had devolved to one long game of keep-away. The boat was rocking side to side from the waves. She slowly stood from her crouch, straightening her legs, towering above me.

Stella dangled the keys with a jangling metallic sound. "You want them so bad?" she said. "But you wouldn't even know what to do with them. You're just a leech, Violet. You're a suck-up. You're the world's biggest fraud and everyone sees it."

What was even happening? I felt dizzy and light-headed, though I'd had no more than a few sips of wine. I clutched the edge of the boat to stay upright.

"Oh, sure," she said, her face shadowed in the starlight. "I've let you hang around. Because I'm *nice*. Because I *pitied* you. And I thought you'd show some pride, eventually. But you never did."

"Why, Stella?" I said. "Why are you saying this?"

"Because it's true!" she shouted.

A wave walloped the boat, knocking Stella from her feet. She grabbed the windshield to keep from falling overboard. The wind had picked up, and the waves were growing larger.

"Stella, *get down*," I said. "You're going to kill yourself."

But she had stood back up triumphantly, her loose bun unraveling, her hair blowing wildly in the wind. She had managed to hold on to the wine bottle this whole time, and now she lifted it, draining the last of the liquid, the glass reflecting the moonlight. She threw it overboard, and the bottle landed in the water with a loud *plunk*. I heard it, but I couldn't see it, because a cloud had moved in front of the moon. The night had gone pitch-black.

The waves crashed and sloshed against the boat. Bile churned in my stomach. "See," Stella said, her voice detached from her body in the darkness. "What I can't stand the most is that—"

It happened in slow motion. Like a dream, or a nightmare. A swelling wave passed beneath. The clouds moved; the moon reemerged. The boat tilted at a steep angle, the bow raked up. For a moment it looked like Stella might, miraculously, keep her footing, her bare feet affixed gecko-like to the sloping surface.

But then the boat reached the apex of its tilt, and as it crashed down, it launched Stella into the air like a catapult. When she came back down, her head hit the edge of the bow with a sickening *thunk*. Even in that split second, I saw her body go limp. She had been knocked out cold, just before she rolled into the dark water.

There was a thick pool of blood visible against the boat's white paint.

This was where instinct was supposed to kick in. A surge of adrenaline: haul her out of the water, stanch the bleeding, race back to shore. But there was nothing. No instinct, no urgency. Only the echo of the words she spoke moments earlier.

Leech. Suck-up. Fraud.

Why are you saying this?

Because it's true.

Leaning over the edge of the boat, at first I saw nothing. Then, the bubbles breaking on the surface. Then a movement in the water. A thrash. A pale white arm reaching blindly for the surface, looking for something to grab hold of. A body fighting to stay alive.

Sometimes, standing on the platform and waiting for the subway in New York, I'd feel the strangest impulse. The sparkle of headlights in the tunnel, the stirring air. As the subway roared into the station, I felt the urge to jump. It wasn't that I wanted to die. It was a kind of curiosity, testing the limits of personal freedom. What would it be like, to do the worst possible thing?

Well, what if you finally did heed that feeling? And not just for one brief moment. For another, and another, and another, until the moments stacked into measurable time. What if that impulse could be stretched from a point into a line? A black slash of finality. The *fin* of a conductor's baton. A heartbeat flattening into silence.

The thrashing gradually slowed. The bubbles broke less frequently, and then not at all. The surface of the ocean continued to slosh against the boat.

All you do is interfere, she said.

This time, I did nothing.

PART THREE

CHAPTER FOURTEEN

"ARE YOU OKAY?" the woman at the motel said. "Do you want me to call someone?"

"I just need a room," I said.

She squinted at my wet hair and red eyes and lumpy duffel bag. Then she stepped out from behind the front desk and peered through the window to the parking lot. "Are you sure he didn't follow you, sweetheart?"

"What?" I said. Her knowing look made it clear she took my confusion for denial. The implication finally clicked. "Oh, no, it's nothing like that. It's just...I had a fight with my best friend. She lives down the road. She kicked me out."

"Oh!" she said, visibly relieved. No shotgun vigil, no 9-1-1 on speed dial in case the abusive boyfriend showed up. "Well, you'll make up with her. I'm sure of it."

"I hope so." I attempted a smile.

"Just one night?" she asked. "We'll need a credit card for the deposit."

She studied my card. "Violet Trapp," she said. "What a lovely name. I had a cousin named Violet. You rarely hear that name these days." She handed back the credit card, and placed the room key on the desk, but kept her hand atop it. She had the distinctive curiosity of a postmenopausal, small-town gossip. "Honey, I have to ask, what were you doing around here at this time of year, anyways?"

My initial plan was to keep the story as simple as possible, answers stripped of detail to prevent further questioning. But there was my credit card, logged in the computer. The careful way she had enunciated my name. The security camera aimed at the front desk. Sooner or later, someone would uncover this particular moment in time. I had to make it look real.

"Her grandparents have a place here," I said. "We're from New York. We were just up for the weekend. She had a stressful week. Actually, her boyfriend just dumped her."

The woman frowned sympathetically. "And she took it out on you?"

"I guess so. She was in a terrible mood, and told me she didn't want me hanging around anymore. She wanted to be alone. So I decided to leave."

"Oh, honey, don't take it personally. There's nothing worse than a broken heart."

A lump formed in my throat. "I'm sure you're right," I said.

"You'll feel better after a good night's sleep," the woman said. "Your room is at the end, nice and quiet. Far from the road."

"Thanks," I said. My stomach grumbled. "Is there anywhere to get something to eat?"

"Best you can do is the gas station across the way." She nodded toward the road. "They have a 7-Eleven that's open all night."

I filled my arms with soda and chips and cellophaned pastries at the 7-Eleven, where the man behind the counter gave me the same appraising, sympathetic-but-skeptical look as the woman at the motel. "Don't get many strangers at this time of night," he said. But when I told him my story, it had a pleasing weight, a satisfying constancy. In the next twenty-four hours, I repeated it several times. To the taxi driver, who took me to the bus depot. The cashier selling the tickets. The person sitting across from me on the southbound bus. It was easy to remember, because it was so very close to the truth.

I was staying with a friend.

We had a fight, a bad one.

She wanted me to leave.

So here I am.

That's where the story always ended: with me, standing in front of whomever I happened to be speaking to. Unspoken was the coda, which—for the time being—only I knew to be true: *and that was the last time I ever saw Stella Bradley.*

I'd never subscribed to the idea of prophecy, of instructions delivered with a psychic thunderbolt: Joan of Arc seeing visions in the garden, presidential candidates claiming that God told them to run. The idea of a higher voice—God, or call it whatever you like—cutting through the daily mental noise to show the way seemed implausible at best, and a ruthless lie at worst. Why does anyone decide to lead a military uprising, or run for president? Because they want power. But it's unbecoming to state that so baldly. Anyone who said that God had spoken to them, I figured, was just looking for cover.

But on the boat that night, I understood how it might happen. After the thrashing stopped, my mind went perfectly quiet. Blank and still. And in that quiet, it was easy to listen to the one small voice that persisted. It was like driving through a desert with only static on the radio, and suddenly coming over a rise where the static gave way to a signal.

When people claimed to hear God speaking, this was what they really meant. The infinite branching possibilities of life had—for that moment, at least—been pruned away, leaving only one option. The path forward was clear and definite. At a pivotal moment, you knew exactly what to do. As I stood on the boat, the ocean slapping and sloshing against the hull, I experienced that feeling of profound relief. One might even call it ecstasy.

I waited for a long time to be sure she was really gone. But the night, despite the wind and waves, was ordinary and peaceful. The world looked no different than it had before.

After I was certain, I began to move quickly. The keys, which Stella had dangled above my head not thirty minutes earlier, had fallen near my feet when she was thrown overboard. It took a few minutes to get used to the boat's steering wheel and throttle. From the compass on the dashboard, I knew that I was pointed in the right direction—west, back toward the Bradley property—but I had to steer in a southwesterly direction to account for the strength of the current. Stella had taken us far offshore, and it was a long time before the lights of the house finally came into view.

When I approached the dock, there was a small pinging noise. There, on the bench seat behind me, was Stella's phone glowing in the darkness. It had just resumed contact with the cell towers. There were several texts on Stella's phone, from her parents and friends and Jamie. I unlocked the phone—her password was her birth year, backwards—and typed replies to each of the messages. Her texts were easy to mimic: lazy and short, affectless except for occasional strings of exclamation marks. The only thing I added was a hint of mystery at the end. Jamie had written to her: You should know that I still care about you and respect you. I don't want things to be weird for us at work. Violet-as-Stella replied: fine, but I don't, and you're still an asshole. we won't be seeing each other again, so save the crap for someone else.

Just as I was about to get rid of her phone, I paused. Even with my adrenaline surging and heart pounding, my mind was calm and rational. I opened her e-mail and spent a few minutes composing a message. Then I scrolled through her recent calls. There was a number, a local area code, that she had called several times in the last twenty-four hours. The man on the other end answered with a gruff "Yeah?"

"Hello?" I said. "Hello? Can you hear me?"

"Who is this?" the voice said.

"Hello?" I said. "You're breaking up."

I kept him on the line for almost a minute before he hung up. I did that a few more times, for good measure, until he eventually stopped answering.

The screen cracked easily under the heel of my boot. I stomped on the phone several more times. Then I picked it up and threw it into the water. My own phone had remained back at the house, which meant it wouldn't betray my movements.

There was a small towel tucked under the bench seat, and before climbing out of the boat, I used it to wipe down the steering wheel, the throttle, the edges I'd clung to in the tossing waves, and the pool of Stella's blood on the bow. After scanning the interior one last time and throwing the towel into the water, I stepped onto the dock and shoved the boat clear. The current was strong, and it quickly carried the boat away from the dock, the white speck diminishing until it vanished entirely.

The story was beginning to formulate in my head. What would Stella need, if she were running away? In the master bedroom, I cataloged her possessions. She had a few hundred dollars in her wallet. Surely she would go to the bank and withdraw as much as she could. But this didn't fit into my plan. Every ATM was equipped with a camera these days. And if Stella wanted to run away, if she really wanted not to be found, she would ditch her credit cards. But the cash in her wallet wouldn't get her very far.

I felt something like tenderness. As if I were truly gaming this out for her benefit. Poor Stella. Beneath her confidence, she was a girl who became easily overwhelmed. How many times had the world told her she was gorgeous and charming and dazzling? Enough times to hollow her out entirely. This was the ending she should have had—an escape from the manufactured pressures of her life. A chance to start over. If people were going to believe that she'd really made a break for it, she needed as much runway as possible.

The gun, glinting on the nightstand, reminded me. In the closet, the safe was still open. The real Bradley treasures were kept closer to home, in their Beacon Hill mansion or in the vault at their bank. But Grandma Bradley's one indulgence was fine jewelry, even up here in Maine. There, in a black velvet bag in the back of the safe: there was Stella's ticket out.

They glittered in my palm. A pair of diamond earrings, a few carats each. A tennis bracelet with a neat row of cushion-cut gems. And a ring, which I recognized from when the Bradleys entertained on a grand scale, hiring caterers and a string quartet while the guests dined at long tables on the lawn, overlooking the ocean. This was the ring that Grandma Bradley would wear on those occasions. A sapphire, hefty like a walnut and blue like the summer sky, ringed by a band of diamonds.

The jewelry was cool and solid in my hand as I closed the safe, pressed the lock button, and wiped it clean. When would anyone bother to check the safe—would it be days from now, weeks from now? I would have to remember to act surprised. *The diamonds were gone,* the Bradleys would say, worrying and speculating. *And so was the gun.*

My hair was tangled and my skin salty from the ocean air, so I took a scalding hot shower. I started to turn off the lights and thermostats, but then I thought, *what would Stella do?* That had to be my guiding mantra. Stella wouldn't bother to check every little thing. She would just *leave*. So the heat remained on. The occasional lamp stayed burning.

The walk to the motel took almost an hour. From a distance,

warm squares of light shone through the lobby windows, and the neon sign blinked vacancy. It turned out it wasn't so hard to cry on command. The water table was high, ready to reveal itself with just a little bit of digging. I cried so much that my eyes puffed and swelled. But it wasn't guilt or distress that I felt, so much as an overwhelming recognition.

You're a heartless snob, my mother once said. *You can't wait to get rid of us, can you?*

That dark impulse, which I'd suppressed for so long. Stella Bradley was dead, and I saw who I really was. Who I had always been. It was the first time in my life that I recognized what I was capable of. Death forces you toward honesty. There is always a perfect understanding between the killer and the killed.

————

Port Authority after midnight: the stores are closed, awaiting the morning rush. The alcoves and nooks near the heating vents are occupied by the sleeping bodies of homeless men. The fluorescent lights are set to a low hum, and the air smells cloyingly of fast food, with a tinge of sweat and garbage. The only motion came from those like me, passengers emerging from the end of long bus rides, moving like ghostly fish toward the exits of this strange aquarium.

But I didn't mind it. I didn't mind any of it. I had slept most of the way, and I was glad to be back in New York. When the cab drove south down Seventh Avenue in the earliest hours of Monday morning, all I could think was *I made it.* I meant this in a very simple sense. Two of us had left the city for Maine on Friday morning. One of us had come back. One of us had what it took to persist, and the other one didn't.

Pete, the doorman, was on duty that night.

"You have a good weekend, Miss Trapp?" he said, as he opened the door of my cab.

"I was in Maine with Stella. She's still up there."

"Nice to get away from the city," Pete said. "Have a good night, Miss Trapp."

I debated how to tell the Bradley family. It had to look real. If Stella had kicked me out and hinted at disappearing for a while, would I be surprised? Alarmed? Or would I think, this is just Stella being Stella? Nonetheless, I called Anne on my walk to work that Monday morning. It was mid-November, and the weather was persistently perfect. The trees held the last of their crimson leaves, crisp temperatures just right for sweaters and football. While waiting for Anne to pick up, I decided that I couldn't remember a more beautiful autumn.

"Violet?" Anne said, sounding out of breath. "I just got out of spin class."

"Oh, I'm so sorry to bother you. I just wanted to tell you about the weekend."

"Are you back from Maine? Stella made it sound like you were staying for a while."

"That's the thing. I'm back, but she's—well, we got into an argument on Saturday night. A pretty bad one. I got a motel room and came back on the bus yesterday. She's still up there. I mean, as far as I know."

"Oh, dear. Oh, Violet, I'm sorry."

"To be honest, Mrs. Bradley, she was seriously upset. Jamie breaking up with her...I think it came as a shock. She wasn't taking it well."

"I wish she had let me come up. The poor girl. She really can't handle this kind of thing by herself."

"I think she just wanted some space from it all, you know?"

"So she didn't say when she'd be coming home?"

"Not to me."

Anne sighed. "And she won't be in trouble at work?"

"Given the ratings on the Danner story"—this, this was the one moment I felt an unsettling flare of heat in my cheeks—"I'm guessing they'll be in the mood to forgive her."

"You'll let me know when you hear from her?"

"Of course. And I'm sorry, Mrs. Bradley, I don't mean to worry you. I just wanted—"

"No, no, I'm glad you called. Thank you, Violet."

Jamie's desk was empty when I arrived around 8:30 a.m. He, like most people in the newsroom, tended to arrive closer to 10. But the habits of my ambitious intern days had stuck. I drank my coffee and caught up on what I'd missed over the weekend. The major newspapers had all covered the Danner story. Danner's spin machine was in high gear, spokespeople reinforcing the message that the CEO had delivered in his interview. They were conducting an internal investigation; they would implement rigorous sexual harassment training; they would make sure this never happened again.

An e-mail pinged in my in-box. My chest tightened when I saw the sender—Willow, the woman in Florida. She had watched the story. It wasn't what she'd been led to believe. What had happened to her was just a footnote. Why, she wanted to know, *why* had I spent so long chasing her down and convincing her that she was the hinge to the whole thing?

I don't expect you to respond to this, she wrote in her e-mail. I could see her, leaning against the doorjamb in her white living room, digging her fingernail into the orange peel, looking at us with skepticism that was, in the end, completely justified. I assume you've moved on and you're already preying on some other helpless victim.

I jumped at the hand on my shoulder.

"Whoa," Jamie said, taking a step back. "What's wrong?"

"Nothing," I said, breathing hard. "You scared me."

"You're really pale."

"Well, you shouldn't sneak up on people like that."

"Let me guess. She said you're not allowed to talk to me anymore, is that it?"

"What?"

Jamie gave me a quizzical look as he dropped into his chair. "Stella."

"Oh," I said. "Oh, yeah. No. I mean, it's fine, we can talk, it's just—"

"Never mind." He shook his head. "Sorry, you're in an awkward position. I don't mean to put you in the middle of it."

I sighed. "I think it's too late for that."

We went to the cafeteria on the third floor to get coffee, and a modicum of privacy. Everyone in the newsroom knew about Stella and Jamie's relationship; it was ideal office gossip, self-contained and slightly illicit. We sat by the windows overlooking Sixth Avenue, people occasionally waving at us as they carried bagels and oatmeal back to their desks. As I told Jamie about the weekend, from Stella's return to the apartment in the early hours of Friday morning to her ultimate accusation on Saturday night, it struck me: had it really happened so fast? Less than forty-eight hours from when Jamie broke up with her to when she climbed atop the bow of the boat. The triangular dynamic of the past year had proved shatteringly fragile.

"And that's when she kicked you out?" Jamie said.

"She said I had sabotaged your relationship. That I was... jealous of you two."

Jamie's expression softened, briefly.

"I told her that was ridiculous, but she wouldn't believe me. She wanted me gone." It didn't feel like a lie. The night in Maine had gone one way, but it so easily could have gone another. "She couldn't stand being around me. That's what she said."

"Jesus." His face had closed off again. "She is a horrible person."

"Don't say that."

Jamie wrapped his hands around his coffee cup. He had removed the lid so the coffee would cool down faster. As he squeezed the sides of the cup, the liquid crept toward the brim. A taut meniscus stretched across the top. He was on the verge of spilling.

"Careful," I said.

He let go of the cup and put his hands flat on the table. "She is, Violet. You're allowed to get mad at her. *I'm* mad at her. She kicked you out? Who does that to their best friend?"

Before that afternoon's rundown meeting, Eliza caught my eye and beckoned me over.

"So you got a little R&R this weekend?" she said.

"I'm really sorry it was so last minute. I should have told you."

"You were up in Maine with Stella? Ginny forwarded me the strangest e-mail from her. It sounds like she's staying up there for a while."

"I think so. I'm not sure."

Eliza shook her head. "You know, Violet, you're really the one who deserves the week off. You've been killing yourself on the Danner story."

"Well, thank you, but I'd rather get back to work."

Eliza smiled. "I never know what to do with myself when I'm on vacation, either."

"I heard you once called into the control room from Maui," I said.

"It was Oahu," Eliza said. "It was our honeymoon. It's a good thing I did. This guy from the Council on Foreign Relations had hijacked the interview. Rebecca was like a deer in the headlights.

They should have pulled her out of there. She seems so in control, they can't always tell when she needs help." She arched an eyebrow. "But I can."

By now, the conference room had filled with the other producers. "Okay," Eliza said, clapping her hands for order, taking a seat at the head of the table. "Let's make this a quick one. Jamie, where are we on the quote from Sec Def's people?"

"No comment at this time," Jamie said. A former DoD employee was suing for discrimination—a man who claimed his female colleague had undeservedly taken the promotion he was in line for. He was, he said, a victim of affirmative action.

"Yeah, I wouldn't offer comment on that clown, either," Eliza said. "What else?"

The meeting only lasted ten minutes. It was one of those days when *Frontline* ran like a well-oiled machine, no last-minute catastrophes to derail our lineup. Our ratings had remained high through last week, after the Danner story aired on Tuesday night, and it buoyed the collective mood. On the whole, Rebecca tried to instill an attitude of indifference—"because what good is it," she always said, "being obsessed with ratings when you're constantly in third place?"—but even she seemed jittery as we waited for the final numbers from the previous week.

"Eliza," Rebecca shouted from inside her office. "Am I reading this right?"

Eliza squinted at her phone. The executives had the ratings e-mailed to them as soon as they came out. The rest of us were left to guess the numbers based on their mood, or wait for the *Deadline Hollywood* story to go up.

"We won the demo last week," Eliza announced. There were gasps in the newsroom—actual, audible gasps. That meant we had drawn more viewers aged twenty-five to fifty-four than any other cable news program in our time slot. That meant we had beaten not only MSNBC but Fox and CNN, too.

"When was the last time this happened?" I asked Jamie.

He grinned. "I don't think this has ever happened."

"Fuck me!" Rebecca shouted. She was pacing excitedly in her office, hollering at the speakerphone. "Ginny! Jesus Christ, did you see this?"

That night, after the broadcast, Jamie and I went for drinks at the bar around the corner. It had been a long time since we'd done this, just the two of us. Stella had seen to that.

"Do you think you eventually get used to this feeling?" I asked. "Like, if you work at the *Today* show, does this become boring?"

"I have no idea," Jamie said. "I've only ever worked here."

"Kiddie Cable News," I said. An old nickname. Ten years ago, when KCN was started, the quality had been so uneven that it seemed like children were running the place.

"It does feel good, doesn't it?" Jamie said. "Stella must have been happy. You told her?"

I shook my head. "We haven't been in touch since I left."

"Really?" Jamie raised his eyebrows. "Well, I'm sure she saw the news. She has a Google alert on herself. I'm kind of surprised she hasn't called."

"Why?"

"To gloat," he said. "It's strange. She was calling all weekend—I had to put my phone on silent—but then she just stopped. The last thing I got was this cryptic text on Saturday night."

"She was probably just embarrassed." Jamie was pulling out his phone, and my heartbeat accelerated. "She knew you were ignoring her."

"Okay, here it is. We won't be seeing each other again, so save the crap for someone else. What the hell does that mean?"

"She's dramatic," I said. "You know that."

Jamie looked pensive as he swiped a tortilla chip through a

dish of salsa. "I should call her. I should congratulate her. It's the right thing to do."

"Wait," I said, as he stood from the table. "Jamie. Wait a second. Be careful."

He laughed at the look on my face. "I think I can handle it. This'll only take a minute. I'll just say—"

But then he pulled the phone away from his ear and frowned at the screen. "That's strange," he said. "Straight to voice mail. It didn't even ring."

"Huh." I reached for my beer and took a large gulp.

"Stella never turns her phone off," he said, perplexed.

"The service can be spotty up in Maine."

"Yeah," Jamie said, sitting back down. "That's probably it."

Tuesday, around lunchtime, my phone rang.

I drew a deep breath and answered. "Hi, Mrs. Bradley."

"Have you heard from her, Violet? She won't respond to my texts. I've been calling and calling but her phone just goes to voice mail."

"That's so strange," I said.

Here it was. The next stage was beginning, and I felt oddly calm.

"I'm starting to worry," Anne said. There was a push-pull in her voice. Creeping panic, and the parallel self-insistence that it would be fine. It would be *fine*. We had been through this before; Anne didn't want to overreact. "I called Ginny. Stella e-mailed her on Saturday night. Something about wanting to take some time to herself. Which is fine, I suppose, but why wouldn't she have her phone on?"

"Jamie tried calling her yesterday," I said. "It didn't ring then, either."

"That's not like her, is it? She always calls me back."

"Yeah," I said. "But you remember that Christmas, when

she left. None of us could get hold of her for, what, a whole week?"

"Do you think that's what happened here?"

"It could be," I said.

"Well, as long as she doesn't miss Thanksgiving next week. But she wouldn't do that." Anne's brittle laugh was meant to reassure herself. "That's a bridge too far, even for Stella."

"I'm sure you're right," I said. "I'm sure she'll be back by then."

Winning the demo called for something bigger than celebratory pizza in the newsroom. Eliza considered waiting for Stella's return, but these victories went stale quickly, and besides, no one could get hold of her. On Friday night, after the broadcast, Eliza rented out the back room of an upscale Japanese restaurant. There was an open bar, waiters circulating with glasses of sake and delicate squares of sashimi, a chef making hand rolls to order. It was like the Christmas party—the same cast of characters, the same level of indulgence—but this was infinitely sweeter. Christmas you celebrated because the world kept turning and inevitably it was December again. But this feeling could be arrived at only by victory. There was no one else in the world celebrating exactly what we were in this moment.

I was standing with a few other producers, listening to Rebecca talk about the time the House Speaker tried to hit on her mid-interview, when she cut herself off and said, "Excuse me for a moment." She wove efficiently through the crowded room and greeted the two people who had just arrived: Ginny, and a distinguished-looking older man. He was tall and elegant in his blue blazer, but there was a cane by his side, and the hands that grasped it looked spotted and arthritic.

Jamie leaned over and said to me, "That's Mr. King."

"*The* Mr. King? Of King Media?"

"The lion in winter," Jamie said. "This is the first time I've seen him in person."

Mr. King was an Oz-like figure, powerful but never visible, a name only invoked by those at the highest levels. He was the one boss that nobody made fun of. I couldn't quite believe that he was here, in the flesh, in the room with us. It was almost hypnotizing.

He had a raked forehead and a serious gaze fixed on Rebecca, who seemed to shimmer from his attention. Working at KCN the last three and a half years had required me to constantly re-assess my understanding of power—the scale of it, and where it really lay. When I was a lowly intern, someone like Jamie seemed to possess everything I could ever want: a desk, a title, a salary. But there were trapdoors in the ceiling that led to another level. There was Eliza, who commanded an entire newsroom. There was Ginny, who had the final say on what made it to air. And then there was Mr. King. Our entire world was, for him, merely one piece of the pie. He had probably just come from dinner at the Four Seasons or the 21 Club, stopping on his way back to his Fifth Avenue penthouse. Even if he stayed at the party for five minutes, standing by the door while his town car idled outside, that was enough. It signaled that this was, in fact, a big deal.

The interns and assistants in the room didn't notice him. It was only the senior staff—Eliza, Rebecca, Jamie—who tuned their antennae to his presence. What a strange feeling it must be, I thought, to move through the world like that. To possess a power that remains invisible to any ordinary person passing on the sidewalk. How many people in America could identify King Media with a real person? A fraction of a percent. His low profile was probably strategic. What had he done to get to this place, to this hard ceiling of power? What had he left in his wake? Mr. King said something to Rebecca, and she laughed. I wondered what they were talking about—the ratings? Or their mutual friends, or their plans for the holidays? It was only when I stopped staring at him that I realized that Ginny, next to him, was staring at me in turn.

A shiver passed up my spine. I smiled as she approached, but her expression remained cold.

"I'm extremely concerned about Stella," she said.

"Oh," I said. "I mean, I am, too. I haven't heard from her all week."

"It doesn't make sense," Ginny said. "We were right in the middle of negotiating her new contract. And then I get this e-mail from her on Saturday night. She needs time to think, she needs time to herself. Where does that come from?"

I thought the question might be rhetorical, but Ginny frowned at my silence. "*Well?*" she said. "You were the only person with her. What exactly happened, Violet? What changed between Saturday morning and Saturday night?"

"I don't know," I said. "She was gone for a lot of the day. I don't know where she went."

"You've spoken with her parents, I assume?"

"Of course. Actually, Mrs. Bradley and I were remembering the time she ran away for a while, at Christmas a few years ago? This could be—"

"I don't see how this is remotely similar. Stella is the next star of this network. She wouldn't walk away from that. Or from three million dollars a year."

I swallowed, trying not to flinch. Three *million?* "With respect, Ginny, Stella has done irrational things before. And the thought of staying at KCN might be too painful for her."

"Why is that?" Ginny sounded irritated.

"She was upset about the breakup with Jamie." I kept my voice low, conscious of Jamie standing a few feet away. "Maybe she doesn't want to work at the same network as him."

Ginny narrowed her gaze. "Your argument on Saturday night. Was it about Jamie?"

"Yes," I said. "She thought I had something to do with the breakup."

"Did you?" Ginny said. "I know that you and Jamie are close."

A waiter approached, holding a plate with red slices of tuna, dotted with bright green wasabi. I shook my head, feeling nauseous. "Of course not. Stella was my best friend."

"Could you bring me a Scotch on the rocks?" Ginny said to the waiter. "A double, please." As he walked away, Ginny turned back to me. "You said was."

"Pardon me?"

"Stella *was* your best friend?"

My pulse started hammering, and my cheeks grew hot. I reminded myself: this is real, this story you're telling. You feel nervous and uneasy because you don't know where Stella is. And isn't that true, strictly speaking? The Atlantic Ocean is a big place.

"The way we left things," I said. "I'm not sure how she feels about me anymore."

"I see," Ginny said. She kept staring at me, unblinking. Jamie came over, grinningly oblivious of what he was walking into.

"Ginny, just wanted to say hello," Jamie said. "This is a great party, isn't it?"

"Sushi has never been to my liking," she said. "But yes, this is nice."

Jamie began talking about a story he was working on, seizing his opportunity to impress the boss's boss. While he spoke, Ginny's gaze flickered back and forth between us. Her distaste was barely concealed. *These two scrabbling opportunists,* she must have thought. These grasping nobodies. Jamie and I weren't her kind of people. We just didn't play the game in the way she saw fit. She made that as clear as possible without being outright rude.

I felt a distinctive surge of anger. Willow's e-mail had been sitting in my in-box, unanswered since Monday. I didn't know what to say. It was my fault, my guilt to bear. Willow had trusted us with her story. Had trusted *me*. But in those long minutes we devoted to his interview, the Danner CEO had easily washed his hands of the crisis. Today, just like last week, or last month, or last year, he could walk into the finest restaurants in New York City and receive a warm welcome. His name stayed firmly lodged in the register of society.

See, the term *money laundering* had it backwards. People don't launder money. Money launders people. Change a few variables and what would you call a man like the Danner CEO? But he would never be known as a pimp, or a criminal. He was too rich. That category doesn't exist on the Fortune 500 list.

Market pressures. That's how the bosses at Danner had justified it, in their coded e-mails and memos. The company had to keep growing. The shareholders demanded greater and greater returns. They weren't *trying* to be evil. They were just looking out for the bottom line. Having a moral compass was a nice idea, in theory. But you got a whole lot further by playing dirty.

CHAPTER FIFTEEN

THE BROKER HAD left a dozen messages. There was a place she wanted to show me in Washington Heights, more realistic for my budget. When I didn't answer her calls, she began sending me texts. They were misspelled and almost incoherent—probably typed with one hand while she rushed around Manhattan in her beat-up Corolla—but I gave her credit for persistence, then I blocked her number. Who knew what the Bradleys would ultimately decide to do about the apartment? But I could enjoy it while it lasted.

On Saturday, I finally cleaned up the mess in the living room. The fragments of glass that Stella had walked across, barefoot and anguished, were marked by her dried blood. But the rug had concealed the stains, and eventually it looked like nothing had happened.

It was a beautiful apartment. I would miss it if I had to leave. The kitchen faced east, the marble countertops reflecting the morning sun. The living room was best in the afternoon, the dancing shadows of tree branches stretching across the wall. It should have been grotesque, the reminders of Stella in every corner, but it wasn't. This was still my home. My first real home.

In the evening, I left the apartment and started walking south. Night fell and the streetlights switched on. Every restaurant was

packed. It was the weekend before Thanksgiving, and therefore the last weekend before it was officially the holidays, when
everything—crowds of tourists, endless rotations of parties—
would ratchet up to an unpleasant intensity until the season
finally burned itself out on New Year's Eve. But this was a
weekend for a cozier kind of pleasure. Families cooking dinner,
couples sharing a bottle of wine. Sleeping with the window
cracked open to let in the cold night air.

By the time I reached the ferry building near Battery Park,
there was a strong breeze off the harbor. Most people were
traveling in the opposite direction, coming into the city for the
night. As I waited to board the ferry, two girls passed me—best
friends by the looks of it, intertwined arms and shrieks of laughter as they tottered down the ramp in stiletto heels and tight
miniskirts. Going out bare-armed and bare-legged in November was unpleasant, but these girls knew the deal: this way, you
wouldn't risk losing your jacket at the club. Plus, the liquor kept
you warm. They looked about twenty-one or twenty-two. I had
turned twenty-six a few months ago. Entering my late twenties
had come with a feeling of relief.

The boat was almost empty as it chugged across the harbor
toward Staten Island. For several minutes I stood at the stern,
watching Manhattan recede as the ferry unspooled a wake behind it. It was almost exactly a week ago that I had been on the
boat with Stella, in Maine.

My preparations had been careful. I'd cut her passport and
driver's license and credit cards into stiff confetti, spreading the
pieces among several public garbage cans. Stella's wallet was
made of a supple leather, embossed with her monogram. Leather
wouldn't burn, but it scorched and blackened as I held the lighter
up to her initials. When I was sure no one was looking, I pulled
the wallet out of my bag, holding it lightly between my fingertips. I let go, and it dropped into the water without a sound.

Next was the gun. I'd wiped it clean of fingerprints, and kept it wrapped in a scarf. Even holding it for just a moment, cold and heavy and alien, gave me a zip of fear. The idea of Stella actually using it seemed ludicrous. But who knew what she was capable of? The weekend could have easily taken a different turn. Dropping it into the harbor was a relief.

There was one thing left. The jewelry in my pocket was recognizable by touch: the twin nubs of the diamond earrings, the railroad track of the bracelet, the knobbly ring. I had taken to wearing the ring when I was alone in the apartment. It fit perfectly, sliding snugly over my knuckle. I'd toyed with the idea of hiding the ring somewhere secure, keeping it for a while. I loved that ring. I would never in my life be able to afford something so beautiful. The thought of it disappearing forever into the muck of New York harbor made me melancholy.

But this was how people got caught—they were too sentimental. They let their desires get the better of them. I had learned the danger of beautiful things. There would be no loose threads in this story. My fist unfurled, and the jewelry vanished into the black water.

———

Detective Fazio hadn't changed in the past three years. Tall and lean, threadbare across the scalp, a face sagging from too many late nights. Anne summoned him to the house on Sunday afternoon. Despite her threats to cancel their annual donation to the police memorial fund, the Bradley money and influence kept flowing, and the detective arrived promptly at 1 p.m.

As the five of us settled in the living room, Fazio looked at me. "You're the friend, aren't you? You were here last time?"

"Yes. I live with Stella." I chose my verb tense carefully.

"She was the last person to see our daughter," Anne said.

"And that was a week ago. *Over* a week ago. We haven't heard anything since."

"There's been nothing at all?" The detective looked at Thomas as he spoke. "No texts to other friends? No updates on social media?"

"Nothing," Thomas said.

"Can't you track her cell phone?" Anne said. "Wouldn't that show her location?"

"Mrs. Bradley, I should be clear. I'm just here to have a conversation with you. But if your daughter truly is missing, and the last place she was seen was in Maine, the folks up there have jurisdiction. Have you contacted the local police?"

Anne frowned. "No."

"You should call them. We'll debrief the sheriff, and he can take it from there."

"I was hoping"—Anne glanced at Thomas—"*we* were hoping that you might remain in charge of this investigation. The house in Maine is in a very small town. They don't have the same resources that we do here."

Fazio's smile was more like a grimace. "That might be... difficult."

"He's right, Mom," Oliver said. "Matters of jurisdiction are cut-and-dried in cases like this. The Rye Police Department doesn't have any standing."

"Oliver, please," Anne said.

"I'm just saying, there isn't—"

"*Oliver!*" Anne snapped. "For God's sake. This isn't one of your law school seminars. This is your *sister* we're talking about."

"Okay, everyone, let's take a moment." Fazio took out his notebook and pen. Like last time, this had a calming effect on Anne. I wondered if Fazio ever wrote anything in that notebook, or if it was just filled with scribbles and doodles, enough to make

the wealthy taxpayers of Westchester County feel they were getting their proper due.

Fazio asked me to tell him what had happened that weekend.
Anne nodded along to my story. She seemed comforted by the
familiarity, like a movie she had memorized.

"And was this typical of your daughter," Fazio asked, turning
to Thomas and Anne. "To get this upset about a boyfriend?"

"She could be...dramatic, at times," Anne said. "But no. She
never seemed to take her boyfriends very seriously."

"But she's done this before," Fazio said. "Like that Christmas,
when she—"

"This is different," Anne snapped.

"I apologize, Mrs. Bradley, it's just that—"

"Don't apologize, Detective," Thomas said, shooting a look
at his wife. "You're right. And the last thing we have from her
is this e-mail, which states plainly that she wanted to take some
time to herself."

"She sent an e-mail?" Fazio said, jotting down a note.

"Not to us," Thomas said. "To Ginny Grass. The president of
KCN."

"Stella's boss," Anne added, impatient with Fazio's questioning look. "And a close family friend. She's always taken such
good care of our daughter."

"Could I see the e-mail?" Fazio asked.

As Thomas scrolled through his phone, Anne leaned forward.
"But this doesn't change anything, Detective. That e-mail doesn't
sound like Stella."

Fazio was now peering at the phone. "It's very short," he said.

"I can tell," Anne said. "Our daughter didn't write that."

I pressed my palms, tacky with sweat, against my jeans. A tiny
tremble in my legs. I'd known this was a possibility, that even
though I could mimic Stella's voice, I wasn't perfect enough to
fool her own mother.

"But, Mom," Oliver said. "That's the whole point. Stella wasn't acting like herself last weekend. Right, Violet?"

I took a deep breath. "Right," I said.

"This boyfriend," Fazio said. "He was her coworker, correct? James Richter?"

"Yes," I said.

"I'd like to speak with Mr. Richter. And with Ms. Grass, too."

Thomas furrowed his brow. "You don't suspect them of anything?"

Fazio closed his notebook. "I'd like to speak with anyone who was in touch with Stella last weekend."

After Detective Fazio left, Oliver and I helped ourselves to lunch. The Bradleys' housekeeper kept the refrigerator well stocked: neatly washed and cut fruit, pasta salad, roasted vegetables, cold-brewed iced tea, prosciutto-and-mozzarella sandwiches on hard Italian rolls. The food replenished itself like magic. The first time Stella and I went grocery shopping together, we left the store and she took a big bite from an apple we'd just bought.

"Don't you want to wash that first?" I said.

"What are you talking about?" she said, her mouth full.

"That apple. It's covered in chemicals."

She raised an eyebrow and took another bite. "Is this one of your weird Florida things? I've literally *never* heard of anyone doing that."

There was a bowl of apples on the kitchen counter. I thought of Stella as I picked one up. The Bradleys always had good apples, carefully selected and washed ahead of time. Somehow they were never mealy or bruised. This one was particularly perfect: the skin tight as a drum, the flesh tart and crisp. Maybe that accounted for the way Stella ate apples—comprehensively, even the waxy casing of the core, everything except for the stem and the seeds. Although if there wasn't a garbage can handy, she'd eat that, too.

The trip wires of the past week were proving to be strange things. The memory of how Stella ate apples; the absence of her dishes in the kitchen sink; the gradually fading smell of her clove cigarettes from the living room. I was glad to be free of the cruel and sadistic person Stella had become, the way she warped the energy at work and at home, but I hadn't accounted for the subtler ways her presence filled the edges of my life. It was calmer and easier without her. It was also lonelier.

"Do you want any of this?" Oliver said, gesturing at a container of broccoli slaw.

"I'm fine." I shook my head. "Not that hungry."

"Are you okay?" He squinted at me. "You look a little pale."

"I'm starting to worry," I said. The words were false, but the nausea was real.

"Do you want to know what I think?" Oliver said. "I think she's trying to punish Jamie. She wants everyone to make a big fuss, and then she'll say it was his fault, and he'll feel awful about it. This is a game to her. It always has been."

"That would be pretty extreme, even for Stella."

"I might be wrong. In which case I'm a jerk for saying what I just said. But you'll keep it between us, right?"

I managed to smile. "Do you mind dropping me at the train station on your way back?"

Oliver smiled back. "Why don't you just drive back into the city with me?"

"I can give you a ride down to the Village," Oliver said, as we crossed the Triborough and the Manhattan skyline came into view against the dark evening sky.

"Are you sure?" I said. "I'll just take the subway downtown."

"Please," Oliver said. He drove past the exit on the FDR that would have delivered him to the Upper East Side, where he lived. "It's nothing."

"And you know," he added, after a few moments of silence. "I've never even seen your apartment. Stella never once invited me over. Crazy, right? My own sister."

"Oh," I said. Oliver glanced at me, then his eyes flicked back to the road. There was a long pause. "I mean, do you want to see it?"

"I'd love to." He smiled.

I had imagined Oliver's car idling in front of our building while he took a brief tour. But there was a parking spot open on our street, and his Audi sedan fit neatly into the space. He locked the car with a satisfied beep. It seemed he was planning to stay a while.

"Wow," Oliver said. As I turned the lamps on, he did a lap around the living room. He ran his hands across the back of the couch and the top of the mantel, squeezed the pillows, tested the springiness of the armchairs. He was like a lion in a nature documentary, pacing his territory and sniffing out intruders. "Did my mom do the decorating?" Oliver said. "This has Anne written all over it."

"She gets the credit," I said.

"When I moved into my place a few years ago, I asked her to help pick things out. You know me, I'm terrible at that stuff." He shrugged and laughed. I laughed weakly, too, although I didn't know Oliver nearly well enough to possess that knowledge. "But she said no. She said that was the kind of thing that a girlfriend would want to do, in the future. You know, when I *finally* got one."

"Oh," I said.

"But for Stella, she'd move heaven and earth." He rolled his eyes as he went into the kitchen. "My perfect little sister. Look. This is our grandmother's china. And has Stella ever used this?"

"Actually, yes. She likes it for her toast in the morning."

"Well, still." Oliver stared covetously at the delicately patterned plate, as if it were a gold medal that a competitor was letting him look at but not keep. "It's obvious who the favorite is."

"No one thinks she's perfect," I said. "And they love you just as much, Oliver."

"They love us in different ways. I hold up my end of the bargain. I work hard and I don't embarrass them. And who wants to be loved for that?" Oliver stopped, surveying the doors that lined the hallway. "Which one is her bedroom?"

"On the left," I said. It was almost too late by the time I remembered—he already had his hand on the doorknob, was already twisting it open. "Oliver!" I shouted.

He jumped and spun around. "What?" he said. "What's wrong?"

Behind him, in the bedroom, glaring evidence stood out: the slept-in bed, the clothing piled on the armchair, the damp towel on the bathroom door. I knew how bizarre and inappropriate this would look, my sleeping in Stella's room for the past week. It was just that her room was so much bigger and nicer than mine. It seemed a waste for it to remain empty.

"Um," I said. "I just remembered. I want to show you this thing in my room."

My bedroom was more like that of a girl who had been missing for a week: airless, pristine, spooky. I looked for something plausible to show Oliver—but what, what? I had nothing worth remarking upon.

"Ah," Oliver said. "Etchings, right?"

"Huh?"

"You had some etchings you wanted to show me. I get it."

He sat down on the bed and leaned back on his elbows, taking in the cheap furniture and the bare walls. "This is more my speed, anyway," he said. "This is kind of what my apartment looks like. You should come see it sometime." He raised an eyebrow suggestively.

Was it possible that I was the stupidest person in the world? Yes, it was entirely possible. Why else would I have practically dragged Oliver to my boring bedroom, were it not because I wanted to have sex with him? He was waiting patiently for me to sit down on the bed so that the obvious part could begin. *Shit,* I thought. *Shit, shit.*

Oliver laughed. He had noticed my crossed arms, the tight expression on my face. "It's okay. I get it. It is kind of weird, isn't it?"

"What is?"

"That she's not here, and it's just the two of us." Oliver stood up from the bed. For a moment, I panicked. Was he going to come closer? Initiate what he thought I was too shy to initiate myself? But instead he said, "I'll get going. It's been a long day."

I walked him out. As he was waiting for the elevator, buttoning his coat and wrapping a scarf around his neck, he smiled at me. When Stella and Oliver stood side by side, you couldn't help but notice the differences between them. But with Stella gone, the similarities were more pronounced. The blond hair, the confident gaze, the lanky height. The way he talked to Detective Fazio, the way he leaned back on my bed: I recognized that easy, satisfied sense that everything will work out as it should. That perfectly bred poise.

The idea wasn't even half formed. But it was enough to stir up a hot feeling of shame, remembering what she said on the boat that night. *You've attached to my family like a leech.* Stella would have hated this. I could imagine the disgust on her face. *My awful brother? What could you possibly see in him?*

Oliver stepped inside the elevator. As the doors started to close, he looked up at me. He stuck out a hand, and the doors slid back open.

"How about dinner sometime?" he said.

CHAPTER SIXTEEN

STELLA WAS OFFICIALLY declared a missing person on Monday morning. The police in Maine examined the house and noted the obvious clues. Stella's car was still there, the keys sitting on the kitchen counter. Her wallet and phone were gone. Many of the lights had been left on, but the door was locked, and there was no evidence of forced entry. There was an empty slip in the boathouse, and Thomas confirmed that the speedboat was missing. He also confirmed that the contents of the safe were missing: the jewelry, and the gun.

Oliver and I drove up to Maine on Wednesday morning, the day before Thanksgiving. It was late afternoon by the time we arrived. I was hoping for a chance to shower and change after the long car ride, but there was a detective waiting in the living room.

"Violet, honey?" Anne said. "This nice man needs to speak with you."

"Oh—sure," I said. The story was an easy routine by now. "Of course."

The detective led me to a small study, considerably shabbier than the rest of the house. Overstuffed bookshelves, boats in glass bottles, stacks of magazines and papers, and a dark leather couch, where I sat while the detective pulled over a chair from the desk.

He was short and stocky, built like a high school football player. He cleared his throat. "Now, Miss Trapp. You were the last person to see Stella."

"Yes," I said. "Saturday night. A week and a half ago."

"Can you walk me through the weekend?"

I described it to him in detail, as I had for Detective Fazio a few days earlier. At the end of it, he frowned. "So there was no one else at the house? Just the two of you?"

"Just the two of us."

"Was Stella with you the entire weekend? Did she ever go out?"

"Um," I said. "She went out for a while on Saturday morning. She took the car."

"She didn't say where she was going?" I shook my head. The detective extracted a piece of paper from his folder. "Do you recognize this number?" he said.

"No," I said. "Two-oh-seven. Isn't that the local area code?"

"Stella was texting and calling this person all weekend. This was the last number she called on Saturday night. Several times, right around ten thirty. We traced the number back to a burner phone. Sold just a month ago, from a convenience store."

"Huh," I said.

"We found cocaine in her glove box, and marijuana in the kitchen. Do you know whether she brought that up with her from New York?"

"I have no idea."

"But she's a regular drug user?"

"I mean, she's twenty-six years old. She goes out. She likes to have fun." I paused, and then decided to plunge forward. "You're guessing that this burner phone was, what, a dealer?"

"It's possible."

"She had friends in the area. People she'd met during the summers. I think there was a guy she got coke from. I never knew his name."

He nodded, took a few notes. "No one thinks about it in these ritzy summer towns, but it's a big problem around here," he said. "Opioids and heroin, especially."

"Stella never did anything like that," I said. "Except, wait. This guy she was dating, he had knee surgery, and gave her his leftover OxyContin. That was a while ago, though."

"Was this boyfriend"—he checked his papers—"James Richter?"

"Oh, no, no. This was several years ago."

"So this has been going on for a long time." He sounded satisfied by his own observation. "Let me ask you about the safe upstairs. There were a few items missing."

"I heard. Jewelry and a gun, right?"

"Why do you think Stella took the gun?"

"How do you know she took it?" I said. "What if someone else broke into the house and took the gun and, I don't know—kidnapped her?"

"There's no sign of forced entry," the detective said. "No damage to the safe. And that's a top-of-the-line model. You can't get it open without the combination."

"Well, maybe they forced her to open it." My voice was getting louder.

"Miss Trapp, I know how distressing this is."

"You're implying that this is all her fault." My righteous indignation almost felt real.

"We're investigating every possibility," the detective said. "But the evidence suggests no foul play. No blood, no damage, no sign of a struggle. That e-mail made it clear that she wanted to get away for a while. Also, the Bradleys have a camera installed at the gate. The footage doesn't show anyone entering the house, except you two."

"A—a camera?" I startled. *How did I miss a camera?*

"See," he said, taking another paper from his folder. A photograph. "Here's you, leaving the house around eleven p.m. on Saturday. That's the last activity the camera captured. Just after Stella made those phone calls. Did you hear what she was saying?"

"I was in the other room," I said. "I couldn't really hear. But she sounded...agitated."

The detective squinted at me, nodded slowly. "Agitated," he said, making a note. "Those phone calls probably are the key to figuring out what her plan was. Wherever she went, she got there by boat. Unfortunately, there's no camera down by the boathouse. Could've shed some light. Damn shame."

"Shame," I echoed dumbly.

"The woman at the motel confirms that you arrived just before midnight." He chuckled. "A small town like this, everyone notices everything. Not many visitors this time of year."

"I can imagine."

"But other than you, there was nothing unusual about that weekend. No strangers coming to town. No one casing the Bradley property." The detective sighed, shut his folder. "Would you do me a favor, Miss Trapp? It's the mother. Believe me, I know how hard this is on her. But she needs to let us do our job. She can't be second-guessing us at every step."

"Anne likes to be in control," I said. "That's how she operates."

"But sometimes parents can't see the truth about their kids. She thinks this drug thing is some crackpot theory. I'm only asking that you help her stay calm. Open-minded. I'm afraid this case might be a lot simpler than she thinks it is."

I had come up to Maine for the police interview, but Anne insisted I stay there for Thanksgiving. She treated me as a talisman. Stella had brought me into the Bradley family. The two of us were a package deal. Surely, by staying close to the family, I'd draw Stella back.

Stella's grandparents arrived with turkey and stuffing and pies prepared by their housekeeper in Boston. "Routine is key," Grandmother Bradley said sternly while we sat at the long dining table, soft strains of Bach in the background. "Anne, you have to keep your wits about you." Thomas, Oliver, and I returned to New York after the holiday, but Anne stayed in Maine. Her daughter had now been missing for two weeks. There had been no activity on her credit cards. The police confirmed with the cell carrier that her phone had been shut off the whole time. Anne's worry had deepened into a more serious panic.

If we were producing this story for TV—and our audience loved a story like this, a beautiful rich girl gone missing—most of the footage would be useless. Anne, berating the police for their inefficiency, channeling her frustration into excessive exercise. Thomas, remaining laser-focused on his work, answering every e-mail and calling into every meeting. Oliver, speculating snarkily about where Stella was. They weren't reacting like they were supposed to, because they didn't know yet how the story ended.

What we needed were the freighted silences, the teary interviews, the panning and zooming of pictures from Stella's childhood against a sentimental soundtrack. We needed the money shot: the bereft mother, breaking down when she realized that she'd ignored the warning signs. Preferably while she was sitting in front of a wall lined with family photos. Keep the camera on her for several long seconds. Let the audience feel her pain.

The Bradleys didn't know how to be vulnerable in public. They were determined to look normal for as long as they could. They didn't want Stella's photo splashed across the news. They didn't want the neighbors organizing a search through forests and fields. They didn't want their dirty laundry aired for all of America to see.

Detective Fazio was retiring from the Rye Police Department at the end of December. After thirty years, he had a pension waiting. But Thomas offered to pay him five times his police salary if he would serve as a private investigator. They would spare no resources in the search. There would be a bonus when he found Stella. *When.* That was the operative word.

Anne called me in mid-December, several weeks into the investigation. It was late, nearly midnight. I could tell that she had been drinking, and crying.

"I'm so worried, Violet." Her voice was thick and quavery. "I know something terrible happened to her. I just *know* it."

"I'm worried, too," I said.

"She was so beautiful. Too beautiful. It makes other people do crazy things. Some nutjob just taking her, doing God knows what to her." She let out a whimper of pain. "I always knew this would happen. I always knew someone would take her away from me."

After Anne had sobbed and recovered and sobbed again, and finally hung up, I lay flat on my back, looking up at the unfamiliar bedroom ceiling.

"That was my mother?" Oliver propped himself on his elbow and gazed down at me, at my naked body draped in his high-thread-count sheets.

"The poor woman," I said.

Oliver ran his fingertips lightly across my bare stomach. He took my hand and lifted it to his lips. "Poor *you*," he said. "Poor Violet. You're bearing the brunt of everything."

I closed my eyes. Oliver meant well, but his sincerity could be cloying. I often worried that I'd give myself away. The mattress distended as he rolled over. When I opened my eyes, his face hovered above mine. He brushed the hair from my forehead. "You're so pretty," he said. "My poor, pretty Violet."

"Oliver—"

But he leaned down and kissed me, and I felt his erection pressing against my thigh. We'd just had sex fifteen minutes earlier, but he seemed to have the pent-up energy of a teenage boy. He was a good kisser. I'd never really been kissed with that kind of affection.

This whole thing was new for me. There were a handful of guys in college and in New York, one-night stands occasionally stretching into repeat hookups. But those were expressions of the lowest kind of desire: how it felt to have a boy grab your ass on the dance floor, how it felt for him to gruntingly relieve himself inside you when he barely knew your name. I treated sex as an obligation to be dispensed with every six months, like going to the dentist. There were men happy enough to oblige me in this. I did this mostly to avoid the judgment of Stella, who talked constantly about sex.

But a man who wanted to take me out to dinner? To gaze at me and compliment me, to have me spend the night and stay for breakfast in the morning? This was a novelty.

It felt deliciously inevitable. After dinner at an Italian restaurant on the Upper East Side, we walked back to his apartment on the pretext of a drink, hand in hand, slightly tipsy. Oliver kept stopping to kiss me. We skipped the drink and went straight into the bedroom. "Why didn't we do this sooner?" he said, afterward.

We both knew the answer to that, but it was as if there were a quota on how often we could say her name. Initially, I took pleasure in how it could trigger Oliver. Listening to him complain about Stella was as satisfying as watching a rant-filled hour of

cable news that confirmed all of your biases. I had years of griev-
ance built up, but Oliver had decades.

"You hate her even more than I do," I said once, laughing. We
were sharing a bottle of wine over dinner, and Oliver was fixated
on some adolescent episode.

But then his eyes, animated with old slights in the half distance, shifted back to the present and locked onto me. "I'm
joking," I said quickly. "Just joking."

"I don't *hate* her," he said, smoothing the tablecloth, shifting
his fork and knife into parallel alignment. Then he looked up at
me. "If you do, that's unfortunate."

"Of course not," I said. "I'm sorry. That was a bad joke."

After that, I was careful. I only mentioned her name enough
to show that I was worried, concerned about the investigation's
lack of progress. For his part, Oliver seemed to accept the police's prevailing narrative: that Stella had gotten mixed up in
a bad crowd. That, if there was foul play, it was of her own
making.

It was when we stopped talking about her that things changed
for the better. The shared heat of our feelings toward Stella—
our frustrations, our jealousies—descended into the unspoken
and charged everything with an electric pulse. Neither of us was
stupid. We both knew that, if she were here, we wouldn't be
together.

But sometimes, when Oliver and I were having sex, I'd close
my eyes and think of Stella. How much she would hate this.
Her words on the boat that night: *leech, suck-up, fraud.* And
now my connection to the family was stronger than ever. Friendship has no legal status, no promise of future offspring. This did.
And who knew what this was, how far this could go? A wedding announcement in the *Times*, a new last name, a classic six
on Park Avenue. A thorough whitewashing of the past that was
only achievable through marriage. If Stella weren't dead already,

the sight of me and Oliver in bed together—naked, flushed, flourishing—might have killed her.

———

"We have to say something," Ginny said. "I'm getting too many questions. The media reporter from the *Times* has been calling every single day."

We were gathered in the Bradley living room, a week before Christmas. I was there as Stella's friend, but also as Oliver's girlfriend. Anne and Thomas seemed unsurprised. These kinds of things happened, like a widow marrying her dead husband's brother, pairings of those unmoored by loss. But when Oliver held my hand or rubbed my back, Ginny's eyebrows arched. I could tell she doubted this performance of sadness, even though she herself was proof that grief makes strange bedfellows. Ginny and Anne had become especially close over the last month. Oliver told me they spoke on the phone multiple times a day.

Increasingly, Ginny was taking charge of the situation. She had summoned this meeting. The office had been gossiping for weeks, aided by the trail of bread crumbs that Stella herself had left. People had seen her lose her temper, or yell at Jamie. Maybe she was the type to just...snap. Or maybe it was leverage. "Her contract is up for renewal," I overheard one assistant speculating to another. "I bet she's trying to drive the price up." Soon the chatter spread beyond KCN. It began on a blog that covered the TV news industry, with a blind item about negotiations for Stella Bradley's new contract being put on hold. It was then pointed out that Stella hadn't been seen on TV since the Danner story. Around the month mark, the rumors were boiling rapidly enough that the steam drifted up to more mainstream publications.

"I don't need the world digging into my daughter's business," Thomas said.

"But it could help," Anne said, touching her husband's arm. "What if someone out there saw something, and that's how we find her?"

"Shouldn't we tell the truth?" Oliver said. "Just say exactly what happened."

"For what it's worth," I said. "There *are* enough people out there who know that she's missing. One of them is going to leak something, eventually."

"A short, simple statement," Ginny said. "No explanation. Just the facts. The family asks for respect and privacy at this time. It's the best path forward."

A few days later, a statement was released simultaneously to the media and to KCN employees. This was an active investigation, and any further questions should be directed to the police. The family prays for Stella's safe return home. They love her and miss her, and they are grateful for the well wishes.

My name appeared throughout the coverage. A picture of us, scraped from social media, accompanied every story. It was strange to see myself this way, a stock player in a larger drama. Violet Trapp, friend and coworker and roommate. Violet Trapp, the last person to see her alive. After the statement, the gossip at KCN went from heated to feverish. I was bombarded with invitations to lunches and drinks from coworkers I barely knew. "In case you need someone to talk to," they said. "I can't even imagine how hard this is for you." People found excuses to stop by my desk, but before long, they always changed the conversation to Stella. The boldest ones presented their own theories of what happened.

But I noticed that no one did this for Jamie. No sympathetic inquiries, no invitations to lunch. The police had interviewed him, but since then he'd been kept in the dark. I counted as family; an ex-boyfriend didn't. Jamie was tainted, possibly dangerous. He was one degree too close to the problem.

"They think it's my fault," Jamie said, staring at his beer, at our usual place.

"Don't say that." I waved a hand. "They're just gossiping idiots. They're bored. Something new will happen tomorrow, and they'll move on."

"I don't mean our coworkers. I mean the Bradleys."

"Oh."

"Well? Don't they?" He was pale, and his face looked cramped with nausea. "And aren't they kind of right? Stella would still be here if I hadn't broken up with her. But—Jesus Christ. How was I supposed to know that *this* would happen?"

Jamie never said what he thought *this* was. He had, I was discovering, a squeamish side.

"Obviously you couldn't know that," I said.

"I thought I was doing the right thing! I was being honest with her! You see that, don't you? You knew how bad things were between us. Right, Violet?"

He looked at me pleadingly, like an altar boy at confession. Jamie was so strident about his innocence. He wanted the world to know that his hands were clean, that it wasn't his fault. This was part of what I found so refreshing about Oliver. "I was a terrible brother to her," he'd said. "But to be fair, she was an even worse sister. Truly awful."

And it's not like Jamie was going to catch any real heat for this. His alibi was airtight. He'd been at the office that fateful weekend, his movements recorded by the security guards and cameras. None of it was Jamie's fault—it would be cruel to think that. But when other people blamed themselves for what happened to Stella, I allowed myself to imagine an alternate universe where it *wasn't* my fault, where it *wasn't* my burden. Because, except for those moments, the weight of that knowledge was always there.

Even when I wasn't fully conscious of it—often the ambient anxiety arrived before the memory itself did. Rinsing the shampoo
from my hair in the shower, standing in line at the coffee cart, riding the descending elevator late at night, I'd find myself thinking,
I'm stressed, but what am I stressed about, again? Then I'd remember, and I'd remember that this problem was unfixable.

"Right," I said finally, after a long beat. "Of course I see that.
And so will everyone else, soon enough. Just let the police do
their work."

He laughed bitterly. "Yeah. Sure. Because they've been doing
such a great job."

———

After the press release, the police in Maine set up a tip line
for anyone who might have seen her. The line was, predictably,
flooded with crank calls and flimsy sightings, information from
people with the most tenuous connections to Stella. The police
weren't making any progress. "God, these people are idiots,"
Anne said, after hanging up the phone with the police one day in
January. "Walter, I am *so glad* we have you on the case."

Walter was what Anne called him, now that Detective Fazio
was officially retired and working for the Bradleys. And it was
true. Fazio caught things that the Maine police didn't. He was
the one who discovered Stella's passport was missing. It could
just be a coincidence—that's what he emphasized. Maybe she'd
lost it, at some earlier point. But Anne knew her daughter. Stella
might be messy, but she wasn't a scatterbrain. She wasn't the
type to lose her passport.

A turning point came when a dead body was discovered in a
town about thirty miles away from the Maine compound. The
police were elated to have something to work with. I was sure
Anne would harass them for constant updates while they worked

to identify the body. But instead, she became very still. She sat on the Bradleys' porch, staring at Long Island Sound, with a tearless silence that was almost serene. It was like a superstition. If she didn't turn around, if she didn't look, Stella would remain alive.

Anne took it as a sign when the body wasn't Stella. This, along with the missing passport, was proof to her that her daughter was alive. Anne had spent dozens of hours online, reading about similar disappearances. Women who vanished and returned alive, weeks or months later. There was something called a fugue state. Couldn't this have happened to Stella? She had forgotten who she was. Now she was wandering the world, waiting to be found.

"Don't you see?" Anne said, brandishing articles printed from the internet in the skeptical faces of her husband and son. "She's lost. She could be anywhere. I have to go find her."

It took me a long time to realize that I was witnessing the unraveling of a family. The brave front the Bradleys presented to the media was convincing. I even believed it myself, for a while. But when January turned to February, and there was no sign of Stella, the Bradleys started to crack. In all my years, I had failed to understand how tenuous their self-assurance was. A life that appeared solid in construction, laid with bricks of wealth and good manners and good genes, was as flimsy as a house of cards.

The Bradleys, it turned out, were just as screwed up as anyone else.

Thomas's workaholism became pathological. Plus, he had decided that he was going to summit Mount Everest before the year's end. He was pushing sixty, in mediocre shape, and had never once expressed an interest in mountain climbing. But ever since Stella disappeared, he had become obsessed with the idea. He would do it in her—not her memory, but her honor. He hired a trainer. He woke up early to go on runs with a weight-filled backpack. Thomas, once taciturn to the point of rudeness, now could not shut up about the best route up the Lhotse wall.

In different circumstances, Anne would have put a stop to this foolishness, but she was consumed by her own quest. There were so many places in the world that Stella might be. Anne packed a gigantic suitcase and bought an open-ended, around-the-world plane ticket. London, she'd start in London, because she had to start somewhere. Then to Barcelona, or Marrakech, or Santorini. She would find her daughter. She would be gone for as long as it took.

CHAPTER SEVENTEEN

WHEN YOU'RE IN a relationship, life becomes easier in ways that seem small at first, and gradually become significant. Take the Monday-morning-in-the-office dance. When a colleague asks about your weekend, and you're single, it's a scramble to come up with the right answers. You have to look busy, with friends and meals and interesting activities, like rooftop yoga and wine tastings. It isn't acceptable to *do nothing* multiple weekends in a row, unless there's a hurricane or a blizzard. If you're ambitious in New York, ambition doesn't end when the week does.

But with Oliver, weekends took care of themselves. We went out to dinner, to museums, to Broadway and off-Broadway performances. Oliver was lobbying for a position on the board of Lincoln Center—at thirty he was young for it, but that didn't stop him—and along with his sizable donations came a subscription to the ballet and the opera. His enthusiasm was both broad and intense, and it was easy to go along for the ride.

"Do you have plans on Tuesday night?" Oliver said, opening a bottle of wine while I cooked dinner. When he finished pouring the wine into my glass, he twisted the bottle so the liquid wouldn't drip down the neck. I'd noticed that if a waiter failed to perform this maneuver, Oliver would frown, and leave a bad tip.

"Other than work, you mean?" I reached for the glass, but he stopped me.

"It needs to breathe," he said. "There's a new show opening at the Public. You can take the night off, can't you?"

"I can't. You know what my schedule is like."

He laughed flatly. "You must really love your job."

I looked up from the shallot, which was turning into a fine dice with the help of the expensive chef's knife I'd bought after my most recent promotion and raise. "Once upon a time," I said, "you thought my job was fascinating."

Oliver wrapped his arms around my waist and rested his chin on my shoulder. "I still think that," he said. "But am I not allowed to resent it for taking away the woman I adore?"

"Nope," I said, resuming the chopping. "We're a package deal. Can you get the water started? The big pot, under the counter. Lots of salt."

"When was the last time you took a vacation?" Oliver said.

"I don't know," I said. "But it's not a great time. I've got a lot on my plate, and—"

He held up a hand. "A long weekend, then. Can't they spare you for a few days?"

"I guess so." The olive oil in the cast-iron pan was sizzling by now, and I dropped the shallots in. After they turned soft and golden, I'd add diced tomatoes. The meal was simple—pasta, salad—but Oliver was impressed by whatever I cooked. He liked to brag about this to his friends. I cooked, and I worked, and I was from real America, not a born-and-bred New Yorker. In other words, I was nothing like the kind of woman that a man like him tended to date.

"Good," he said. "I'll take care of everything. You can try the wine now, if you like."

———

The police were cautioning the Bradleys against hope. By now they assumed Stella was likely dead, but with no body and no weapon—and no sign of the boat—the leads were scarce.

At KCN, without new information to fan the flames, the gossip had finally died down. My visitors and lunch invitations slowed to a trickle. People are scared of loss. They'd rather say nothing than risk saying the wrong thing. This wasn't fun for them anymore.

Occasionally Eliza would call me into her office, close the door, and express concern. Was I taking care of myself? Did I have someone to talk to? I always answered by saying that work was a good distraction. When I finally asked for a day off, Eliza smiled gently. "Good," she said. "You need a break."

Oliver and I drove out to Long Island on a Thursday night in early April. It was late when we arrived at the hotel—a small place in East Hampton, gray shingles and white trim and green lawn. A woman appeared at the sound of our knock and showed us to our room.

"Special occasion?" she asked.

"It's our four-month anniversary," Oliver said.

After she left and closed the door, I said, "It is?"

But Oliver was already in the bathroom, turning on the faucet in the clawfoot tub. He held his hand under the stream of water, adjusting the knobs. "Let's take a bath," he said. He shucked off his shoes, started unbuttoning his shirt.

When the tub was full, soft drifts of jasmine-scented bubbles on the surface, I undressed and slid into the water. It was almost too hot, but the pain released its grip in a few seconds. "I didn't realize you were keeping track," I said, settling into the tub's curved back, closing my eyes against the flickering candles around the edge.

"What kind of a boyfriend would I be if I didn't?" Oliver said.

Checklists were Oliver's way. Expensive hotel, bubble bath, candles—and I could bet there'd be champagne and oysters later this weekend. His predictability was a pleasant change after Stella. After a moment, I opened my eyes. Oliver, in his bathrobe, was sitting on a stool and gazing at me. "Aren't you getting in?" I said.

"I'm savoring this moment." He smiled.

"You're sweet, Ollie," I said.

"Excuse me?"

"Oh—God, sorry. I'm sorry. I forgot you don't like that nickname."

"I *hate* it," he said, teeth bared. He stood up and walked out. From the bedroom came the blaring sound of the TV, much louder than it needed to be.

"I'm sorry," I called out. "Oliver. I'm really sorry."

When he came back several minutes later, his face was dark. He stood with his arms crossed, towering above me. "You realize that she was the only one who ever called me that?"

"Who was? Stella?"

"She knew how much I hated it. She *relished* saying it, just to drive me crazy. And look—now she has you saying it, too."

"It was a stupid slip. It won't happen again."

"You know, Violet, sometimes I look at you"—he gestured at the tub, and I became hyperaware of my naked body—"and all I can see are the ways in which she left her mark."

"She was my best friend," I said. "Of course she rubbed off on me."

"You're thinking about her right now, aren't you?"

"We're *talking* about her, Oliver."

"This was supposed to be a nice weekend. A getaway."

"It is, it's—"

"Not when it's all about Stella," he said coldly.

A draft came from the open door. In the guttering candlelight, the hollows and shadows of Oliver's face stretched and retracted like a yo-yo. Then he sighed. "I'm sorry, Violet. But my whole life, she's been the center of attention. After she disappeared, I thought this was the silver lining."

My heart was thudding faster. My face flushed, pricking into sweat. "This?"

"*This,*" he said, smiling. "Us. Finally getting free from her."

I felt light-headed. A laugh track from the sitcom on TV, loud and false, echoed off the hard tile walls.

"I'm turning into a prune," I said. "Pass me that towel?"

I was aware of Oliver's gaze tracking me as I stood up, the water sucking at my limbs. I wrapped myself tightly in the towel, but he stood in the door to the bedroom, blocking my way.

I shivered. "I need to get some clothes on."

"You loved her, didn't you?" he said, gazing at me.

"Are we still talking about this?" I tried to get past him, but he shifted in response.

"Please answer the question," he said firmly.

I stopped. Looked up, and stared him right in the eye. "Of course I loved her."

"But you love me more." It was a statement, not a question. His words hung in the air for a long beat. Oliver took a step closer, and ran his hands down my bare arms. I let the towel drop to the floor.

After we had sex—good sex, charged and sparking—and I went into the bathroom to pee, the candles around the tub had extinguished down to waxy stubs. Only one was still burning, a tiny flame dancing above a pool of clear wax. A romantic prop that had outlived its moment. I licked my fingers and pinched it out with a small hiss.

When I woke up the next morning, the bed was empty. Oliver's note said he had gone downstairs for breakfast.

"You'll love this place," Oliver had said, on the drive out from the city. "It's known for its food." He thought a love of fancy cuisine had to accompany my love of cooking. He tried so hard, paying attention to every little detail. But I was the last person who could fault him for that.

"There you are," he said, when I came into the dining room. There was a fire crackling in the fireplace, the smell of wood smoke and coffee in the air. The table was covered with plates of fruit, a basket of bread and pastries, several newspapers. Oliver had already worked his way to the op-ed pages of the *Wall Street Journal*.

"What's our plan for the day?" I said. The bread was dense with raisins and pecans, the bright yellow butter dotted with flakes of salt. It was, I'd admit, delicious.

"I have a tee time at Maidstone. Do you want to use the spa this afternoon? And we could walk on the beach before lunch."

"Sounds nice," I said.

The warped intensity of the night before was gone. Instead, it was like Oliver and I were reading from a script, a performance of normalcy. Our words sounded so rote, so trite. I felt detached from the scene, watching from above and wondering, *is this really how couples talk?* Could two idiosyncratic, complicated people really be reduced to these clichéd exchanges? The man on the golf course, the woman at the spa. But maybe this was just what it was like to be in a relationship. How would I know?

I was reading a novel from the free shelf at work—publishers sent everything to us, even though the only authors we ever had on *Frontline* were politicians hawking their campaign books— when my phone started to buzz. "Do you need to take that?" the pedicurist said, already rising from her stool.

This wasn't one of those spas with hushed voices and silenced cellphones. They knew the reality of their clientele. How much work had been conducted from this very chair, by New Yorkers pretending to take vacation but really just relocating their career-focused selves a hundred miles east? Negotiations, conference calls, divorce settlements, you name it.

"It's fine," I said, gesturing at the frightened-looking woman to sit down. She probably had PTSD from previous clients. "Just a few e-mails. No problem."

A tornado had ripped across Kansas the night before, and Rebecca was going to anchor from the scene for tonight's broadcast. The rundown was being scrapped as a result, including a story I had worked on. It was one of those Community Cares segments, a feel-good story about a New Jersey mother with an autistic toddler who had formed a support group for other parents like her. She was genuinely lovely, and shy, and hadn't wanted the publicity. I had to twist her arm to allow a camera crew into the support group. Now I'd have to call and tell her the segment had been bumped. And by bumped, I mean it would never air, but I wouldn't say that.

"I have to make a quick call," I said to the pedicurist. "But you can stay."

She nodded, and continued applying polish to my toenails, wearing that expression that so many waiters and taxi drivers and housekeepers and executive assistants have managed to perfect—those whose job it is to pretend they have gone temporarily deaf.

After making the phone call and answering several e-mails, my mood improved. I didn't feel like myself if I wasn't working. I tried to explain this to Oliver at lunch—a luxurious lunch with wine and oysters, check and check—when he looked at me crossly for responding to e-mails between the appetizer and the entrée. He had taken the day off; why couldn't I?

See, the things that Oliver liked about me now were the

things that would eventually have to disappear, if we stayed together. That's how it was done, in his world. He wanted to be the kind of man, he thought he *was* the kind of man, who was progressive and modern and supportive of his ambitious partner. But he also lived in a world of definite rules. After marriage, the women gave up their high-powered jobs. They hired caterers for the dinner parties they were expected to host. Society absorbed them. It was forgotten that they had ever lived anywhere that wasn't New York. This weekend felt like an audition for that role. The woman painting my toenails had no idea that I'd grown up in the cruddiest town in Florida.

Oliver wanted to go for a drink before dinner, at a place in Sag Harbor that made the best martini on the East End. This wasn't just his opinion; the *New York Times* had declared it so. He treated culture like big-game hunting, bagging specific items for his collection. But when we got there, the door was locked and there was a sign in the window: CLOSED FOR RENOVATIONS. REOPENING ON MEMORIAL DAY.

"Damn it," Oliver said. "I wanted you to see this place."

"Should we head straight to dinner?"

Oliver looked at his watch. "But our reservation isn't until 7. This is so frustrating." He frowned, and glanced down the street. Summer was several weeks away, and the town was quiet. He said, "There. I guess we can get a drink there instead."

The bar was on the next block. It was shabby but comfortable, neon signs in the window and TVs behind the bar tuned to a basketball game. We took a table in the corner, the legs uneven and rickety, the surface sticky with spilled beer.

"Well." Oliver looked annoyed. "Not exactly what I had in mind."

"You know, it's the weirdest thing," I said. "This place feels familiar."

Oliver arched an eyebrow. "Have you been here before?"

"No," I said. "I've never even been to Sag Harbor."

Our conversation was stilted and stiff, a hangover from our lunchtime bickering. We made our drinks last, the melted ice turning them watery, Oliver checking his watch every few minutes. Whenever the Knicks scored, and the men at the bar erupted in cheers, he startled.

Finally, it was time to leave. Oliver paid the bill and I lingered in the restroom, smoothing my hair and reapplying my lipstick. Dating Oliver initially felt like payback. Stella had taken over my turf—well, I could take over hers, too. And he reminded me of her in certain comforting ways. But sometimes I thought, *what am I doing?* Oliver thought he had finally found someone who preferred him to Stella. But that's ultimately where the problem lay. Oliver wasn't an adequate replacement for Stella; I'd never love him the way I loved her.

I left the restroom and saw Oliver outside, hands shoved in his pockets and jacket collar turned up against the springtime chill. At the door, I glanced back one more time. That's when I spotted the man clearing the empty glasses from our table. Rolled-up sleeves, tattooed forearms, bar towel tucked in his back pocket.

He saw me at the same moment I saw him. Then, suddenly, I put it together.

"Stella?" he said, stepping closer. "It's Stella, right?"

"I—uh, I'm not sure—"

"I remember you." He smiled. "It was, what, three or four years ago? You came into the bar over in East Hampton."

My mouth opened and closed without making a sound.

"Don't you remember me? I'm Kyle. We, uh, you know." He blushed. "I always wondered if I'd run into you again. And here you are. Stella. You don't forget a name like that."

"I think you have the wrong person," I finally said. Outside,

Oliver was glancing over his shoulder, looking impatient. "I'm sorry. I have to get going."

"Wait!" he said. "You're making me feel crazy. You really don't remember?"

"I just—sorry. I have no idea what you're talking about." I could feel Kyle's eyes following me as I walked away. I had to grip the doorknob hard to keep my hand from shaking.

———

The world is a place of brutal chaos, which is what makes it so easy for a crime to remain unsolved. If the criminal has done an adequate job of erasure, the world will supply infinite explanations to fill the vacuum. What happens to the missing woman? Maybe she has a psychotic break and slips away from her life in the middle of the night. Or she crosses the road at the wrong time and is hit by a car. Or a man kidnaps her and takes her prisoner.

This is why, from the very beginning, I knew my plan would work. Stella, who blazed through life with equal parts dazzle and risk, supplied enough material for dozens of theories. She was part of that sisterhood of glamorous women who met untimely ends, the Diana Spencers and Grace Kellys and Marilyn Monroes of the world. No one would say it out loud, because it reeked of victim-blaming, but I'm certain there were people who looked at Stella Bradley's story and thought, *that girl was always trouble.* A sickening thought pattern, but for my plan to work, I had to take advantage of it.

Because when you have a woman like that at the center of the story—beautiful, wild, trouble—then who bothers to look very closely at the peripheries of her life? Suspicion sweeps through the darkness like a lighthouse, illuminating the ex-boyfriend or the town loner, but it doesn't linger for long. Especially not on those who are quiet and ordinary, whose very faces indicate their forgettability. Who, as Thoreau would put it, will go to the grave with their song still in them.

A person, in other words, like me.

As we drove back to East Hampton, I kept my eyes fixed on the road. Oliver was talking but I wasn't listening. That night with Kyle—it would be four years ago in November—that night when I used Stella's name, it had imparted a kind of magical confidence boost. It made me bigger and brighter. More memorable than I'd ever been. It turned out it was easy to become a completely different kind of person. How much had I told him, those years ago? Had I given him a last name? This was a risk I hadn't foreseen. A chink in the armor.

"Stella used to come out here a lot," Oliver said. I snapped back to attention. "A friend of hers had a house on Georgica Pond. Did you ever go there?"

He glanced over at me. "I don't mean to dredge up old memories," he said. "But this drive always reminds me of her."

There was a sign on the side of the road, reflective white letters on green paint. We zipped past it. "What did that say?" I asked, certain I hadn't read it correctly.

"Oh." Oliver smiled. "The name of the road. Around here it's called Lost at Sea Memorial Pike. Isn't that poetic?"

My stomach gave a painful lurch. "Can you pull over?"

"What's the matter?"

"Oliver," I said. "*Please.*"

The car hadn't even come to a stop when I opened the door and hurled the contents of my stomach onto the gravel shoulder. The waves kept coming, even when there was nothing left to expel. I spat and coughed the bitter bile from my mouth.

Lost at Sea. I closed my eyes and saw Stella: her eyes vacant and her mouth agape, her hair floating loose in the dark ocean water as her dead weight tugged her deeper.

Guilt wasn't as simple as you might believe. It wasn't remorse or regret. It wasn't a desire to go back in time and do things differently. It was walking around with knowledge that you alone possessed. Knowledge that takes up more space because there's no one to share it with. In its specificity, in its intricacy, in its persistent details—the sloshing of the waves, the dark smear of blood, the coin-like moon—the truth weighed more than a hundred theories combined.

———

"Did you hear about the shake-up?"

It was rare that Jamie beat me into the office, but Oliver and I had driven back that Monday morning, to extend the weekend. Jamie watched me drop the duffel bag to the floor and kick it under my desk. "How was the Hamptons?" he said.

"Fine. Too cold to swim. What's the shake-up?"

"They want fresh faces. Out with the old, in with the new!" Jamie spread his arms wide in punctuation. Then he grimaced. "Guess how many times I've heard that line."

"What does this actually mean?"

"It means they fired a bunch of people because they were getting bad ratings. They're revamping the nine o'clock and ten o'clock hours, and the Sunday morning show, too."

"*Bill of Rights*? I kind of like it the way it is."

"At least we'll be rid of that terrible name." Jamie shook his head. "Fire the anchor named Bill and you can't really call it that, can you? That's the biggest change. New studio, new anchor, whole new staff. Bill's EP was fired, too."

My computer booted up, and I opened my e-mail. I was happy to be back to work. Even being out for one day on Friday felt funny. I could keep track of the action, the e-mails and texts flying back and forth, but I couldn't be a part of it. Not really. The important stuff happened face-to-face.

Case in point: Eliza and Rebecca, standing in a corner of the newsroom. The expression on Eliza's face was slightly grim. In theory, *Frontline* had nothing to worry about during this shake-up. Our ratings had been rock-solid since the Danner special. Rebecca was the critical darling of KCN, and the cash cow to boot. But change was always dicey. What if the new 9 o'clock anchor was a star, and they decided to groom him or her to take Rebecca's place? The shoddy state of 9 o'clock and 10 o'clock wasn't of concern to Rebecca or Eliza. In fact, the worse everyone else was, the better we looked. *Frontline* generated the lead-in that pushed a healthy audience into subsequent hours. As long as we were the best, the executives couldn't touch us.

Rebecca and Eliza and Ginny: an outsider might think they were on the same team, but their goals were often at odds. If Rebecca and Eliza wanted a moat of mediocrity around the shining example of *Frontline,* Ginny wanted the opposite. It was her job to make sure that KCN was the best—or at least competently good—in every hour. I always thought of Ginny as the referee between the high-strung personalities in the newsroom. But who would be the referee if it came down to Rebecca versus Ginny?

Later that day, as we emerged from our afternoon rundown meeting, I saw Ginny waiting for Eliza. The printer was conveniently located near Eliza's office. I lingered over it, pretending to examine some papers while the two of them talked.

"We're down to a few finalists, and I'd like your opinion," Ginny said.

"Does it really matter?" Eliza said. "I won't be working with them."

"Of course it matters." Ginny sounded irritated. "And you may very well be. They could wind up filling in when Rebecca's on vacation."

"Well, don't tell her that. She'll have a fit."

"Don't coddle her, Eliza. She knows the reality. I'd like her to meet the candidates, too."

The next morning, Ginny brought the first person to the newsroom. This woman was in her late thirties, had ditched law school for journalism school, was currently a reporter for a network affiliate in Washington. She was pretty, although she wasn't doing herself any favors with her chunky heels and polyester skirt-suit. I watched Rebecca give her a quick up-and-down glance and mouth "No way" at Eliza. What made that woman so appealing to Ginny was also what made her problematic to Rebecca. The raw potential: she was intelligent and authentic, just waiting for a professional to cut and polish her skills. But there was only room for one smart and attractive brunette in prime time.

Ginny returned an hour later. The next candidate was a man. I glimpsed him from behind before he went into Rebecca's office. He was tall, with a deep voice and an evident comfort; he had taken off his suit jacket, draped it over one arm. From Rebecca's office came his booming laugh.

That laugh. That's what did it for me.

When he and Ginny left Rebecca's office, I stood up from my desk. He caught my eye, and his smile dropped away. Confusion replaced it, and then delight. "Just a second," he said, touching Ginny on the arm and walking toward me.

"Corey Molina," I said.

He smiled. "Violet Trapp."

When I was in high school, Corey had seemed like such a grown-up. But he had been just a kid back then, an overcaffeinated stick figure in a baggy suit. Now, when he hugged me, I felt his broad back muscles straining beneath his shirt. His face was tanned, his hair salted with strands of silver. He'd gotten better with age.

"This is so weird," he said.

I laughed. "Tell me about it."

"Not often you see someone from our neck of the woods in Manhattan, huh?"

"I'm sorry to break up this little reunion," Ginny interjected with a brittle smile. "But I have to get Mr. Molina to our next meeting."

Corey's gaze flicked between Ginny and me, sizing up the dynamic. "Of course. Just had to say hello to an old friend." Before he followed Ginny to the elevator, he murmured, "I'll send you an e-mail, okay?"

"You know him?" Rebecca said, after they walked away.

"His wife was my history teacher in high school. He worked for the CBS affiliate in Tallahassee. Small world."

"Ex-wife," Rebecca said.

"What?"

"No wedding ring."

"I didn't even notice."

She shrugged. "I meet a guy who looks like that, that's where my eye goes."

I laughed. "And how does Mr. Rebecca Carter feel about this tendency?"

"You're funny, kid. Number one, you don't get to talk until you've been married a hundred years like me. Number two, it's an old habit. Waitressing, I learned to check."

"The single guys tipped better?"

"Nope. The married guys who wanted to pretend to be single for the night. Eliza!" Rebecca shouted across the newsroom. "So what did you think?"

"He looks the part," Eliza said. "I don't know. Six out of ten."

"Tough crowd," Rebecca said. "Violet here can vouch for him."

"Really?" Eliza cocked an eyebrow. "Do tell."

"Let's do this over lunch," Rebecca said. "My date canceled

and there's a table at Michael's with my name on it. You're coming with us, Violet. We want the gossip."

When I got back from lunch, there was an e-mail from Corey waiting in my in-box.

Dinner on Friday? the subject line said. In the body of the e-mail: I'm new here, so you name the time and place, city slicker.

As the week crept by, my initial reaction to seeing Kyle—tremors, vomiting—seemed overblown. Each passing day was a step toward freedom. By Tuesday he would have said something, surely. By Wednesday I was almost starting to relax. And then, on Thursday morning, Anne called.

"Someone saw her," she said, before I could even say hello. "Some bartender on Long Island. Walter is driving out right now, to talk to him."

"Wow," I managed to say.

"I'm running to catch a flight home." She sounded breathless. Behind her was the babble of an airport announcement in another language. Italian, or maybe Spanish. "You and Oliver should plan to come up tomorrow morning. We need a family meeting right away."

"Of course." I squeezed my eyes closed, took a deep breath.

"Oh, God, Violet. I *knew* she was alive. I knew it."

Oliver was spending the night at the apartment. Around midnight, he switched off the TV and stood up from the couch. "Aren't you coming to bed?" he asked.

"I won't be able to sleep," I said. My mind was spinning through the same frantic loop. What would Kyle say? If they put it together, my borrowing Stella's name so many years ago, how bad would that look? I reached for the remote and flicked the TV back on. I found it soothing, the blare and repetition of news and commercials, news and commercials.

Oliver looked at me like I was a simpleton. "The police get these bogus tips all the time. Walter probably only brought this up because he's trying to justify his salary."

"That's pretty cynical."

"My sister is gone, Violet. Whatever happened happened." He yawned, stretching his arms above his head. Oliver was truly a sociopath. "Don't let this get to you."

Fazio was stuck in traffic and running late. The wait was excruciating: Thomas and Oliver talking stiffly about work and Thomas's preparations for Everest, and Anne chattering about her travels, the times she was *certain* she had spotted Stella, only to realize it was someone else, which made sense now, given that Stella was on Long Island. Ginny nodded and held Anne's hand, glancing over at me several times, skeptically. My pale exhaustion must have been obvious, even with concealer and blush.

Anne liked having Ginny there. She filled the role Anne was no longer capable of filling: the levelheaded woman, the person who kept track of the details. When Fazio arrived, Ginny answered the door, took his coat, offered him coffee. Anne herself was nothing but nerves, crossed legs jiggling as the detective took his seat.

"I talked to this young man last night," Fazio said. "The bartender who claims he saw Stella. He says he first met her over three years ago, and recognized her as she was leaving the bar last Friday night. It took him a few days to put together that this was the same person he'd been hearing about in the news."

He paused. "I hesitated to bring this up. I'm afraid this might not get us anywhere. But it's been a while since we had a fresh lead, and I know you like to be kept in the loop."

"Of course, of course," Anne said, nodding vigorously. She

had been calling Fazio every day for updates. Oliver looked at me and raised an eyebrow.

"Well, here's the catch," Fazio said. "The bartender says she didn't look like the picture on the news. Similar, but not the same. She didn't answer to the name Stella when he approached her, and then she left the bar abruptly. I asked him if he was certain this was the same person. He said it could be, accounting for the makeup that TV people wear."

"And where precisely was this, Mr. Fazio?" Ginny said.

"In Sag Harbor. At a bar called the East End Tavern."

"That's where we were on Friday," Oliver said.

"*What?*" Anne said.

"Violet and I," Oliver said calmly. Across the room, Ginny's eyebrows shot up. "We had a drink before dinner. The American is under renovation right now, which is too bad. But if Stella was there, she was doing a good job hiding. We must have been there for, what, Violet, an hour? Right around the time this man claims to have seen her."

"Was there a security camera?" Ginny asked.

"No," Fazio said. I felt a ping of relief.

"This *cannot* be a coincidence," Anne said. "Stella appearing at the same bar as Oliver and Violet? She's getting ready to come home, isn't she? Maybe she's been watching us! Doesn't that make sense?"

Anne's eyes were wild with hope and pain, looking for someone to agree with her theory. "*Well?*" she said, when the five of us remained silent. "She wants to see how we're doing, doesn't she? She misses us. She wants to be with her family."

"Anne," Ginny said quietly, taking her hand again.

"Unfortunately, Mrs. Bradley, I think this guy may be another crank," Fazio said. "I was hopeful at first, too. He seemed certain. But maybe he recognized Oliver from the news. Or maybe he overheard them talking about Stella. He figured this was his chance for attention. And Oliver and Violet being at the same bar that night would give his story some credibility."

"No," Anne said. "No. I don't get it. Why would he do that?"

"In a case like this, you get a lot of bad tips. We've had them from the beginning."

"Should we talk to him?" Thomas said. "See if anything he says rings a bell?"

"With all due respect, Mr. Bradley, I spent several hours questioning him. I can show you the footage of the interview, if you'd like. And he's been in for larceny, breaking and entering, a DUI. He's behind on his alimony. I suspect this is a scheme to make money."

The tattoos on Kyle's forearms. The soft eyes, concealing some long-ago mistake. He was a kind man, an honest man, but certain things are held against you forever.

"So, what? We just ignore this?" Anne said. "We haven't made any progress?"

"Mom," Oliver said. "Calm down. You're making yourself hysterical."

"Don't you condescend to me," she snapped. "What the hell is wrong with all of you? Why don't you *care?*"

I felt nauseous. I had thought Anne might react to Stella's disappearance like before, with a cool and correct bearing. But in these months without closure, the raw pain had transformed her. Her color was high. Her hair was long and her skin tanned. She looked younger, inflamed with purpose. Her old armor of cashmere and pearls and La Mer had concealed the resemblance. But with that discarded, it was staggering.

She looked just like her daughter.

Thomas's eyes brimmed with tears as he watched his wife snatch up her purse and car keys. Oliver was staring at the floor. Ginny hovered behind Anne, murmuring softly. But Anne refused to be consoled. The pain hadn't lessened as the months went by. Now it was springtime. The air softening, the trees shimmering with green. The world was renewing itself, but Stella was still gone. Anne shook her head and said, "This is useless. If *you* won't look for her"—she pointed at Fazio, then Thomas, then Oliver—"then I'll just keep doing it myself."

In the silence after Anne slammed the front door, Thomas retreated to his study. Ginny hugged Oliver goodbye. "I'm sorry about your mother," she said quietly. "We're going to make this right." She stepped back, then she gave me a cold stare.

After Ginny left, Oliver shook his head. "I knew it was nothing." He sighed. "What a waste of time. Should we head back to the city?"

But as we were gathering our coats, Fazio appeared in the foyer. He cleared his throat. "Miss Trapp, could I speak to you for a minute?"

Oliver frowned. "We really should get going."

"This won't take long," Fazio said. "I just need a few minutes with you." He held out an arm, ushering me back into the house.

CHAPTER EIGHTEEN

"I'M GOING TO get more coffee," Fazio said, waggling his empty cup. "Can I get you anything?"

I shook my head. "No, thanks."

He smiled. "Back in a minute."

Fazio disappeared into the kitchen. The living room was eerily lifeless with the leftover remnants of the conversation, half-drunk cups of coffee on the side tables, a crumb-covered plate—Oliver was the only one to partake of the biscotti. His blasé calm was so weird. I could see him on the bench in the foyer, typing on his phone, occasionally glancing at his watch.

But why was it weird? What did he have to worry about? Sometimes I forgot that Oliver was actually innocent. His resentment, his bitterness, his long-held grudges against Stella. He had every motive to want his sister dead. But motive didn't make you guilty. Actions made you guilty.

This might be the moment when everything came crashing down. My mind scrambled for a justification, a way to spin it. I hadn't technically *killed* Stella. But the night itself had long ago become secondary. What was worse, what would cause the most trouble, was the lie. I was a bad person; I had become remarkably comfortable with this. The thing that really scared me, that sent me panicking, was the judgment of others—how fucked up was that?

Fazio came back in. Before he sat down, he closed the pocket doors that separated the living room from the hallway. The last thing I saw, as the doors squeaked on their tracks, was Oliver looking up at the sound in surprise.

"I think we'll want some privacy," Fazio said. "So, Miss Trapp. Another call came into the tip line last week. And it concerns you."

My mouth was dry, my tongue thick and gluey. I nodded.

"It was your parents," he said. "They saw your name and picture in the news. They said they haven't seen you, or spoken to you, in years. Is that true?"

I nodded again.

"Well, they had a lot to say. I won't give you chapter and verse, but the gist is that they insisted that I couldn't trust you. That you had been deceptive in the past."

He looked at me, squinting. "Does that sound like your parents?"

I coughed. "Yes," I said. "Unfortunately."

"They had no idea you worked at KCN," he said. "They didn't know a thing about you. At first, I thought they were like this bartender. Just making it up. But I ran their names through the system and, sure enough, they're your parents."

I sat perfectly still, saying nothing.

"You seem shocked," he said.

"It's just...I haven't talked to them in years."

"Look. They clearly have an agenda. They want to get you in trouble, or maybe they want to get on TV themselves. But they've got a long rap sheet between them, and you're obviously a good kid." He sighed. "I know how it goes. My father was an alcoholic. My mother left him, but he still managed to make our lives hell. Some people are just bad parents."

"Bad is an understatement," I said.

Fazio let out a gruff *heh,* and I took what felt like my first breath in minutes.

"I'm sure this isn't pleasant to hear," he said. "But I thought you should know. If they're looking for a spotlight, they might contact the media next."

"Really?"

"People want their fifteen minutes."

My heartbeat was finally beginning to slow down. "Is that it, though? That's all they said?"

He nodded. "Can I give you some unsolicited advice, Miss Trapp? Maybe reach out to them. Try mending the fence. It could save you a big headache in the long run."

As we drove back into the city, I told Oliver about my conversation with Fazio. "Hmm," he said. "Your parents? Weird." And that was it. He spent the rest of the drive talking about the new case he was working on. He had to go back into the office that night, which was good, because that night was my dinner with Corey Molina.

After a shower and change of clothes and a double espresso, and a walk through the cold spring air, I arrived at the restaurant feeling better. In fact, almost buoyant with relief. It was a sleek nouveau space in Chelsea, white walls and open kitchen and minimalist menu. Corey was already waiting at the table, a glass of wine at his elbow.

"I thought you didn't drink," I said.

He smiled. "Good memory."

"I guess things might have changed in—how long has it been?"

"Almost eight years. You forget that I was basically a kid back then, too."

"Yeah, but twenty-six seems so grown up to a seventeen-year-old."

Corey pinched the stem between his fingers, moving the wineglass in tiny circles so that the liquid formed a whirlpool. "You're probably that age by now. Do you feel grown up?"

I laughed. "It depends on the day. I feel far away from high school, I can tell you that."

"The drinking thing," he said, after I'd ordered my own glass of wine. "That was always Diane's idea. She was Mormon, you know?"

"I remember."

"I'd go out to the bar after work most nights. She never guessed. Sometimes I'd come home completely hammered and she was just—she had no idea." He shrugged. "It seems obvious now, doesn't it? That marriage was never going to last."

"When did you break up?"

"Two years ago in June, but we'd already been living apart. I've been at the Phoenix affiliate for almost four years now."

"And now you're ready for the big leagues."

"Ah." He smiled. "I see you've been drinking the Kool-Aid."

"What do you mean?"

"KCN's ratings aren't exactly setting any records."

There was a pause as the waiter brought our appetizers, Corey leaning back in his chair to make room. I squinted at him. "You're not taking the job, are you?"

"I have a better offer from CNN. They're putting me on a fast track to becoming a foreign correspondent, which is what I've always wanted. I played through with KCN to get leverage on my contract. Don't tell Ginny."

He grinned. Rebecca was right. He *was* handsome. Broad smile, stubbled tan. He raised his glass toward me. "Although I had second thoughts when I saw you."

My heart was thrumming. "What do you mean?" I said.

"I mean you're brilliant, Vi. If KCN has managed to hang on to you for this long, they must be doing something right. How great would it have been for us to work together."

"Oh," I said, feeling diffusely disappointed. I had to remind myself that this was better than a come-on. You don't want someone tripping over himself just because you look pretty that day. You want someone willing to alter the course of his career because of your talent.

But there was a term for those who never married, who were wedded to the job instead: a news nun. There's a reason they don't write fairy tales about brainy career women.

"They are." I cleared my throat. "I mean, I guess they are."

Corey had warm brown eyes. "Are you happy?" he said.

"I—of course, I'm…" But I floundered, and fell silent. I tried again, but I didn't know what to say. It was such a simple question. How had I never answered it?

"I'm sorry." Corey reached for my hand. "I'm sorry, Violet. I didn't mean to upset you. That's a pretty personal thing for me to ask."

I blinked. "I just—I guess I don't know. I never thought about it."

"Most of us don't," he said. "Until we have to."

After a pause, he let go of my hand. "Here's what I meant to say," he said. "Sometimes you don't know if you're happy until you go somewhere else. It's a big world. There's a risk to becoming a lifer. Even if you make it to the top of the ladder—they'll still remember you as the person you were on your first day."

"But what if you love your job?"

"Usually that's more a reflection of you than of the job."

I drank from my water glass. It was satisfying to crunch the ice cubes between my teeth, the cool water rinsing away the salt of the appetizer, the tannins of the wine. "I like that," I said. "But you are suspiciously wise."

Corey laughed. "I've been reading a lot of self-help lately."

"Post-divorce malaise?"

"That, or maybe it's impending middle age."

Hours later, the restaurant was nearly empty, the music cranked up in the open kitchen, dessert cleared and the check long since paid. Neither of us made a move to stand up. The conversation was effortless. This was part of what I loved about journalists. The news we reported represented only one small slice of reality. Beneath the official quotes and statements and statistics, there was so much more gossip and speculation—the hidden depths of the iceberg, teeming with life. Corey and I didn't talk much about home, but I didn't have to strenuously avoid the subject, either. It was the opposite of Oliver's indifferent *hmm* when I mentioned my parents. Every question Corey asked was tinged with the knowledge of my past—my real past.

When the waiter finally interrupted and said they had to close, Corey and I moved to the sidewalk. The glow of the restaurant dimmed behind the windows, and the staff clustered around the bar for their shift drink. It reminded me of the end of a broadcast, when the director shouts "Clear" and the anchor exhales. If you hang around in the minutes that follow, you witness the rapid disassembly: the bright lights turned off, the stage swarmed with crew to reset for the next day. It always felt melancholy, the abrupt end to the magic, the resumption of real life.

"What time is it?" I said.

"I'm staying nearby," Corey said. "Come back to my hotel for a drink."

"I really should get to bed."

"Really?" he said. That big grin. "Aren't you having fun?"

"Maybe this isn't what you mean," I said carefully. "But I should tell you that I have a boyfriend."

"Ah. The truth comes out." He smiled, offering me his arm in a smooth transition to chivalry. "Then at least let me walk you home."

As we started walking, he said, "That was only half of what I meant. I actually do want to know what you think about the ambassador to the UN. But while we're on the subject"—he bumped his shoulder against mine—"who's the lucky guy?"

"His name is Oliver. He's a lawyer."

"Oliver the lawyer. How did you meet?"

Corey had heard of Stella, of course. Everyone in the industry had. He went quiet, after I explained. "So you and Oliver have been dating since...?"

"Since December."

"Right after Stella disappeared."

Corey glanced at me. He wasn't smiling anymore.

"What?" I said. "What does that look mean?"

"Isn't it kind of gruesome? Do you manage to talk about anything except her?"

"We do fine."

"Do you love him?"

"*What?*" I said. "What kind of a question is that?"

"A valid one. You've been dating for four months."

"I have no idea," I lied. But why should I lie to Corey? "No. I don't love him."

"Then what are you doing?"

The truth, unutterable, was that I didn't really know. "That family has been through so much," I said, instead. "I feel like I have to be there for them. Or for Oliver, at least. For now."

"That's what I was afraid you were going to say," Corey said.

"Is that such an awful reason to stay with someone? Compassion?"

"Yes," he said.

Our conversation, which had flowed so easily before, had become jagged. Short words spiking through the silence, like an erratic heartbeat in an EKG.

"It's going to be hard," I said. "If I break up with him."

"You've done harder things than that," Corey said.

Another stretch of quiet. Corey was probably a very effective interviewer. Lies require noise and misdirection to blend in. Silence is the best way to draw the truth to the surface.

"He does remind me of Stella, in some ways," I finally said. "But I like that about him."

He smiled sympathetically. "You miss her."

"Of course I do."

"But she's gone, Violet. You're not going to get her back."

For a moment, I wanted to tell Corey everything. What I had done that night, in the name of self-preservation. He knew me. He knew how hard I'd fought, to get to this point. He knew how easy it was to backslide. *He gets it.* He'd understand.

But did I really know Corey? On the sidewalk we passed a group of girls, NYU students most likely, shrieking and shivering in skimpy clothing. His up-and-down glance was almost imperceptible, but not quite. One of the girls, a baby-faced blonde with breasts quivering in her strapless dress, caught his eye and smiled.

See, Corey was good at his job. He made you feel like you were at the center of the universe, like he was talking right to you. But there were so many other people who felt the exact same way. That's what TV anchors were trained to do. I was just an old friend from his hometown. Someone he liked, but someone for whom he was willing to keep a horrible, incriminating secret? Not a chance.

"What I'm saying," he said, "is you can't change what happened. Staying with Oliver because you feel bad for him won't help anything. And even if he reminds you of Stella, he won't ever replace her."

A few blocks later, we stopped in front of my building.

"This is where I get off," I said. "Thank you for dinner."

"You're a good egg, Violet." He hugged me tight. "I hope you know that."

When we stepped apart, he added, "We'll see each other again, right?"

"Of course," I said, though I suspected the odds were low.

He smiled. "Call me when you can have that drink, okay?"

The office on Wisconsin Avenue was boxy and unremarkable from the outside. It might have contained anything: logistics companies, medical device sales, tax preparers. The inside wasn't much better, with gray carpeting and poor lighting, and reporters who had to do their own hair and makeup. D.C. lacked the glassy glamour of the New York studio. It was a different beast entirely. But that's why I was here.

"I heard you're good," Trish said, as I took the seat across from her. The corner office was new to her, but she'd been based out of D.C. for many years, and her voice was familiar to me from the control room. "Eliza doesn't say that about everyone. Although I bet she'd hate to lose you."

"She's been understanding," I said. "She knows there's a ceiling for me at *Frontline*."

Two weeks after my dinner with Corey, it was announced that, with *Bill of Rights* now canceled, Trish had been hired as EP of the new Sunday morning show. She was looking for a senior producer to help revamp it. It took me a few days to work up the nerve to talk to Eliza about it, but she was unsurprised by the request. "I knew this day would come," she said. "I won't ask you if you're sure. You look sure."

"It's a long shot," I said. "But I'd like to try."

"You'll get the job," Eliza said. She wrote, "CALL TRISH RE: VT" on a legal pad, circling it twice. "They'd be idiots not to hire you."

On the train to Washington, that Monday morning in mid-

May, I reviewed my notes. I'd crammed like this was a final exam: watching tape of *Bill of Rights,* noting what worked and what didn't, studying our competition to see what we could learn from them. The other Sunday morning shows had their advantages: NBC was slicker, CBS had gravitas, ABC was wonky and worldly. CNN was able to make everything feel like an emergency, and Fox and MSNBC just covered whatever their audience wanted. KCN had been lost in this shuffle for years. Bill, of *Bill of Rights,* ended every show with a monologue about treating the Constitution as a living document. It was interesting if you forced yourself to pay attention, but death for the ratings.

KCN was ripping the show down to the studs. We had an empty hour, forty-two minutes of programming that wasn't bound by any tradition. I started to think about how we might build it from scratch. I read the white papers and speeches of every halfway important politician in Washington. I studied the techniques of the great political interviewers, the Frosts and Walters and Russerts of the world. My current job kept me on my toes, but it had been a long time since I'd stretched my mind in a sustained way, forming new ideas and connections.

I had gotten this far in life with the help of existing institutions. Places and people whose language I could learn. College, *Frontline,* even the Bradley family. But I wanted a blank slate. I wanted to prove that I could make something happen, something good and lasting, with my own hands and my own will.

"So tell me." Trish leaned back in her chair. "What should we do next?"

"I knew you'd kill it," Jamie said, the next day.

"You know what you want?" the waiter barked at us, materializing next to our table with pen and pad in hand. Never mind that we'd sat down sixty seconds earlier, hadn't even opened the laminated menus. We always ordered the same things.

"Spinach and goat cheese omelet," I said.

"Bacon cheeseburger deluxe," Jamie said. "And a Coke."

Lunch was usually a maximally efficient affair, but on days when we could escape for a bit longer, Jamie and I liked to go to a diner on Ninth Avenue. After almost four years, we had finally achieved the status of regulars.

"I don't know about *that*," I said. But I couldn't help smiling.

"The work paid off?"

Jamie had helped me prepare for the interview, peppering me with mock questions, walking me through the hierarchy of the Washington bureau. Mr. King was not fond of D.C. and was never willing to allocate the bureau the resources they needed. "Everyone and their mother wants to be the next Woodward and Bernstein. Let them have it," he was said to have proclaimed. "We can break stories where they aren't paying attention." Hence *Bill of Rights* lasting years longer than it should have. Hence the worn carpets and shoestring budgets. Apparently Ginny had pushed him to retrench in D.C. Why not just close the bureau entirely, if we truly didn't care? He was so annoyed by her provocation that he doubled their budget.

I nodded. "Although I never got the chance to show Trish my impressive grasp of parliamentary procedure."

He smiled. "It'll come in handy someday."

On the walk back to the office after lunch, while we waited for the light to change on Eighth Avenue, Jamie tilted his head back and closed his eyes, and spread his arms wide. It was the first hot day of the year, July temperatures in May. "Man, that feels good," he said.

"You're crazy," I said. "Summer is the worst."

He laughed. "So says the girl who grew up in Florida."

As we crossed the avenue, a ragged-looking man walking in

the other direction scowled at Jamie. One hand kept his pants hitched up, and the other hand pointed at Jamie's checkered button-down. "Stupid shirt!" he shouted.

"I am going to miss this city," I said.

"And me and my stupid shirt, right?" Jamie said.

"You and your stupid shirt can come visit." It felt reckless to talk this way, as if I had the job already. But I had begun to trust my own instincts. That's what this work did to you.

On Saturday night, Oliver and I were going to see *Tristan und Isolde* at the Met. Oliver would be wearing a tuxedo, which meant I had to rent a dress, because nothing in my closet was fancy enough. I took my time getting ready, a long bubble bath with a glass of wine. I preferred the bathtub in Stella's room, which sat beneath a frosted-glass window, open to the May afternoon. The exposed parts of my skin pricked with goose bumps in the breeze, which made it even more luxurious to sink deeper into the hot water. When I moved down to Washington, I'd have to live somewhere boring and cheap. I'd miss this beautiful apartment. The night felt valedictory—one of my last Saturday nights in New York.

Later, I stood in a bathrobe in front of Stella's mirror and laid out my makeup. My rented dress was hanging from the shower rod, wrinkles loosening in the steam. Over the wheezy drone of the blow-dryer, I didn't hear him coming. He appeared behind me in the mirror, like a ghost.

"What the *fuck!*" I said, nearly dropping the blow-dryer.

"I wanted to surprise you," Oliver said, pulling flowers from behind his back. "Calla lilies. Your favorite."

"Oh." I didn't even like calla lilies; he did. "Thank you. But Jesus, Oliver. Did you have to sneak up on me? How did you get in?"

He dangled a set of keys. "We all have keys to this place."

"We?"

"Your landlords. Anne, and Thomas, and me." His smile and his smirk were nearly identical. "I'm going to put these in water. Why are you in here, anyway?"

"It's . . . it has better lighting. For doing makeup."

"Good idea," he said. "You don't want to look garish."

I scowled in the mirror after he left. I was tempted to wear blue eye shadow and neon lipstick, just to spite him. But when I emerged a half hour later, he said, "You look beautiful." My makeup was tasteful and minimal. The dress was strapless, navy blue, formfitting and flattering. My hair was straight and smooth over my shoulders, and I wore a sparkling rhinestone necklace, rented along with my dress.

Oliver stared at me. Then he said, "It would look better with your hair up."

I crossed my arms. "Hair up doesn't work with the necklace."

"Get rid of the necklace. Earrings go better with a dress like that."

As I unfastened the necklace and pulled my hair into a chignon, I wondered why I was even listening to him. But the mirror confirmed it: he was right, his way was better. He and Stella both had this quality—an unerring instinct for what looked good.

The performance began at 6:30 p.m., and it was 6:25 by the time the cab pulled up at Lincoln Center. "Hurry," Oliver said, already several steps ahead of me.

"We still have five minutes." I was moving as fast as my heels permitted.

"When they say six thirty, they mean six thirty. Not even a minute later."

"Well, that's not friendly. What if your subway gets stuck?"

He turned and shot me a look. "Then you should have planned better."

I rolled my eyes at his back. We reached our seats with seconds to spare. Oliver took my hand as the lights went down, but I pulled it back into my lap. He looked at me crossly. Then he whispered, "By the way, you can't look at your phone during the performance. Your job will have to wait."

"I'm not an idiot, Oliver."

"Good." He turned his gaze back to the stage as the orchestra began playing.

At the first intermission, as we took our seats at the Grand Tier restaurant, Oliver spotted someone he knew. "He's on the board of Lincoln Center," he said. "The nominating committee, in fact. I have to say hello. I'll be right back."

The first part of the opera had left me unmoved, but the building was another thing. Alone at our table, I was free to gawk: the red carpeting, the starburst chandeliers, the murals. It was like an exquisite jewel box. And the people! The men in tuxedos, the women in long dresses, holding glasses of champagne and greeting one another with intimate recognition. It felt part of another era, St. Petersburg in the time of tsars and tsarinas, Fifth Avenue in the Gilded Age. Across the restaurant, Oliver laughed heartily with a silver-haired gentleman. Oliver was confident he'd be asked to join the board soon enough. There were a few board members pushing ninety, in poor health. He was, he said, just waiting for one of them to die.

In a weird way, I admired this about Oliver, the brutal clarity with which he understood his own ambition. We had this in common. There were boxes to check, and he checked them no matter what. Maybe this was why I had once found myself attracted to him.

But there were factors holding Oliver back. He was too many generations removed from the origin story, the great-grandfather who made the Bradley fortune. Wealth was the ultimate safety

net, but it made your edges duller. Born into different circumstances, Oliver could have been a corporate killer, the guy who
started in the mailroom and wound up in the corner office. But
this world, the world of tuxedos and ball gowns and board seats,
only countenanced that bloodlust in the first generation. Oliver
could make partner at his law firm, but he would never be on
the cover of *Forbes*. He could run for the Senate, but never for
president. There were very few heirs and heiresses who avoided
this trap, who kept their edges razor-sharp. Stella, strangely, had
turned out to be one of them.

"Success?" I asked, when Oliver returned to the table.

"Time will tell," he said.

The performance was nearly five hours long. At the second
intermission, back in the restaurant, a woman approached our
table, an old family friend of the Bradleys. Oliver stood and kissed
her on the cheek.

"How *is* your family?" the woman said, gripping Oliver's
forearm, leaning in close. Old people loved Oliver. "Your poor
parents."

Oliver changed his expression to look solemn. "We're holding
up," he said.

"I just can't stand it," the woman said. "That beautiful girl. I
hope whoever did this to her—well, I hope that when the police
find him, they shoot him on sight."

Oliver grimaced. "I agree. Although I wouldn't count on the
police. They've been, let's say, less than efficient."

"How dreadful."

"But you know my mother," he said. "She's taking matters
into her own hands. She's up in Maine right now, in fact."

"She is?" I said.

The woman smiled politely at my interjection. Then she
turned back to Oliver. "That sounds just like Anne," she said.
"You'll let me know if I can help in any way?"

After she left, I said, "You didn't tell me your mom was back in Maine."

Oliver sipped his espresso. "I thought I'd spare you. You don't seem to like talking about the investigation."

"But I still care," I said. "And you're the one who hates talking about her."

"It doesn't matter." He shrugged, as if to say *why should a pair of sociopaths like us split hairs?* "It's pointless. A wild-goose chase. But it makes my mom feel better. That's why she keeps doing it."

"What's she looking for?" I was annoyed. Why had Oliver kept me in the dark?

Oliver cocked his head. "An explanation, of course."

The third act was interminable. My dress was too tight, my heels pinched my swollen feet. I crossed my legs one way, then another, unable to get comfortable. I didn't understand how you were supposed to keep track of the action on the stage, and also the subtitles on the tiny seat-back screen. Oliver had explained that most of the audience was already familiar with the story. They didn't need the subtitles to follow along.

Well, I didn't get it. These performers, singing grand words about love and passion and betrayal, without even a remotely plausible story upon which to hang the emotions—it made no sense. It required more than just a willing suspension of disbelief. Delusion, maybe.

But clearly I was a philistine. The audience, minus me, was rapt with attention as Tristan died in the arms of Isolde. The opera was underpinned by the philosophy of Schopenhauer—I had read about this on my phone, in the cab uptown. It had something to do with needing to renounce the material world in order to achieve true peace. Of course, the audience watching the performance probably possessed a collective wealth larger than the GDP of Slovakia. If their Patek Philippes and diamonds weren't the apotheosis of the material world, I didn't know what was.

There were now several performers on stage. I had completely lost track of the action. I felt disoriented, and suddenly panicked. I didn't belong here. My heart was beating too fast. The music was overwhelming, the tone of voice prosecutorial. Someone had betrayed someone else. But I didn't even know who I was supposed to care about. There were a thousand faces turned toward the stage, and I was the only person who couldn't see what they all saw.

When I squeezed out of the aisle, several people grumbled. The usher at the door said, "You won't be able to go back in, miss."

"I don't care," I said. "Where's the bathroom?"

After I'd splashed water on my face, and sat down in the stall for several minutes with my dress unzipped, letting my rib cage reinflate, I felt better. Scrolling through e-mail, firing off responses while I waited in the bright lobby: it was like a fast-acting drug, erasing the panic I'd felt in the darkened theater.

But. But. Anne was stubborn, just like Stella. My tracks were covered, my alibi was intact—or so I thought. But how could I be sure? What if something had changed?

The doors to the theater opened, and the audience exited in a steady stream. When Oliver caught sight of me, he looked so righteously pissed off that I considered turning around and getting my own cab.

"I can't *believe* you did that," he said, as we walked outside.

"Why? I had to go to the bathroom."

"That was unacceptable."

"Just stop," I said. "Stop talking to me like I'm a child."

"It's a breach of etiquette. And right at the finale. It is beyond rude."

"I don't care!" I snapped. "I don't care about the opera, and I don't care about the etiquette. This is so not my thing, Oliver."

He raised his eyebrows in surprise. "But it's *my* thing, Violet." He was doing his best to soften his tone. "It's important to me. Doesn't that matter to you?"

I ignored him, moving north on Broadway to get upstream of the other people trying to hail cabs. When we climbed into a taxi, I said, "I'm leaving, Oliver."

"What are you talking about?" he said.

"You know how I was in Washington on Monday? Well, I was interviewing for a job. And I'm pretty sure I'm going to get it."

He was quiet for a long time. "You said you were there to work on a story," he finally said. Then he added, "You *lied* to me."

"I didn't want to say anything until I knew it was real."

"But why? Where is this coming from?"

"This is a big move for me, Oliver. Plus"—I paused, took a breath—"I need a fresh start."

"A fresh start from *what*, exactly?"

There was a new kind of anger in his face. For the first time, I was frightened of Oliver. Maybe I'd gotten it wrong. Maybe he was exactly as cutthroat as his sister.

"Say it," he said in response to my silence. "I want you to say it out loud."

"From Stella," I said. "From everything."

He closed his eyes for several seconds. Then he opened them and said, "No."

"Excuse me?"

"I'm not going to let her win. Not this time."

"You're not letting anyone win. This is something I'm doing for me. For my career."

"You need a fresh start?" he said. "Well, if it weren't for

Stella disappearing, you wouldn't be leaving New York. Isn't that true?"

What could I say? Yes, but that was beside the point, because if it weren't for Stella disappearing, Oliver and I would never be together in the first place.

Oliver smirked at my lack of retort. "No," he said again. "She ruins everything, but I'm not going to let her ruin this."

CHAPTER NINETEEN

THE NEXT WEEK, after wrapping Wednesday night's broadcast, Rebecca and I wound up in the same elevator. "I hear we're about to lose you," she said.

"Nothing's definite yet," I said.

"The way Trish has been talking, I'd say it is. She's thrilled, you know. Most of the good people want to stay in New York. Washington isn't exactly glamorous."

"That's what I like about it."

"You'll be back, though." We walked through the lobby, toward the street. Rebecca's black town car was idling by the curb. "They'll give you a few years to turn that place around, then they'll call you back up to the majors."

As I walked home that night, I wondered if what Rebecca said was true. If the tether of KCN eventually reeled me back to New York, I'd be returning as a new person. Washington would be a fresh start, and this chapter would become a tragic footnote. There were a lot of people in television like Corey, who had married young and then realized their ambition was so much larger than that of their spouse. So they divorced, and it was unpleasant, but eventually the memory receded. It seemed like half the people in TV had failed starter marriages. Maybe Stella had been mine.

At home, when I unlocked the door, the lights in the apartment were on. I froze in the doorway, keys in hand.

"Hello?" a voice called, from inside the apartment. "Violet? Is that you?"

Oliver appeared, holding two glasses of wine.

"You let yourself in?" I said. "Oliver, you have to give me some warning."

He handed me a glass and smiled. "You know, this apartment is growing on me. I'm thinking I might give up my place and move in here."

Oliver had been acting strange since the opera on Saturday. His charm had become more brittle than usual, his conviction absolute. He seemed determined not to relive any of the weekend's unpleasant arguing, but the result was that he said outlandish things—like "I'm moving in"—and before I could respond, he quickly changed the subject.

Well, so be it. I only had to tolerate this for a few more weeks. The next morning, in the kitchen before work, I said, "Will you let me know if I need to do anything about the apartment—paperwork or anything like that?"

Oliver was reading the paper, waiting for his coffee to cool. "I doubt it," he said, idly turning a page. "The apartment is under my parents' name. It's simple enough for me to move in. I'm immediate family."

"I meant taking my name off," I continued. "When I move out."

He looked up, smiling and tilting his head, as if befuddled.

"I have to pack this weekend," I said. "Trish, my new boss, she was talking about a start date in early June. I might go down to D.C. on Sunday to look for an apartment."

"But you haven't been offered the job yet, right?" Oliver said.

"Not technically," I said. "She'll probably make the offer today."

Oliver shrugged. "Why get ahead of ourselves? If you get the job, then we can talk about the particulars."

"I *am* getting the job, Oliver."

"I wouldn't be so sure of that," he said, returning to the newspaper.

At work, later that same morning, Ginny asked me to come to her office.

Compared with the newsroom, the executive floor was quiet and elegant. The carpeting was thicker, the furniture a richer shade of walnut. There were no eager young interns and assistants running around to oil the machinery. Here they had executive assistants, serious middle-aged women who sat sentry in the hallway, their desks pristine except for the occasional vase of flowers. The woman outside Ginny's office said sternly, "Are you Violet Trapp?"

"Yes," I said, standing up straighter. *She* wasn't my boss, after all.

"Ms. Grass is ready for you." She gestured at the open door.

Ginny was reading something on her screen as she motioned for me to sit down. She let out a small, frustrated "hmmph."

"Busy morning?" I ventured.

Ginny raised her eyebrows, suggesting that the nature of her morning was absolutely not my business. "I spoke to Trish yesterday," she said. "You're not going to Washington."

I had guessed this might be the reason for the call. A counteroffer, an attempt to make me stay. I'd already rehearsed my response: "I'm very grateful for every opportunity *Frontline* has given me. But, with respect, this role would be a new challenge. And I think I can be an asset to the Washington bureau. With that in mind—"

Ginny shook her head. "No," she said. "I'm not trying to convince you to stay. You *are* staying. You didn't get the job in Washington."

"I—I'm sorry? I'm a little confused."

The look on Ginny's face confirmed what I'd always suspected: she hated me. Completely hated me. "I don't see what
there is to be confused about."

"It's just that Trish, and also Rebecca and Eliza, they were
even talking about start dates—it just seemed like..."

Ginny wasn't going to help with my floundering silence.

"I don't understand what changed," I said finally.

"I'm the president of KCN's news division," Ginny said.
"That means Trish reports to me. So does Rebecca, and so does
Eliza. If I think they're making a foolish decision, I have the
power to overrule them."

There was a credenza behind Ginny's desk with a number of
framed photographs, most of them with politicians and digni-
taries. She didn't have a single family photo. *That's because she
doesn't have a family,* I thought spitefully. She's a miserable old
woman. Cold and lonely and miserable. Even her own sister
didn't love her enough to stick around.

But there was one photo—Ginny as a younger woman, with
two blond children in her lap. I recognized the children. How
could I not? They were Oliver and Stella. Especially lately, the
Bradleys were the closest thing to family that she had.

"Did you talk to Oliver?" I said, interrupting her.

Her surprise showed, briefly, before she composed herself.
"Yes. I did."

"You're doing this because he asked you to." It made perfect
sense. Oliver and Stella both knew how to use these connections
to their advantage.

"The factors that went into my decision aren't any of your—"

"Admit it," I said.

She stared at me. Ginny might have been the master of civility,
the epitome of decorum, but she was realizing that her skills
were wasted on me. Well, good. If we could just admit our ani-
mosity, we could get to the point.

"Fine," she said. Then she laughed. "Do you really think I have time to sit here and contemplate every low-level producer who wants a new job? This wasn't even on my radar until Oliver called. So, yes. I did it as a favor to him."

"Why?"

She arched an eyebrow. "Why wouldn't I? That poor boy has been through enough. The last thing he needs is the stress of his girlfriend leaving him."

"You think I'm going to stay with him after this insane stunt?"

"That's a selfish reaction, but I expect nothing less from you." She picked a bit of lint from her jacket lapel. "The truth is, once I started thinking about it, I realized I don't want you in Washington, either. I want you here, where I can keep an eye on you."

A flush of heat rose in my face. I had to pivot. "You respect Rebecca and Eliza, don't you?" I said.

"Rebecca and Eliza are two of the most talented people here," Ginny said.

"Well, they believe in me. They like my work. And they know me better than anyone. If you trust their judgment, why don't you let them make this decision?"

"I never said I trusted their judgment," Ginny said. "Most of the time, yes. But not always. That's why I'm here. It's my job to be the gatekeeper. To keep everyone's tempers in check." She emitted a short laugh. "Someone has to. Otherwise, you reporters and producers—you'd do anything for a story. You'd watch someone die just to get the tape."

I froze, but I kept my gaze level. "That's a ridiculous thing to say," I said.

"Is it?" Ginny's stare was unblinking. In the silent cocoon of her office, the only thing I heard was my heart thumping in my chest. Then she said, "And I disagree with your premise. I know you far better than Rebecca or Eliza ever will. I've seen you outside this office. I have a much better grasp of your true nature."

A loud knock made me flinch in my seat. The executive assistant opened the door and said, "Ms. Grass, there's a call for you—you asked me to put him through?"

"I'll take it. You stay there," she said to me.

While Ginny was on the phone, I looked around her office, as if searching for—what? An eject button? A trapdoor? Her office was so exquisite that I wondered about the work she actually did. In Eliza and Rebecca's offices, there were messy piles of paper, stacks of unshelved books, rolling racks of dry cleaning. Ginny had midcentury modern furniture, Abstract Expressionist prints, an orchid on the coffee table, a bar cart in the corner. It was annoyingly perfect, which is why the strange object caught my eye.

Amid the spines on her bookshelf was a large red cube. It was made of neoprene-like material, and a zipper ran around the side. I shifted in my seat to get a better look. There was a symbol emblazoned on the red case: a heart with a lightning bolt through it. A defibrillator.

It brought back a memory. Ginny, on the porch in Maine, almost two years ago. Her bracelet had caught in the candlelight, a flat metal plate engraved with writing, Stella leaning closer to look at it. I'd overheard bits of the conversation as I shuttled plates back to the kitchen.

A medical bracelet, Ginny had said. *I have a heart condition. A form of arrhythmia.*

Is it serious? Stella's voice, syrupy sweet.

If I keep an eye on my diet, I'm fine.

"As I was saying," Ginny said, after she hung up the phone. "Trust is a privilege, not a right. You've done nothing to earn my trust. As long as you're working at KCN, I'm going to make sure it's right here, under my supervision."

"With respect, Ginny, I've done nothing but work hard since my first day."

She laughed. "Young lady, you could win all the Emmys in the world and it wouldn't matter to me. I've gotten a long way by trusting my hunches. And I have a hunch about you. You're not telling the truth about Stella Bradley."

There it was. For the first time, someone had said it out loud. And I felt strangely calm. It was almost a relief.

"And why do you think that?" I said.

"I know what it's like to lose someone. After my sister died, I could barely get out of bed. But you—you haven't seemed the slightest bit upset."

"Maybe I'm just tougher than you," I said.

"Or maybe you're glad she's gone," Ginny said. "You've got Oliver to yourself. You're the only one left to take credit on the Danner story."

"This seems like quite a leap," I said. "Are you just projecting this onto me because you're frustrated the police haven't solved it? Fair enough. But that's a cheap shot, pinning it on a...what did you call me? A low-level producer?"

There was another knock. The executive assistant said, "Ms. Grass, your eleven thirty is here."

"Thanks so much, Violet," Ginny said loudly, for the benefit of her assistant and the person waiting outside her office. "I'm glad we got this chance to talk."

"Likewise," I said.

"I look forward to our next discussion," Ginny said. "In the very near future."

That night, I asked Oliver to come over. It was time to end things for good. How could he have thought this plan would work? But he was shortsighted in the same way Stella had been, constantly looking one move ahead, with no idea that he was marching toward the edge of a cliff. Or maybe he didn't care. He just expected that there would always be a cushion to his fall. Money, power, privilege, connections—those things could always be traded, in some fashion, to ensure a comfortable outcome.

Not this time, though. There was nothing that could make me stay.

Near midnight, the door opened. "We need to talk," I started to say, but when Oliver came into the living room, he was breathless, and his eyes were manically animated.

"Did you hear? Did she call you?" he said.

"What are you talking about?"

"My mother!" he said. He went into the kitchen and got a glass of water, drinking it fast and then refilling it. "I couldn't get a cab. I ran here from the office."

"Oliver, *what* is going on?"

"She found the boat," he said. "Some lobsterman in Maine, a few towns up the coast, he hauled it in. It's just been sitting there, right in the middle of the marina."

"The boat?" I said, weakly.

"*The* boat!" he said "The one that's been missing since that night in November."

———

Arriving at KCN on Friday morning, jittery and jacked up on caffeine, I wondered how much longer this would be my life: walking to the office, waving to the security guard, riding the elevator. Either I'd be found out and everything would come crashing down—or it wouldn't, and I'd keep doing the same thing as the past four years, trapped under Ginny's watch.

I honestly didn't know which prospect was worse.

The idea began forming that morning. There had to be another way out. The job in Washington was going to be my chance to start over. Freedom had nearly been mine, by inches.

When Jamie arrived, he looked anxious. "What the hell happened?" he said.

"What?" I said, panicked. That very question had just been running through my mind. What *had* happened, to bring me to this moment?

"The job," he said. "I thought it was a sure thing."

"Oh."

"I got an e-mail this morning. Now they want me to interview for the position? What happened? Did you change your mind?"

Before I could explain, Eliza appeared in the doorway of her office. "Jesus fucking Christ," she said, shaking her head. The newsroom was still relatively empty, which meant Eliza could curse freely without an intern reporting her to HR for abusive tactics. "Trish just called from Washington. She is *furious*."

"I'm confused," Jamie said. "Can somebody explain?"

"Ginny didn't think it was a good idea," I said. "For me to take the job."

"What? Why?"

Eliza leaned against her doorjamb, crossing her arms. "I have seen some petty shit in my day, but this takes the cake." To Jamie, she said, "It's a power move. That's all. Ginny wants to remind everyone that she's in charge." Then to me: "Unless you did something to piss her off?"

"That's ridiculous," Jamie said. "A power move? Trish wants to hire Violet, and Violet wants to work for Trish. What's the point of interfering?"

"But that *is* the point," Eliza said. "You act spiteful, it shows how much capital you can afford to squander."

Eliza's ringing phone drew her back to her desk. Jamie blew out his cheeks. "I think she's been reading too much Sun Tzu," he said.

"Ginny or Eliza?"

"Both," he said. "So how should I respond to this e-mail?

It's from Ginny. She wants me on the train to Washington this afternoon."

"Well," I said, "that depends on what you want to do."

"Are you kidding? That job belongs to you, Violet. And even if they don't give it to you, I'm staying away from this stupid game." He sat down at his computer. "No, the only question is how rude I should be in my response."

Jamie cleared his throat, made a show of rolling up his sleeves. "Dear Ginny, aka Führer Grass," he proclaimed loudly, while pecking out the letters. "F-Ü-H-R-E-R. Umlaut. Comma. New paragraph. Okay, what now?"

I laughed. I laughed so hard I started crying. And then I was just crying.

"Oh, come here," Jamie said, opening his arms. "I know this sucks. I know."

There was a spare office on the floor, which we often used for talking confidentially with sources. Jamie led me inside and closed the door. He didn't say anything. He held me in a hug, my head against his chest, and I sobbed. His hand on my back, the rise and fall of his breathing, the smell of laundry detergent on his shirt—they were permission to let go. Toughness extracts a price, eventually. Nothing comes for free.

"Hey," he said, when my tears finally slowed. "Hey, Violet. You know you can talk to me, right? What's really going on?"

"I ruined your shirt," I said, touching the black smudges from my mascara.

"There's a spare one in my desk," he said. "Learned that trick from the movies."

"Ha," I said, hollowly.

"Violet, I'm serious. Let me help you."

"Help me with what?" I said. "I'm screwed."

Jamie squeezed my hand. "Why don't you tell me what this is actually about?"

"Why? What's the point?"

"Because you don't have to be alone with it."

I closed my eyes again. He was a good man. Jamie, holding his arms wide, ready to receive my problems, not so that we could dissect and analyze and solve them, but simply so he could share the burden for a while. That the problem remained inarticulate didn't matter. What mattered was not to be alone. He was, perhaps, my best shot at happiness.

Years ago, when I spurned Jamie's advance, I thought I didn't need his love because I had Stella. Months ago, when I let Stella sink into the ocean, I thought I didn't need her love because I had myself. But this meant that I had stepped outside certain boundaries, and I wasn't sure if I could ever come back in. The world looks at you and sees you in the context of other people. Relationships radiate out like the delicate strands of a spider's web. The politician talks about his hardworking parents, or his loving wife. The mother is willing to sacrifice anything for her children. These are always the first nouns people reach for. I am a daughter, a sister, a mother, a wife. I am a friend.

I thought I could survive without those words, without those silken strands. But surviving isn't the same as living. And didn't Jamie love me, in a way? The kind of love that comes from a thousand late nights, a thousand fires extinguished, a thousand problems solved. I visualized it. I visualized opening my eyes, telling the truth. You can't imagine the things I've done, Jamie. You can't imagine the cruelty I am capable of. It is the loneliest feeling, and I don't want to be lonely anymore. I want to open up to you, Jamie, I want to tell you the truth.

And what would that look like, if I told him? What if he forgave me, and what if I trusted him? What if, bit by bit, he helped me climb out of this bottomless black well?

But love has its limits. Kindness can't fix everything. Trust is a gamble. Everything I'd worked for could be gone in an instant.

So I shook my head and looked away from his gaze. "Yes, I do,"
I said. "That's how this works."

Ginny had a nickname at KCN: the Ice Queen. Often it was
said with respect; she used her steeliness to successfully negotiate
interviews with Middle East dictators or Kremlin officials. But
it cut both ways. She took a frosty approach to conflict. She
didn't like firing talent, especially because their contracts usually
required a full payout in the event of termination. Instead, she
marginalized them. Anchors were demoted to reporters. They
were given fewer hits. They were denied access to hair and
makeup. Eventually, dignity required them to quit.

It didn't matter how much Rebecca and Eliza liked me. They
could talk shit about Ginny behind her back, but at the end of
the day, she was their boss. She controlled their budget. If it
came down to defending me versus preserving their own careers
at KCN, it was obvious which would win. I understood this;
in their situation, I would do the same. Ginny would ban them
from writing reference letters or tapping their contacts to find
me a new job. Ginny would make sure I failed. She would leave
me alone, on a tiny floe of ice, to drift and drift until finally I
gave up and drowned myself.

But here's the thing: it's far easier to keep someone out in
the first place. Once the franchise has been extended, good luck
taking it back. Once a person like me has a foothold in your
world, good luck driving them out. That's why the British fought
so hard in 1940. That's why, to an extent, the universe favors
progress. An inch of incursion soon becomes a mile. Ginny never
really understood the relentlessness of an outsider. I had tasted
the possibilities. I wasn't giving up that easily.

CHAPTER TWENTY

ANNE CALLED WITH frequent updates from Maine. The police were putting more resources into the investigation. A picture was starting to come together.

Irregular currents had kept the boat close to shore. The lobsterman who found the rusted and salt-bleached boat didn't recognize it from the police description. He left it in the care of the dockmaster, who had vague plans of fixing it up before the summer season. Anne had been visiting every town in that part of Maine, asking questions and showing pictures of Stella. She stopped in this particular small town for coffee. While a fresh pot was brewing, she waited on the deck that overlooked the harbor. That's when she spotted it.

The police were performing a full forensic workup, but the boat was badly degraded by saltwater and wind and rain. The best they could do was guess at what had happened. If Stella had made it to her intended destination, the boat would have made it, too. But the drifting boat—at sea for several months, based on its condition—pointed to a simpler explanation. Over three thousand Americans die from drowning every year. That's what they told the Bradleys. Almost every single day, someone dies in a boating-related incident. As time went on, it seemed the most likely answer.

Anne had crossed the hemispheres of the world, searching for the crack through which her daughter had slipped. And here it was: an accident. The crack turned out to be ordinary and commonplace. There was some comfort in this. Even though the police were suggesting that Stella was finally, conclusively, inescapably dead, at least they had dropped their theory about the burner-phone mystery man, about the drugs, about Stella getting mixed up with a bad crowd. Drowning was tragic, but it was dignified. If Anne had to resign herself to losing Stella forever, at least her daughter could remain as perfect in death as she had been in life. Closure, perhaps, was possible.

But Anne wasn't the person I had to worry about.

———

It was almost two weeks later, on a Friday, when I arrived to a strange tension in the newsroom. There were several interns whispering in the corner. Eliza, who on a good day barely acknowledged the interns, beckoned one to her office and closed the door.

Rebecca's assistant studiously avoided my gaze as I walked past her desk. "What's going on?" I said, but she shook her head without looking at me.

All morning, Jamie's desk was empty. His computer was off. No jacket, no bag, no coffee cup and muffin wrapper in his trash can from his usual coffee cart. He hadn't said he'd be late. When he had to field-produce, he always told me ahead of time. I felt a ripple of unease. In the past two weeks, since the police concluded that Stella was dead, Jamie had been miserable with a new bout of guilt. Miserable enough to do something drastic.

Later, when I went to the kitchen for a cup of tea, there were two assistants hovering, with low voices and furtive whispers. My heart began to race. *Act normal,* I thought. When I went to the refrigerator for milk, one of them grabbed my wrist and hissed, "Stop!"

"Seriously, *what?*" I snapped. "Why is everyone acting so possessed?"

"You have to make sure the coast is clear," one of the assistants said. She leaned over, looking toward the door. "Okay," she said, "but make it fast."

The middle shelf of the refrigerator had been cleared to make room for a large tray with a clear plastic lid. Inside was a cake, with white frosting and lilac roses. The script across the top read, "HAPPY BIRTHDAY REBECCA."

"Oh my God," I said. "Is *this* why everyone is so jumpy?"

"It's a surprise," the assistant said. "For after the show tonight."

Jamie was finally back at his desk, looking frustrated and rubbing the side of his neck. "I think I pulled something," he said. "I knew it was too heavy to carry."

I was so relieved that I almost laughed. "Something for the birthday girl?" I said.

"Twenty-four bottles of Veuve Clicquot. Eliza wouldn't even let me take an intern to help. She has them all working on decorations."

In that morning's meeting, Rebecca swept into the conference room with a smile on her face. But the glow dimmed when we failed to greet her with anything beyond an ordinary hello. "Nice of you to join us," Eliza said, looking at the clock.

"Well, ex-*cuse* me," Rebecca said. Her hair was freshly blown out. She was wearing a new dress, a particularly flattering red sheath. An outfit to defy the gravity of a fortieth birthday.

After the meeting ended, with Rebecca flouncing out and saying that she had to meet her husband for lunch at Jean Georges because today was a *very special* day, Eliza loosed a gale of laughter. "Oh, she is pissed," she said. "She is going to waste that three-hundred-dollar lunch yelling at her husband about how awful I am."

"I thought Rebecca hated her birthday," I said.

"She says she does," Jamie said. "But she hates it more when people forget."

"Not that she'd believe me if I pretended to forget," Eliza said. "So I told her last night: 'Listen, Becks. I know you hate your birthday. So we'll just do a quiet drink after work. Nothing fancy.' She was trying so hard to pretend that just a glass of wine and my company would make her happy." Eliza laughed. "Yeah right. She's turning forty. This woman wants a fucking party."

I'd pitched Eliza on a story that morning, but she asked for more information before green-lighting it. By this point, I'd produced several serious pieces. It didn't really get any easier—pitching an idea in front of a big room, asking Eliza to divert resources to my story, bracing myself for rejection—but I was getting better at bearing the pressure.

Eliza saw me in the doorway and beckoned me inside. There was a voice on speakerphone: Ginny. Eliza said, "So I was planning to say a few words, welcome everybody, and then hand it over to you to make the toast. Sound good?"

"That's fine," Ginny said. "I'm going to practice my speech in the car."

"Where are you, anyways?" Eliza said. Simultaneously she was reading the paper I'd handed to her, circling things and jotting notes in the margin.

"Out on Long Island."

"For work?"

"No," Ginny said. "A personal errand. I had to look into something."

"Got it." Eliza handed the paper to me, scrawled with notes, and gave a thumbs-up.

"If the traffic isn't too bad, I'll be back in a few hours," Ginny said. "I'm leaving Sag Harbor now."

"Huh. Sag," Eliza said, after she'd hung up. "And I always thought Ginny was more of an East Hampton lady. You got what you need, right?"

Maybe it's a coincidence, I thought. But on the walk back to my desk, my hand had a fine tremor, the paper vibrating like a leaf in the wind.

When Rebecca went down to the studio for the broadcast, the newsroom sprang into action. Space was cleared for tables and tablecloths. The caterers hurried in with platters of crudités and cheese and rows of glass flutes for the champagne. Balloons were inflated, decorations strung up. Someone had made a paper crown from a repeating pattern of golden Emmys. Seven in total, which was the number that Rebecca had won.

As the show drew to a close, with minutes left to go, we turned off the lights. In the darkened silence, we could hear their voices as they walked upstairs—Rebecca complaining to Eliza about how third-rate the guest was in that last segment. When they reached the top of the stairs, Rebecca said, "Oh, good God."

She looked genuinely stunned when the lights came on and everyone yelled "SURPRISE!" Rebecca wheeled around toward Eliza, who was laughing. Rebecca was laughing, too, as she whacked Eliza on the arm.

Later, Ginny clinked a fork against her glass. It was objectively strange that Ginny was the one giving the toast when Eliza was Rebecca's best friend, her partner, the only one who could skewer her with affection. But this party was also an exercise in appearances, a way for KCN to show how much it valued its prime-time star. Ginny was the boss, which meant she took the credit. So she spoke platitudes about what an honor it was to work with Rebecca, how she was an inspiration to us all.

After Ginny's toast, Rebecca lifted her glass. "I have to take a moment and thank all of you," she said. "And there's no teleprompter in sight, so forgive me as I wing this."

But when Rebecca began speaking, it was clear that she'd written this ahead of time. Maybe her show of surprise was just that: a performance. Her words were beautiful, thoughtful, precise. After she thanked Ginny in a suitably lengthy manner, Rebecca turned to Eliza.

"Lize," she said, a catch in her voice. "What can I even say? Except that I hope everyone in this room gets to experience what we've experienced. You've made me so much better. Every single day, you challenge me and fight with me and push me to work harder. It may not be pleasant, but as I get older, I see the truth, which is that I need you. I'd be nowhere without you."

Eliza smiled. She put her hand over her heart, mouthed, "I love you."

Rebecca laughed, lifting a finger to catch a tear before it spilled into her makeup. "I'm getting soft in old age," she said.

"Wrap it up," Eliza said. "Thirty seconds 'til commercial."

The room rippled with laughter. "See what I mean?" Rebecca said. "Okay. I'll stop, because brevity is the soul of ratings. Right, Ginny? I just want to say thank you. Life is about the people we surround ourselves with. And I feel so lucky to be surrounded by all of you."

At that moment, the lights dimmed, and two assistants emerged from the kitchen, bearing a cake covered in flickering candles. When Rebecca leaned forward for one long moment, she was the only thing illuminated in the room. After she blew out the candles, and everyone applauded, she leaned into Eliza. Just for a second, she rested her head on Eliza's shoulder and closed her eyes. Eliza kissed the top of Rebecca's head, an automatic and unthinking movement. The two of them, their friendship a version of unconditional love.

I blinked and shook my head. Standing beside Rebecca and Eliza was Ginny. She was staring at me. It was clear that she had been waiting for me to notice her.

She knew.

And, I realized, I wouldn't be able to avoid this forever.

"Want another drink?" Jamie said. "I'm empty."

"Actually, I need to..." I glanced around the room. Ginny was now talking to someone else, laughing in a fake way, her hand lifted to her chest like a prim Victorian lady, her fingertips resting lightly above her heart.

"I forgot," I said. "I have to run an errand. I'll be back."

"Now?" Jamie said. "Violet. Where are you going?"

It's not like I was stupid. I knew I needed an insurance policy.

The week before, I visited an unassuming public library branch out in Queens, to use the free online browsing on their clunky computers. I wore a baseball hat, my hair tucked under the cap. My cover story (I was in med school, and my laptop was broken, and I was writing a paper about heart arrhythmias—specifically, the chemical triggers of ventricular fibrillation) wasn't necessary. The library, with its dusty afternoon light, was a place of purposeful anonymity.

When the police were investigating Stella's disappearance, they found the drugs she brought to Maine. But they never found her stash in New York, beneath the loose floorboard in the back of the coat closet. That night, I left most of it where it was. I only needed a tiny amount, the plastic bag practically weightless in my pocket. The human heart is a delicate thing.

When I returned an hour later, the party was dying down. Half the crowd had left, responsibly avoiding hangovers, and the half that remained was drunk. Jamie was one of the responsible ones.

The room emptied as the clock neared midnight. Rebecca left, and then so did Eliza. There were a few diehards in the corner, clutching beer bottles in one hand while steadily attacking the remaining birthday cake with the other, gossiping at a careless volume, their eyes too glazed with booze and sugar to notice me at my computer.

Then Ginny appeared beside my desk. "You're still here," she said.

"It seemed like you had something you wanted to talk about," I said.

"I think this conversation requires a drink," she said.

At the bar, she poured two Scotches. "It's time to go home," Ginny said sternly to the drunken cake-eaters, who scurried away in shame, leaving us the only people in the newsroom.

Ginny led me into the spare office. She sat behind the desk, and I took the guest chair. "I was in Sag Harbor this afternoon," she said. "Kyle, that was his name. Detective Fazio was so quick to dismiss him, but I wasn't so sure. It bothered me.

"And then," she said, swirling her Scotch, releasing the peaty aroma. "After the police found the boat, I thought to myself: something doesn't add up."

She took a slow sip of her drink. "You're very quiet," she said.

"I'll let you finish," I said.

Ginny's upper lip curled. "People are impressionable, especially in the face of power. You know what it means to lead the witness? That is exactly what Fazio did. He showed a picture of Stella to Kyle, and he said, could this be her?

"But what he should have done," Ginny said, "and what I did today, is say to Kyle, describe her for me. Forget about the pictures you've seen. Close your eyes and tell me exactly what this person looked like—this person who you remember as Stella Bradley."

Ginny smiled. "Well, Violet, this man has *quite* a remarkable memory. Dirty-blond hair, parted on the left. About five foot seven. Brown eyes. Bitten-down fingernails. And a scar, just above the right eyebrow."

She touched her forehead, mirroring the location of my scar. It was small, but clear enough if you were looking for it.

"He told me about the first time you met," Ginny said. "Thanksgiving, several years ago. You told him your name was Stella Bradley. You told him about your family. He remembered everything about your little...encounter. With affection, in fact. Which is why he was so upset to hear you'd been lying to him."

"It was an old game we used to play," I said. "Stella and I switched names all the time. Haven't you ever given a fake name to a man hitting on you?"

"Then why not clear up this simple confusion? Why not explain to Fazio that the bartender, in fact, spotted you that night?" Ginny paused, noting my silence. "Because it's not simple confusion, is it?"

"Maybe it's embarrassment." I met her gaze, level and straight. "That's all."

"I doubt that." She arched an eyebrow. "From what I can tell, you lack the gene for shame."

"Ginny, honestly, I don't understand where this is coming from."

"Stella has been driving that boat since she was eight years old. Her grandmother started drilling her in swimming even before that. She practically grew up on the ocean. She knows what she's doing. So what happened? She simply fell off the boat? She *drowned*, as the police seem to believe so fervently?" Ginny laughed harshly. "I don't buy that for a second."

"You seem very confident," I said. "But what if Stella had been drinking?"

"There's no evidence of that."

"Well, I was there. And I can tell you, Stella had been drinking plenty that weekend."

I set my glass of Scotch down, leaned back into the chair, recrossed my legs. Ginny's confident expression slackened. She looked, for the first time, vaguely apprehensive. She didn't know where this was going.

"I saw those pictures in your office," I said. "You loved Stella. You never had a family, but she was the closest thing you had to a daughter, wasn't she?"

Ginny twitched, but stayed quiet.

"It's so sad," I said. "It happened with Anne and Thomas and Oliver. And now it's happening to you, too. The grief is driving you crazy. You're seeing things that aren't there."

"This isn't going to work on me," Ginny said.

"Think about it. The police have been investigating for months. If there was foul play, wouldn't they have found evidence by now? Even a shred of it? You have to twist yourself into knots to think that she was murdered."

"*No,*" Ginny said, sitting up in a confident posture. "That's exactly my point. It's not complicated if you were on the boat that night. And you were, weren't you? What do they always say?" Ginny counted on three fingers. "Means, motive, opportunity. The ocean is the perfect place to hide a dead body."

"She was my best friend," I said. "What motive are you talking about?"

Ginny gestured, indicating the newsroom outside. "Do you know what makes me good at my job?" she said. "I can recognize ambition. That's why I poached Rebecca, years ago. It didn't matter what we had to pay. She was worth it. You can see it in a person's eyes—that thing. Stella had it, too. So the idea that she'd give it all up? The idea that she'd make a mistake like this?"

Ginny let out an exasperated laugh. "That is ridiculous. We were in the middle of negotiating her contract. Stella wanted to be the next Barbara Walters."

"Stella was fickle," I said. "The only thing she really wanted was attention."

"And you think Barbara Walters doesn't?" Ginny smirked. "All of these people want attention. They thrive on it. If they didn't, they'd go work at a newspaper. But that desire makes them good at their jobs. It means they'll do whatever they have to do to stay on top."

"You make it sound like Stella was the one willing to commit murder," I said.

"Let me finish. That's one kind of ambition," she said. "But there's another kind. It's the person who doesn't show her cards. She's willing to let other people think she's there to help them. Her ambition isn't so naked. It cloaks itself in teamwork and niceties. It's the more dangerous kind. And I'm good at recognizing that, too."

"*Niceties,*" I said. "Aren't you describing yourself?"

Ginny shook her head. "There's a difference between you and me. I come from a good family, Violet. I have a reputation to uphold. I have a sense of shame, you see? But you don't. You come from nowhere. And a woman with nothing to lose—I don't trust her for one second."

She paused. "I'm going to show you something," she said. "You talk about motive. I wonder what the police would think of this e-mail."

Ginny's purse was on the floor, beside her chair. She leaned down, her head ducked low while she rummaged for her phone. Her half-drunk glass of Scotch, lipstick rimming the edge, sweated into the paper napkin beneath it. It took me only a second to do it, slipping my hand into my pocket and passing it above her glass in one fluid motion. When she sat up, I had rearranged myself to look perfectly normal.

"From Stella," she said, sliding her phone across the desk. "The police are so fixated on that last e-mail she sent to me. But she sent this one, too, a few days earlier. And this one, I know that Stella wrote for sure."

> one more thing, can u make sure Violet has nothing to do with
> my new show? i need to pick my own producers. she is insanely
> jealous and will make things complicated. nasty attitude on the
> danner story. cld be an issue for us.

"Why show me this?" I said.

"Because I want you to know that I'm not joking."

I laughed. "No offense, Ginny, but no one *ever* thinks you're joking."

"What you're doing right now," Ginny said. "That arrogance? That will be your downfall, Violet. But soon enough, I'll look back on this moment and savor it." She lifted her Scotch toward me. "I was here before you, and I'll be here long after you're gone."

She took a last, long swallow of her drink. Her eyes were glimmering and satisfied.

"I guess that's true," I said. "And speaking of, I should get going. I have to pack."

"Skipping town?" Ginny said, smugly.

"Not exactly," I said. "I have a job interview. In London."

"You what?" she said. But I stood up and walked out of the office. Turning my back on her, ignoring her, was exquisitely satisfying. She followed me out and said, her voice tight with anger, "What are you doing?"

"Don't worry," I said. "I'll be back in a few days to wrap everything up. Assuming all goes well with Ashley Fong."

"Ashley *Fong?*" she sputtered.

"Yes. Would you like me to give her your regards?"

Ginny's breath, through her flared nostrils, was ragged. "I pick up the phone tomorrow morning," she said, "and the interview is off."

"Oh, sure. You can try that. But as Ashley explained, she doesn't report to you. The European bureau has its own mandate. They're very independent over there."

"I'll take this all the way to Mr. King," Ginny said. "You are not getting that job."

"You know, I wondered for a long time—why didn't you just fire me? I'm just a low-level producer, after all. But you've got this flaw, Ginny. You care too much about what other people think. You won't tell anyone about your sister. You won't admit that your beloved Stella was a narcissist with a drinking problem. And if you fired me, people would talk. Because I'm good at my job. They *know* I'm good." I cocked my head. "What would they say? Is Ginny threatened by Violet? By this nobody from nowhere?"

Ginny was as red as a tomato. Or a choking victim.

"So you'd rather keep up appearances. You'd rather not admit to anyone just how much you hate me. That would be so— *unbecoming.*"

"You are nasty," she spat. "You are a nasty, evil girl."

"True," I said. "But it's gotten me this far, hasn't it?"

"One phone call!" Ginny shouted, as I stepped into the elevator. The tweed suit, the pearl necklace, the coiffed bob—but her eyes were wild and panicked. She was an animal caught in a trap, nothing like the composed businesswoman people believed her to be. That's the thing about perfection. Remove one card, and the whole house crumbles.

The gap between the doors was narrowing. "Don't think I won't do it!" she shrieked.

PART FOUR

CHAPTER TWENTY-ONE

IT TAKES SO little to uproot a life. A phone call to the Bradleys to let them know I was leaving. My personal mail forwarded to KCN until I found an apartment. One box of winter clothing, sent on the slow boat because it was July, and two suitcases for the plane. On the day of my flight, after checking the apartment one last time, I left the keys with the doorman. He nodded politely, but there was no tearful farewell.

None of this had ever really belonged to me, anyway.

The airplane took off from JFK in the thick heat of a summer night and landed at Heathrow in a morning of autumnal gloom. Low gray skies, cool temperatures, intermittent drizzle. The cab driver told me this was unusual for July, that the weather would improve soon enough. I told him I didn't mind, that in fact I preferred this weather.

"Where are you from, miss?" he said, catching my eye in the rearview mirror.

"I flew in from New York."

"New York!" he said. "You'll see there's quite a lot of New Yorkers here. London is a big city. You'll feel right at home."

"Well, I'm not really from there," I said. "I'm from Florida."

"Florida." He sounded disappointed. Then his eyes brightened. "Like Disney World?"

"Yes," I said. "Like Disney World."

The hotel was in Soho, just a few blocks away from KCN's office. The driver was right: London did feel like New York, at least this part of it. It could have been the West Village, with the jumbled streets and white-walled coffee shops and narrow restaurants. But when we turned a corner, the street opened into a quiet green square, lined soldierlike with elegant Regency houses. London had history that made the Bradleys look like new money.

The driver stopped in front of the hotel. My door was opened for me from the outside. I was distracted, searching for a tip, so it wasn't until he laughed and said, "You're not even going to say hello?" that I looked up.

Jamie, with a big smile on his face.

Two weeks earlier, in London, Ashley Fong asked if I had really thought about this.

"It's not like the New York office," she said. "We're tiny, compared to them. And every year we have to do more with less."

"That's the appeal," I said. "I'd like to try something different."

"You've been with Rebecca and Eliza for how long?"

"Four years."

"And you're ready to get out of there."

Trish, the executive producer in Washington, had been unsurprised by my back-channel phone call. This was a lesson learned from producing: never let a door close. After we expressed mutual disappointment that we wouldn't be working together, Trish called me a few days later with an idea. Her friend Ashley Fong, the head of KCN's London bureau, was hiring. If I was interested, Trish would put in a good word.

In fact, the London bureau was hiring for multiple roles. Ashley needed two senior producers. The TV screens in her office were tuned to the BBC and CNN International and Sky News. Jamie sat in the office next door, interviewing with Ashley's deputy. Later, Jamie and I would switch places, a silent smile flashing between us in the hallway.

"I am," I said, in answer to her question. "And so is Jamie."

"I take it you two are a package deal?"

"We've just about reached the point of finishing each other's sentences."

"Good," she said. "But I'll be honest with you. We're in a major jam right now."

"How so?"

"We're short a reporter. How hard should it be to convince someone to move to London? Very, apparently. The bosses keep sending us these twenty-three-year-old kids. Who know nothing about the world. Not great for a foreign correspondent. They wash out after a few months, and we're back to square one."

"That must be frustrating."

"But when I try to hire a more senior reporter, guess what? The reporters want to stay in New York. How are you going to suck up to the executives when you're all the way across the Atlantic?" She made a face, then shook her head. "That sounds petty, but it's true."

"Yeah," I said. "A lot of backstabbing goes on."

"You have no idea. A few years ago, I was on deck to oversee the morning lineup. But at the last minute, Ginny intervened. Instead she wanted me to head up the Hong Kong bureau. Know why?" Ashley gestured at herself. "She's a racist."

"Really?"

"She wasn't explicit about it," Ashley said. "But she thought I didn't have the right sensibility for morning. That someone like me—who *looks* like me—couldn't connect with real America. Couldn't cut into Fox's base. Like she understands it so well? Guess what, bitch. We're *both* from New York. We *both* went to Spence."

I laughed.

"Well," Ashley said, "it worked out. Hong Kong and London were like a trip to the spa after New York. It's liberating. You'll see. You'll love it."

"Does this mean I have the job?" I said.

Ashley smiled. "Very direct. That's why Ginny doesn't like you, right?"

"Ginny hates me. I've never known why."

"Welcome to the club," she said. "Unfortunately, we still need her. She has to convince *someone* to come over here and take this correspondent job."

"Actually," I said, "I might have another idea."

———

The day after returning from that first trip to London, Corey agreed to meet me for lunch.

"You must really love Cuban food." He slid into the booth across from me. "Otherwise there's no good reason to drag me out to Tenth Avenue."

"It's the best ropa vieja in the city," I said. "But, more importantly, no one from KCN comes here."

"Ah," he said. "*That* kind of lunch. So what? You're ready to jump ship?"

"Nope. I already have a new ship. And I want you to join it."

As I started talking, Corey laughed and tried to interrupt: he had just started at CNN, he was happy there. When I told him to be quiet and listen, he looked surprised. Then he looked bemused, then serious. The plan, as I laid it out, didn't sound crazy.

It sounded kind of perfect. By the time our food arrived, Corey was chewing a thumbnail, thinking hard.

"You wanted a fast track to a foreign correspondent job," I said, lifting a forkful of rice and beans. "Doesn't get faster than this."

"This feels too good to be true," Corey said. "There has to be a catch."

"Well, for one thing, CNN won't want to let you out of your contract. That'll be an ugly fight. But so what? Make your agent earn his percentage."

"What about this Ashley Fong? Do you like her?"

"I like her enough." I shrugged. "Look, Corey. I'm being self-ish. I like you, I know you, and I think we'd work well together. My colleague Jamie Richter is coming to London, too. He's one of Eliza's original protégés. Our mandate is to remake the place. We want the new face of the bureau to be someone really good. Who makes us look good, in turn."

"It's tempting." He had a dreamy look in his eyes. "London, huh?"

"They call this a win-win," I said.

———

Oliver wouldn't look at me. In his apartment, he was staring at the floor, pouty and embarrassed, like a small child being punished.

But defiant. A child who doesn't feel he's done anything wrong—now, or ever.

"I don't get it," he said. "Why do you want to leave so badly?"

"I already told you. I need a fresh start."

"If you loved me, you would stay."

"But I don't," I said. "I'm sorry, Oliver."

He finally looked up. "There's no one left," he said. "Stella.

My mother, my father, they've basically gone crazy. I'm completely alone. You must understand that."

His words were pathetic, but his eyes were angry. Those words weren't a plea. They were an imperative. He was commanding me to feel his pain, and to nurse him through it. And if this had been four years earlier, I might have. The fancy homes, the vacations, the life of luxury: once upon a time, that would have been sufficient compensation for this kind of emotional labor. But it wasn't four years earlier. I knew better, by now.

And besides, he tried to fuck up my career. That was unforgivable.

"I have to go," I said. "I have a lot to do."

Oliver punched a button on his phone and held it to his ear. "I'm calling Ginny."

"That won't work. She doesn't oversee the London bureau."

He frowned. "No answer. Never mind. I'm going to leave a message."

"Do whatever you want," I said. "And take care of yourself, okay?"

"Ginny," he shouted into the phone. "This is Oliver Bradley. Can you please—"

But I closed the door behind me, blocking the sound of Oliver's voice.

———

I left New York on Saturday, arrived in London on Sunday, and would begin the new job on Monday. Ashley said we could take more time—adjust to the jet lag, find a place to live—but none of us cared about that. We wanted to get to work. Later that week, Corey would be reporting from Baghdad on their parliamentary elections. Jamie would be field-producing for him. My plate was full, too: there was a G8 summit happening in Germany, the conclusion of the Tour de France, a new encyclical from the Pope. The first week would be intense.

It was a strange feeling, walking around a new city, imagining what shape my life might take here. Charmingly crooked streets, lush green squares, tall red buses: one day, these novel things would become familiar. I spent that Sunday wandering alone, getting pleasantly lost. The clouds cleared in the late afternoon. The sky was bright and the air was rinsed clean. Latitude and season meant that the sun wouldn't set until after 9 p.m.

There was a pub around the corner from our hotel, which Jamie and I had passed on our way to breakfast that morning. A heavy wooden door, white walls and green shutters, old-fashioned lettering on the facade. "Check it out," Jamie said, peering through the window. "There's a fireplace. And a bed for a dog."

As if on cue, a springer spaniel ambled toward us. The dog's snout had gone white with age. Jamie squatted down and extended a hand. The dog sniffed, then licked Jamie's palm a few times before disappearing through the propped-open back door to the pub. Jamie stood and brushed his hand on his pants, looking wistful.

"We can come back tonight," I said. Jamie's family had springer spaniels when he was a kid, dogs trained for duck hunting in the low country of South Carolina. It was one of the things he missed most about home.

The evening sky was still light when I arrived at the pub, but it was cool enough that there was a fire crackling behind the grate. The room smelled musty and old, in a good way. The springer spaniel was asleep in front of the fire, hind leg twitching. The young woman behind the bar put down her book and said, "What can I get you, love?"

I had arrived early. Jamie and Corey were coming straight from dinner with one of the legal scholars who had helped draft the Iraqi constitution, getting briefed in advance of that week's elections. Ashley was delighted by this. *Taking initiative, what a concept!!!* she had e-mailed me. *Honestly it is depressing how happy this makes me.*

The table closest to the fire was occupied by an elderly couple, the man with his pint and the woman her glass of wine, each of them reading a newspaper, occasionally sighing in disapproval. "Dreadful news these days," the woman said, setting the paper aside. "Quite enough for one night. Come on. Off to bed."

I took the table after they left. Among the papers was a copy of the *New York Times International Edition,* carefully refolded. I scanned the front page, curious if the story merited international coverage. The sensational headlines had mostly died down after the police and coroner made it clear that they suspected no foul play. Still—the media loved cataloging turmoil in their own world.

It was tragic, everyone agreed on that. According to the coroner, the heart attack happened in the earliest hours of Saturday morning, not long after she returned from the office, but it took several days before the super finally broke into the apartment and discovered the body sprawled across the bedroom carpet. Her death was an eerie echo of her sister's: the wealthy woman who lives alone, her absence unnoticed for far too long. The defibrillator in her bedroom was only ten feet away from where she collapsed, but no one was there to administer it or to call 9-1-1. And she was susceptible; she had a weak ventricle. The stories reveled in the details, the minutes and hours and days that ticked by before someone finally thought to ask, where is she?

There was a lengthy obituary, a star-studded funeral on the Upper East Side. By now, the story had migrated to the business section.

In Wake of Executive's Death, a Shake-Up

People in the office were sad, but not upset. There's a difference. Solemn faces, teary eyes, lowered voices. But no one doubted that the ship of KCN would continue to run smoothly with Eliza Davis at the helm. Maybe even better than it had before. Big changes like this always happened suddenly. But within days, people forgot that it had ever been different.

The article described Eliza's long tenure at KCN. She was known as an uncompromising journalist, a beloved mentor, the secret mastermind of Rebecca Carter's career. She would be the first African-American president of KCN, or any cable news network. In her statement, Eliza said the right things: Ginny had left big shoes to fill. In the wake of this awful tragedy, she wasn't in any rush to make sweeping changes.

It seemed Mr. King was, though. He appointed Eliza to King Media's board of directors, a position Ginny had never held. Eliza was both glamorous and down-to-earth. Her husband was the chief of pediatric oncology at Columbia and they lived in a brownstone in Morningside Heights—things I never knew, and which I learned by reading the paper. Mr. King loved her. The media loved her. She was their new star. Everyone was rooting for her.

A jingle from the front door drew my gaze. "Sorry we're late," Corey said.

"Was it helpful?" I asked.

"Very," he said. "Everyone's drinking beer, right?"

While Corey went to the bar, Jamie crouched down and scratched behind the spaniel's ears. "That's a good girl," he said. "Hey, so Corey's no slouch."

"Not just a pretty face, right?"

"I like him a lot."

I smiled. "I knew you would."

Corey came back with his hands triangled around three brimming pints, setting them down on the table among us. "What do we owe you?" Jamie said, taking out his wallet. But Corey waved a hand. "Never mind," he said. "It'll even out over the long haul."

"I'm getting the next round, then," Jamie said.

"And then me," I said.

Corey lifted his beer. "Who would have thought? Three rednecks like us in London. We've come a long way."

A long way. But there were still nights when I woke up in a cold sweat. Stalked by memories as vivid as reality. The slosh of waves against the boat, the arm reaching for the surface. I could soothe myself back to sleep with the thought that she'd done it to herself. Repeat it like a mantra: *she did it to herself.* She was sloppy drunk, standing on the bow in rough ocean waters, wild with agitation. I had merely done what I should have done much earlier: stand back and let her suffer the consequences of her actions.

But even I didn't believe that. I had made an active decision that night on the boat, a horrifically cruel decision: that Stella didn't deserve to be saved. That the world was better off without her. *I* was better off without her. In that moment, playing God, I had finally decided that there was no more room for forgiveness, that this was the last of her nine lives.

The perverse thing was, she would have been proud of me. *Finally standing up for yourself.* I could imagine the bemusement in her voice. *Didn't think you had it in you.* My mother, too. Violence was something she could respect. Letting Stella drown: I thought that it would cleave me from the past, distance me from the person I had been before. But sometimes I feared that it had only brought me closer to my dark, twisted roots.

I watched Jamie and Corey talking excitedly about their upcoming trip to Baghdad, and thought about what they had done

to get here. Jamie had given up a show he loved, a chance to become Rebecca's EP after Eliza's ascension. Corey had divorced
his wife, moved from city to city, torn up a brand-new contract.
It was naive to think that other people were perfectly happy.
That other people didn't feel compromise, or conflict, or sadness.

There were things they didn't know about me. Things they
could never know about me. But they knew me better than anyone else in the world. This was how I comforted myself. If it
had been Jamie on the boat that night—or Corey, or Rebecca, or
Eliza—I would have hauled him out of the water immediately. I
would have administered CPR, raced back to land, called 9-1-1.
I would have done anything to save him.

Food, water, warmth, shelter. These things are necessary to
survive. It had taken me time to realize that people fit into this
equation, too. Love fits into this equation, too. Jamie, in the
empty office, holding me while I sobbed. Eliza, on my last day
in New York, telling me how proud she was. There are people
you cannot live without. To remember this is to remember your
humanity.

You say that now. A little voice, in my mind. *But what if Jamie
betrays you, like Stella did? What if he tries to ruin your career,
like Ginny did? Wouldn't you put ambition over love?*

It was just a passing thought. A synaptic blip. So why was my
heart racing, my palms sweating, my face flushing?

"Hey," Jamie said, putting a hand on my knee. "Violet. You
okay?"

I shook my head. "Just tired."

Corey smiled sympathetically. "Long day."

"Do you want to go home?" Jamie said.

"I'm fine," I said. "I'll stay."

Calm down, I told myself. Take a sip of the cool beer. Feel the
warmth of the fireplace. Listen to the sound of their voices. This
is all in your head. This is merely theoretical. There are people

right here who love you, and no one is actually asking you to decide. You're ambitious, sure, but no one is asking you to commit murder. No one ever said that cruelty was a necessary condition to success.

But—the dark, terrifying voice in my mind—*doesn't that just prove the point?*

To be selfish. To be cruel, at times. To harden your heart so that you need no one else. When you realize how powerful this makes you, you keep it to yourself.

ACKNOWLEDGMENTS

For two books now, the most brilliant people in publishing have had my back. Three fierce, fabulous women in particular have made all of this possible: my agent, Allison Hunter; my editor, Carina Guiterman; and my publicist, Maggie Gladstone. I'm more thankful to them—my powerhouse trio—than I know how to say.

I'm deeply grateful to everyone at Little, Brown for their belief and dedication: Asya Muchnick, Reagan Arthur, Judy Clain, Craig Young, Ashley Marudas, Lauren Harms, and Pamela Marshall. At Janklow & Nesbit, I also owe great thanks to Clare Mao.

Several people generously lent their insight and expertise about the world of broadcast news. I could not have written this book without Molly Battles, Katie Wiggin, Kira Kleaveland, Paul Needham, and others (who know who they are!). A special thanks to Kira and Paul, who read an early version of the manuscript and offered sharp-eyed advice. I also found invaluable illumination in the writings of Gabe Sherman and Brian Stelter, who allowed me to understand the behind-the-scenes dynamics of this world.

In the midst of writing this novel, I read Richard Ben Cramer's masterpiece *What It Takes*. It's the best portrait of ambition I've ever encountered, and his observations made a permanent groove in my imagination. There are journalists who write like novelists, and I'm grateful to them for so vividly capturing the drama and comedy and tragedy that resides in the real world, not just in fiction—and for deepening our understanding of the world as a result.

Lastly, thank you to my family, the people who offer me grace and love, who allow me to find joy and meaning in both the hard times and good times. To my parents, Ed and Kate; to my sister, Nellie; and to my husband, Andrew: I love you so much.